Frances Anne Bond was born, brought up and still lives in the town of Scarborough, North Yorkshire. She has worked in shops, in a coffee bar, as a clerk in a building society, as secretary to a headmaster in a private preparatory school and in the social services. She is married and has two grown-up daughters. She has been writing since she was a child and has previously had articles, short stories and one novel, *Dance Without Music*, published.

Also by Frances Anne Bond from Headline

Dance Without Music

Return of the Swallow

Frances Anne Bond

KNIGHT

Copyright © 1990 Frances Anne Bond

The right of Frances Anne Bond to be identified as the Author
of the Work has been asserted by her in accordance with the
Copyright, Designs and Patents Act 1988.

First published in 1990
by HEADLINE BOOK PUBLISHING PLC

First published in paperback in 1991
by HEADLINE BOOK PUBLISHING PLC

This edition published 2003 by Knight
an imprint of The Caxton Publishing Group

10 9 8 7 6 5 4 3 2 1

ISBN 1 86019 6683

Typeset in 10/10$^1/_4$ pt Times
by Colset Private Limited, Singapore

Printed and bound in Great Britain by
Cox & Wyman Ltd, Reading, Berkshire

Caxton Publishing Group
20 Bloomsbury Street
London WC1B 3QA

For my husband, Peter, with love.

Acknowledgements

Researching this novel, I read many books but two in particular should be mentioned. *The New Look: A social history of the forties and fifties in Britain*, by Harry Hopkins gave me invaluable details about everyday life. So much we forget! The fate of youngsters shipped off overseas after the Second World War first caught my interest when I read an article about them in July 1987. Thereafter, I collected every scrap of information I could find on the subject. In 1989 *Lost Children of the Empire* by Philip Bean and Joy Melville was published. Within the book were the voices of the child migrants who provided information through letters to the Child Migrants Trust. Their accounts made absorbing though harrowing reading and were of tremendous help to me in my work. I would like to express my grateful thanks to the authors of these books.

I must also mention two special people in Australia: Ken Moon of The University of New England, Armidale, N.S.W. who vigorously followed up leads on my behalf, always with good humour; and Brian Underwood, a 'real life' opal miner. Bombarded with queries, Brian patiently replied, writing fifteen- to twenty-paged letters describing day-to-day living conditions in the Outback and searching out details of life in Coober Pedy and opal mining there during the fifties. And he's never even met me! Thank you so much Brian. I'll even wish for you that the Australians continue to win the Ashes. Thanks also to Jane Sloane of Tourism, South Australia for her help.

Lastly, thanks to my family and friends for their

support, and to Jane Morpeth, my editor at Headline, who boosted my confidence by praising the book and then, with tact and grace, showed me how it could be improved.

PART I
FLEDGELINGS

Chapter One

At the height of the celebrations, in the middle of the street party and half-way through eating a sausage roll, Dorothea Bellows had one of her 'funny turns'. Her movements slowed, then stopped. Her large, greeny-blue eyes, her one claim to beauty, widened into a blank stare and animation drained from her face like sand through an egg timer.

The attacks had started four years ago when Dorothea was twelve years old. She had been entombed in the bombed-out house for twenty-two hours when the rescuers found her. She was lucky, they told her. The solid oak table she had sheltered under had protected her from physical hurt. After her first attack, the family doctor had reassured her parents. Time would heal, he promised. It was the shock. And they didn't last long; a couple of minutes then she would start, shake her head, and be a normal girl again. She had been lucky, he repeated, remembering the shattered bodies he had been called to attend during the Hull air raids of 1941.

Dorothea preferred to ignore them. She had no prior warning of her 'funny turns'. One minute she was there, then she wasn't! Yet, in a curious way, she *was*. It was as if she detached herself from her body and floated up into the air, like some ludicrous, plump angel. She never told anyone. How could she? The whole business made her feel a freak. She'd read in a paper once about a girl who saw visions but that girl had been a nun. She was just a sixteen-year-old lass who worked at the Metal Box Factory. Yet now, in some strange way, Dorothea

3

floated above Warren Street and looked down at the street party.

It was a cheerful scene. Mr Gill had been to the Town Hall for permission to close off the road and put tables down the middle. It seemed that even with something as important as celebrations for Victory in Europe Day, formalities had to be observed. The fluttering Union Jacks looked colourful and a surprising amount of food had been unearthed for the occasion. In the centre of each table stood a large, highly coloured jelly, especially for the children. Yet the youngsters seemed subdued.

From her omniscient viewpoint, Dorothea nodded understandingly. Children were creatures of habit. Meals in the street disturbed them, as did the sight of grown-ups laughing, rushing about and even kissing their neighbours. Dorothea spotted her best friend Nancy, behaving perfectly in character by kissing Bill Thomson.

'Poor Bill,' murmured Dorothea.

He was one of the few young men attending the party, there because of Nancy, of course. Seated next to Bill was Mrs Mason. Her two sons had been killed in the war, one in France, one in North Africa. No one had ever seen Mrs Mason cry but now, watching her bent head, her fingers worrying away at the sandwich on her plate, Dorothea wanted to cry for her.

With her sharpened vision, Dorothea also noticed that the reason Mrs Johnson hadn't taken off her apron when all the other women had, was because she looked to be over five months pregnant and everyone knew Mr Johnson had been in a German prisoner of war camp for eighteen months. He'd be coming home now. Dorothea's mouth tightened. She felt angry with God. If she *had* been a real angel, she thought, she would have told him he made a right mess of things sometimes.

To calm herself, she glanced away from the scene of the party and looked about her. She noticed the bunting draped from the lamp-posts had slipped askew and the Union Jack flying above the corner shop had a hole in it. All the houses showed some sign of bomb damage. Windows were boarded over with plywood and near the bottom of the road, like a drawn tooth, a gaping hole cordoned off with rope marked the place where numbers thirty and thirty-two Warren Street had once stood. The contrast between the jollifications of the party and the gaunt, sombre surroundings struck Dorothea as peculiar.

'Ow!'

She came back to a stinging pain in her ankle. Nancy had kicked her.

'Sorry, but I had to. You give me the creeps when you blank out like that.'

Dorothea blinked and rubbed her ankle. Noise crashed round her head like the breaking of a wave. A nearby toddler, having dropped her cake, was screaming her head off.

'Are you all right?'

'Yes.'

'Good. You're getting some colour back into your face.'

Reassured, Nancy took a jam tart, put it on her plate then unbuttoned the top of her dress and blew down her front. She smiled seductively at the reddening Bill.

'Hot, isn't it?'

'More like August than May.' With a shaking hand, the young man raised his teacup and drank. 'Keeps you cool, tea does, in hot weather.' His eyes adored Nancy.

She decided he bored her, and turned back to Dorothea. Impulsively, she reached out and grasped her friend's hand. 'Just think, Dorrie, it's really over! There'll be no more sleeping in smelly air-raid shelters, no more buzz bombs, no more rationing . . .'

Dorothea was back to normal. She grinned at Nancy. 'No more black-out,' she chanted. 'No more wooden-soled shoes. Why—' she paused as the advantages of peace crowded in on her '—we'll be able to buy face-cream and . . .'

'Silk stockings,' finished Nancy.

They stared at each other, their faces ecstatic.

'Nancy.' Mrs Dempsey approached them. Nancy's mother was good-hearted, stout, red-faced, and always out of breath. 'Pop home for some more bread, love. These blessed kids! First they won't eat at all – now they won't stop. And you, Bill Thomson,' she fixed him with a steely stare, 'come with me. There's a wobbly table you can fix. That damn tea urn will topple over and scald someone before we're finished.'

She departed, followed by a sheepish Bill. Dorothea watched him walk away.

'He's really sweet on you.' She spoke without rancour. How could it be otherwise? Half the lads in the Hessle Road area of Hull were sweet on Nancy. With her trim figure, curly hair and large brown eyes she attracted admiration as naturally as water ran downhill.

Nancy pulled a face. 'I know. And he's awful, isn't he?' She pushed back her chair. 'Come back with me, Dorrie.'

Arm-in-arm, the two girls strolled to Nancy's home. When Nancy pushed open the unlocked front door, Dorothea's nose wrinkled at the odour of fish. She bit her lip and glanced at Nancy, hoping she hadn't noticed. Mrs Dempsey worked hard at keeping her home clean – Dorothea was sure there would be no piles of fluff under the beds of the Dempsey household as there were in her house – but Mr Dempsey worked as a 'bobber', landing fish all day long, and there was no disguising the fact.

Dorothea felt glad her dad worked for the railways. She knew the original Hessle-Roaders were proud of their unique way of life, but for relative newcomers like Dorothea and her parents, the all-pervasive scent of fish, particularly when the wind blew over the fish meal factory which produced animal feedstuff seven days a week, became over-powering. Nancy banged shut the door behind her.

'The bread's in t'pantry, Dorrie. I'll get the

6

greaseproof paper. Be quick, we don't want to miss anything.'

She walked towards a large oak sideboard which occupied a good third of the small room, then paused to look out of the window.

'Oh, you'll never believe it!' She laughed. 'Mr Gill's outside with a damn great megaphone. Where on earth did he find that?'

With a petulant gesture, she pushed aside a lurid, coloured portrait of the King and Queen which her mother had cut out from a magazine and propped up in the window.

'I can't see what's going on because of this ruddy thing,' she complained.

'Better leave it,' warned Dorothea. 'You know how your mam feels about the Royals.' She waved a large loaf of bread at Nancy. 'Want me to slice this up?'

'I suppose so.'

Nancy was reluctant to leave her observation post. 'Your little lad's here – the one that follows you about. He's got a cheek. He doesn't live in the street!'

'What little lad?' Dorothea joined her friend at the window. 'Oh, Rob Steyart, you mean.'

'Who else?' Nancy dimpled. 'How many other school kids have a crush on you?'

'Pack it in, Nancy.' Dorothea frowned. 'It's not like that. He's lonely, that's all. It's not easy, fitting into this neighbourhood, you know.'

She spoke with feeling. It was all right for Nancy, she had been born into the Hessle Road community, but Dorothea had not and remembered only too well her own experience of being made to feel an outsider. 'I told him he could come. They're a lot of old miseries in his street. They haven't even bothered with decorations. Anyway,' she poked Nancy in the ribs, 'what about this bread your mum wants? Let's get on with it, shall we?'

Obediently, Nancy replaced the magazine picture in the window and turned to her friend. 'There'll be lots of changes now, won't there, Dorrie? All the young chaps will be coming back.'

'Not straight away.' Dorothea paused to push away a wisp of fine, mouse-coloured hair from her broad forehead. 'Still the Japs to sort out, remember.'

'Pooh, that won't take long.' Nancy began to spread margarine on to the slices of bread and to wrap them in greaseproof paper. 'And the blokes over here, they'll be leaving,' she mused. 'The Free French, they always have lovely manners, the Poles and—' she paused '—the Yanks.'

'Yes, they *will* be missed.'

Nancy gave Dorothea a suspicious look but her companion, her face turned away, continued to slice the bread.

Nancy grinned. 'Yes, they will,' she admitted. 'They're good fun and know how to treat a girl. You ought to come out with me more often Dorrie, then you'd know. They're ever so kind, too. Look at the sweets they give to the kids. Of course,' she sighed, 'they have plenty of money. They seem to like it over here, don't they? Strange when you think of all the shortages.'

Dorothea shrugged. 'There's shortages and shortages,' she murmured. 'Come on.' She picked up the packages of bread. 'Let's get back.'

The party lasted all day. The local brass band turned up to play rousing tunes, there were games for the youngsters, and Mr Gill delivered a speech.

Dorothea felt particularly hungry. She always did after one of her turns. Most of the food had been eaten now but a plate close by her held one solitary iced bun. She frowned and looked away. I don't really want it, she told herself. Nearby, Nancy, despite what she had said earlier, was flirting with Bill Thomson. It wasn't fair. Nancy had an enormous appetite and yet look how slim she was. Gloomily, Dorothea took the bun and bit into it.

'Not finished yet, Dorothea?'

Although her mother's voice held only mild criti-
cism, Dorothea spluttered, then choked. She put the
half-eaten bun back on her plate. 'Yes, I have.'

'Good. Then you can help me clear the tables.
We're to make space for Mr Garman. He's bringing
out his piano so we can have a sing-song.'

Hazel Bellows' eyes were shining. Dorothea looked
at the auburn curls dancing on her forehead and
wished, not for the first time, that her mother looked
older.

'I'll help you in a minute, Mum. I want to pop home
and see if Jake's OK. The noise might upset him.'

'You and that animal . . .'

But Dorothea had escaped. As she emerged from
the dark passageway which led round to the backyard
of her home, she heard the strains of a tinkling piano.
She pushed open a wooden gate and a chorus of
enthusiastic singers struck up with 'There'll Always
be an England'. A low growl erupted from the dog
lying half in, half out of his kennel. Then followed the
clink of a chain and the muffled thumping of his tail.

'Did you think I'd forgotten you?'

Dorothea's voice softened as she crouched down
and ruffled the coat of the mongrel dog. Jake nuzzled
her hand and his chestnut-coloured eyes clouded with
love. Their meeting, three years ago, had resulted in a
case of mutual adoration. Dorothea had been an
unhappy thirteen year old and Jake a peculiar-
looking, half-starved stray. They needed each other.
Now, Dorothea gave Jake's flapping ears an affectionate tug and fed him half a spam sandwich.

'We'll go for a walk later,' she promised.

An hour later she was placing cups and saucers on
the table when her parents came in.

'I met your dad at the end of the street, Dorothea.'
Hazel Bellows covered her best dress with a floral
apron. 'You never came back, love.'

'No.' Dorothea put the salt and pepper shakers in
the centre of the checked tablecloth. 'Time was
getting on and I knew Dad would be in for his tea.'

9

'It's a pity you missed everything, Dennis. It was smashing.' Hazel's face was animated. 'There were games for the kids, and Mrs Baker took a piece of my cake and said it was the best she had ever tasted.'

Her husband grunted. 'Some of us have to work for a living.' He picked up a newspaper. 'What's for tea?'

Hazel's chatter ceased. She turned away. 'Kippers, is that all right?' Dennis did not reply. He sat down and turned over the page of the newspaper.

'Would you like one, Dorothea?'

She winced at the forced brightness of her mother's voice.

'No thanks. I've had enough to eat for today.'

'Are you sure? I've got plenty.'

Dennis looked up. 'Leave her be, woman. It will do her good to miss a meal. Doesn't look as though she's starving, does she?'

Before her mother could reply, Dorothea spoke, her voice composed. 'Kettle's on, Mum. I'm just going upstairs to decide what to wear tonight.'

Outside the kitchen door, she breathed deeply. Did he do it on purpose? she wondered. When she was small she had been good friends with her father, but now . . . Well, Mum could scurry about looking after him but she'd be damned if she would. She'd made her plans and when the right time came she would leave and nothing her father could say would stop her.

She went up to her bedroom. Her best dress was freshly ironed and laid out on the bed. Her mother must have seen to it before she went to the party. Dorothea sighed. She felt her usual mixture of love and exasperation. There was a tap on the door. Hazel had followed her upstairs.

'All right if I come in?'

'Of course.' Dorothea clenched her hands.

Hazel entered the room and perched on the edge of the bed, being careful not to crumple the dress. 'Don't let your dad upset you, love. He's tired, and when he is, he's not very tactful.'

Dorothea looked away. 'I'm not upset, Mum.'

Hazel examined her fingernails. 'You'll be out with Nancy tonight, I suppose?'

'Yes. Why?'

'Oh, nothing.'

In the short silence that followed, Dorothea fought down her irritation. 'We're going dancing,' she eventually volunteered.

'That's nice.'

Her mother fingered the material of the dress. 'I used to love dancing,' she confided. 'Your dad and me will be going out; I suppose everyone will be doing something tonight.' She sighed. 'What I'd really like,' she said, 'is to go and see Bette Davis in "Dark Victory". It's on at the Regal, but I suppose your Dad will want to go to the Club. My,' she paused, 'it will get a bit lively on the streets, I bet.'

'I *can* look after myself, Mum.' Dorothea's voice rasped with ill-concealed impatience. 'Now, if I can get on . . .' She pulled open the drawer in her dressing-table and rummaged through her underwear. Hazel stood up and straightened the counterpane.

'I know you can.' She offered her daughter a timid smile. 'Only, when you dress up, you look older than you are. And that Nancy . . . well, she's a cheerful girl but her reputation . . .'

Dorothea snorted. 'You don't have to worry about me, Mum. I'm not exactly beating young men off with a stick!'

Hazel twisted her wedding ring with agitated fingers. 'Don't talk like that. You're an attractive girl.' She pressed her lips together at Dorothea's ironic look, and continued doggedly: 'You *are*, love. Of course, you need to fine down a little and you will, as you get older. It would help if you smiled more. When you were younger you were always making people laugh, but lately . . .' Her voice trailed away at Dorothea's expression. She moved to the door.

'Well, I must get on with your dad's tea.' She waited, but Dorothea refused to look at her mother.

11

Instead, she sorted through a pile of stockings, looking for an undarned pair.

Hazel's shoulders drooped. 'Don't be late in,' she said, then added in a soft voice, 'I only want you to be happy.'

She retreated downstairs and Dorothea straightened up and stared at herself in the mirror. 'Oh, I mean to be, Mother. Much happier than you've ever been!'

Chapter Two

Rob Steyart was there when the party ended. He helped to push the piano back to Mr Garman's house. He cleared the debris from the plates into brown carrier bags and and carried stacks of glasses and cups into Mrs Dempsey's kitchen for her. He even offered to help her wash up.

'No, lad. You've done enough. Away with you, and play. A young man like you doesn't want to do women's work.' Mrs Dempsey delved into her capacious handbag and produced a threepenny piece. 'Take this for your trouble.'

Rob shook his head and a blush mantled his cheeks. 'No thanks. I've enjoyed helping, honest.'

'Well, if you're sure.' Mrs Dempsey replaced the coin in her purse. 'Off you go, then.' She watched as he walked, with some reluctance, towards her back door. 'Give my regards to your granny.'

The door closed behind him.

'He's a funny lad, that,' she confided to her next-door neighbour who had rolled up her sleeves and donned a wrap-round apron in preparation for a mammoth washing-up session. 'Very polite, but fancy wanting to hang around here.'

Her friend added washing soda to the steaming water in the sink. 'He's no Hessle-Roader, that's for sure. Why, I can't remember any of my lads giving me a hand around the house.'

She smiled contentedly and plunged her work-roughened hands into the hot water. She was proud of her four boys who all topped six feet in height and worked on the Boyd Line trawlers, fishing in the Arctic Circle.

Rob walked home through quiet streets. It was early evening. The men had come home from work and would now, he knew, be eating their evening meals or washing and brushing up in preparation for the evening celebrations. The street parties had been for the women and the children. The night belonged to the men, and perhaps a few of the younger women as yet unencumbered by husband and children.

As Rob passed by the open door of a small terraced house, a toddler appeared, swayed unsteadily on the step, raised a hand to wave at him then toppled over and hit the pavement with a smack. The child howled. Rob hesitated, but before he could move a curly-headed young man, dressed in blue overalls appeared, swept up the baby in his arms and went back in the house, closing the door behind him. Rob's eyes felt suddenly hot and scratchy. He blinked furiously, then went on his way.

'I expected you earlier.' Thelma Steyart, Rob's grandmother, was dressed in her outdoor clothes, a dark brown shapeless coat and a matching brown beret which perched on her thin grey hair like a saucepan lid. 'I suppose you went to that street party? I hope you did; because it's too late for tea. I'll have to go now, Rob. I'm late already. You could come along with me. The Boys' Club's open tonight.'

He shook his head. 'No, I'm all right.' He gestured towards the clock on the wall. 'You'd better hurry, Gran.'

She hesitated, looked as if she wanted to say something, then gave an imperceptible shrug, picked up her prayer book and left the room. Her shadow momentarily flitted against the window as she hurried past, on her way to the Anglican church of St Barnaby's. Thelma Steyart was a great church-goer, unlike the majority of her neighbours who went to church three times in their life: to be christened, married, and later, buried.

14

Left alone, Rob listened to the silence. He was glad his grandmother had her church to comfort her. Today must have been rotten for her, too. Not that she ever said anything. The fate of Alec Steyart, her son and Rob's father, was a subject never discussed. On a sudden impulse, Rob went over to the green-painted kitchen cabinet which stood in the corner of the room and pulled at the bottom drawer. It opened reluctantly. In this drawer reposed all the items long ago discarded, or preserved for special occasions. There was a nut-cracker, usually brought out once a year at Christmas time but ignored the last four years. There was a bottle opener, though Thelma Steyart drank only tea or water. There were rusty screws and parts of equipment the main bodies of which had been consigned to the dustbin long ago. There was a cracked stone hot water bottle and there was a photograph.

Rob had found it one day when he was rummaging in the drawer looking for a piece of string. His grandmother was out shopping so he had an opportunity to sit back on his heels, take out the photograph and study it in detail. He had recognised the faces immediately though it gave him a funny feeling to see his grandmother as a slim, unlined young woman instead of the gaunt, stern-faced person she now was. In the photograph, she was seated with her arm loosely around the shoulders of a boy about eleven, Rob's age now. He had looked down at the face of his father and devoutly wished he resembled him more. The young Alec looked nothing like himself. With gentle fingers Rob touched the fair curly hair and the laughing mouth of the boy in the photograph. He had stared at the picture a long time before putting it back beneath the hot water bottle. His grandmother, he realised, must have forgotten its existence, but he did not tell her of his discovery. She had an album of photographs in the drawer next to her bed, but she had never offered to show him any of them and he never asked.

Now Rob sighed. He took out the old photograph and went to sit down at the kitchen table. She must have loved her only son very much. What had happened to make things go wrong?

He had been four years old when he had first met his grandmother. He couldn't remember much about it, but he remembered he had looked up at her unsmiling face, and shivered. 'Is she a witch?' he had asked, burying his face in his father's trouser leg. For some reason, his query had broken the tension. His father had stopped gripping his shoulder so tightly it hurt and had smiled, bending down to pick him up. Looking fearfully at the grim old lady, Rob had been relieved to see a reluctant smile steal across her thin features.

'He has your imagination then, Alec,' she had commented dryly.

His mother had not accompanied them on that visit. It was later, when Rob had been at school for two years, that the whole family had visited Hull. After that, they had been to see Grandmother twice a year. Rob was quite happy to go, particularly when his father took him to see the boats, but it was always better to go home again, back to their little house in Manchester. Now the house was gone, his mother was in hospital, and his father . . .

The boy started at a burst of laughter out in the street. It was eight o'clock. The revellers were on their way out. He replaced the photograph in the bottom drawer then moodily crossed to where his grandmother's budgerigar slept in its cage, its head under its wing. He rattled the bars. Annoyed, the bird ruffled its feathers and squawked at him. Rob stared into bright little eyes. 'I wish I was grown-up, Joey,' he said. 'I wouldn't be stuck in this kitchen with you. If I was grown-up, I'd . . .' He paused. 'I'd take Dorothea Bellows out.'

Dorothea watched the trolley bus approach them. 'I mustn't be *too* late home,' she murmured to Nancy. 'Mum's got it into her head we're going to the dance at the Church Rooms. She's worried about trouble when the pubs turn out!'

Nancy fluffed out her hair. 'Wonder where she got that idea from?' She grinned at her friend. 'Nobody in their right mind would go to the local hop tonight.' She adopted an American twang: 'We're for the bright lights, sister.'

They hopped on to the trolley bus and Nancy bought the tickets, then she nudged Dorothea. 'Relax, Dorrie. The dance finishes at a quarter to twelve and if no one decent offers to take us home, we'll catch the last bus back to Hessle Road.'

Dorothea smiled and nodded but she wondered if she had done the right thing, coming out with Nancy. She had a good idea who would end up with an escort home!

They had met when the Bellows family had been re-housed in the Hessle Road area of Hull after their home had been bombed-out. At thirteen, Dorothea had been priggishly contemptuous of Nancy. At school, Dorothea worked hard, already planning her future, dreaming dreams. Nancy messed about in lessons, laughed when she came bottom of the class and thought of nothing but boys. Then Dennis Bellows had injured his back. He was off work almost two years and at the end of that time Dorothea's dreams suffered a setback. When she was fifteen she left school and went to work at the Metal Box Factory. There she worked alongside Nancy.

At thirteen, life was simple; at fifteen it became more complicated! Naturally a loner, self-conscious about her strange attacks, Dorothea found growing up a difficult and confusing time. But Nancy! Fascinated, Dorothea watched her blossom effortlessly into womanhood, and in the process came to appreciate Nancy's friendliness. The girls who worked at the factory were a rough lot and didn't like Dorothea Bellows. They mistook her quietness for arrogance and, anyway, the Bellows family were not Hessle-Roaders! They were as good as foreigners. So goodnatured Nancy became her former classmate's champion.

Patiently, she coaxed Dorothea out of her protective shell. They sat together at tea-breaks, went on walks together and moaned about their respective parents. And, gradually, Nancy introduced Dorothea into the exciting world of dates, half-understood jokes and boyfriends. The word sex was not often used, but in Nancy's company Dorothea could experiment with make-up, giggle over the problem page letters in magazines and sigh over film stars. In Nancy's company Dorothea could believe that growing up was fun. On her own, she was not so sure.

'This stop.' Nancy elbowed her. 'Come on. God, look at the crowd!'

They left the bus and joined the jostling pack of people waiting outside the Majestic Dance Hall. Nancy grinned and waved at a group of nearby sailors who stamped their feet and whistled back their approval. Dorothea averted her eyes and gazed down at her new ankle-strap sandals. Because they were light and flimsy, they did make her feet look smaller than usual, she thought, but how she wished she could wear high heels. She sighed. She was five feet eight inches tall; high heels would remain an impossible dream. Nancy always wore high heels. Glancing down at her, Dorothea reflected that being friends with Nancy brought a mixture of pain and pleasure.

The doors opened and the crowd surged in. The dance hall was a large building, but tonight no building was large enough. The orchestra struck up with a smoochy Glen Miller number and immediately hundreds of couples flocked on to the floor, some gesturing, waving, shouting across to friends, others ecstatically clamped to their partners, all of them caught up in the euphoria of victory.

Emerging from the cloakroom, Dorothea blinked. The lighting was romantically low but the overhead, revolving globe splashed flickering pools of silver on the mass of tightly packed bodies. The hall buzzed with talk and laughter, and intermittently blasts of perfume assailed her nose from passers-by who had been over-enthusiastic with their 'Evening in Paris'. She swayed. The dancers, she thought, looked like a shoal of silver mackerel twisting and turning in a fisherman's net. For her the music faded, and she closed her eyes and dropped her head. Oh, please, no, not twice in one day!

'You OK, Dorrie?' Nancy touched her arm.

'Yes.' She took a deep breath. 'Hot, isn't it?'

'Yeah. I'll get us a drink when the crush round the bar thins out.' Nancy glanced round the room. 'Plenty of blokes here tonight. We should have a good time.'

Dorothea nodded. 'I can see two free seats, near the band. Shall we sit down?'

'Good grief, no. We'll never be seen sitting there!'

Nancy had already been 'seen'. A tall RAF officer came up and whisked her off to dance a foxtrot. No one asked Dorothea to dance. She pasted a smile on to her face and waited. The next dance was a waltz. A small man in khaki approached her. He was middle-aged and balding but she rewarded him with a brilliant smile. On their second circuit of the floor her partner gave up attempts at conversation and blissfully rested his head on her bosom. With stony gaze, Dorothea stared over him. When the music ceased, she escaped and crossed the floor to where Nancy stood, now surrounded by a group of people.

'Here she is.' Nancy waved. 'This is Hank.' She pointed to a tall, rawboned GI. 'And this is Val, she's in the Land Army. And I think he's called Lewis . . .' She reeled off a string of names. Eyes sparkling, cheeks flushed pink, she was truly in her element, thought Dorothea admiringly. Hank must have agreed. He put his arm about Nancy's shoulders, already staking his claim.

'Let's sit down. There's a free table over there.'

'I think they've just got up to dance,' murmured Dorothea but Hank rushed on. 'Grab a couple more chairs, Lou. I'll get some drinks.'

There followed a flurry of activity as the group sorted itself out then a sudden exodus as a Military Two Step started. Dorothea found herself alone at the table except for one other person.

'Say, do you folks really *enjoy* doing that?'

Startled, she looked across. The speaker was a black man! Her mouth dropped open. During the rush to claim the table, she had not noticed him but now he claimed her full attention. His voice was wonderful, she thought, like rich treacle. He was looking at her, an amused expression on his face. Hurriedly, she closed her mouth. Then she said shyly, 'I suppose they must like it. It's not one of my favourite dances.'

'That's OK, then.' He grinned, his teeth showed startling white in his face. 'Maybe they'll play something halfway decent soon, jive or something, then we'll show 'em.'

'I can't jive.' Conscious that her voice sounded stilted, she blushed then felt glad the lights were low. She didn't want him to think she was prejudiced. Living in Hull, she was accustomed to seeing foreigners on the streets but this was the first time she had spoken to a coloured man. She felt relieved to see him smile again.

'That's OK, kid. With me as your partner, we'll dance everyone else off the floor. I'm *real* good!'

She laughed. She thought he was fascinating. He had a long, lively face and eyes the colour of old pennies. His build was slim and he looked, she thought, about twenty years old. What a pity he's black . . . The thought surfaced in her mind and made her ashamed, but she also felt excited and on edge. She watched his long dark fingers tap on the table in time with the music. No, it's not a shame, she decided. She was glad he was different. But they had been silent for too long. Feverishly, she searched for something to say.

'Do you come here often?'

His shout of laughter caused the people at the next table to turn and smile.

Dorothea blushed again.

'Gee, I'm sorry. But don't you know that's *my* line?' He choked back his laughter and tapped open a pack of American cigarettes. 'Want one?'

She shook her head. He lit a cigarette for himself, and leaning back in his chair blew a smoke ring at the ceiling. She watched every move. He seemed so relaxed, so easy in his own skin, she felt the tension leave her. He blew another smoke ring then rocked his chair forwards. 'If you really want an answer, no, I haven't been here before. I've just checked in to Wenlock Barracks. But I've seen a bit of England. I was stationed in the south.'

'Oh.' She watched his nostrils flare as he drew on his cigarette. His nose was straight, his features well defined. He was the most beautiful man she had ever seen. Just sitting near him made her feel funny. She swallowed.

'Do you like it over here?'

He hesitated. 'Hey, that's kind of a loaded question, Dorrie. It is Dorrie, isn't it?'

She nodded.

'Well, it's real interesting. It's such a little country but there are so many differences: I like your countryside, all those neat fields, and up here the moors – they're something else.'

He fell silent and she edged her chair closer to his. Another dance had started and she hoped fiercely that no one would return to the table and disturb them. He was so unlike anyone she had ever met and she wanted him to herself. Also, he was treating her as an adult!

'Go on,' she said.

'Well, folks are generally friendly. And, my goodness,' he shook his head, 'you've had it rough. Here in Hull, for example, looks as though you've had a real pasting from Jerry. But . . .' He hesitated. 'I can't help feeling you're almost *too* patient, *too* polite about things. I mean, no one kicks up enough fuss, gets things put right. Back home, I reckon some of these ruins would be pulled down by now.'

21

He fell silent and a sheepish look spread across his face at Dorothea's change of expression.

'How dare you!' She sat up straight in her chair, forgetting the attraction she felt for him. 'What do you know about it? Maybe if you'd been bombed out of your home, kept awake night after night by air-raids, lived on the rations we've had to put up with, you wouldn't find it so easy to "kick up a fuss"!'

'I'm sorry.' He frowned. 'But you did ask me. I think your country's swell, really. It's just . . . back home, I'm used to trains and buses running on time, and although England's always great when it has its back to the wall, it seems to slow down when it comes to picking up the pieces afterwards.'

She glared at him. 'America's wonderful, is it? It should be! It hasn't exactly been in the thick of things, has it?' Her voice wobbled. 'All right, it's four years since Hull was badly bombed, but since then there's been nothing we could use to repair the buildings and no man-power. We had a lot of casualties, you know, and later on we had the buzz-bombs.'

'Hell, I've really upset you, haven't I?' He reached over and took her hand. 'I'm sorry, kid. I'm inclined to shoot my mouth off. I'm really sorry, and you're right – I don't know anything.'

Her anger faded. His hand felt so warm, his skin so smooth. Her own skin tingled. Her voice quietened.

'No, you don't know. We're just tired, you see. The war seems to have lasted for ever.'

He squeezed her fingers. 'Will you forgive me enough to dance with me? That's a quickstep they're playing, a *real* dance. Come on.' He stood up. 'We're celebrating victory, remember?'

He hadn't lied. He was an excellent dancer. For a few minutes he guided her skilfully through the tightly packed couples but inevitably they became caught up in the throng of dancers swaying in the centre of the floor. Pressed close against him, Dorothea thought she could feel the beating of his heart. She closed her eyes and savoured the moment. He was tall enough for her to rest her head on his shoulder and when she dared to do so, she felt his hand tighten on her back. For the first time in her life, she felt attractive. When the music finished she felt another surge of delight for he did not lead her off the floor but loosely linked her hand in his and waited.

'I don't know your name,' she said.

'Gabriel – Gabriel Barrand.' He grinned, then pulled a face. 'My Mamma, she's a great Bible reader. Gabriel means "Man of God". It sure takes a lot of living up to!'

She smiled. 'My name is just as bad. Can you imagine anyone christening a baby Dorothea?'

His eyes twinkled. 'Our folks didn't do us any favours, did they? Still,' he squeezed her hand, 'Dorrie's not so bad. And my friends call me Gabe. Will that do for you?'

She nodded, the music started and they danced. All too soon it ended again. 'Look, Hank's finally made it with the drinks. Let's go back.' She didn't want to, but when he looped his arm about her shoulders she felt happy again.

Nancy's eyes rounded like saucers as she watched them return. 'My, oh my,' she whispered to Dorothea. 'Where did you find him?'

Dorothea took her seat without replying. Back with the group, her old uncertainties returned. Nancy was so pretty and petite, Gabe was sure to be attracted to her. She looked round. Everyone was chattering. Vi mentioned she was hoping to attend university now the war was over which brought forth the information that Gabe would go to college on his return to the States.

Then Nancy piped up: 'My friend Dorrie should have gone to college. She's really clever, always top of the class, particularly in maths.'

Dorothea kicked out under the table but Nancy, having consumed three ports and lemon, had turned slightly belligerent. She stared ferociously at Vi.

'You upper class lot think you have all the brains,

23

but working-class girls can be just as good. Dorrie has ambitions, too.'

Dorothea's face reddened. 'Don't listen to her,' she whispered.

Gabe leant forward and grinned his lop-sided grin. 'No, tell us, Dorrie. I'd like to hear.'

Fearful he was mocking her, she glanced at him shyly through lowered eyelashes, then seeing the encouragement in his gaze she held up her head. 'I did have plans to stay on at school but it wasn't possible. Anyway, I've been inquiring about further education, maybe night-school. If I can pass exams, get qualifications, I'll try for a different type of job.'

'Well, now,' Hank was bored with this conversation, 'I know I'm just a country hick but I know a good tune when I hear one. And with a gorgeous girl like this around . . .' he pulled a giggling Nancy to her feet '. . . I know what I want to do.'

Other members of the party rose to their feet. Dorothea stared down into her glass. She was sure Gabe would ask Vi to dance now.

He was holding out his hand to her. 'Come on. When I find a partner I enjoy dancing with, I stick with her.'

The next three hours were pure magic for Dorothea, then things became hazy. Hank, in his own estimation, was a country hick; but he had a knack of weaving his thin body through the impatient crowd at the bar and returning with drinks in record time. As the evening faded people were affected differently. One couple went to dance and never returned, Nancy's laugh grew louder and Gabe's drawl more pronounced. Vi brought the house down by climbing on to a chair and impersonating Winston Churchill. A GI jumped up on to the stage, grabbed the mike and sang an Al Jolson song, then a local man followed him and sang 'The Laughing Policeman'. Everyone was very, very happy.

During the last waltz Dorothea clung to Gabe, overcome not so much by passion as the need not to fall down. The lights were dim, and all about her she could hear voices crooning: 'Who's taking you home tonight?' She wondered hazily what would be the expression on her father's face if Gabe took her home, and for some inexplicable reason she found the idea so funny she rocked with laughter.

'Hey,' he put his finger under her chin and forced her to look up at him, 'you've taken too much on board tonight, Dorrie. Not used to drinking, are you?'

'Of course I am.' She stopped laughing and straightened up. 'I'm not a kid. I'm . . .' she put three years on to her age '. . . I'm nineteen.' Then she hiccupped.

He sighed. 'I should have realised.' He put his hand under her elbow and guided her off the dance floor. 'Stand there,' he said, and walked away.

She stood still and stared in front of her. He's gone, she thought. A moment later, he reappeared.

'Nancy tells me there's a bus in five minutes, at the end of this street.'

Dorothea refocussed her eyes. 'Nancy . . . where is she?'

'She's leaving with Hank. I'll take you back. Get off at Rayner's, she said?'

He *was* taking her home. This beautiful creature was taking *her* home! A wide smile spread across Dorothea's face. 'The Star and Garter, actually,' she said.

'Sorry?'

'The pub, it's really called the Star and Garter.' She pronounced her words carefully. 'The fishermen always call it Rayner's. I don't know why.'

'Never mind, I'll sort things out. Let's go and collect your coat.'

Carefully, she turned and followed him.

They caught the bus, alighted at the Star and Garter, and he walked her home. When they arrived the house was in darkness. Dorothea's parents had retired to bed.

'Sure you'll be all right?'

'Yes.' She raised her face and closed her eyes. After a pause, he kissed her on the cheek. She was bitterly disappointed. In her mind she had already assigned a role to Gabe. He was the handsome hero, wise and sensitive enough to perceive the fascinating creature hidden behind her dull, ordinary exterior.

'Well . . .'

He couldn't be going!

She opened her eyes. Perhaps he caught the mute appeal by the light of the gaslamp for he hesitated, then said: 'You really can dance, you know. Hank and me, we were thinking of visiting a dance hall in Albert Avenue, Newington, next Thursday. Do you know the place?'

She nodded her head vigorously. She didn't but Nancy would. 'Perhaps you could both come along, we could make up a foursome?'

'Oh, yes.' Her eyes grew enormous with happiness. He touched her face with his hand. 'Great. See you there, about eight?'

She nodded, then watched him as he turned and walked rapidly away. Then she let herself quietly into the house and went to the kitchen for a drink of water. Her head was muzzy. In the back yard Jake whined and in direct contravention of her father's orders, she released the dog and allowed him in the kitchen. He snorted a greeting and jumped into Dennis's chair. She stroked his head.

'I've met someone wonderful tonight, Jake,' she said. 'I think I'm in love with him.'

A sentimental tear squeezed itself from her eye and plopped on to Jake's paw. He licked it away, snuggled himself into a more comfortable position on the chair and closed his eyes.

Chapter Three

One way for the girls employed at the Metal Box Factory to enliven the monotony of the working day was to use their tea breaks to gossip about their amorous adventures of the night before. Nancy's name was invariably mentioned; Dorothea's, never. So, the day after the Victory Dance, when Nancy let slip that Dorothea had been taken home by a gorgeous black American GI, there was a collective intake of breath.

'Never!'

Nancy's small, vivid face clouded with uncertainty as the girls, sprawled on metal chairs, mugs of tea clasped in their hands, turned their be-turbaned heads towards her friend. Nancy realised she had let her mouth run away with her yet again.

A blowsy, red-headed girl was the first to comment. 'Go on – you're pulling our legs.'

'It's true, isn't it, Dorrie?'

Dorothea stood by the table. She filled her cup from the large metal teapot, and nodded.

'If it *is* true, tell us about him then.' The redhead's voice held a sneer.

Dorothea was silent. Nancy, eager to make amends, spoke for her. 'She doesn't have to tell you if she doesn't want to, Mary Timpson.'

'Yes, she does.' Mary's eyes sparkled. 'We're interested. We talk about our chaps, she can tell us about hers. Tell me, Dorrie Bellows, is it true what they say about black men?'

Nancy, flags of colour flying in her cheeks, opened her mouth but remained silent when

27

Dorothea frowned at her. There was an amused, avid silence.

Dorothea thoughtfully stirred her tea. They really dislike me, she thought. The realisation, instead of upsetting her, made her brave. She thought of the lads *they* courted, then she thought of Gabe. She turned and faced them.

'What's the matter, Mary? Why should you want to know? Is it because that weedy boyfriend of yours can't manage it?'

Mary's eyes widened in shock and disbelief. 'Why, you . . .' She jumped up from her chair. 'My Dave's worth two of any negro. I've heard about them! No decent lass would go out with one – they have to take the leavings.'

Dorothea's face whitened but now Nancy entered the fray.

'You take that back, Mary Timpson! If you went up to town more often you'd know how smart the black men are. You see them with lovely girls. Not that you'd know. Your boyfriend will only take you to the local pub.'

She stopped. Nancy was no coward but Mary was a big girl. Now she was shaking with temper and clenching and unclenching her huge hands. It was rumoured she had laid out her own father one night when he was bashing Mary's mother. Nancy decided it was time to change the subject. 'Anyways,' she hurried on, 'I thought you wanted to know what happened when Hank took me home and Mum and Dad were still out . . .' She winked at Dorothea as the girls turned back to listen to her. All except Mary, that was; she pushed past and stalked outside.

Dorothea drank her tea quickly and went back to her machine, rubbing at the stains on her hands with an old rag. God, how she hated this place! A gale of laughter came from the group of girls still clustered around Nancy. Her voice rose and fell. How much of what she said was true and how much was fiction? Dorothea shook her head. She would never know.

The whistle blew, the girls went back to work and the noisy machines whined into action. Dorothea took a sheet of metal and fed it into her machine. The draughty barn of a building in which the girls worked was as hot as hell in summer and freezing in winter, there was dust everywhere and no comfort, but at least the work was so undemanding your thoughts could roam free. Dorothea thought about her workmates. It was generally understood in the area that the roughest girls went to work at the factory. She had elected to apply for a job there because it paid higher than a shop job. She had no intention of staying any longer there than she had to, however. Her father was recovered now and as soon as she managed to save a few more pounds she would be off.

She glanced around. The rest of them would stay there until they married and started a family. Some of the girls were already engaged. The insular nature of the Hessle-Roaders meant the girls by and large married boys they had gone to school with. The lads left school and went to sea in trawlers or else worked on the fish dock; the first child was usually born when its parents were still in their teens. It meant living with in-laws, screaming babies and money worries. Dorothea knew the fishermen were generous with money when they had it but most of them became heavy drinkers. It was a local joke that they all wore the customary square-toed boots to allow them to stand closer to the bar. And the women didn't seem to mind. When their men were at sea they found companionship and support with their mothers and grandmothers who always lived close by.

Well, it wouldn't do for her, nor for Nancy. As if on cue, her friend staggered past carrying a pile of boxes. The sun, streaming through a dusty, fly-blown window, haloed her curls and made her look positively angelic.

She paused next to Dorothea's bench. 'Sorry I blabbed, Dorrie.'

'Don't worry.' Dorothea shook her head. 'You'll

catch it if the foreman sees you with your hair uncovered.'

'Pooh!' Nancy grinned, then crossed her eyes. She went on her way, singing. Dorothea smiled as she looked down at her work. Rules and Nancy didn't get on. For the first time, it occurred to her that Nancy truly valued their friendship. Dorothea knew she was considered an outsider but what about Nancy? True, she had been born in the area but Nancy was a rebel. She would flirt with local boys then say she despised them. She looked further afield for her serious boyfriends. Dorothea knew local mothers warned their daughters against Nancy. Would Nancy stay in the Hessle Road area? Dorothea shrugged. It was no good broaching the subject. Nancy never planned ahead. Dorothea didn't understand her at all.

The foreman dumped a pile of metal rods on her workbench. 'Here's another lot, Dorrie. That 'ull keep you going.'

She reached over and pushed them into a tidy group, then flinched as a sharp piece of metal caught her finger. She sucked away the blood. She was getting as bad as Nancy. She knew she should always wear protective gloves.

She wondered again about Nancy's tall tales. Did she really allow boys the liberties she hinted at? Dorothea shivered. She could never imagine allowing boys to do such things to her. No, her energies were totally concentrated in escaping this kind of life and finding something better. But she'd have to be careful. Sometimes, when Nancy spoke of French kisses and adventures in The Cut, the local courting lane, Dorothea felt hollow inside. And look at the feelings she had experienced when dancing with Gabe . . . She cut off such dangerous thoughts and concentrated on her work. She managed to do this so well, she was surprised when the leaving whistle went. As she tidied her bench, Nancy, who had already hurried out, reappeared and shouted across to her: 'Hey, Dorrie, must be your lucky week. You've an admirer waiting outside.'

Dorothea started to ask who it was, but Nancy had disappeared again. An admirer . . . surely not . . . ? She ran a comb through her hair and picked up her jacket.

Outside, leaning against the brick wall of the factory, was Rob Steyart. When Dorothea appeared, he straightened up and took his hands out of his pockets.

'Hello, Dorrie.'

'Oh, it's you, Rob.'

Her voice was curt. I could have done without him, she thought. Then she looked at his expression and felt ashamed of her flash of irritation.

'Didn't mind me waiting for you, did you?'

'No, of course not.'

The tall girl and the smaller boy walked along the road together. 'I'm off for some chips, see.' Rob lengthened his stride manfully to keep up with Dorothea's quick steps. 'And I thought, Dorrie will be leaving work – I can tell her my news.'

'Oh, Rob.' Dorothea halted. 'Is there news of your dad?'

Rob Steyart had come to live with his grand-mother five months ago. From local gossip, Dorothea knew his mother was in hospital in Manchester suffering from TB and his dad was posted 'missing at sea'. Now, seeing him look down at his shoes and shake his head, Dorothea cursed herself. What on earth had made her say that?

Rob looked up at her. 'I'm going to visit my mum next week. The doctors have arranged it.'

'Why, that's great news. Won't she be pleased to see you? She must be improving, Rob, if she's allowed visitors.'

'I don't know.' He looked up at her. 'My gran says I must prepare myself. She says Mum's not long for this world. But,' he hunched his shoulders self-protectively, 'I reckon that's daft! My mum's not forty yet. She didn't even look ill last time I saw her. People don't die that young, not unless they're in an accident or something.'

Dorothea looked down at the boy. He walked beside her with tight, jerky movements and she could hear his shallow, uneven breathing. She realised he was close to tears and resisted an impulse to put her arm around his shoulders. If I do, she thought, he's sure to blub and then he'll never forgive me.

'Old folk tend to look on the black side, Rob. I don't suppose your gran knows any more than you do. When you get to the hospital, the doctors may have good news for you.'

He nodded and they walked in silence until they reached the fish and chip shop. Despite the warm weather a queue had formed outside and the smell of frying wafted through the still air. Dorothea paused. 'I'd better get home.'

Rob joined the end of the queue. 'Can I walk Jake with you at the weekend?'

She hesitated, then nodded. 'Of course.'

He smiled. 'Thanks. I'll see you then.'

She nodded again. She wondered, as she turned into Warren Street, if Rob was having as much difficulty in making friends as she had done. She had spoken to him about it a couple of times when she had been taking Jake out and had seen him wandering about on his own but now she seemed to be always falling over him. The lad should find friends at school, not tag around after her.

Perhaps Nancy was right and he was developing a silly crush on her. He had recently taken over a newspaper round and one day he had stood outside her house and warbled a few notes of 'The Donkey Serenade' before he delivered the paper. Dorothea pulled a face. Her mother had enjoyed a good laugh over that!

As she entered the house she heard her father shouting: 'I've said it before and I say it again, Hazel, that dog has to go!'

A frown spread over Dorothea's face. She heard her mother's indistinct murmured reply then her father again: 'The bloody animal makes fools of us all! Dorrie knows he should stay fastened up but no, she lets him off and he's away thieving again.' Dennis Bellows broke off his tirade as his daughter entered the room.

'Oh, you're home, are you?'

'Yes, Dad.'

Dorothea fought to keep the tremor from her voice. Dennis was a small man but when he was angry he was a formidable sight. Now the veins stood out on his forehead and his face was choleric red.

'What's happened?' she asked.

A swift glance about the room showed her the offending party was nowhere in sight. She relaxed slightly.

'What's happened! What usually happens when he's off his chain? He's slipped off, that's what. Been in every house in the street with an open door. Frightened Mrs Gill silly, and pinched a chicken off Mrs Smithers's table. Ate it all too. And don't say it's not your dog because there's a trail of feathers right into our backyard and the chicken's head is by our dustbin.'

Dorothea bit her lip.

'What's Mrs Smithers doing with a chicken? She must have bought it on the black market. I know for a fact she bought a pound of sausages at the butcher's on Monday so she had no meat ration left this week.'

'What the hell has that to do with it?' Dennis stared at her, his brow furrowed. 'You're supposed to keep that animal under control. I'm up for election at the management union meeting tomorrow – do you think they'll elect me now? What sort of bloody fool does it make me look when your dog's pinched stuff off all my mates?'

Dorothea hung her head. 'I'm sorry, Dad.'

33

'So am I. He goes, understand!' Dennis glanced at his watch then swore again, this time under his breath. 'Now I'm going to be late for the shift.'

He slammed out of the house. Dorothea sighed and looked at her mother. 'How long has he been missing?'

'All day, but he's all right.' Hazel Bellows went into the backyard and unbolted the coal house door. A scruffy, wriggly body shot into the kitchen and fawned over Dorothea.

'He turned up five minutes before your dad was due home. I realised he'd been up to his old tricks so I pushed him in there, out of the way.'

'Mum, you're a brick. But what about . . . ?'

Hazel looked at her daughter's anxious face. 'Don't worry. Your dad will forget it. He's worried about the meeting tomorrow. I'll go shopping, see if I can find a bit of black market stuff myself. If he has a decent meal tomorrow night, he'll calm down.'

Dorothea looked sternly at Jake. 'I should punish him, I know, but it never does any good.'

'No.'

They looked at Jake who grinned up at them, his tongue lolling from his mouth. Then Dorothea turned to her mother and squeezed Hazel's arm. 'Dad won't be back until morning, will he?'

'No, why?'

'Well, Jake's certainly had his exercise for today and I've four shillings going begging. There's "The Seventh Veil" on at the Ritz. Want to go?'

'Oh, I'd love to!' Hazel clasped her hands together. 'Brenda from next door has been and said it was marvellous – she cried buckets.'

'Good. I'd better chain Jake up.'

Hazel began to laugh. 'He pinched more than that chicken, you know. He put a scrubbing brush and kneeling mat underneath our mangle, and I'd no idea where they'd come from until I popped down to the corner shop for a loaf of bread. Then Mrs Cotter came out on to her step and shouted to me: "That bloody dog of yours has taken my brush and mat! Why don't you send him round tomorrow for the bloody bucket, then you'll have the lot!" Oh, Dorrie, I was so embarrassed, I almost ran home.'

They stared at each other then dissolved into peals of laughter. Half an hour later, unusually companionable, they strolled arm-in-arm in the direction of the cinema.

Chapter Four

Dorothea hurried to where Gabe waited for her. She felt excited and on edge. It was their fourth date but this time would be different, she thought. Previously they had been with Hank and Nancy, in crowded dance halls where it was difficult to talk. Today it was just the two of them. Gabe turned and saw her and his face split into an infectious grin. He waved.

'Hi.'

She crossed the road and walked up to him, suddenly shy.

They had arranged to meet outside the Queen's Gardens and Dorothea had brought bread with her to feed the ducks. However, the day was cool, the sky overcast. She shivered.

'Not so good, is it?' He tucked her arm through his. 'What shall we do?'

'I *did* think we'd walk round the gardens first.' She held up her brown paper bag. 'For the birds,' she explained.

'OK.' He turned up the collar of his jacket and peered upwards. 'Maybe the sun will come out later.'

The gardens were deserted. A flotilla of ducks, spying the couple, paddled over and noisily and voraciously snapped up the bread which Dorothea crumbled into tiny pieces and threw in the water. Gabe sat down on a nearby garden bench and watched.

'Didn't know there were gardens here,' he said. 'I've done some exploring these last two weeks but I've not been here before.' He watched her shake out the last of the bread, split open the paper bag and hold it out over the lake. 'Good country for bike riding – really flat. Have you a bike, Dorrie?'

'Yes.' She came and sat down next to him. 'Look at that,' she said. A bossy drake chased away his wife and greedily choked down the last of the bread. 'Just like a male!'

'Don't you like males?' teased Gabe.

'Not most of the ones I know. Born selfish, they are!'

'What a cynic for one so young.' He grinned. 'I'd better come along to your neighbourhood and look at these guys.'

Dorothea didn't smile. 'I shouldn't bother. It's drab and dull and boring and nothing ever happens.'

Gabe leant back and stretched his arms along the back of the bench. 'I should think you've had enough excitement in Hull,' he said. 'Like I say, I've been looking around. The bomb damage is horrific. Surely you're glad of a quiet life now, even though it can be a mite boring?'

'I sound a right misery, don't I?' Dorothea looked at him. 'I'm sorry. Things are a bit difficult at home right now, and work is horrible. But you're right, I should be thankful the war's over.' She paused, then seeing Gabe was looking at her, listening to her, she went on: 'We were bombed out, you know. That's why we had to move to Hessle Road. I remember that the air-raids were awful, and yet exciting in a way. You'd hear the planes, they came over at three-minute intervals, then the searchlights would be switched on and there was lots of noise from anti-aircraft guns. We'd pile off to the shelters and pass round flasks of tea and play with other kids, and it was like being in one large family. Even people who hadn't spoken for years made friends again.

'The morning after a raid there'd be the gossip. I remember when Reckitts & Colman bought it, and then Hammond's store went up.' She laughed. 'Hammond's held a sale of fire-damaged stock and Mum queued for hours for some sheets. When we

38

opened them up there were scorch marks all over them. One night we slept in the open, in the grounds of Hesslewood Orphanage. That was queer, that big, red sky. It was like a great adventure, you know, then you'd hear that someone you knew had been killed and you felt awful.' She stopped, surprised to find there was a tear rolling slowly down her cheek.

'I'm sorry,' she apologised again. 'I don't know what's got into me lately.'

'Don't cry, Dorrie.'

'I'm not!'

She was silenced. Gabe kissed her. It was a proper kiss, the first one he had given her. She was mute with astonishment, her tears dried. She stared at him.

'The ducks have deserted us,' he said calmly. 'What next?'

She gulped. 'We could walk along to Princes Dock and you could see all the shipping and go along the Pier. The paddle steamer goes from there to Barton-on-Humber. We could go on that, if you like.'

'Up you get, then.' Gabe sprang from the seat and held out his hand to her. 'It's too chilly to sit here any longer.'

As they left the gardens the cold wind snapped at their ankles like a stray dog but Gabe pulled Dorothea closer to him and she felt warm with happiness. They went to watch the paddle steamer load up with cars but decided it was too cold for the crossing. When a splatter of rain came they ran for a Corporation bus which conveniently turned the corner of the road.

'Picked the wrong day, didn't we?' he said as they climbed on to the bus. 'I might be able to wangle a pass for Saturday. Want to meet me?'

'Oh, yes.' Dorothea's face shone.

The bus was full but Gabe spotted two seats at the rear. They sat down. 'I'll get away about . . .'

A voice interrupted them. 'I'll take that seat, mister.'

Dorothea looked up to see a tall, blond US captain in front of them. His face was handsome but set in harsh lines. He stared at Gabe.

'Did you hear me?'

Dorothea stiffened and looked back at Gabe. He was staring straight in front of him, his face grim. One or two of the passengers were now looking round, interested, a little apprehensive. The captain caught hold of the back of a seat and braced his body as the bus rounded a corner. His eyes never left Gabe.

'Answer me, boy.'

Gabe's reply was quiet. 'I heard you.'

'Well?'

The captain swayed towards them and Dorothea flinched. She felt Gabe take her hand and squeeze it. A murmur spread around the bus. The conductress, an extremely fat woman, came padding down the aisle. The captain did not notice her approach. He still stared at Gabe. 'You coloured boys are taking too much on yourselves over here,' he said.

Dorothea wondered if the man was drunk for his blue eyes looked glazed, and hectic spots of colour showed on his cheeks. He tapped Gabe on the shoulder. 'In fact, I've decided – the best place for you is off the bus, not just off the seat. Of course, your lady,' he sneered the word, 'your *lady* is welcome to stay.'

Gabe half rose from his seat, his face stormy, but Dorothea pulled him down. The conductress had reached them. Her heavy hand fell upon the captain's arm.

'Only one person's getting off at this stop, my lad, and that's you!' With a deft movement she pressed the bell and as the bus slowed she twisted the captain on his heel and propelled him off the bus. Then she rang the bell again.

'Sorry, sir,' she thrust her head out to say. 'It's an old rule. Last on, first off.'

The incident occurred so quickly the captain was speechless. He stood on the pavement open-mouthed as the bus drove away. The passengers stared back at him through the windows and a ripple of amusement spread through the bus. The conductress brought them to order. 'No standing on this route,' she

40

announced, her face impassive, until she passed Gabe and Dorothea and allowed herself a faint grin.

Gabe still held Dorothea's hand but she felt his grip slacken as tension drained away.

'About Saturday,' he said, 'you still want to go?'

'Of course I do.'

He smiled at her. 'Do you like swimming?'

'Yes.'

'Let's go swimming then.'

She nodded. If he didn't want to talk about that awful man, neither did she. But the incident had shaken her and for the rest of the bus journey she was silent. She kept stealing glances at Gabe. Ever since they met she had seen him as an exciting, exotic hero-figure. Something like a prince in a fairy tale, she thought wryly. What a kid she was! He was just a man, a man with a different coloured skin. She thought of the calm way he had handled the captain's aggression and smiled. He was, she decided, a man she wanted to get to know.

Gabe's pass had only been for the afternoon so Dorothea was home early. The house was empty. Dennis Bellows was at work but Dorothea was surprised to find her mother out. At first she was pleased. Hazel would have asked what Dorothea had been up to, and there was no way she was going to tell her mother about Gabe. He was her secret. Nevertheless, the empty house made her feel dismal. Her father had placed a pile of leaflets on the table with a terse note, demanding rather than requesting that Dorothea fold them and put them into the waiting envelopes, 'if she had time'. Dorothea scowled. Why should she help her father with his rotten Labour Party work? He wasn't interested in anything she did! On the table there was also a covered dish containing potted meat and a tomato for Dorothea's tea. She had eaten a snack in a café with Gabe before he returned to the Barracks but the colder weather had made her hungry so she cut a thick slice of bread and plastered it with the potted meat. Then she went and released Jake and allowed him into the kitchen.

The dog gave her his usual rapturous welcome but as she munched her tea, Dorothea's melancholy increased. It was her day off, she thought, and she had nowhere to go and no one to go with. But that wasn't the true reason for her depression. Putting down the bread, she lifted the mirror from the wall and propped it on a chair. Then she twisted and turned in front of it, trying to see as much of herself as she could. She looked terrible, she decided. Her hair, supposed to turn under in a page-boy style, had come uncurled and hung drably to her shoulders; her face was too broad, her mouth large. Nancy kept telling her she had lovely eyes, but what was the good of them when the rest of her was so awful?

She looked down at her figure. She was just a big awkward lump. She *couldn't* go swimming with Jake! She remembered what Mary Timpson had said about black men taking the 'leavings' and tears stung her eyes. But Gabe wasn't like that. He hadn't even made a proper pass at her. She only wished he would! She sighed and replaced the mirror on the wall, then sat down and took a huge bite of bread. The knock on the door made her jump. Her spirits rose. Perhaps it was Nancy coming to see if she could go out? But no, she remembered, Nancy had arranged to see Hank that evening. She went to answer the door. It was Rob Steyart.

'I found this tennis ball.' He showed her. 'I thought Jake would like it.'

'Come in.' She led the way into the kitchen. Even Rob was better company than her own thoughts. 'Want a potted meat sandwich?' He nodded and sank down on the clipped hearthrug next to Jake.

'Here, boy.'

Jake nosed the ball, licked Rob's hand but kept his eyes fixed on Dorothea preparing the sandwich.

'How did the visit to your mum go?'

'Not bad. She seemed awful tired though, didn't talk much.'

Dorothea handed him the sandwich. Immediately,

he broke a piece off, put his hands behind his back then offered two clenched fists to Jake. 'Which one, boy?'

Jake yawned, then delicately prodded the left fist.

'He always knows.' Rob opened his hand and allowed Jake to eat the bit of sandwich. 'He's very intelligent, isn't he?'

'I think he can just smell the food.'

Jake, seeing Rob eat the rest of the sandwich, stood up and padded to Dorothea. He sat on her foot and rested lovingly against her.

'He really loves you.' Rob's voice held a wistful note.

'Yes.' Dorothea caressed Jake's ears.

'Tell me how you found him.'

'Oh, Rob I've already told you.'

'Tell me again.'

'It was just after we'd moved to this house . . .' Obediently, Dorothea told her story. 'A family called Lombard lived at number thirty-two. They had a little girl of four and a dog, a beautiful labrador called Sadie. One day, Jake came along. He,' Dorothea paused, wondering how to phrase the words delicately enough, 'saw Sadie and fell in love with her.'

'Just like grown-up people do?' asked Rob, his eyes fixed on her face.

'More or less the same,' agreed Dorothea. 'He sat outside their house and wouldn't go away. He was a bit of a nuisance, actually.' She suppressed a smile. 'My dad fell over him one night. It was in the black-out, see. He went a right bump. One night there was a terrible air-raid and Mr Lombard's house was hit. He was away fire-watching and his wife and daughter were visiting relatives so they were lucky, but poor Sadie was in the house. The firemen and the air-raid wardens came and put out the fires but the house was just a pile of rubble. Yet still Jake wouldn't go away. It was awful to see him, he got thinner and thinner and he was filthy. No one could catch him. Every night he haunted the ruins of the house and howled. All the children were warned not to go near him, but I couldn't bear it. I used to lie in bed and hear him howl.'

She fell silent, remembering herself as a lonely unhappy child, in a new area and a new school. Cold-shouldered by the local children, particularly when she proved to be clever, teased for being plump, she remembered how her heart had gone out to the starving stray dog that no one wanted.

'One day,' she continued, 'I took some food and water and sneaked under the ropes cordoning off the bombed house. I just sat down and waited and eventually he came to me.' Remembering, a lump in her throat prevented her from continuing.

'He trusted you.' Rob's shining eyes watched her.

'Yes.' She smiled at him. 'My dad saw me, on his way home from work, and he went mad, ordered me to come away. It wasn't just the dog,' she explained, 'the ruins were unsafe. He was frightened I'd get hurt. I was going to go but Jake whined and nudged me. He wanted me to follow him, so I did.'

'And you found Sadie!'

'Yes. She was buried but they got her out alive. Jack Lombard was in tears. His daughter had been pining for her. They dug her out and wrapped her up and took her away, and nobody bothered about poor old Jake.'

'You did, Dorrie.'

'You bet I did.' She grinned. 'I made my dad's life a misery until he agreed I could keep him.'

Rob sighed. 'I wish I could have a dog, but my gran won't let me.'

'Never mind.' She studied the youngster. 'You can have a bit of Jake if you like.'

'Can I? Which bit?'

She laughed. 'Take your pick.'

Rob studied Jake, his short legs, long tail, floppy ears and ungainly body. 'His head, I think.'

'A wise choice, that's his best bit.'

They were both laughing when Hazel Bellows

walked in. Dorothea thought how attractive her mother looked in her red swagger coat, a wisp of a hat perched on her upswept hair. She must have been wondrously pretty when she was young. What on earth made her marry Dad?

'Guess where I've been, Dorrie?'

'Haven't a clue.'

'Brenda and I have been to a Spiritualist Meeting! We went for a laugh really, but it was wonderful.' Hazel clasped her hands together. 'There was a woman who spoke with a man's voice and gave messages to people in the audience. I was frightened to death she'd speak to me, but she didn't. Then another man stood up and he said there was a person in the audience who possessed great gifts and could become a fine medium. And Dorrie—' Hazel looked at her daughter, wide-eyed '—he looked straight at me!'

Dorothea frowned. She knew her mother was always getting enthusiasms for different things but she didn't like the sound of this at all. 'Wasn't it Brenda who took you off to see a fortune teller last week, Mum?'

'Yes, she did.'

'Well, do you honestly think you should get mixed up with such things?'

'Why not? It doesn't do any harm.'

'I'm not so sure, and I know Dad wouldn't approve.'

'If you don't tell him, he won't find out. He's so involved with his Union work.'

That's half the trouble, thought Dorothea savagely. If Dad took more notice of Mum she wouldn't need to go off chasing things to occupy her mind and time.

'What's a Spiritualist Meeting, Mrs Bellows?'

The two women had forgotten Rob.

'Oh, just a Church Meeting, Rob.'

Hazel removed her coat and changed the subject. 'And what are you up to?'

'Nothing.' He looked depressed.

'Yes, you are,' said Dorothea. 'You're going to help me.'

She picked up the leaflets. 'Did my dad say anything about these to you, Mum? I don't know why they can't see to forms down at the Labour Club!'

'Yes, dear.' Hazel's voice was vague. She turned away and gazed blankly into space.

Oh, Lord! Dorothea gave an inward groan. She'll be communing with spirits now. God give me strength.

She pushed half the leaflets towards Rob. What a pair we are, she reflected. What was that old saying, about picking your friends but not your family . . . ?

'Did I see you coming out of Mrs Bellows' house, Rob?'

'Yes, I went to see Dorrie.'

Thelma Steyart said nothing else but she sniffed and Rob's heart sank. His grandmother's sniff was a marvellous vehicle for expressing disapproval.

'Mrs Bellows has started going to church, Gran.' Rob's expression became crafty. He knew it was Dorrie's mother, rather than Dorrie herself, who was the object of the old woman's disapproval. Several times he had heard his grandmother comment on Hazel Bellows' short skirts and bright lipsticks. She had also said it was scandalous for a woman with a grown-up daughter to look so young. Rob thought it must be wonderful to have a mum so lively and vivacious. Hurriedly, he pushed out of his mind the image of his own mother, so weak and listless, her face bleached as white as the pillow-case on which her head rested.

'She told us all about it when she came in,' he said.

'You mean, she's been to a service today?'

Rob opened his mouth, and then paused. His grandmother's gaze had sharpened. He wriggled on his chair like a fish on a hook. 'I *think* so,' he said.

'I know of no church that holds services on a Wednesday afternoon.' Thelma tapped thin fingers against her pale lips. 'Think carefully, Rob. Tell me exactly what she said.'

Rob wondered if he could possibly change the subject. He remembered Dorrie's mum had said she didn't want Mr Bellows to know about the Spiritualist Meeting. And now he thought about it, he was sure his grandmother wouldn't approve. She didn't even like the Fishermen's Bethel Mission, although that was where most of the Hessle-Roaders went . . . those who went anywhere to worship. His grandmother was really funny about religion. When he first arrived to live with her, that's what most of her questions had been about. Had his mother taken him to church regularly? Things like that. Then, when he had mumbled that he never went to church, speaking in a low voice because he knew her views on the subject, she had actually smiled. Now, as then, he felt confused and took refuge in mock stupidity.

'I don't know, Gran. She and Dorrie were talking but I wasn't really listening. I was helping Dorrie fold some ballot papers. Oh!'

He stopped. He had tried to escape from one trap only to fall into another. His grandmother hated the Labour Party. He looked at her from beneath lowered eyelashes. Fortunately, she was too busy following her own line of thought to listen properly to what he was saying.

'I'll check the church announcements in the evening paper,' she said. 'It could be one of the Primitive Methodists. Well, well, fancy Hazel Bellows turning towards religion.'

Thankful his grandmother had forgotten him, Rob slid quietly out of the back door. He hoped she didn't find out the truth. He wanted Mrs Bellows to keep going to the Spiritualist Meetings. Then Dorrie could tell him if people really did float up into the air and talk in foreign languages.

Chapter Five

Gabe Barrand left the Barracks and walked to the nearest bus-stop. Thank goodness he had arranged to meet Dorrie this afternoon, he thought, as he strode briskly along the road. She would raise his spirits. She was always such a lively kid, and bright too. He couldn't believe she was stuck in a factory job. He remembered Nancy blabbing away the night they met about Dorrie's dreams and ambitions. How embarrassed she had been. He sure hoped she'd make it one day and get a job worthy of her. His ruminative smile faded. Thinking about Dorrie's ambitions reminded him of the letter he had received that morning from his father.

It wasn't that he didn't care about his family; indeed, he thought the trouble was, he cared too much. And he wanted so badly to please his old man and make him proud of his son. He venerated the wise old guy with the work-hardened hands and soft voice who had worked so hard for them all. He also deeply loved his bustling energetic mother and three mischievous, giggling sisters, but . . . Gabe sighed. Why did he have to be the only son?

He had grown up knowing the hopes of his family rested solely on his shoulders. And when his scholastic achievements, first in junior school and then high school, had reinforced his father's suspicions that Gabe was exceptionally bright, those hopes and ambitions had soared to dizzy heights.

From growing up knowing that he must get a good job to ensure his own success and help his sisters make suitable marriages, Gabe was shown new horizons by his ambitious father. He could pass scholarships, gain entry to a top college. Maybe he should study law . . . How the old guy's eyes had sparkled. 'You have been blessed with talents, boy,' he had said. 'With God's blessing you will help not only your own family but black people everywhere!' And eighteen-year-old-Gabe's eyes had sparkled too. He had been young and idealistic. He worked hard, thought of nothing but his studies – and then he had been drafted!

He found himself in an alien world, often hard and brutal but also exhilarating. For Gabe, it proved a revelation. For the first time in his life he was free of responsibilities. Initially reserved, he gradually blossomed in the company of his fellow soldiers. He developed a relaxed style and became popular with both men and women. He was lucky in his postings. Too lucky, his innate streak of responsibility told him, but what the hell – it was nothing to do with him. He found he particularly liked living in England. He liked the country and he liked the people.

Dorrie now . . . his lips turned up in a smile as he thought about her. He had reached the bus-stop. He checked his watch. Good, the bus should be along soon. He always looked forward to meeting Dorrie. God, she was in so much of a hurry to grow up. She made him feel like an old man sometimes. His smile widened. She'd be a sexy little baggage, given half the chance.

Oh, he'd picked up the signals all right but – his smile disappeared and he sighed – it wouldn't do. He'd be posted soon and she'd be left behind, convinced her heart was broken. He sighed again and a sudden wave of irritation hit him. He hadn't really changed at all. He put on such a show of being cool, relaxed, but that's all it was – a show. He worried about people all the time and then, sometimes, he got sick of worrying, sick of feeling responsible for other people. His father's letter had been full of

plans for the future. Gabe didn't want to consider
the future, not yet. It was *now* that was important!
And this business with Dorrie – sure she was a great
girl, but why should he feel so responsible for her?
She had a mind of her own, she worked in a factory,
surely she knew the score? The guys in his unit would
die laughing if they knew he was dating a virgin.
He'd bet his bottom dollar she'd never been with a
man. Yet she could be so damn provocative. Provocative yet gut-wrenchingly innocent! A sudden
image of what Dorrie might look like, naked in bed,
flashed into Gabe's mind and he swore, conscious of
a stab of desire.

He saw with relief the bus he was waiting for
round the corner of the road. He climbed aboard
and took a seat. His mental picture of Dorrie faded
from his mind. An old lady sitting opposite stared at
him curiously then flushed as he smiled at her. A
second later, she shyly returned his smile. Gabe
smiled again, more broadly this time, then stared out
of the window. Resolutely, he tried to forget his
father's letter.

Dorothea edged her way out of the changing rooms.
Whilst she had been undressing she had heard shouts
and children's laughter, but now she was in the pool
area she was relieved to see the place was not unduly
crowded. She was a good swimmer and she wanted
Gabe to know it. She looked about her. He was waiting by the poolside, seated at the top of the steps, his
legs dangling in the water. She looked at the slope of
his wide shoulders, his lean brown back, and her eyelids pricked. She wanted so much for him to like her.

The floor tiles were wet and slippery but she
walked as quickly as she could towards him. If she
could reach him before he turned and saw her, she
thought, it would be better. She knew the swimsuit
she had bought especially for today suited her but
she still felt dreadfully self-conscious. The suit was a
turquoise-blue colour which brought out the colour

51

of her eyes, and the one-piece style flattered her figure, showing off her trim waist. She also hoped it minimised the size of her chest and thighs. She took a deep breath and touched his shoulder. He turned and greeted her.

'There you are.' He jumped into the pool and held out his hand.

Gingerly, she lowered herself into the water, gasping at the sudden chill. Gabe grinned at her and ducked down below the surface, then emerged, laughing, the water streaming from his face.

'Go on,' he said. 'You do it. Much the best way.'

She stared at him. His dark curling hair, cropped close to his head, was silvered with tiny beads of water; his eyes were narrowed. She blamed the cold water for the contraction of her chest and lungs which left her breathless, the hairs at the nape of her neck prickling. She turned her gaze away, held her nose and submerged herself. When she surfaced, her hair slicked back from her face, coughing and spluttering, he caught hold of her.

'You look like a mermaid in that suit,' he shouted, and kissed her.

She clung to him. Blast him! she thought. His kiss was light and teasing, a butterfly kiss. She put her arms about his neck, allowed her lips to part. He drew away, his smile fading, then pulled her towards him again. His hands slipped from her waist down to her hips and lingered there. His mouth came down on hers. Around her, the splashing and shouting of the other bathers retreated into the distance. The chlorine taste of the water on her lips was like nectar.

When he lifted his mouth from hers, she shivered, felt empty. She saw with disbelief that his face had resumed its usual half-teasing expression.

'Race you,' he shouted, and struck out strongly, his arms cleaving a sweet, clean line through the blue water. She watched him, struggling to regain her composure. Then she went after him, determined to beat him. She swam well but was no match for Gabe who won easily.

They swam several lengths of the pool then lounged

around in the shallow end, watching grim-faced youngsters practising their breaststroke and a couple of mothers supporting chubby babies adorned with water-wings. A flaxen-haired child in a red bathing-suit bobbed by then disappeared in a splutter of bubbles. Gabe reached out and yanked her to the surface. The girl's eyes widened at the sight of a black man, then she grinned her thanks and doggedly struck out again.

'That's one thing I like about this place.'

'What's that, Gabe?'

He grinned at her. 'No one seems to give a damn what colour you are.'

Dorothea remembered the captain on the bus. 'They do back home?'

'Jeez, baby, if only you knew! Why, in some states in the South, I'd be in jail if I went into a whites' pool.'

'Honestly?' Dorothea was shocked.

'You just don't know!' He looked at her fondly, seeing her shiver. 'Come on, we'd best go.'

They were making their way towards the changing rooms when someone shouted. Another man, also black, approached them.

'Gabe! Gabe Barrand. So this is where you get to!'

Dorothea sensed, rather than saw, Gabe recoil.

'This your little lady?'

Gabe shrugged. 'Hi, Vince.' He looked at Dorothea. 'This is Vince Teller. He's in my Unit.'

Vince was built like a truck. Next to him, Gabe looked puny. The huge man eyed Dorothea, particularly her figure. Then he said, 'This here's Rona,' and pushed forward his companion. Rona was blonde, in full makeup and wearing a bathing suit which looked as if it would disintegrate in water. She did not speak but nodded, clasping possessive hands around Vince's massive forearm.

'Pleased to meet you.'

Dorothea resisted a strong urge to place her hands over her breasts to stop Vince staring at them. Gabe rested a hand on her shoulder. 'Can't stop and talk, Vince. We're both cold. Maybe see you later?'

'Sure, sure.' Vince leered at them. 'Don't like to think of anyone being cold. You go and get warmed up. Come on, Rona.'

They walked away and Gabe and Dorothea continued in the direction of the changing rooms.

After dressing, they went along to the cafeteria for a cup of tea. They sat in silence for a while, locked in their own thoughts, then Dorothea spoke.

'You didn't spend long talking to your friend, Gabe. Why?' Her voice quavered. 'Were you ashamed of me?'

'What the hell does that mean?' She was astonished to see anger on Gabe's face. 'Anyway, Vince Teller isn't a friend.'

'Oh? I thought he was.' She fiddled with her teaspoon. 'That Rona, wasn't she beautiful?'

Gabe looked even more annoyed. 'OK, she was pretty.' He stared at Dorothea and continued, 'And nothing like you.' He saw the expression of hurt on her face and relented. 'For your age, Dorrie, you sure are naive!' He ignored the blush mounting in her cheeks, leant forward and spoke rapidly.

'Rona's a certain type of woman.' He shrugged. 'Look, Dorrie, you must know negroes are a bit of a novelty over here. Hell,' he shrugged again, 'we're not complaining. Back home . . .' He paused and a humourless smile flitted across his face. 'Back home we'd be in bad trouble if we dated a white girl. Maybe not in the North so much but where I come from . . .' He sighed. 'Then we come over here and girls seem actually to prefer us. "My, oh my," we think. "This place is paradise, man." '

He fell silent and gazed down into his teacup. Dorothea watched, waiting for him to continue.

'Then we get wise.' He pushed away his cup. 'Or some of us do. It isn't *us* that's the attraction, it's our colour. And you know what?' He raised his head and looked at her. 'That's almost worse, because you end up by feeling like some performing monkey!'

'Oh, Gabe.' She reached for his hand. 'I'm sorry. I never thought.'

He stared down at their joined hands, white on black. 'That's why I like you so much, Dorrie. You're straight. I'm just another guy to you, not merely a scalp for your collection. I think I realised that when you lit into me when I criticised your home town at our first meeting.'

Remembering the mixture of emotions she had experienced on the night they met, Dorothea fought down a pang of guilt. It's not like that now, she told herself. She laughed, then apologised. 'Sorry. It was just the thought of me having a collection of scalps. You're flattering me, Gabe. My only other admirer is an eleven-year-old boy.'

He grinned and she was pleased to see the strained look leave his eyes.

'Then the guys round here must be blind. They don't know a real dish when they see one.'

'Oh, Gabe,' she clutched his hand, 'you really mean that?'

'Sure I do.'

'You always treat me like a kid. I was beginning to think there was something wrong with me.'

He stared at her and something glimmered at the back of his eyes. 'Let's get out of this place,' he murmured.

It was good to be in the fresh air after the chlorine-filled atmosphere of the swimming baths. After the cold snap, the summer weather had returned. Soot from many chimneys had rimmed the fresh green of the trees but the birds sang and the yellow sun hung low in the blue sky.

Beneath the shade of a chestnut tree, Gabe kissed her again. She touched his lips with her fingertips. 'I'm glad we talked,' she said. 'Now we can be a proper couple.'

He shook his head. 'Don't get heavy, kid. I like you a lot but we have to face it – before long I'll be shipping out of this place.'

She made a wordless noise of dissent.

'It's true. They reckon the Japs will give in soon and then we'll be sent home. It might only be a matter of weeks.'

'I don't care about the future. You're here now. I love you, Gabe.'

'You're just a kid . . .'

'Don't say that!' she interrupted him. 'I'm *not* a kid. I'll show you.' She pressed herself against him, arching her back so her breasts pressed against his chest. She heard him catch his breath and smiled triumphantly. She knew she was behaving shamefully and she didn't care at all. She would *make* him love her!

When he pushed her gently away from him, she couldn't believe it. 'You're taking things too fast, Dorrie. You'll regret it later.'

'I won't, I won't!' She burst into tears. 'You said I was dishy,' she wept, 'but you don't fancy me at all, do you? I'm just too fat and ugly!' She sobbed out loud and an elderly gentleman walking along the road looked up with alarm then crossed to the other side.

Gabe sighed. He pulled her back into his arms and stroked back her hair. 'You really mean it, Dorrie? You want me to make love to you?'

She nodded.

'Well then, honey, you're surely wrong about me not fancying you.' He tightened his hold on her. 'I try to live up to my Mamma's ideals but it's not easy.' He chuckled. 'Let's see what I can arrange.'

Hazel owned a silk underslip, a treasure from pre-war days. Dorothea sneaked in to her parents' room and took the slip from its nest of tissue paper. The silky fabric slid through her fingers like a whisper. She shivered, folded the slip into a small parcel and placed it in her pocket. Her mother wouldn't miss it. Dorothea knew she rarely looked into the bottom drawer where mementoes of her youth were stored. Perhaps she found them too painful to contemplate. Poor Mum, thought Dorothea. Mum just had boring old Dad whereas she had Gabe!

Safely back in her own bedroom, Dorothea put on the underslip then hastily slipped into a freshly ironed cotton dress. She wished she could have bought something new for this day but her clothing coupons had all gone. One day, she told herself, she would have a wardrobe of beautiful clothes. She brushed her hair until it shone and applied a dusting of powder to her face and just a touch of pink lipstick to her lips. She knew Gabe didn't like to see girls wearing too much make-up. Before she went downstairs, she looked round her room as though saying goodbye. When she returned she would be different.

Gabe met her off the bus and they walked along looking for Wilberforce Avenue.

'It's just round this corner, I think.' He stopped to get his bearings, and smiled at her. 'A chap called Willis put me on to it. He's a Scot and sometimes his wife comes up for the weekend.'

Dorothea smiled but did not reply. She felt absolutely nothing.

'Here it is.'

They stopped outside a green-painted front door. Gabe produced a key. Dorothea stared down at the step. Some kid had chalked rude words on it, she felt a wave of panic. It wasn't supposed to be like this!

When Gabe touched her arm, she jumped.

'It's all right, Dorrie. We don't have to.'

Immediately, love flooded through her. She smiled. 'We do.'

Once inside, she felt better. They had climbed the narrow flight of stairs and gone through the half-glazed door at the top. The room was large with square windows. One corner had been fitted out with a gas ring and a sink unit. There were blue-edged cups and saucers displayed on white painted shelves. There was also an easy chair, a small wardrobe and a large old-fashioned bed complete with brass head-board. A gaily patterned quilt was spread over the bedclothes. Dorothea took one look at it then averted her eyes.

Gabe removed his uniform jacket, crossed to the easy chair and sat down. 'Come here.' He spoke softly.

With hesitant steps she walked over to him. He pulled her on to his knee. 'Relax, Dorrie.' He rested his cheek against hers and rocked her, gentling her as though she was a child. 'Stop worrying. We don't have to do anything you don't want to.'

'No, no.' She clung to him. 'I do.'

He made her look at him. 'It's the first time, isn't it?'

She tried to look away but he caught hold of her chin, forcing her to look in his eyes. 'Why are you looking like that? Christ,' he gave a soft laugh, 'it's nothing to be ashamed of.'

'The girls I work with,' she stammered, 'they seem to know everything! I . . .' She stopped and burrowed close to his chest.

He was silent for a moment then said, 'Just calm down. There's no rush, no hurry. We'll only do what seems right.'

For a long time they clung together not speaking. The sun moved round the room, slanting tender fingers of light on to their chair, the cooking utensils and, finally, the bed. Afterwards, Dorothea remembered it as their closest communion, wordless and perfect. Then Gabe stirred. She looked at him inquiringly then got to her feet. 'What is it?'

'Sorry, honey.' The laugh was back in his voice. 'Cuddling you was sweet but the fact is, I've got cramp in my leg!'

'Gabe!' She knelt down in front of him. 'Which one?'

He indicated his left leg and she pushed up his trouser and rubbed his calf. He winced.

'Idiot,' she scolded him. 'You should have told me earlier.'

She kneaded away at his muscles until she felt them relax. Then she looked up and caught her breath. He was watching her with the same expression he had worn in the swimming pool. Even before he reached for her, that look had penetrated her shyness and dispelled her fears.

He bent forward and kissed her. Her lips parted and his tongue explored her mouth gently. When he moved away from her she gave a moan of protest.

'Hush,' he said. He stood up, pulled her up to stand beside him and kissed her again. He kissed her forehead and the line of her jaw, laughing as he did so. 'Such a stubborn jaw you have, Dorrie.'

She laughed with him, a catch in her throat. In his beautiful eyes she could see a tiny reflection of herself. She loved this man, she told herself, and she wanted him.

As his long, slim fingers undid the buttons on the front of her dress she tried clumsily to help him. The dress fell to the floor and he slipped his hand down into the silkiness of her borrowed underslip and rested his fingers on her taut, hardening nipple. She gave a choked-off, little sob. The room dissolved into a kind of shimmer. Her only consciousness was of herself and Gabe. It was she who pulled him towards the bed.

'Steady,' he said. There was still the hint of a laugh in his voice but his breathing was ragged. He broke away to remove his clothing, and as he did so she slipped out of the rest of her clothes and lay on the bed, praying he would find her beautiful. He turned and looked at her and she trembled with feelings she could not fully comprehend. Then he came to her, lay beside her, stroking her face and quietening her.

'Gabe?'

'Hush.' His eyes were bright. 'You're beautiful, Dorrie. I want this to be good for you, but I . . .' He shook his head. His fingertips traced her shoulders, moved down over her ribcage and across her taut stomach. Then he bent and his lips closed on her breast. She cried out and clung to him. He calmed her again. They lay still until he began to bring her to new awareness of her body as he caressed her hips and thighs, to go deeper. Her breath came in great gasps.

'I want . . .'

'Hush,' he said again. The sunlight lay warm on their naked bodies as he caressed then teased her. Then, finally, he eased his body on top of hers. She closed her eyes. This joining, this sharing, was more natural, more wonderful, than anything she had ever imagined. She savoured the sensations rippling through her body then his movements increased, became urgent. There was a stab of pain, she cried out and he stopped moving.

'No,' she shouted. 'No!' And pounded his chest with frustration.

His body moved within her again and the pain was lost in a feeling of heat which flickered then flared inside her. The heat filled her until she could bear it no longer. She cried out Gabe's name.

They lay exhausted. His breath was warm on her ear and she cried a little. He did not speak but took hold of her hand and kissed it.

'You were wonderful, Dorrie.' His voice was serious. 'I mean that. You've a talent for loving.'

'So have you.' She shivered.

'Hey, you're cold. Hop into bed. Properly, I mean.' He grinned.

'Then we'll have a cuppa. Isn't that what you call it? Just like an old married couple.'

She looked at him and his grin faded. 'Ah, well.' He went to make the tea. She slid under the bedclothes and watched as he moved about the room, totally unconcerned about his nakedness. Dorothea had never seen a man naked before. She thought surely no other man could be as beautiful as Gabe.

'Here you are.' He climbed back into bed. Still, she stared at him.

'Why, Grandmama, what big eyes you have,' he mimicked, a self-conscious expression creeping across his face. 'What's the matter?'

'You are.' She swallowed. 'I love you, Gabe.'

'Sure you do.' He took her hand and placed it flat against his own, spreading out her fingers. 'Look how little your hand is against mine.' He stared down, gave a brief shake of his head, and closed his hand on hers.

'I guess that right now,' he said, 'I love you, too.' He shook his head again at the look in her eyes. 'But it won't do, Dorrie.' He released her hand. 'Are you really nineteen?' When she did not reply, he gave a quick sigh. 'I should have guessed.'

She frowned. 'Why does my age matter?'

He picked up his cup of tea. 'You have a lot of growing up to do.'

'All right, old man,' she cried, stung to anger, 'and how old are you?'

'Almost twenty-three.' He took a sip of tea and gestured towards her cup but she turned her face away.

He sighed. 'Don't sulk, honey. That just shows you're still a baby.'

'I don't understand you.' Dorothea's eyes filled with tears. 'We've just made love and it was wonderful. At least,' she drew a quavering breath, 'it was for me.'

'It was for me, too.' He banged his cup down. His face held a baffled expression. 'You were just great, Dorrie, but . . . Hell, how can I explain?'

He drew his knees up beneath the bedclothes and rested his hands on them. 'You don't know me at all, Dorrie. And I don't know you, not really. You think that's not important, but it is. Look, I'm black. I was born in the South and, believe me,' his face set in grim lines, 'you can't know what that means. I've a daddy who broke his back to get me a good education, and when I go home I'll be attending college, not just for me but for the whole of my family. There's no way I can get serious with any woman right now, not here, not at home.'

'I'd wait, Gabe. I wouldn't mind doing that. I could get on with that studying I was telling you about, and then come to America to be with you.'

Her rush of words was stopped by his vehemently shaken head.

'You're day-dreaming, don't you see? I know that you've made up your mind that you love me but you're still a kid, Dorrie. You'll change, probably love a lot of guys before you get married.'

'I won't! I'll prove it to you. I won't mention it again, Gabe, but when you have to go away I'll write to you. I don't care how long we have to wait – I know we were meant to be together.'

'You're in love with love, kid. Just because we're great in bed doesn't mean you love me.' He stopped, shaken by the hurt on her face. 'I'm sorry, maybe I shouldn't have said that. But you're still not seeing things properly, Dorrie. If I took you home, you'd hate it.' He paused. 'No one would accept you. My family would think I'd betrayed them and white folk would automatically rate you "white trash". You just wouldn't fit in, and that's the truth. Why not just make the most of what we have right now?'

The bleakness of his voice appalled Dorothea. She wanted to scream and shout at him. Tell him she didn't fit in anywhere. Beg him to consider taking her home with him. But she looked at his unhappy face and remembered how he had loved her. She knelt beside him, ignoring the covers falling away from her, and linked her hands behind his neck. She felt the unresponsive rigidity of his body as she kissed his lips. 'I'm sorry,' she said. 'I guess you're right. I don't understand. Still,' she kissed him again, 'you paid good money for this room. It's a pity to waste time arguing.'

For a brief moment, he resisted her then his arms went around her, crushing her to him until she gasped for breath. And in this, their second act of love, it was she who was the giver, instinctively knowing how to make him forget his burden of responsibility. She watched his face grow young again and put his need before her own. And, unbeknowing, she herself changed from child into woman.

Chapter Six

Rob Steyart stood at the end of Ruby Street and gloomily watched the weekend traffic rumble along the road. Behind him was his grandmother's house. In there, he had moped away the morning hours, fingering the ornaments on display, teasing the budgerigar, even sneaking into the hallowed sanctum of the parlour in a vain attempt to find something to do. Then his gran had ordered him outside.

'Drive me demented, you will,' she complained. 'Always under my feet. What with you and the Robinsons, I'll end up in an early grave!'

The Robinsons lived next door. There were five children in the family and they fought, howled and argued incessantly. The adjoining walls between the two houses were thin. No wonder Thelma Steyart, who had no interests except for her home and her religion, turned to the Bible for solace. She read it by the hour, her fingers stuffed into her ears in a vain attempt to block out the racket from next door. Rob, on the other hand, enjoyed hearing the rumpus. It was better than silence. He sighed. Gran's house was always silent.

He glanced downwards and saw a thick layer of dust had coated his new shoes. He rubbed first one then the other toe of his shoe on the back on his socks. His gran didn't like him to be untidy. He privately thought his gran didn't like *him*, but on his arrival she had told him she would do her best to give him a good home and that, he now knew, meant keeping him properly clothed and teaching him respect for his elders. Unfortunately, his gran's ideas as to upbringing brought him in direct conflict with his classmates.

The boys at his school came from poor families. Their poverty did not seem to bother them. Rob knew they found many ways to make extra money. The boy he sat next to in school sold old paperback books to the trawlermen returning to sea and always had money in his pockets, but his profits went on cigarettes, not clothes. The Hessle Road lads considered anyone neatly dressed a 'cissy', and dealt with them accordingly.

Rob heard a guffaw of laughter and his slight form stiffened as three boys rounded the corner of the street and walked towards him. He could go back into the house . . . He debated the point in his mind, then clenched his hands in his pockets and stood his ground.

'Why, look who it isn't!'

Stanley Daniels, a bulky thirteen year old not noted for brains, stopped in front of Rob. He screwed up his face in a grotesque parody of a genteel lady and asked: 'Going for a walk with your darling granny, then?'

His companions exploded into laughter at his heavy witticism. Rob's face reddened, but he eyed his antagonist steadily.

'No, I'm not.' Damn! His treacherous voice had wobbled. A spurt of pure rage ran through him when he saw Stan's thick lips broaden into a smile.

'But if I did,' he continued, reckless of the consequences, 'at least my gran would be able to walk in a straight line – which is more than your parents can, after they've been to the pub!'

Stan's smile froze. His eyes bulged and he reached out and grabbed hold of Rob's shirt front. Rob closed his eyes and the two boys accompanying Stanley buzzed with anticipation. Then a window banged and his gran's voice rang out.

'Clear off, you lot.' Her head appeared at an upstairs window. 'It's Stanley Daniels, isn't it?

You're the spit of your father. He was a troublemaker, too! If you don't leave immediately, I'll contact your headmaster. He'll know what to do with you!'

Stanley released Rob. Thelma Steyart was tiny in stature but she was a grown-up and therefore 'authority'. Also, Mr Willinson, the boys' headmaster, *did* know how to deal with unruly pupils. A caning from him left you with bruised hands for a week! Stanley pushed Rob away but his eyes were hard, cold stones as he hissed through his teeth: 'I'll get you later, nancy boy.' Then he turned and shambled down the street followed by his pals.

Rob drew a shaky breath then relaxed. He knew Stan meant what he had said but with the insouciance of boyhood Rob could forget about him for now. With a bit of luck Stan Daniels might get knocked down by a bus before school on Monday. He wondered whether to thank his gran but when he looked up at the house she had already closed the window and disappeared from sight. He knew she wouldn't want him back indoors yet. He pulled on his lip, deliberating. Stanley had been heading for the billiard hall; he'd better go the opposite way. Rob's face brightened. He'd go and see if Dorothea Bellows was at home.

'No, love.' Hazel's voice was abstracted. She had managed to purchase a length of cotton dress material and was painstakingly cutting out a skirt length on her kitchen table. 'I don't know where she's got to. She went out ages ago.'

Rob hesitated. 'Well, could I take Jake for a walk? I'll look after him.'

'Drop him off the pier, if you like,' Mr Bellows's voice came from behind his paper.

Hazel pulled a face in his direction then smiled at Rob. 'Of course you can, love. Only, I should keep him on his lead. Sometimes he runs away, you know.' She waved her hand towards the back door. 'The lead's on that hook.'

He took the lead and went out to collect Jake. The dog quivered with anticipation. On his best behaviour, he sat down and allowed the lead to be clipped on to his collar then trotted next to the boy out of the yard and down the street. Rob patted his head.

'Come on, Jake. We'll go to the park.' He turned left and was pulled up sharp. Jake had lain down in the road.

'Come on.' Rob tugged on the lead. Jake refused to move. Rob looked down at the dog's mournful expression. 'Oh, all right, then.' He walked to the right. Jake bounded up and wagged his tail. He was an urban animal. Dorothea had deduced long ago that he preferred the streets. He enjoyed the lampposts; the dustbins with their lids half-off; the delicious, to him, smells that accompanied the dark patches against walls and doorsteps. His short legs stumped busily along, his quivering tail was held high and his eyes moved constantly from side to side in the hopes of seeing a stray cat!

Up and down the streets they went, Jake sniffing and depositing infinitesimal drops at regular intervals. Finally, they came to St Andrew's Dock. The 'Wet' side of the Dock, the area which seethed with life in the early hours of the morning when the 'bobbers' unloaded the fish, was silent now, deserted. It was so quiet that Rob, contrary to instructions, let Jake off the lead.

The dog ran about pursuing strange scents and Rob strolled along towards the 'Dry' side of the Dock. Here trawlers came to be checked over after a rough trip to the Arctic. Inevitably repairs were needed, and weekend overtime was undertaken to ensure they were seaworthy enough to meet the third tide. Rob watched a chippie busy with some exterior work, cleaning away the rust and corrosion caused by salt water. Then Jake's snorts of boredom brought him round again to retrace his steps to the fish unloading section. Rob had been to the Dock before but he had never seen it so quiet. The only noise he could hear was the slap of the water. In the air was a smell of freshly caught fish and a tang of salt. It was not unpleasant.

Rob sat down on a conveniently placed pile of wooden fish crates and stared into the sun-dappled water. The smell of the sea turned his thoughts, as always, to the fate of his father. Where was he now? The boy's eyes probed the surface of the water. He had an awful feeling that, if he stared down long enough, he would see his dad, his eyes wide but unseeing, his thick hair floating and moving about his bleached face, his body wreathed in seaweed, fish darting about him. He groaned and covered his face with his hands. Aloud, he said: 'He isn't dead, he isn't!'

Deep inside, Rob knew he could bear the thought of his mother's death more easily than that of his father's. His mother was gentle, loving, but she had always been like dim candlelight against the vivid flame of his father and now, with her husband presumed dead, it seemed as though her light was slowly flickering out. Rob scrubbed his eyes fiercely. His dad would be ashamed of him! When he returned, he must never know his son had doubted his survival. Rob sighed and looked round for Jake. The dog had disappeared. Rob jumped up.

'Jake! Where are you, boy?'

There was a clatter and from behind a pile of rusting barrels, Jake appeared. In his mouth he had a large cod's head and from the smell reaching Rob, it had been out of the water some considerable time.

'Oh, hell.' His heart sank. 'Come here, Jake,' he coaxed.

Jake grinned his doggy grin and disappeared from sight. Rob pursued him as he scuttled from the back of the piled-up rubbish and shot off down the dock. Then he lost him. Rob spent an hour looking for the dog then admitted defeat and retraced his steps to Warren Street. At the corner, paws neatly together, Jake awaited him.

'You little devil!' Rob snapped on the lead and sighed with relief.

'Any trouble, was he, dear?'

Hazel had now tacked together the material and was trying on the skirt. Rob blushed and looked away from her. When she twisted round like that, you could see bits of pink flesh through the gaps in the stitching.

'No, he was fine.'

'Good.' Hazel challenged Dennis. 'There you are! He behaves perfectly well with *some* people.'

Jake wagged his tail perfunctorily and disappeared under the chenille tablecloth.

'Help yourself to a cup, Rob.'

'Thanks.' He poured himself a cup of tea from the large brown teapot and perched on the edge of a wooden kitchen chair. 'That looks nice, Mrs Bellows.'

'Thank you, Rob. I'm not sure if red's my colour but you have to make do with what you can get nowadays.' Hazel smiled at the boy. 'Any news about your mother?'

Dennis rattled his paper warningly. Rob wondered what there was in the newspaper to keep him interested for so long. It was one of those big, thick newspapers though, he conceded, and Dorrie had told him her father was interested in politics.

'No,' he answered Mrs Bellows. 'She's just the same, I think.'

There was a short silence then Dennis spoke. 'A lot's going on now. There's new drugs about. That Penicillin – wonderful stuff.'

Rob shifted on his chair and wondered whether Mr Bellows expected a reply.

'Yes,' he said.

Hazel glanced at the clock. 'I can't think where our Dorothea's got to,' she mused. 'Never said anything to you, did she, Dennis?'

'Not much likelihood of that,' muttered her husband.

Rob stood up. 'I'd better go . . .'

The door opened and Dorothea entered the room. Rob gaped. He thought she looked like a film star. Dorrie's eyes shone, her skin glowed, she lit up the dark kitchen with a radiance. Rob's heart skipped a beat. Something wonderful had happened to her, he just knew it. He felt a peculiar kind of stomach ache. He was glad for her happiness, of course, but suddenly she seemed far away from him. He looked at her parents. Surely they noticed? Absurdly, they had not. Hazel swivelled round to face her daughter.

'What do you think, Dorrie? Does it fit?'

'Lovely, Mum.' But Dorothea didn't look, just stood there and exuded happiness.

Dennis put down his paper. He stared at her.

'You're late home, Dorrie. Where have you been?'

There was a sudden tense silence. Rob froze in sympathy with Dorrie. Then, strange retching noises came from beneath the table. Jake, his tail between his legs, emerged and walked stiff-legged to the hearthrug. There, he was violently sick.

Chapter Seven

Dennis Bellows was elated when the Labour Party swept to victory in the General Election of July 1945.

'Clem Attlee will put this country back on its feet,' he exulted. 'They're saying Aneurin Bevan will be Minister of Health; now we'll get the National Health Service moving. And houses – they'll build for the working classes now.'

Hazel looked up from her sewing, interested for once. Dennis could be so boring when he went on about Union matters but now she could contribute something to the conversation.

'Mrs Jackson's been round one of those new "pre-fabs". She says it was lovely, with lots of cupboards and everything.'

'They'll do for a while. Bevan says he'll have the housing problem licked by 1950.' Dennis nodded to his wife. 'When our Dorothea's old enough to get a steady boyfriend, there'll be lots more opportunities around.'

Hazel folded her work into a neat parcel. 'I think she's already got herself a chap, Dennis.'

He grunted. 'Been telling you things?'

'No.' Hazel looked pensive. 'I wish she would, but you know Dorrie.' Her expression brightened. 'But she's a different girl now. She's happier and she hasn't had one of those queer turns for weeks. She was singing before she went to work yesterday and you know how she hates that factory.'

'Well, so long as she's all right.' Dennis consulted his watch. 'How about you and me going to the pictures? You'd like that, wouldn't you? If we leave now we'll catch the first house and then we'll have time for a drink at the Club before closing time?'

Hazel quickly combed her hair and applied fresh lipstick. It's a good thing, she reflected, that Dennis is so wrapped up in the Election results. Any other time he would be pushing to find out more about Dorrie's possible boyfriend.

Dennis meant well, he tried to be a good father, but the truth was he and Dorrie were too much alike. They both liked getting their own way. He was heavy-handed with Dorrie and she retaliated by going into sullen silences. Hazel sighed.

But did she do any better? Other women that she knew had lovely, intimate talks with their grown-up daughters. Dorrie never told her anything. Lipstick in hand, Hazel gazed at her reflection in the dressing-table mirror. She wished she knew what sort of man Dorrie was involved with.

Dennis shouted and she jumped. 'Just coming.'

Her pleasure at being taken out by her husband was dimmed by his choice of film. 'The Lost Weekend', a study in dipsomania, was not her idea of entertainment, and not for the first time she wished her husband was less serious. But then they went to the Club and finally to Carver's for a fish and chip supper so she enjoyed the evening after all. Later, snuggled up in bed, her cold feet resting on Dennis's warm legs, Hazel felt a rare happiness. I hope he's a good man, she thought, remembering her worry over Dorothea. Hazel was a generous woman. Dennis had winked across at her when they were in the Club and their subsequent love-making in their old feather bed had been sweet. She yawned and pressed closer to his broad back. If Dorothea married a good, hard-working man like Dennis, she'd be all right. Conveniently, she forgot her husband's quick temper, the obvious irritation he showed when she uttered what he considered foolish remarks. As she drifted off to sleep she thought what a pity it was that elections were held so infrequently.

* * *

On the 6th August the first atom bomb was dropped
on Hiroshima. The news affected people in different
ways.

'It can't be right.' Hazel pressed a handkerchief to
her lips. 'All those children and babies.'

Dorothea glanced apprehensively at her father but
even Dennis was subdued.

'It had to be, Hazel. It's finished the war damn
quick and that's what counts.' He went to her and
patted her shoulder. 'Our lads will be coming home
now.'

When Hazel remained silent, he shrugged and went
to turn off the radio. Dorothea stacked the dirty
crockery into a pile, then carried the tray of utensils
over to the sink. How would this new, frightening war
development affect her? she thought. She turned on
the hot water tap, feeling ashamed. The bomb had
killed hundreds, maybe thousands, yet all she could
think about was whether Gabe would be sent home!
Yet she couldn't help it; Gabe was her whole life.

Nancy's boyfriend, Hank, had already left Hull.
Nancy had gone about looking miserable for a week
but already she had a new chap. Dorothea shook her
head. 'Not me,' she whispered passionately, 'never
me.' She clashed two saucers together so fiercely, one
of them cracked.

'I reckon about four or five weeks,' Gabe sighed as
Dorothea turned her face away and tapped her feet to
the music. They had gone to the Majestic to celebrate
the anniversary of their first meeting three months
previously. The same band played the same tunes, the
revolving globe glittered silver and practically the
same crowd of people circled the dance floor but,
thought Dorothea, the wonderful glow of happiness
had disappeared. How could she recreate that magical
night? She jumped to her feet.

'Come on, Gabe. They're playing "Green Eyes".
You promised to teach me how to rumba.'

75

He shook his head but followed her on to the floor. As he grasped her lightly about the wrist, she smiled at him.

'Love you,' she mouthed.

He did not smile back.

'Oh, don't be a grouch!'

He stopped dancing and stared at her, ignoring the mutters from couples bumping into them. 'You won't face facts, will you, Dorrie?'

'Not until I have to.'

His lips tightened but he took hold of her and guided her around the floor in time to the music. She glanced up at him.

'Gabe.'

'What?'

'You're hurting my arm.'

'Sorry.' He loosened his grip. 'We have to talk, honey. Don't you see that?' He sighed. 'Hell, I wish I didn't feel so responsible for you.'

Dorothea's face grew sullen. 'If you really felt responsible, you'd *do* something. You could fix it for me to follow you to America. Lots of girls are planning to do just that.'

Again he stopped dancing but this time he snatched at her hand and led her off the dance floor.

'Not that again! How many times do I have to tell you? It wouldn't work.'

She twisted her hands together. 'It would, Gabe. We would make it work.'

'For God's sake!' Unaware of the attention they were attracting, he glowered at her. 'Grow up, can't you?'

Dorothea flinched. Gabe's mouth was set in a grim line, his eyes blazed. She had never seen him look like that before. Summoning up her pride, she hardened her voice.

'You needn't worry, I was just teasing you. I knew all along what you would say. Anyway,' she stuck out her chin, 'why should you feel responsible? I'm grown up, and if you remember it was *me* that persuaded you to take me to bed!'

An intake of breath from a couple standing nearby

reminded Gabe they were being overheard. He put his hand on her arm. 'Come and sit down. We'll talk this through.'

'No.' She pulled away from him. 'I don't want to talk any more. Actually, I just want to go home.' Her voice wavered. 'I'm sick of talking, Gabe. Perhaps it would be better if we just said goodbye now, then we'd be done with the whole rotten business!'

Her voice broke on a gasp. She turned and blundered away from him, rushed into the cloakroom, retrieved her jacket and dashed outside. The night air was cool on her tear-stained face. She half ran along the pavement, her unfastened coat billowing out behind her. At the end of the road she paused and put out her hand to find something she could rest against. Her eyelids were fluttering and she felt the strange drifting-away of consciousness which heralded one of her attacks. In her unhappiness she almost welcomed the sensation.

If only, she thought, I could drift away somewhere and never come back!

She closed her eyes and bright circles spun round and round in the darkness.

'Come on, honey. Come on.'

It was Gabe's voice, husky with concern. Dorothea blinked. He seemed to be half carrying her along the street.

'Gabe?'

'Yeah, that's right.' His voice lightened with relief. 'Who else would be carrying you about at this time of night? There's a café a few yards further along. Think you can manage it?'

'Yes.' Strength flowed back into Dorothea's body. She straightened up. 'You came after me.'

'Darn good job I did! What's the matter, Dorrie? Should I call a doctor?'

'No, no. I'm all right now, really. I feel better already.' She leaned against him. 'You mustn't worry. I've had attacks like this before. They're not serious. I'm glad you followed me, though.'

77

'So am I.' Gabe held her close. 'Here's the café.'

He shepherded Dorothea to a chair, looked at her to reassure himself she was not about to faint, then crossed to the self-service counter and asked for two mugs of coffee. He carried them carefully over to the table and sat down, smiling with relief.

'You look much better now. You really scared me, you know.'

'I'm sorry. Maybe I should have told you, but I haven't had an attack for ages so there didn't seem any point.' She sipped her coffee. 'This is good.'

An old man shuffled to the counter to pay his bill then left, banging the door noisily behind him. They had the place to themselves.

Gabe looked at Dorothea with a serious expression. 'Did you mean what you said, about saying good-bye now?'

She shook her head.

'Good.' His gaze was steady. His dark brown eyes looked black with the intensity of his stare. He reached over and took her hand. 'Dorrie, I might be here for ages yet. Let's just enjoy what time we have?'

She nodded, forcing a smile, but a knot of unhappiness tightened in her chest. She had cherished a faint hope that he would change his mind. Now she knew he never would. He was hers for the next weeks. After that . . . She pulled her hand away and picked up her coffee. A detached part of her mind noticed how the mug trembled in her grasp.

As the rich tints of summer faded into the browns and yellows of early autumn, for the first time in her life Dorothea lost weight without even trying. She lost so much weight, her mother became concerned.

'Maybe you should see the doctor,' she worried. 'Go to the hospital for an X-ray. Your uncle Alfred had tuberculosis, you know. I'll try and get some shin beef tomorrow. A good broth, that will pick you up.'

'Mum, will you leave me alone? I'm perfectly all

right. You nagged me to lose weight and now you nag that I'm getting thin. I feel fine.'

Hazel was unconvinced. 'Look at the dark shadows under your eyes! You should stay in more. You're always gallivanting about. You need some early nights.'

Dorothea wanted to scream. Instead she spoke in a soothing voice. 'I really am OK, Mum. And don't worry,' she paused by the back door, 'I'll be having lots of early nights soon.'

She left without further explanation but as she walked to work the thought drummed in her mind: When Gabe leaves, when Gabe leaves . . .

She approached the factory gate with dragging steps for, truly, she felt exhausted. She saw Gabe at every opportunity and when she was with him, was bright and lively. They went to the cinema together, rode bikes out into the countryside and drank beer in country pubs. Whenever possible they went to the room in Wilberforce Avenue. Their love-making increased in passion. It was as if they were both defying the spectre of separation. Away from Gabe, Dorothea felt only half alive. She seemed to argue with everyone.

Nancy had fallen out with her.

'I thought we were friends, Dorothea Bellows. Ever since you met Gabe, you never have a minute for me. Fine friend you are!'

Even Rob Steyart voiced disapproval.

'You don't seem to take Jake out as much as you used to, Dorrie. You always told me a dog needs regular exercise.'

'Jake's fine. Perhaps you should mind your own business, young man!' Dorothea had flared up at Rob then stopped when she really looked at him. His pointed face had a pinched look which appalled her. She should ask him what was the matter but she didn't. She had enough to cope with, sorting out her own troubles.

'I'm really busy, Rob.' She offered him a half

apology. 'I wonder, if I gave you a shilling a week, would you . . . ?' She stopped. Knew immediately she had made matters worse.

'You don't have to *pay* me. I'll collect him after school every day.' Rob stalked away, hurt indignation showing in every step. Dorothea sighed. Everyone was so touchy.

In the third week of September it happened. By then, Dorothea was so emotionally drained, she felt almost relieved. She had been to town to have her hair cut and had arranged to meet Gabe in Albion Street. She was early and as she waited for him, looked about her. Albion Street was in the middle of an area of Hull which had been heavily bombed but now Dorothea saw that huge clumps of rose-bay willow-herb and yellow ragwort had grown and rioted over the derelict sites. She smiled, looked up and saw Gabe. Immediately, she knew.

He came up to her. 'Dorrie, I have to . . .'

'Don't,' she said. She thrust her arm through his and turned so they faced the bombed-out site, rehabilitated by nature into a place of beauty. 'I remember,' she said, 'there used to be some lovely old railings on this side of the street. Still,' she smiled up at him, 'the buildings were ugly. I think I prefer it as it is now.'

He pressed her arm. 'I don't have to tell you, do I?'

She shook her head. He put his arm around her shoulders. 'Let's go to our place.'

Twice as they walked along towards Wilberforce Avenue, he stopped and kissed her. It was the first time he had shown her public affection since the day at the swimming baths. Dorothea wondered whether he had refrained from doing so for her sake or his own. She would never know now. There were so many things she would never know about Gabe.

They climbed the stairs to the flat and made love. Afterwards they talked.

'When do you go?' Finally, she asked the question.

'Two days.'

'So this will be the last time?'

'Yes.' He smoothed back her hair. 'I didn't say, did I? Your hair looks pretty. It suits you short.'

She turned her face away. 'Where are they sending you, Gabe?'

'Back home.'

'That's good. You must be so looking forward to seeing your family again.' She stopped, conscious that tears were thickening her throat. No tears, no pleading.

'I'll never forget you, Dorrie. You must believe that.'

'I do.'

He kissed her lips. 'Will you promise me something?'

Her heart leapt. 'Anything.'

'You remember, the night we met, you spoke about getting on in life, studying.'

'Oh, that.'

He shook his head. 'You've never mentioned those plans since and I know it's my fault. But now I'm leaving, I want you to promise me, Dorrie. Don't give up on those plans of yours. You're too good to be stuck in a factory. Please, do it for me.'

A pang of resentment flashed through her. Why should she promise him anything? Then she looked at his face and relented. Gabe had always been totally honest with her. It was she who had woven dreams and fantasies. She promised.

'Good girl.'

Her heart sank when she saw him glance at his watch.

'I have to report back at six o'clock, Dorrie and it's almost four. Listen, I've just collected my pay. I thought I'd take you out for a slap-up meal, all the trimmings. What do you say?'

He looked at her and smiled but his eyes pleaded.

He doesn't want a traumatic scene, she realised. He wanted happy memories to take back to America with him. And although her heart was breaking, she smiled and agreed. God only knew how she would force down food.

As they left the room, she paused and looked back. Here she had learnt the joy and pleasure of love but also the heartbreak. As she gently closed the door, she wondered if growing up was worth it.

Chapter Eight

A smell of chalk, sweat and wellington boots met Dorothea as she entered the Institute of Further Education. She wrinkled her nose. The aroma reminded her of schooldays; unhappy schooldays. A queue of prospective students waited in the hall. Dorothea checked the scrawled information on the blackboard near the entrance then went to stand behind a woman with tightly permed hair who was suffering from a cold.

'Excuse me, this is the line for Higher Maths and Book-keeping?'

'Yeath.' The woman nodded, sneezed and blew her nose.

Dorothea nodded her thanks, took a step backwards and stared round at the crowd.

What a collection! she thought. There were a few housewives in turbans, a sprinkling of grey-headed grandads and several spotty youths. More sympathetically, Dorothea looked at the men in the queue. She knew who they were. There was a joke going round that you could tell a demob suit from half a mile away. A steady stream of people entered the hall but the lines of patiently waiting applicants did not seem to move. Dorothea didn't mind, she was used to queuing. You queued for everything nowadays. The Utopia her father had optimistically envisaged was a long time arriving. Butchers' shops were shut down for five days each week, eggs were rationed to one a month, and even cigarettes had gone 'under the counter'.

'Yes, young lady?'

Dorothea blinked. Deep in her own thoughts she had failed to notice her particular queue had split into two sections. She was now the nearest person to a desk behind which a man waited.

She stated her requirements. The man listened, then shook his head. 'Sorry, the book-keeping course is full.'

'It can't be.' Dorothea's face showed her dismay. 'It's only the second enrolment evening.'

With his forefinger, the man pushed his spectacles higher on his thin-bridged nose. He was in his middle sixties and wore a stiff white collar and a blue suit. 'I'm afraid so. There's been an enormous flood of applications this year.' He allowed himself a brief smile. 'People have been reading their newspapers.' He quoted:' ''Better education standards and qualifications will lead to better jobs for the able.'' ' He looked at her sympathetically. 'Why not try something else?'

'What's the point? Figure work is the only thing I'm any good at.'

The flatness of her voice must have focused the man's attention for he studied her pale face, the circles of fatigue around her eyes, and asked, 'Would you like to sit down for a minute?'

Dorothea did not reply. Like black night the terrible depression she had suffered on Gabe's departure returned to threaten her. The first week had been a nightmare. She had tried so hard to act normally but through her misery she had been aware of her mother's anxious looks and her father's short temper, which she knew was caused by a mixture of irritation and concern. She had struggled through the miserable days, hating her work, her friends, and mostly herself. But the spark of anger inside her had saved her. The anger was against Gabe for not loving her enough and against herself for allowing the hurt. No one was worth such unhappiness. She had forced herself to come along to the Institute. She must pick up her life again. Also, she had made a promise.

What was the old man saying? She blinked. 'Sorry?'

'There's a few places left on the Office Studies course. Typewriting, shorthand . . . would they interest you?'

'Oh, no.' She shook her head.

'Shorthand's rather like maths, you know. It's a very exact science.' The man's glasses had again wandered down his nose. He pushed them up. 'With shorthand you have a good chance of employment in a bank or office.' He chuckled. 'I'm an enthusiast, you see. I teach the subject.'

He was a funny old boy but friendly. Dorothea hesitated. She might as well sign up for something and classes would keep her mind busy. She asked for the relevant forms.

Every Tuesday evening for two months she regretted her decision. After a dull day in the factory she was tired and it was a long walk to the Institute. The classroom was always cold and she thought the other students unfriendly. Not realising it was her forbidding expression and unwillingness to join in conversations that kept them at a distance, she told herself it was her schooldays all over again. She shrugged. She didn't care. She'd come to work. And work she did.

'What do you do?' asked Nancy, who had forgiven Dorothea and was once more her friend.

'Write page after page of horrible little squiggles. It's so boring, and typing's even worse.'

But as she progressed, Dorothea's interest grew, especially in shorthand. Provided you followed the rules, the precise little marks never let you down. She liked that. She began taking her Pitman Shorthand book into her bedroom and practised writing the outlines. It was better than sitting in the kitchen with her mother and parrying Hazel's probing conversation as to why she didn't go out any more.

By the time the class had reached lesson fifteen, Dorothea was up to lesson twenty and attempting to take dictation from the wireless.

'Don't go too fast,' warned her teacher who she now knew was called Mr Spence. But his eyes twinkled behind his glasses and she knew he was delighted at her enthusiasm. She practised diphthongs and wrote a few outlines for Rob.

'Here you are. That's your name.'

He studied the paper. 'It's not proper writing. That,' he pointed, 'looks like the picture of a wigwam.'

She explained, 'That's because the outline represents sound. It's totally different from ordinary writing.'

'Like a code, you mean?'

'In a way. When I learn more I shall be able to write really quickly, over one hundred words a minute.'

'Gosh.' His eyes rounded. 'Will you teach me? It would be useful when I'm a private eye.'

Rob had become a devoted listener to 'Dick Barton, Special Agent'.

'Perhaps.' She ruffled his hair.

Like Nancy, Rob had made friends again. Perhaps because she was now so lonely, Dorothea found him congenial company even though he was so much younger than she was. She discovered he possessed a sly sense of humour and she liked the way he asked questions about things and showed interest.

'How's school?' she asked.

'Not bad. I did a special project on birds in Nature Study and Miss Hopkins gave me top marks. I stuck pictures and bits of information I got from the newspaper into a scrap book and she's hung it in the hall so other people can look at it.'

'That's smashing. I bet your gran was pleased when you told her.'

'I think so. She didn't say much. She's not been very well.'

Rob threw a stone for Jake. They were strolling along on a piece of waste ground waiting for the dog to finish digging up old tins, sniffing and exploring.

'I remember now, Mum said she saw her coming out of the doctor's.'

86

Rob stopped walking to pull up his socks. Then he glanced at Dorothea. 'She keeps getting a pain in her side. She's fairly old, isn't she? Do you think she'll die soon?'

'Rob – what a question!'

'Well,' he cleared his throat, 'I have to think about it. The last time I saw Mum, she looked awful and if Gran dies too, what's going to happen to me?'

Dorothea bit her lip. 'You mustn't get morbid, Rob. I know you've had rotten luck but your gran will be OK. She's as strong as a horse by the look of her. As for your mum . . .' She paused. 'She's been ill a long time. Maybe when you are weak and in pain, dying doesn't seem so terrible. Have you ever thought about that?'

He nodded. 'That's what I think.' In a matter-of-fact voice, he continued, 'Sometimes I think I wouldn't mind being dead.'

Upset, Dorothea dug him savagely in the ribs. He jumped. 'Ow!'

'What a stupid remark! You're not ill, my lad. You're young and strong and you have all your life in front of you.' She caught hold of him, dragged him round to face her.

'Maybe you're not happy now but things change. No one has a *right* to happiness, you know.' For a moment her voice wavered, then it hardened again. 'Why do you think I'm going to evening classes? I'm going to make something of myself. I'm going to get a good job and make lots of money. Then I'll do all the things I want to. And you're a boy. It's easier for them. You're going to be fine, do you hear me?'

Rob stared at her, open-mouthed. Dorothea dropped her eyes and wondered what had possessed her. Then Jake rushed up to them.

'Oh, look at you, you little devil. You're covered in mud!'

But she greeted him with relief. Sometimes Jake came in very handy.

* * *

Nancy thought Dorothea should start going out again.

'I do go out.'

'Where? To work, to the pictures with your mum, and to night-school. That's not going out! Come with me on Saturday, Dorrie. You'll grow old and grey staying at home and talking to that daft lad, Rob Steyart.'

'He's not daft, Nancy. He's just lonely.'

'Well, he shouldn't be! Where are his friends? I suppose he scares them away, he looks so miserable.'

'You're hard, Nancy Dempsey. Of course he's sad. His mum died last week.'

Nancy was unabashed. 'He'd get over it quicker if he knocked about with kids his own age. His mum's been poorly ever since he came here. She's been at death's door that long, it can't have been a surprise when she actually went through!'

'Nancy!' Yet Dorothea had to repress a laugh. Rob's present quietness tended to deepen her own ache whereas Nancy's vitality acted as a tonic.

'So you *will* come on Saturday?'

'I'll think about it.'

'Don't think, say yes. Please, Dorrie,' Nancy wheedled. 'There's a Norwegian trawler due in. Some of the crew may go to the dance at the Church Rooms. I can't go by myself!'

Dorothea sighed. 'All right. I'll call round for you, about eight.'

On Saturday Dorothea washed and set her hair and put on her last pair of nylons. Despite herself, she was looking forward to a night out. She went to call for Nancy. Mr and Mrs Dempsey were out so Nancy daringly unearthed a bottle of sherry put away for Christmas and poured out two large glasses, then the two girls went along to the dance. As Dorothea entered the church hall, her mood of anticipation faded. Had local 'hops' always been so awful?

Two brave girls danced on an otherwise deserted floor. There was no sign of Nancy's Norwegians, just local lads who stood in groups and leered at the girls. When Dorothea refused to go and dance with Nancy, her friend pouted and returned to the cloakroom to 'powder her nose'. Dorothea stood by the doorway, a glass of lemonade in her hand, and fumed when a skinny runt of a boy nearby loudly assessed her good and bad points.

The Church Hall was a spartan building with uncurtained windows. There was a poster on one wall advertising extra orange juice for expectant mothers and, on the facing wall, a copy of the painting *A Stag at Bay*. The room smelt of polish and, strangely, boiled cabbage. Dorothea sighed and wondered whether to sit on one of the hard-backed wooden chairs which were placed around the room. She decided against it. Half the chairs were already occupied by girls, all dressed up in their finery, touching their hair self-consciously, talking together with unusual animation and stealing surreptitious glances at the boys. Someone placed another record on the record-player and a few more couples took to the floor. The skinny boy who had been discussing her with his friends bore down on Dorothea. He was at least five inches shorter than she and his rubber-soled shoes squeaked on the polished floor.

'Want to dance?'

'No, thanks.'

'No!' His voice soared on that one word, expressing his surprise and indignation.

'No.' She stared at a point above his head.

He muttered a rude word and turned on his heel; his face glowed red. In the corner, his mates sniggered. 'Suit yourself. There's plenty of skirt here to choose from.'

Dorothea closed her eyes tightly to subdue a sudden rush of tears. Oh, Gabe! She opened them to see Nancy, who was now on the floor dancing with one of the few presentable men in the room. They were gazing into each other's eyes and Dorothea saw a bright red lipstick mark on the man's cheek. She watched them circle the floor then went and put her glass on a table. She turned and bumped into Bill Thomson.

'Why, it's Dorrie Bellows. I haven't seen you for ages. Enjoying yourself?'

'No,' she replied. 'I'm just leaving.'

Nancy swirled by again, laughing loudly at something her partner said. Bill winced. He walked with Dorothea to the exit.

'Mind if I walk along with you?'

'If you like.'

Walking along the dark street, Bill silently matching her steps, Dorothea felt a mixture of irritation and compassion.

'Still carrying the torch for Nancy?' she asked.

He kept his gaze fixed on the ground before them. 'Aye, daft isn't it? I know it is but I can't help it.'

They came in sight of Rayner's pub and Bill stopped. 'Come and have a drink with me, Dorrie. It's Saturday, after all.'

She shrugged. 'Why not.'

Inside Rayner's there was music, loud laughter and thick cigarette smoke. Most of the Norwegians Nancy had hoped would be at the dance were in the pub. Dorothea looked round, hoping to see a free table.

'What will you drink, Dorrie?'

'Anything, half a bitter . . .' The last word was cut off short.

At the end of the bar stood two black GIs. They were nothing like Gabe but Dorothea's heart lurched. She caught her breath then gave Bill a dazzling smile. 'Could I have a short?'

'Of course you can. Gin and tonic, whisky?'

'You choose. I'll be over there.' She waved her hand.

She pushed her way through the couples, the uniformed men. Why had Gabe been sent away when there were still so many soldiers, sailors and airmen around? He'd be back home now. She wondered if his parents were already sorting out a suitable girlfriend for him, a slim, dark girl with a college education!

Bill brought her a brandy. She had never tasted it before and she liked it. He went for two more. She looked over the rim of her glass and thought of him more kindly. He had long eye-lashes and a snub nose. Dorothea decided Nancy was mean. She should appreciate Bill more. 'Time' was called and Bill said he must see her safely home. His hand, when he reached for hers, felt rough but warm and friendly. When they reached Dorothea's house he put his arms loosely about her. 'Give us a kiss, Dorrie.'

She kissed his chin. He must have dabbed on some aftershave because he smelt nice, clean and fresh. When he kissed her on her lips, that was nice, too. His mouth was soft, his lips smooth. When he pulled her closer she did not resist. He kissed her again and this time his hand grasped her breast. She pulled away.

'Pack it in, Bill.'

'Sorry.'

He sounded abashed, uncertain whether to be angry or ashamed.

She patted his hand. 'Go on home,' she said. 'Forget about it.'

He hesitated. 'You won't . . . I mean . . .'

'I won't tell Nancy,' she promised.

You poor fool, she thought as she watched him hurry away. She stood for a moment and looked up at the stars. How cold and pure they looked up there in the velvet darkness of the sky. Bill wasn't the only fool. When he first kissed her there had been a moment when the blood had quickened in her veins. It would have been so easy to have encouraged him. She sighed and felt ashamed of herself. She cared nothing for Bill, and he cared nothing for her. They were lonely, that was all. She remembered how she had protested to Gabe. She would wait for him for ever, she had said. He had known better. Nancy's mother was always warning them about men. They all had an

91

animal in them, she said. It was up to the woman to keep them in order. What a pity no one acknowledged that women could feel the same! She took a last look at the stars then took out her key and unlocked the door with fingers that trembled.

Chapter Nine

John, Nancy's new friend, was a Leeds man. He worked in his father's newsagent's and had come to Hull to visit his grandma. Nancy was ecstatic when she found he had travelled to Hull in his father's car. She told Dorothea all about him as they worked at the Metal Box Factory. That was the only time Dorothea saw her for all Nancy's spare time was now taken up. Dorothea was happy to listen to her chatter. At least the new boyfriend stopped Nancy fretting about Dorothea's non-existent social life.

She went back to her shorthand studies. At night-school she found she could take dictation at one hundred words a minute when the rest of the class struggled to reach half that speed. Mr Spence began finding special pieces of dictation for Dorothea. As each session drew to a close he would read out a parliamentary report or medical paper, especially for her. Some pupils became impatient and a few would laugh when, on transcribing her work, Dorothea stumbled over words like 'duodenum' or 'bureaucracy'. Then, Mr Spence would frown at them and gently correct her pronunciation. One evening he asked if she would be willing to come in an hour early for special tuition.

'But why?' she asked. 'I'm already doing well. I should easily get my certificate at the end of the course.'

'It's an idea I have,' said her teacher. 'I'll explain later, and it would be interesting to see how fast you really can go.'

Because she liked Mr Spence, Dorothea agreed.

Every Tuesday evening she would sit alone in the draughty classroom and take dictation. At first, her fingers would be stiff with cold and she would shift uncomfortably on her hard chair. Then her concentration would deepen and she took pride in the growing speeds she attained as her pencil travelled over the pages. She was delighted one evening when Mr Spence presented her with a special Waterman shorthand pen.

One evening, she was disconcerted to find two strangers seated at the back of the room. She waited for Mr Spence to say something but he merely placed his stop watch on the top of his desk and opened his book.

'We'll start at one hundred and fifty words a minute,' he said. 'It's a report on the environment. Some of the words may be unfamiliar but don't let that bother you.' He cleared his throat and began to dictate.

Conscious of the silent onlookers, Dorothea began badly, then the thrill of capturing her teacher's words took over, and the knowledge that in places she was actually waiting for him delighted her. She read the work back without one omission. Three more pieces of dictation followed, each read at a higher speed. As she read out the final item of work, Dorothea's cheeks glowed like poppies but she read the transcription perfectly. Mr Spence's glasses flashed triumphantly. He turned to the two men at the back of the class. 'There you are! I told you, she's a natural.'

The strangers smiled. They came over to her and shook her hand. They represented Pitman's College, they explained. If Dorothea could reach a speed of two hundred words a minute or higher, they wanted to arrange for her to take part in a series of demonstrations around the country. They would, they hastened to add, pay all expenses, hotel bills and travel.

Her heart began to race. She hurried home that night, anxious to tell her parents of her success.

'What are they paying you?' Dennis's face showed

suspicion. No bloated capitalists were going to exploit his daughter.

Dorothea's hands clenched. 'They didn't mention payment. It's an honour, Dad.'

He snorted. 'Then the answer is *no!*'

'But, Dad,' hating herself, she pleaded with him, 'I'll get to stay in proper hotels, see the country, all at no expense.'

'The matter's closed.'

'It isn't, Dad!' Dorothea swung round to her mother for support. 'What do you think?'

Hazel glanced uneasily from her daughter to her husband. With their chins stuck out like that, she thought, they looked like two pit terriers squaring up for battle. 'I don't know,' she said. 'How would it affect your work at the factory, Dorrie?' Another thought struck her. 'And what if you had one of your attacks when you were away from home?'

'I won't!' All her loneliness and frustration exploded within Dorothea. 'And if I did, I'd manage. I'm not going to hang around at home all my life because I might have an attack. Even if *he*,' she glared at her father, 'wants me to. Do you think I'm going to work at the factory for ever more? I hate it there.'

'You'll not give up a good job until you've found another one, miss.' Dennis was outraged.

Dorothea tried to control her temper. 'But if I do these demonstrations, I might be offered another job. A better job, away from Hull.'

'Ah, that's it, isn't it? Hull's not good enough for you. *We're* not good enough for you, are we?'

Dennis thrust his face up against Dorothea's.

'Now, just calm down a bit.' Hazel, seeing things getting out of hand, strove to restore the balance. 'Let's find out a bit more about it before we fall out. You could see if the factory will allow you to take time off for these demonstrations, Dorrie. And you, Dennis . . .' She shook her head. 'How often do you talk about opportunities for the working class? It seems to me you should encourage your daughter a bit

95

more.' She saw, with relief, both Dorothea and Dennis drop their eyes. 'I'll make some tea,' she said.

'Deep breath, my dear.'

Mr Spence nodded to Dorothea then ran his finger around the edge of his stiff collar. Dorothea hid a smile. Poor man, he was more nervous than she was. The noise level in Thoralby Hall rose as the rows of wooden seats became occupied by groups of chattering people. Dorothea surveyed her audience with interest. She was secretly surprised anyone would wish to attend an exhibition of speed writing, even if it was free. She had expected a few students and teachers but the hall was now three-quarters full. Then she spied the table in one corner set out with cups and saucers and plates of biscuits, and smiled. A cheap night out, she thought.

She crossed to her place on the raised dais and sat down, pressing her legs together, partly to stop her knees from shaking and partly so that no one could see up her skirt. Introductions were made and Mr Spence caused a stir when he dropped his notes all over the floor. Amazingly, Dorothea felt calm and relaxed. She settled herself in her chair. I wish those cows at the factory could see me now, she thought. Mr Spence started dictating. She ducked her head and concentrated on keeping up with his smooth flow of words.

At the end of the demonstration she was rewarded with admiring applause before the audience lined up for their tea and biscuits. Dorothea noticed many people left the brochures they had been given on their chairs. She felt a sense of despondency.

'I don't suppose one person in that audience would have noticed if I'd missed a great chunk out of that transcription,' she said to Mr Spence.

'Maybe not.' Her teacher collected his overcoat and placed his trilby hat carefully upon his grey hair. He sent her a look of reproof. 'But I would have done.'

That first demonstration was held in Hull but before long they were travelling further afield. They visited Helmsley and Harrogate and as far as Manchester. Dorothea loved every minute, particularly when they stayed overnight in a hotel. She loved being shown to her own room, to slide into a bed made up with fresh linen and feel, in the mornings, her bare toes touch soft carpet instead of cold lino. Their contact with Pitman's College expressed himself delighted with the interest the demonstrations aroused so Mr Spence and Dorothea travelled further, to Birmingham, Peterborough and Chester. During their trips, Dorothea watched Mr Spence closely. She learned how to use the correct cutlery at mealtimes and began to read newspapers properly so that she could enter into conversations with the people she met on her travels. On average, their trips took place every five or six weeks and they became the high spot of Dorothea's life. The everyday routine of work at the Metal Box Factory slipped by in a mindless blur. Yet she was uncomfortably aware that something must change soon. Already her father grumbled about the drop in her wages.

'And when are you going to get this wonderful job you talk about?' he asked her.

'Soon, Dad. Very soon.'

But would she? The many compliments she received about her shorthand writing skills were never backed up by the firm offer of a job. Mr Spence offered his opinion that employers were frightened of her speeds. Not everyone can dictate, he told Dorothea. She had smiled at his little vanity but the smile soon faded. It appeared from having no qualifications, she was now *too* expert!

The wet miserable summer of 1946 slipped away. During early autumn Dorothea faced conflict at home, this time with her mother. The newspapers had been full of details about the psychopathic sex murderer, Neville Clevely Heath.

'He preyed on women staying in hotels.' Hazel

perused every lurid headline with fascinated horror. 'Oh, Dorrie, it might have been you!' In vain did Dorothea protest she was the last person in the world Heath would have picked.

'He was after women with money. Middle-aged ladies, Mum.'

Useless to explain that even if she had met the handsome murderer with his waved hair and casual, blue-eyed charm, she would have stayed immune. Dorothea had decided she was finished with men. In the factory, she even refused to embroil herself in the constant discussions as to whether Princess Elizabeth should marry Lieutenant Philip Mountbatten. She told her mother to stop worrying about silly things and fixed up with Mr Spence to attend a demonstration in Carlisle.

Throughout November and December, Dorothea and Mr Spence doggedly stuck to their schedule, travelling on unheated trains and often delayed by increasingly atrocious weather. The dawn of 1947 brought even greater discomforts. Blizzards gripped the entire country and power supplies were regularly cut off.

One night Mr Spence sat opposite Dorothea in their railway carriage and watched her blow on her hands in a vain attempt to bring back some feeling. 'I think, my dear, we really must cancel further travelling until this dreadful weather improves. If it ever does.' With a gloomy face, he stared through the train window.

Dorothea pushed her hands back into the pockets of her coat and nodded agreement. Travelling was horrible at the moment. Yet she found the thought of working at the factory with no trips to look forward to depressing. Damn the weather! She curled up her toes in her new ankle-length rubber boots.

Demonstration over, they headed back immediately to the railway station. Already in the streets snow piled up at the side of the pavements like miniature alps. They made their train connection but halfway through their journey the railway points froze and after a long, cold delay passengers were informed they would be diverted to York. On arrival there, the railway employees were apologetic. Yes, they had intended laying on a fleet of buses to enable travellers to reach their destinations but that was now impossible.

'Look at it.' The Stationmaster waved his arm at the heavily falling snow.

Dorothea and Mr Spence left the railway station and walked into a snowstorm. It was late evening and when Dorothea sneaked a look at her companion she didn't like what she saw. Mr Spence was an elderly man and now, with his face tired and pinched with cold, he looked positively frail. She addressed him with false cheerfulness.

'Come along, Mr Spence. We can't stand here. We look like snowmen already.'

He looked at her with a worried expression. 'But, Dorothea, what shall we do? I thought we'd make it home tonight. I don't have a great deal of money with me. I did not anticipate this delay.'

'Don't worry.' She slipped her arm through his, unobtrusively helping him walk on the slippery surface. 'We'll manage.' A thought struck her. 'We'll book into the first place we can find. We can telephone Mr Hollis at Pitman's and explain the situation. I'm sure he'll agree to the hotel sending him our bill. You do have his telephone number with you?'

Mr Spence nodded. 'If you're sure,' he muttered.

'Quite sure.' She guided him round a snowdrift. She realised she enjoyed being in charge.

Years later, when Dorothea was old enough to be contemplative, she would play the 'what if' game. And the one occasion she would invariably think of was that evening in York with Mr Spence. What if they had turned left instead of right? But they did turn right, and slipped and shuffled their way along the deserted icy footpaths until they came on a board, half-shrouded in snow, standing in a small city garden. The lettering read: 'Bonne Vista Hotel'.

'This will do.' Dorothea forced open the gate. Tugging Mr Spence behind her, she carefully climbed the steps leading to the front door and went into the building.

Inside the hotel she stopped, nonplussed. After the howling emptiness outside she was bemused by the activity within. People were everywhere, stamping snow off their clothes and shoes, clamouring for attention. A thin young man staggered past her and caught her shins with the edge of the large suitcase he was carrying. Behind a reception desk a black-haired woman parried questions and repeatedly banged a bell as she handed out keys and shouted requests for silence.

Dorothea gulped and swayed. The noise was like a wave around her. Her eyes began to flicker. She tried to focus her gaze on something. She stared at a suitcase on the floor near her. It was covered with snow. She watched the snow change and melt and marvelled at the crystalline images revealed to her.

From a distance she heard Mr Spence's voice. 'Dorothea, are you all right, my dear?' Someone was shaking her. Mr Spence's face swam into view. She tried to speak and couldn't. Her head felt stuffed with cotton wool and her legs shook. She heard another voice.

'I'll look after her, sir. Don't you fret. It will be the heat, I expect, after the cold outside.'

Someone caught hold of her elbow, pushed her through a doorway and into a kitchen.

'Sit down.'

Thankfully, she collapsed into a shabby, basket-work chair. Her head was beginning to clear. The man who had placed her there hurried over to a huge gas cooker. She saw he was small and sandy-haired with a kind, monkey-like face.

'Kettle's on.' He came and looked at her. 'Feeling better, are you?'

'Yes, thank you.'

'That's good.' His brown face creased into a smile. 'You just sit quiet.'

'I will. In a few minutes, I'll be fine. Look,' her brow furrowed, 'please don't stay with me. You're so busy.'

'I'll go through in a second.' He made her a cup of tea, placing it carefully in her hand. 'My brother used to go like you when he was young. Perfectly all right; then he'd black out. I recognised the signs. Now you stay there.' He jerked his finger at the door. 'I'd better get back. Denise, my wife, will be going spare.' He laughed. 'We only took this place over three months ago. We're doing it up. Didn't expect custom yet, you see. But since this weather started we've had people on our doorstep day and night, every time the trains stop. Ah, well.' He grinned at her. 'Come through when you feel better.'

That night, Dorothea slept deep and dreamlessly. She didn't hear the blizzard raging but when she awoke the snow lay thick outside. It was early morning but she dressed and went downstairs. She wanted to thank the hotel proprietor for his kindness to her. She pushed open the door that led to the kitchen. The woman she now knew was called Denise was there, setting out rows of bowls on the table. The thin boy who had barked her shins was at the sink and the sandy-haired man had just staggered in through the back door, hauling indoors a sack of potatoes liberally encrusted with snow and ice. They looked at her.

'Sorry, I don't mean to intrude. I just wanted to say thank you, but I can see you're busy so . . .' Dorothea fell silent. They all looked tired out. 'Look,' she said impulsively, 'can I help in any way?'

'Help?' The little man looked scandalised. 'But you're a guest!'

'Does that matter?' Dorothea turned towards his wife for support. 'Your husband mentioned last night that you've only recently moved here and hadn't expected all these guests. Surely I could help? I'm not used to sitting about, and by the look of the weather outside we're all going to have to stay here some time.'

The dark-haired woman spoke to her husband. 'Go on, Norman, say yes. You know you want to.'

'It's not proper,' he muttered.

'Oh, blow that!' His wife grinned at Dorothea. 'Norman likes things to be proper. Comes of him being an officer's batman in the war. If you really mean it, we'd be delighted, miss. We're new to the business, see, and we hadn't bargained on this lot.'

'Right, what can I do?' Dorothea advanced into the kitchen and rolled up her sleeves.

She helped set out the breakfast tables, made toast, then went to Mr Spence's room to see how he was feeling. The old gentleman blushed when he answered the tap on his door for he was still in a threadbare checked dressing-gown. He admitted he was feeling shivery so Dorothea sent him back to bed then took his breakfast up on a tray. She rang Mr Hollis at Pitman's and explained their situation to him. He agreed the hotel bill could be forwarded to the College and she returned to the kitchen, smiling.

'What next?' she enquired. 'Shall I peel the potatoes for lunch?' She was thoroughly enjoying herself.

The terrible weather kept the hotel guests virtually prisoners for a week. The proprietors, who Dorothea now knew were called Norman and Denise Gill, managed as best they could. They were a few grumbles when the fresh vegetables ran out and power cuts rendered hot water an impossible luxury, but on the whole everyone made the best of a difficult situation. One evening when the electricity was off, everyone gathered in front of a meagre fire in the main lounge. They wore their outdoor clothes, and in the flickering candlelight a belated bond of companionship was formed. Each traveller vied with his neighbour to tell of horrific travelling experiences and by the time the weather had improved enough for them all to resume their interrupted journeys, genuine friendships had formed.

'We'll be sorry to see you go and that's the truth of

it,' said Norman Gill to Dorothea. She had come to say goodbye to them all before she and Mr Spence left on the afternoon train. 'Saved our bacon, you did.'

'Nonsense, I only helped out.' Dorothea smiled at the couple. 'Did you hear all the nice things said about you when the other guests left? I have the feeling your hotel is going to be a great success.'

'I hope so.' Norman's face grew serious. 'We've put all our savings into this place.' He looked towards his wife and then at Dorothea. 'There's something we'd like you to think about on your journey home.'

'Oh?' A frown creased her forehead. She had a feeling Norman Gill was going to say something important.

'It's like this. We've listened to you talk during the last week, about wanting a new job, and we wondered . . .' Norman scratched his head. 'You've just said you think this hotel will be successful. Well, we think so, too, and we know we'll need more staff. No, hear me out, Dorrie.' He raised his hand when she started to interrupt him. 'I've heard the place next door is coming on the market next year. I've been wondering . . . If we do well, I might buy next door and knock the two properties into one. Now, that *would* be a hotel!'

He grinned. 'But even with this place, we're short-staffed. Billy here is a good lad, we have two girls coming in for the bedroom work and Denise is a marvel, but we need someone with a nice manner to see to reception, take bookings, sort out accounts, pay the bills, things like that. What about it, Dorrie? If you did agree it would be a godsend. I hate figure work and Denise manages it but it takes her a long time. There's so much more she should be doing.'

Dorothea stared at him.

'Not offended, are you?' Norman looked anxious. 'It's not exactly office work but I reckon it could be more interesting. Of course,' his laugh was embarrassed. 'We might still ask you to peel the spuds when there's a rush.'

'I'd love to, but . . .' Dorothea's mind was racing. 'I'm sorry, Norman. I don't mean to be rude, but you've only just moved in here. Can you afford a receptionist? I don't know, but I shouldn't think there are many people staying in hotels right now.'

'Don't you believe it.' Norman's voice sounded more confident. 'I read, I hear things. I tell you, this country will be booming before long. The war's changed things. People expect more now. In the paper just yesterday it said car manufacturers can't keep up with the demand. Cars mean travel, holidays.'

Dorothea thought about what he had said. 'I'd live in, of course?'

'Yes, there's a nice little room on the top floor you could have.'

She considered his proposition. She'd be in York, a place she had always admired. She would meet lots of people. She had already realised she enjoyed being involved in hotel work.

'There's one thing, Norman, or perhaps it should be Mr Gill if I'm to work for you?'

'Don't be daft, lass,' he replied comfortably. 'What is it?'

'I have a little dog. I wouldn't want to leave him behind. Could he come?'

'Well . . . I'm a cat man, myself.'

Norman's wife Denise, who had remained silent while they talked, now spoke. 'That's OK, Dorrie. We could do with a guard dog. You'd have to keep him in your room or in a kennel outside. He mustn't annoy the guests.'

'Oh, he's well behaved.' She crossed her fingers behind her back.

With a speed that was surprising, everything was fixed up. Dorothea would move in before Whitsuntide. That would give her time to give in her notice at the factory and yet be available to help the Gills with the hoped for holiday influx. She went off to catch her train with a light heart.

During their journey home, Dorothea told Mr

Spence the news. She was relieved when he wished her well. She had thought he would be disappointed at the cessation of the shorthand demonstrations but he admitted that he had found the lasting spell of bad weather and the necessary travelling exhausting. He would be quite happy to stay at home, he said. He wished her luck and settled down in his corner seat for a snooze. Sleet splattered against the windows as the train chugged slowly through scenes of winter desolation but Dorothea did not look up. She was busy listing all the things she had to do and wondering how to break the news to her parents.

'York! Oh, Dorrie, we'll hardly ever see you!' Hazel's eyes filled with tears.

'Of course you will.' Dorothea patted her mother's shoulder. 'You can come through and stay with me. There's some lovely shops at York.'

'I knew you wanted another job but I did hope you'd find one in Hull.'

'He's offered a fair wage, you say?'

'Yes, Dad.'

'That's something. But hotel work.' Dennis shook his head. 'Funny business. What kind of hours will you work? There's no proper union representation, see?'

'They'll treat me fair, Dad. The work can't be any harder than in the Metal Box Factory.'

Dorothea watched as her parents looked at each other. She decided to change the subject. She knew she would go to York whatever they said.

She looked downwards. Jake was sprawled across her feet. After a week's separation, his greeting had been ecstatic but now his weight was giving her cramp in her toes. 'Move over, Jake.' She pulled her feet away and he gave a gusty sigh and immediately rolled back on to them. She smiled. 'I see he's wormed his way indoors.'

'We couldn't leave the poor thing in his kennel,' said Hazel. 'Even your father agreed that would be cruel.'

Dennis sniffed. 'Nothing but a damn nuisance,' he

complained. 'Forever under your feet and he makes terrible smells!'

To hide a smile, Dorothea bent forward and stroked Jake's rough coat. 'With all this snow I suppose he couldn't go out much, but Rob Steyart's been round, hasn't he?'

She looked up, puzzled by a sudden silence. Eventually Hazel answered. She sounded nervous. 'Rob's not in Hull any more, Dorrie.'

'What?' Dorothea gaped at her mother.

'A lot can happen in one week.' Hazel sighed and sat down. 'Thelma Steyart was taken real bad. I know because I saw her. Her neighbours called out to me when I was passing their house. I'd been shopping. They said they had heard a bump. When we got into the house, she was laid on the floor. Looked awful, she did. The side of her face was all drawn up, like a sneer. We called the doctor and he came and she was rushed into hospital. I waited at the house until Rob came home from school. Do you know, he never said a word when I told him? Just looked at me with his big eyes.' She paused and looked across at Dorothea who said nothing. She just listened to her mother and pulled at Jake's ears.

'I brought him here to spend the night but the next day the authorities stepped in. They came to see me while he was at school. I thought it better for him to go, until we knew what was happening. Anyway, they said Thelma Steyart was seriously ill and they would take charge of the boy. They didn't even tell me where he was going.'

'Didn't you *ask*!' Dorothea broke her silence. Her voice sounded aggressive.

'Don't you shout at your mother,' Dennis answered. 'She did what she could for the lad but Rob Steyart's no relative of ours. It's the council's job to look after such matters. It's obvious Thelma Steyart won't be coming out of hospital.'

'But we have to find out what's happened to him, Dad.' Dorothea stood up. 'I'll ring the Town Hall tomorrow. Maybe they'll tell us something. Poor, poor Rob. That's what he was frightened of, you know. That one day he'd be left with no one.'

Her voice broke on a sob and she mumbled something and ran from the room. Hazel mopped her eyes with a handkerchief and Dennis sighed. He picked up the evening paper and went to sit in his chair. Tail between his legs, Jake crept to sit beside him. The dog whined. Hazel's tears dried with astonishment when Dennis, instead of shouting at Jake, dropped a heavy hand to rest on his head.

Chapter Ten

Built of bilious-looking yellow brick, the large, square-shaped house squatted in the middle of a stark, bleak garden. No green showed through the snow-blanketed lawn, no weeds defaced the wet gravelled path leading to the front entrance. Rob climbed the three steps and stared upwards at the words emblazoned above the doorway: 'St Wilfred's School for Boys'. They blurred and he blinked as dizziness swept through him. He thought about Dorrie and wondered how she felt when she had one of her attacks. Then he wondered if perhaps they were catching and he had caught them! He shuddered. In view of everything else that had happened to him, the idea seemed likely.

His escort muttered something beneath his breath and pressed the doorbell once more. He had proved to be a short-tempered man and Rob decided he didn't like him. The lady who had travelled with him on the train had been friendly. She had bought him a comic and chattered about the dreadful weather. Scared half out of his wits, Rob had ignored her. Now he was sorry. This man had collected him at the railway station as though he was an inconvenient parcel. Rob stared downwards. He noticed soot from the train on the bottom of his mackintosh. His gran would be cross. That is, he fought back a fresh wave of nausea, if she was still alive.

The door opened.

'Here's the boy.' His companion gave Rob a little push to indicate he should enter the house. 'I won't come in. Damn train delays again! The kid's ration book is in his case. Other documents to follow in due course.'

He turned up the collar of his overcoat and faded away into the fast gathering dusk. Rob stepped through the door and found he was in a high-ceilinged, sparsely furnished front hall. He was vaguely aware of dark-painted walls and a smell of disinfectant but before he could observe his surroundings properly the man who had opened the door spoke to him.

'Put your case over in that corner for now, son. Don't want anyone to trip over it, do we?' He shook hands with Rob. 'My name's Dick Marr. I'm to take you to the Principal's office. He's waiting to meet you.'

Dick had a freckled face and a friendly expression. His movements were quick and economical. Rob felt a little happier as he followed him through a door and down a long narrow passageway. The man knocked on a heavy oak door and waited, then in response to a voice within, he opened the door and gestured for Rob to enter.

The Principal of St Wilfred's, a man called Hugh Carlisle, was seated behind his desk. A shock of black hair gave an initial impression of youth but a second glance dispelled that notion. Carlisle's coarse pale skin showed tell-tale splotches of age and a fine network of wrinkles criss-crossed his forehead and cheeks.

'Come in, my boy. Welcome to St Wilfred's.'

Carlisle waved him to a chair placed by the side of his desk, then picked up a typewritten letter. He scrutinised the contents, leant back in his chair and stared thoughtfully at Rob.

'You've certainly had troubles, young fellow.'

Rob gripped his hands together and said nothing.

'I see your grandmother, Mrs Steyart, is extremely ill and it is unlikely you will return to her. However,' he put down the letter and rested his hands palms downward on his desk, 'in some ways, you're lucky.'

He paused, as if inviting comment, but still Rob was silent.

Carlisle frowned but continued, his voice even, 'St Wilfred's is a fine school and it's not often we have vacancies. We don't accept everyone, you know; only boys whose fathers have died bravely fighting for their country.'

Rob stared at the man's hands. They fascinated him. They were huge, the fingers thick and splayed-out, with dark grizzled hair covering the backs.

'My dad's not dead,' he said. He swallowed hard when he saw the hands on the blotter tense. He sneaked a look at Mr Carlisle's face. He noticed the two deep fissures running down his cheeks and the stony look in the pale blue eyes. He dropped his gaze but repeated stubbornly, 'My dad's not dead. He's down as missing, but that doesn't mean he's dead.'

'Ah.'

Rob's gaze had returned to those huge hands. Now he saw them relax, the fingers curl slightly inwards, and risked another look at the Principal's face. The thick lips beneath the beak of a nose wore a faint smile.

'We have a dreamer here, a child who refuses to believe what he is told.' He paused as if lost in thought, then said, 'Think what you like, Steyart, but you should know Navy personnel regard your father as dead otherwise you would not be here.'

Rob opened his mouth but something, the atmosphere in the study, cautioned him to silence.

'Mr Marr.' He jumped as Carlisle bellowed his assistant's name.

Dick Marr opened the study door.

'Rob and I have had our chat. Now take him to his dormitory and explain the rules. Don't take too long about it. I want to discuss the kitchen extension with you. Anyway,' Carlisle's lips parted in a smile, showing large, yellowing teeth, 'you'll soon settle in, Steyart. Boys are adaptable.'

He was wrong about that, thought Rob. Try as he

might, he found his first week at St Wilfred's almost unbearable, but what could he do but bear it? He moved through the days totally disorientated. From early morning until bed time, bells clanged and everything seemed to be conducted at a mad dash. The house was old and full of stone-flagged corridors leading to twisty staircases and gloomy corners. Rob was perpetually lost and always late. He ran to meals, to prayers, to Matron for items of St Wilfred's uniform, primarily grey flannels and the compulsory green blazer which stamped him as an inmate. Rob privately called the clothes his prison uniform. When he had the chance, he ran to try and find somewhere to be alone, so that he could ponder on the massive change in his life. But privacy was unknown at St Wilfred's. The building was awash with boys, fighting, swearing, screaming, sweating, and playing weird ritual games from which Rob, as a new boy, was excluded.

The only good thing about the whole place was that Rob never saw Mr Carlisle after his initial interview. And yet, the Principal's personality dominated the working of the Home. And if a member of staff, driven to fury, threatened a visit to him, instant silence descended, even if it only lasted for five minutes. Twice, Dick Marr sought Rob out and said a few words to him, which helped, but the rest of his waking hours were passed in a state of confusion and misery. Rob gritted his teeth and hung on; things had to get better.

Gradually, they did. He made no friends, but the layout of the house became known to him and the rules and routines began to make sense. Then he began to distinguish a few faces. On his ninth day at St Wilfred's he was, as usual, late down for breakfast. The dining hall, an echoing room painted battleship grey, was always cold but this morning it was freezing. Outside, hail rattled against the long, uncurtained windows and inside the panes of glass, the condensation had frozen into ice pictures. Rob shivered and looked in vain for an empty space. The boys sat on wooden forms and ate from long tables. Rob hesitated. He had been at St Wilfred's long enough to realise that if he didn't hurry up and eat he would go to school breakfastless. The normal breakfast of two slices of bread and margarine and a cup of luke-warm cocoa was unappetising but he craved the warmth the food would generate for his walk in the snow. So it was with relief he spied a white hand waving to him from the middle of the end table. He hurried over.

'There's space here. Move up, Enwright.'

The voice was squeaky, hesitant, but the speaker gave Rob a brief smile as he squeezed his thin shanks further up the form to make room.

'Thanks.'

Rob climbed into the space provided. He reached for the enamel jug holding the cocoa and slopped some of the liquid into a mug. Good, it was still warm. He drank, then turned to his neighbour. 'It's . . .' He groped for the right name. 'It's Dale, isn't it? You're in the corner bed in my dorm?'

The boy nodded. He swallowed his last bit of bread and licked his fingers. 'That's right. Steven Dale, but everyone calls me Spider.'

Rob could see why. Dale was a long, thin boy with fair, almost colourless hair falling forward over a high forehead.

Rob remembered Spider because he had noticed the boy was a loner, like himself. Instead of running with the pack, Rob had seen him moving quietly around the building on his own or, more often, in the empty dormitory, sitting tailor-fashion on his bed reading, always reading. He was an odd-looking character, stooped and gangling, but he had made a gesture of friendship and Rob appreciated that. He looked down at his last uneaten half slice of bread and margarine then pushed it over to his neighbour. 'Want it? I've had enough.'

'Sure?' Rob nodded and Spider's face lit up. He

113

took the bread and ate it rapidly. A bell clanged and Rob groaned. 'Here we go again!'

'Don't you like school? I do. I like learning about things, and it's better than staying in this hole.' Spider walked alongside Rob as the boys filed out of the dining room and went to a cloakroom to collect coats and wellington boots.

'It's a bit different to what I've been used to,' said Rob guardedly. He had found, to his amazement, that he was expected to attend a catholic school. When he thought about it, he remembered his mother used to go off somewhere every Sunday morning but she never took him with her, and his father had never gone to church at all. His gran was very definitely Church of England. Rob hoped she never found out about his new school because if she did, even if she was now getting better, the shock would surely kill her!

The crowd of boys rushed down the driveway, pushing each other and slipping and sliding on the ice, than dispersed into smaller groups as they walked along the pavement towards the school which was only two streets away. Rob sneaked a look at Spider. The taller boy moved like a disconnected puppet, feet shuffling, arms moving jerkily, elbows stuck out, hands flopping on skinny wrists. Rob sighed. Spider was not exactly the kind of friend he longed for.

'You ought to get those fixed,' he said.

Spider had stopped to take off the spectacles he wore. He rubbed the eyepieces with a grimy finger. They were the most dilapidated pair of spectacles Rob had ever seen; the side frame was twisted, the bridge part held together with a dirty piece of sticking plaster. Spider, realising he was intensifying the lack of vision rather than improving it, stopped rubbing and glanced at Rob. With a sense of shock, Rob looked back into eyes of the calmest, deepest grey he had ever seen.

'I get through two pairs of glasses a year. Mr Carlisle won't allow me any more. He says people like me will bankrupt the Health Service, if it ever gets going.'

As he spoke Spider replaced his spectacles and Rob saw, with a queer feeling of relief, that he was just a spotty, skinny boy again.

They walked the rest of the way to the school without speaking, then separated to go to their different classes. At four o'clock, Rob left the building, hesitated then waited near the school gates, hoping to catch sight of his morning companion. Spider finally appeared, moving along with his queer gait. He seemed surprised to find Rob waiting for him. 'Did you want something?'

Rob felt embarrassed. 'No. It was just . . . I was late out myself.' He put his hands in his pockets and strode off. 'Just thought we might as well walk back together.'

His quick steps took him halfway down the road before he heard Spider running after him. He turned.

'Just a mo.' Spider leaned against a wall. His breath came in wheezy gasps.

'You sound awful.' Rob was impressed. 'Something wrong with you?'

Spider's breathing eased. He pushed himself upright and fell in step with Rob.

'I get asthma. It's worse in cold weather.' He glanced at Rob. 'Sorry about just now. I was a bit surprised, see.' He straightened his spectacles.

Rob shrugged. 'Doesn't matter.' He stooped, picked up a handful of snow, moulded it into a snowball and flung it with some force at a lamp-post. It missed.

Then Spider said, 'It will be all right, you know. It's awful at first, but you'll settle down.' He stepped back and eyed Rob. 'You're not tall but you look pretty fit. Do you like games?'

'Most of them, why?'

'That helps. A couple more weeks and you'll be OK. But,' he hesitated, 'perhaps you'd better not hang around with me too much.'

Rob wanted to ask why but with a sinking sensation in his stomach he realised he already knew the answer. There had been a boy like Spider at the school in Hull. Not physically like Spider. The Hull boy had been short and fat with darting eyes and nervous gestures. He had sweated a lot, hence his many and varied nicknames. Rob bit his lip. He had sweated because he was a victim, an easy target for bullies. Rob had not bullied him but he had kept well away. He sneaked a look at Spider, a frown on his face. Now he knew why Spider needed two pairs of glasses each year. Then he remembered his shock on looking into the other boy's eyes. No, Spider wasn't anything like the boy in Hull!

He sighed then said, 'Look, I brought a Meccano set with me. It's in my locker. Want to see it when we get back?'

Spider hesitated then smiled his reply. The sweetness of that smile kept Rob warm all the way back to St Wilfred's.

Rob's unlikely friendship with Spider attracted a few sniggers and whispers but nothing of note happened until the following Friday evening. On Fridays, the boys had a proper bath. The wash-house adjoined the main building. It was a draughty place with rattling metal pipes which carried the boiling water to individual cubicles housing the baths. Rob was one of the first to enter the wash-house. Spider had told him it was better to be in the first group of boys. The water was piping hot then. Also, if the bathers messed about too much the staff member in charge would often make late arrivals share a bath. Rob went into one of the cubicles and undressed. Outside he could hear the arrival of other boys. There was the usual horseplay, the scuffling, the howling when someone's bare feet were stamped on, the uncomplimentary jeers and remarks as to certain parts of the anatomy. Rob turned on the bath tap and flinched back from the gushing stream of hot water. Hurriedly he turned on the cold water tap.

Then he paused. The intermittent shouts and laughter had ceased. There was utter silence. A silence that, somehow, shouted menace. Rob waited. The silence continued. He hesitated, then wrapped a towel about his waist and stepped out of his cubicle.

A group of boys was clustered at the end of the room. Prominent among them towered the figure of Boots Gillan. Rob knew Boots was the largest boy in the school. Spider said he was normally good-natured but possessed of a terrible temper. Next to Boots stood a boy called Terry Smith and Rob's heart thumped when he saw, grasped firmly between the two, the naked, shivering figure of Spider. Rob swallowed. His mouth felt suddenly parched. He forced himself to walk towards the group of boys.

Whatever had happened was serious. As Rob drew closer he could see black anger on the face of Boots. Spider held his head high, even though his arms were painfully twisted behind his back. Terry Smith's face was alight with malice. The other boys seemed frozen in fascinated horror. As Rob approached, Terry released his hold on Spider and went to kick open the door of the nearest cubicle. He went in and turned on a tap. Rob clearly heard the hiss of the boiling water and saw Spider flinch. Rob stared at Boots.

'What the hell's going on?' He was glad his voice held firm.

'Well, if it isn't Spider's new friend.' Terry had rejoined the group. He stood at Rob's elbow. 'Fancy anyone *wanting* to be friends with Spider!'

A titter ran round the watchers.

'I asked a question.' Rob kept his eyes on Boots.

'I'm going to teach this bugger a lesson.' Boots shook Spider until the thin boy's teeth rattled.

'Why, what's he done?' As he spoke, Rob's eyes left the red face of Boots and glanced round, hoping to see authority in the shape of a member of staff.

'No luck, new boy.' Terry's smile was triumphant. 'One of the younger kids slipped and hit his head. Mr Sharpe has taken him to Matron.'

His glee made Rob's skin crawl. 'I'm not talking to you.' Again he faced Boots Gillan. 'I want to know what he's done?'

'The bugger pushed my vest and pants down the toilet then shat on them!'

Rob blinked and suppressed an hysterical urge to scream with laughter. 'I don't believe you. Spider would never do anything like that.'

'He did. Terry saw him.'

Rob turned to the silent on-lookers. 'Anyone else see?'

No one spoke.

'He did it.' Boots shook Spider again. 'I'll give this sod a bath he'll never forget!'

Rob risked a glance through the open door of the cubicle. The bath was now half full. The water still ran, red-hot. Bubbles swirled as if in anticipation.

'Come off it, Boots.' His voice held desperation now. 'You can't do it. If you put him in there, you could kill him.'

'Then I'll kill him – you, too, if you like.'

For the first time, Spider said something. 'Leave it, Rob.' The words came out in a shrill rush. Rob shook his head. He appealed to the watching boys. 'Come on. You know Spider. Would he do such a thing?'

There was a hush, then from the anonymity of the crowd a voice shouted: 'Ask him, Boots.'

Boots gaped at the boys then shook Spider again before releasing him to slide into a crumpled heap on the paved floor. Rob bent over him. 'Tell us, Spider.'

Spider stared upwards. Without his glasses, his face looked more naked than his body. 'I didn't put his clothes in the toilet,' he whispered. 'I never saw his clothes, but . . .' He paused. 'I got undressed and I needed to go, you know. Terry Smith said all the lavs were in use, except the one at the end.' He gestured. 'So I went in. I didn't know. I hadn't my glasses on. I couldn't see.'

'You *did* do it, you bloody little . . .' Boots choked and reached out for Spider.

'Oh, Christ!'

Rob knew Boots would probably kill him, but if he didn't do something, he would certainly kill Spider. He put his head down and ran into the older boy. He felt rather than heard the breathy sound as his head connected with Boots' stomach and then it was simply a blood-hazed mêlée, a fight to stay alive.

Fortunately, Rob was on his feet before Boots, so he was able to let go a left hook and two satisfying body blows before Boots regained his balance. He heard the onlookers screaming encouragement then his foot slipped on the wet floor and he fell heavily. Boots hurled himself on Rob's recumbent body, and grabbing the younger boy's ears proceeded to bang his head on the floor. Rob's senses slid away. Lights exploded behind his closed eyelids and when the punishment stopped, he simply thought he must have died. Then the pain in his head eased. He opened his eyes and looked up into the face of Mr Carlisle. 'Get up.'

The ice in those two words took away any remaining breath he possessed. He tried to push himself up from the floor but his legs failed him.

'Get up, I said.'

This time he managed it, with help from Spider and another boy. To one side stood Boots, his head hanging forward on his chest.

White about the mouth, the Principal swung round on Terry Smith. 'Where is Mr Sharpe?'

'Taken a boy to First Aid, sir.'

'Fetch him.'

Terry disappeared with alacrity.

Lucky devil, thought Rob, muzzily. He swallowed. There was a metallic taste of blood in his mouth and he thought he had lost a tooth.

'The rest of you get dressed and get out. I'll speak to you tomorrow. You two,' Carlisle eyed Boots and Rob with distaste, 'report to my office in ten minutes.'

He turned and left, grasping the arm of Mr Sharpe who bumped into him in the doorway and hurrying him out.

Wincing, Rob put on his clothes. Spider clucked round him like a mother hen. Rob wished he would go away and leave him on his own.

'I'm all right,' he was saying irritably when Boots put his head round the cubicle door. Rob froze.

'You ready?' Boots was rubbing his stomach. Rob nodded.

'Come on, then.'

They walked slowly towards Carlisle's study.

'Bloody good punch you have.'

Rob nodded, then asked: 'What will he do?'

'Thrash us, hard.'

'I thought so.'

'Well,' Boots felt his stomach again, 'you'll get over it. He's whacked me three times. Last time I couldn't sit down for a week.' He grinned, entirely without malice. 'Tough old sod. Doesn't like boys, you know.'

'I gathered that.'

The door of the study came into view.

'Like football, do you?' asked Boots.

'Yes.'

'Good.' Boots sighed. 'We play round the back sometimes. I'll see you get a game.'

They stopped outside the study door. Rob felt in his mouth, trying to locate the site of the missing tooth. 'All right. Only if Spider's left alone, though. He'd never have done that on purpose, you know.'

'I know – hasn't got the bloody guts.'

'Spider's got guts,' said Rob stiffly.

'If you say so.' Boots dug in his trouser pocket and produced a penny. 'Toss you for first.'

'Heads.'

'Tails.' Boots pocketed the coin. He entered the study. Rob listened. He heard only the swish of a cane. He counted ten strokes. Boots's face was suspiciously red when he emerged but he managed a wobbly grin. 'Get the bugger one day, I will,' he whispered.

Rob nodded, took a deep breath and stepped past

him. When he reappeared, walking carefully, he found Boots waiting for him.

'Welcome to St Wilfred's.'

'Thanks.'

The two boys grinned at each other and limped down the corridor in perfect accord.

Chapter Eleven

After six weeks at St Wilfred's, Rob felt he had lived there forever. After eight weeks, he found to his alarm that memories of his former life were fading fast. Life at the Home was so self-contained. True, the boys attended the local school but once there, they automatically closed ranks, presenting a united front to the rest of the pupils. They knew they had a reputation of being rough and unruly and they gloried in it. *They* didn't go home to loving mums and dads. They were half-way to being men and they acted accordingly. They swaggered around the playground and smoked fags behind the toilets, usually sticking the butt end of the cigarette on to a pin so everyone could enjoy a drag. They talked in lessons and slouched in their seats when told to sit up straight. In short, they were an irritant and a nuisance to the teachers.

But times were changing. Before Rob arrived, the school had been run by elderly men and women. Now younger teachers were returning from the war. The ex-soldiers took it upon themselves to discipline these loutish boys. The whack of the cane was regularly heard through classroom walls. The St Wilfred's boys blew on their hands, blinked back tears and boasted no teacher could hit as hard as Mr Carlisle.

Without consciously realising it, Rob Steyart established his own niche in the hierarchy of the St Wilfred's community. He was with them, yet not wholly of them. After his fight in the washroom and his subsequent beating by Carlisle he became quite popular. He was asked to join card schools and played footer on the muddy patch of land behind the

123

Home which the lads laughingly called their sports ground. Boots, in particular, sought him out, still shaking his head in wonder at the thought that Rob, who only came up to his shoulder, had succeeded in flooring him.

Yet there was something in Rob which fought against total integration with his peers. At school, he avoided boys from the Home. He didn't want to waste his school hours. He remembered Dorothea Bellows's insistence on working hard. He also remained friends with Spider.

'What do you see in that little runt?' Boots was genuinely baffled.

Rob groped for the right words. 'He knows about all sorts of things,' he said. 'I just like him.'

Boots shook his head and went off to find a pal who swore his uncle had sent him a 'dirty' book. Rob went to find Spider. As usual, he was in the dormitory reading.

'Don't you ever get sick of books?' Rob's voice was irritated. He flung himself on to his bed. At last the horrific winter had ended, and during the last week the air had smelt of spring and growing things.

'No.' Spider looked up and smiled. 'There's so many interesting things to read about.'

'Jim Lawson's uncle has sent him a mucky book.'

Rob stared down the room, depressed by the identical iron bedsteads, the unbleached sheets and scratchy grey blankets. He felt restless.

Spider turned over a page. 'I've seen it. It isn't mucky. It's about art. It's full of pictures of Greek statues.'

Rob rolled over on to his stomach and cupped his chin in his hands. 'There's naked women in it, isn't there?'

'Yes.'

'Then I want to see it. That's about the nearest we'll ever get. This dump's a prison!'

Spider laughed. 'You see girls at school.'

'Oh, yeah. They'll be interested in a St Wilfred's boy, I don't think!'

'They might be.' Spider put down his book. 'You're not bad looking, Rob. Women seem to go for moody-looking chaps.'

'I'm not moody.'

'No, of course not.' Spider's gaze returned to his book.

'Ever had a girl friend, Spider?' Rob wished he hadn't asked when he saw the blush run up Spider's neck. 'I just wondered,' he hurried on, 'because girls like brainy chaps. I thought maybe someone at school?'

Spider shook his head.

'I had one in Hull. At least . . .' Rob chewed on his finger. He decided to be honest. 'She wasn't a proper girl friend. She was older than me. But we went walks together.' He fell silent, remembering. 'She had a smashing dog.' He sighed.

'Go on.'

'Nothing, really. I thought she might have written to me, you know.'

'Was she pretty?'

'Not exactly.' Rob sat up. He felt an overwhelming desire to tell Spider about Dorrie, to describe her. Deep down, he was afraid he was beginning to forget how she looked.

'She was tall with ordinary sort of hair and she had funny eyes, they changed colour.' He gulped, over-come by a need to be with her again, to hear her laugh, to be able to pat Jake's shaggy coat.

Spider studied Rob's face. 'Maybe she hasn't your address?'

'She could have asked my gran.'

'But you told me your gran's had a stroke. Maybe she's so ill she can't have visitors. Maybe she can't speak. If I were you,' Spider's hand sneaked forward towards his book, 'I'd write to her.'

'Think so?'

'Why not.'

Rob chewed his lip. 'All right, I will.'

Three weeks later Rob crept up behind Spider, upended him then sat affectionately upon his stomach.

'I've had a letter.'

'Have you?' Spider tried to push Rob away then gave up and wheezed.

'Sorry.' Rob jumped up. 'You were right. It's from Dorrie, that girl I told you about. She's written three pages. She didn't know where I was, but she tried to find out. She says she's pleased I wrote. She works in York now and she's going to send me a photograph of Jake, that's her dog.' He helped his friend to his feet. 'Thanks, Spider. I owe you!'

'You do?' Spider's eyes gleamed. 'There's a book I want. It's in Woolworths and it's only a shilling, but I've no money left. It's about insects. I'll write down the title. You can get it for my birthday next week.'

Spider was a gentle boy but he could be forceful when it came to enlarging his meagre library.

Rob went in search of Boots.

'Lend us a bob.'

'You must be joking. When do I have any money?'

There was one other person to try. Dick Marr listened to Rob's request. 'You know the rules about lending money, Rob.'

'Yes, sir. But there's a special reason for buying Spider a birthday present and when I broke the window in the greenhouse, Mr Carlisle docked my pocket money for a month.'

Dick Marr was an amiable creature. He advanced Rob a shilling and even checked the date of Spider's birthday.

Rob gave Spider his birthday present after breakfast. They were in the cloakroom, preparing for school.

'What is it?' inquired a red-headed boy called Allan. 'Is that what you *wanted*?' he continued when the brown paper was removed to disclose the book.

'Exactly,' said Spider. He beamed at Rob. 'Thanks.'

'Happy birthday.' Rob clapped him on the shoulder.

'What have we here, a pair of poufs?' Unobserved, Terry Smith had come into the cloakroom. 'Your birthday, is it? Funny, I never thought of you being born. Always knew you never had a dad!'

'Pack it in, Smith.' Rob watched his friend blink and turn away. He could never fathom Terry's hatred of Spider. What had Spider ever done to him? With a flash of wisdom, he wondered if it was because all Terry's spiteful digs and venom never really penetrated his friend's serenity.

Ignoring Rob, Terry danced nearer to Spider. 'Let's see what your boy friend's bought you.' He snatched the book from Spider then deliberately pushed it straight into the boy's face. The spine of the book caught Spider's glasses and there was a crunching noise. A lens broke and a piece of glass caught the side of Spider's nose.

'Oh, dear. You'll have a job reading it now!'

Rob saw the scarlet flower of blood. He knew Spider was helpless without his glasses and knew Carlisle would refuse to replace them. He went for Terry.

'You're a bastard, Terry Smith.' He hit him with all his strength and Terry's nose spread across his face and bloomed brighter than Spider's.

Rob knocked on the door and entered Mr Carlisle's study. His spirits rose when he found Dick Marr inside. However, the man's face was stern. 'It won't do, Steyart. This is the second time you've been caught brawling.'

'Yes, sir.'

'Going to tell me what happened?'

Rob hesitated. There was a strict code of conduct at St Wilfred's but why should he cover for a toad like Smith? He explained.

Dick Marr went to stare out of the window. 'Doesn't excuse your behaviour, Rob. However,' he took the cane which Carlisle kept at the side of the desk, 'in the Principal's absence, it's my job to administer punishment.' He hesitated. 'I think four strokes will be sufficient.' He indicated to Rob to bend over. 'You didn't *quite* break Smith's nose!'

As Rob was leaving the study, Marr said: 'Find Spider and send him to me.'

Rob turned. 'But, sir, he didn't do anything. And it's his birthday!'

'Do as I say, please.'

White-faced, Spider listened to Rob. 'Wish I'd never mentioned my blooming birthday,' he muttered.

He was missing a long time and Rob prowled around restlessly. It was evening when his friend finally reappeared. Rob rushed over to him. 'What happened?' He stopped talking at the look on Spider's bruised face.

'He took me to town.' Spider spoke in an awed whisper. 'We went to order new glasses, then we went to tea at a Lyons cafe, then we went to a sports shop. Look.' He held up a pair of binoculars. 'He said it was time I had a decent birthday present.' His eyes moistened. 'Honestly, Rob, this is the happiest day of my life.'

'Gosh.' Rob was struck dumb, but not for long. He eyed the binoculars covetously. 'Let me see through them,' he begged.

Spring became summer. In August, the boys were taken on a camping holiday by Dick Marr and other members of staff. Mr Carlisle stayed behind. The weather was good and the boys enjoyed the break from routine. They ran wild through meadows, looked for birds' eggs in honeysuckled hedgerows and huddled under their blankets when they heard unaccustomed night sounds from birds and animals.

They camped in a farmer's field outside a small village. One morning Boots found a forgotten cache of thunder flashes in an old lean-to in the grounds of an empty property occupied in the war by army personnel. He showed them to Rob and Spider. Spider had, of course, read all about them. They decided to see how they worked. The three boys detonated them beneath a woman's wooden peggy tub. The bang, the woman's hysterics, and the destruction of the peggy tub which blew into a thousand pieces, enthralled the boys. They agreed the punishment they suffered for the escapade was well worth it.

By the time the holiday was over, the trio had become welded into a strong, if unlikely, friendship and back at St Wilfred's they became a force to be reckoned with. Spider's life improved beyond all recognition. As time went by each boy contributed something to the friendship: Boots provided the brute strength, Spider the brains, and Rob, to his own discomfiture, became the leader.

'Why me?' he would ask when the other two fell silent. They shrugged. They couldn't explain, it was just right.

The autumn term commenced and Rob had to have new trousers. He had grown two inches and his thin frame had broadened considerably. In the 'real' world the New Look exploded on the fashion scene and was roundly voted frivolous and absurd by the Government and the daily newspapers. The continuing shortages led to a wonderful variety of major and minor fiddling and a new word, 'spiv', was coined.

In the enclosed world of St Wilfred's the daily conversation centred around what would be the pudding that evening or who Mr Carlisle had it in for. Only a few boys had outside contacts; the majority functioned, reasonably happily, within their secluded environment. Rob had become completely reconciled to his life. Remembering the uncertainty and loneliness he had experienced living with his gran, he felt nothing stronger than regret when he was informed in early October that Thelma Steyart had died in her sleep.

As Christmas approached the older boys were

allowed to go into town on their own to buy Christmas presents. Rob's opinion was that shopping was a waste of time but he relished the opportunity to be by himself for a few hours. He made vague excuses to Spider and Boots and wandered around the busy streets. He spent some of his money on a cinema trip to see a Marx Brothers film then went into Woolworths and bought a box of Christmas cards. He would send one to Dorrie, of course, the one with a spaniel holding a sprig of holly in his mouth. There was Dick Marr, Boots and Spider and Mr and Mrs Bellows might like one, too. He didn't have much money left but that was all right because he didn't have anyone to buy presents for. Spider and Boots had already agreed with him that it was soppy to buy for friends.

A group of young girls passed Rob as he stood at the corner of a street. One laughed and he thought how much it sounded like Dorrie's laugh. On a sudden impulse, he counted the money in his pocket, squared his shoulders and marched into the nearest jeweller's. He would buy a present for Dorrie.

'Yes?'

The lady in the shop had grey hair which made him feel better.

'I'd like . . .' He paused for inspiration, then noticed the shop assistant was wearing earrings. 'To see some earrings, please.'

'Clip-ons or pierced?'

He gaped. 'Pardon?'

'Does the lady have pierced ears?'

He thought. 'No.'

'Clip-ons, then.' She opened a drawer at the back of the counter and brought out two trays of earrings.

Rob's eyes widened at the price tags. He reddened. 'I can't afford *real* jewels,' he said.

The shop assistant suppressed a smile. It had been a long, hard day but she had children and grandchildren of her own.

'These aren't real jewels, son. Perhaps,' she

paused, 'you might find something suitable on the stalls in the market.'

'No.' Rob pulled out his money and laid it on the glass counter. 'I want something from a proper shop. Something in a box.'

The woman looked at Rob's face. She had recognised the St Wilfred's blazer. She thought a moment then said, 'Just a minute.'

She disappeared into the back of the shop and returned, holding a small box in her hand. 'What about these?' She put the box on to the counter and removed the lid. 'These earrings were withdrawn from stock because they became a little tarnished at the back, but no one can see that when they are worn and they are so pretty. The stones are opals, real ones.'

'Oh!' breathed Rob. He gave a smile of delight as he looked at the varying bluish-green of the small stones. 'They're perfect. They look just like Dorrie's eyes.' His smile faded. 'Are you sure I can afford them?' She mentally calculated the total sum of the coins spread out on the counter. 'Just the right amount.'

She wrapped up the box and watched Rob leave the shop, and although her feet hurt and it was still three hours to closing, she realised with pleasure, that she actually felt Christmassy.

Back at St Wilfred's the three tallest boys were hanging paper chains and Rob could hear a carol service on Matron's radio. He realised he felt happy. His school report had been good and in the spring he was moving up a class. He took a writing pad from his locker and started a letter to Dorrie. She wrote to him every month. He wondered how long it would be before he could see her. In the spring, she had said, before the hotel became busy. Rob wrote that he hoped she enjoyed Christmas and that Jake was being good. Then he chewed on his pencil. He would have to ask Matron for a strong brown envelope in which to post the earrings. He hoped she would like them.

Boots lumbered into the dormitory and Rob quickly covered up the letter with his arm. Boots thought all girls soppy.

'I've been looking for you,' said Boots. 'We have to go and see Carlisle.'

Half an hour later, Boots, Spider, Rob and three other boys left Carlisle's study. Boots laughed and scuffled with two of the boys as they walked down the long corridor leading to the main hall, but both Spider and Rob were quiet. In the hall, Spider touched Rob's arm.

'See you later,' he whispered. 'I want to think.'

Rob nodded and watched Spider walk outside without going for his top coat. He shook his head when Boots suggested a game of footer. 'I'm writing a letter.'

He returned to the dormitory. His pencil had rolled off his bed and on to the floor. He retrieved it, then stared down at the piece of paper. Finally, he wrote:

I don't think I'll be able to come and see you in the spring. I've just found out – after Christmas, I'm going to live in Australia!

PART II
MIGRATION

Chapter Twelve

Dorothea read her letter for the third time then stared down into the box containing the opal earrings. The suspicion of tears in her eyes made the stones sparkle brightly. She blew her nose, put the letter in her overall pocket and went downstairs to find her employer.

'Can you spare me a moment, Norman?'

'Of course I can.' He looked sympathetic. 'What's the matter, bad news?'

'Not exactly. It's that youngster I write to, Rob Steyart. He's sent me a letter and a Christmas present. He says he is being sent to Australia.' She paused. 'I feel guilty, Norman.'

'Australia, eh? My goodness, that's exciting! But why should you feel guilty?'

'I don't know, but I do.' Dorothea spoke slowly, trying to clarify her feelings. 'I suppose it's because I know how important I am to Rob whereas, to be honest, I rarely think about him.'

'But that's natural, Dorrie. Your life's moved on.'

'Yes.'

Her expression was abstracted. She remembered her many walks with Rob, their conversations. It seemed so long ago. She realised how much happier she was, working in York. She met so many people. The Bonne Vista had established a regular clientele of visitors and commercial travellers. There were cheery groups of racegoers who booked in at the hotel during race meetings. And Norman predicted life would get even busier. The news of Princess Elizabeth's engagement had sent her employer's natural optimism soaring.

'Foreigners love a royal wedding,' he pronounced. 'And there's not so many kings and queens around nowadays. Mark my words, there'll be crowds of visitors coming here for the wedding.'

Denise Gill shook her head. 'Don't get carried away, Norman. If they do come, they'll stay in London.'

Her husband refused to be discouraged. 'No, they'll travel about; if they have the money.'

Dorothea smiled as she listened to them wrangling. They were happy together even though they never seemed to agree on anything. Sometimes, observing their closeness, she felt lonely, for outside the world of the hotel she had made few friends. Still, now that Arnold James, the chef Norman had recently employed, had moved in, she had someone of her own age to talk to.

'This lad's an orphan, you say?'

Norman's voice recalled Dorothea's wandering thoughts.

'Yes.'

'Perhaps he writes to you, sends you a present, because he has no one else?'

'That's exactly why I feel guilty! Poor Rob, there's no one to care what happens to him. In his letter, he says he will be taught farming. That's crazy! Rob's not interested in farming. Why can't he stay in his own country?'

Norman scratched his head. 'It does seem queer. Maybe the people who run the Home think he will have a better life in Australia. Look, are you really worried about him?'

'Yes, I am. He says so little. I don't think he wants to go.'

'If you have the full address of the Home, I should be able to find out the telephone number. Would you like to speak to someone about it?'

'Oh, Norman.' Dorothea touched his arm. 'That's what I hoped you would say.'

'Let's try, then. Maybe they'll allow you to speak to the boy.'

They didn't. Mr Carlisle, when he spoke to Dorothea, was polite, reasonable, and ever so slightly annoyed.

'It's a wonderful opportunity, Miss Bellows. Australia offers a fine future for hard-working youngsters. Steyart should do well there.'

'I just wanted to know,' Dorothea strove to keep her voice even, 'that Rob was given the chance to decide.'

There was a pause before Carlisle replied. When he did, he sounded amused. 'Do boys of twelve *know* what they want? Steyart has no living relatives in England. He could stay at St Wilfred's until he's eighteen. Unless *you* are prepared to offer him a home, I really can't see the point of continuing this discussion.'

He paused and Dorothea searched feverishly for the right answer but she waited too long. She heard a clipped 'Good-bye' and the sound of the telephone receiver being replaced.

'Any luck?' asked Norman.

She shook her head and went out into the back garden of the hotel where Jake was kept during the day. He came to meet her and rested his head against her knee.

'Good boy.' She stroked him. 'I did my best,' she whispered.

For the next few days Rob's fate worried her, but there was nothing she could do and then the preparations for Christmas occupied all her attention. The Gills allowed her to go home for Christmas Day but she was back and working hard on Boxing Day. During the New Year celebrations, she thought of Rob and wondered if he had started his journey; what he would think of Australia. She had replied to his letter and sent him a postal order for three pounds for Christmas but didn't expect to hear from him again. After the holiday Norman Gill had the top floor of the hotel redecorated and Denise and Dorothea reorganised the reception area so, once again, she was kept busy. Gradually, Rob's fate slipped to the back of her mind.

In June Dorothea passed her examinations and gained a Diploma in Hotel Reception Management. She celebrated by going shopping and bought herself a dress in the New Look style. When she saw her reflection in the dress shop mirror, she was pleased. The long, swirling skirt and pinched-in waistline suited her shapely figure. Long ago she had realised she would never be slim but at least her puppy fat had melted away and her hectic work schedule ensured she kept trim and fit. Remembering her insecurity and bad moods of two years ago, Dorothea was glad she was now nineteen. Why, since she had moved to the Bonne Vista Hotel even her strange attacks had ceased. She moved closer to the mirror and examined her face critically. Much too round and chubby, she thought. How she would love to resemble Vivien Leigh, but she never would. The shop assistant asked her if she wished the dress wrapped. Dorothea shook her head. She would wear it back to the hotel.

Arnold James saw her when she walked into the lounge. The next day he asked her if she would go to the pictures with him. She said she would think about it. During the past year two young men, guests at the hotel, had asked her out. She had refused. Try as she might, she couldn't forget Gabe. She had long ago accepted she would never see him again, but somehow other men held no interest for her.

'What should I do?' she asked Denise. The two women were working on the accounts together.

'Go out with him.' Denise ran her pen down a column of figures. 'You should mix with young people more, Dorrie. And Arnold's a smart, respectable young man.'

Dorothea hesitated. 'He's very serious.'

'What's wrong with that? Arnold has plans. He wants to open his own restaurant. He's a determined chap, I wish him luck. Anyway, he gets excited sometimes. Remember the nectarines?'

Dorothea giggled. She certainly did. Arnold loved cooking. As all foodstuffs were still strictly rationed, he often became frustrated in his attempt to produce attractive meals with the meagre ingredients available. One day, Dorothea had been in the kitchen when Denise returned from shopping and tipped out a bag of nectarines on to the table. Arnold's face had positively lit up with enthusiasm. That evening he produced a fantastic dessert for the guests.

Dorothea studied Arnold for a couple of days. He was a good-natured young man and almost attractive. She agreed to go to the cinema with him, and two days later they went for a walk together. She noticed he had good manners and always walked on the outside edge of the pavement. He didn't say much but Dorothea saw from his eyes how he admired her which made her happy. And the first time he kissed her, he did so with commendable firmness. Dorothea enjoyed being kissed and kissed him back with enthusiasm.

After the awkwardness of the first date, they both relaxed. They started to go out together on a regular basis. Dorothea found out that, in his own quiet way, Arnold was as ambitious as she was and they encouraged each other in their plans for the future. As to the possibility of a future together, Dorothea was carefully non-committal. She wasn't ready for a serious relationship and when Norman began cracking jokes about the 'resident lovebirds', she would frown rather than smile.

Dorothea would be forever grateful to her employers for giving her the chance to work at the hotel but at times she found their total involvement in her life intrusive. Perhaps it's because they have no children of their own, she thought. Still, they don't have to act as if they've adopted me!

Dorothea had noticed Arnold never spoke of his family and he never went away from York during his short holidays. She therefore assumed he was alone in the world and felt sorry for him. Her own relationship with her mother and father had improved since she had gone to work at the hotel and she often went home for a couple of days. One day, on impulse, she asked if he would like to go through to Hull with her for a day. He agreed immediately, and so enthusiastically she wondered if she was doing the right thing. But it was too late now. She went to ask her employer if that would be possible, half hoping he would say one of them would be needed at the Bonne Vista, but Norman greeted the idea as enthusiastically as Arnold.

'You two young people go off and enjoy yourselves. The hotel's quiet at the moment. We can manage. Stay overnight, if you want.'

He gave her a broad grin.

Dorothea responded with a faint smile and said thanks, but one day off would be fine. They fixed a day and she wrote a note and posted it off to her mother to let her know when they would arrive.

The Hessle Road area of Hull looked virtually unchanged since her last visit. Approaching her parents' house, though, she noticed the front door had been repainted and there were new curtains at the window. Her father opened the door to them. He wore a stiff collar and an uncomfortable expression. Dorothea frowned. She had asked her mother not to fuss. When Hazel appeared, she looked pink and flustered.

'I did the best I could with the food,' she whispered to Dorothea as the two women went into the kitchen. 'I've made a shepherd's pie, and put a dash of stout into the fruit cake mixture to liven it up.' Her forehead creased. 'I wish you hadn't told me Arnold was a chef. You know what I'm like at cooking!'

'Stop worrying.' Dorothea gave her mother a hug. 'Remember the cake you made for the VE Day party? That was lovely.' How long ago it was, she thought.

After an initial, embarrassed quarter of an hour everyone relaxed and the visit went better than Dorothea had anticipated. Her father, discovering Arnold shared his political beliefs, began an animated discussion with him regarding the recent strikes, and when she went through to help her mother wash up the dishes after the meal, he was showing the younger man a photograph of the LNER experimental 4-6-4 locomotive, affectionately known as 'Hush-hush'.

'Your Arnold seems nice.' Hazel poured boiling water from the kettle into the sink. 'Get on well, do you?'

'Yes, we do.' Dorothea picked up a teatowel. 'But we're only friends, Mum.'

'Umm.' Hazel looked unconvinced. 'Do you know, most of the girls you worked with at the tinworks are married now, and some of them have kiddies.'

'Don't be in such a rush to marry me off.' Dorothea gave the plate she was drying a particularly hard rub. 'I'm not even twenty yet; there's more to life than getting married.'

'Yes, I know.' Hazel put a wet hand on Dorothea's wrist. 'I must say, you look blooming. Had any of your turns lately?'

'No, thank goodness. Not for ages. I'm hoping I'm done with them for good.'

'Nancy Dempsey's engaged.' Hazel placed another cup gently upon the wooden draining board. She had used her best crockery. 'You'll never guess who to.'

'Who? She never told me. Still,' Dorothea laughed, 'she's not much for writing.'

'It's Bill Thomson.'

'Never!' Dorothea paused in her work. 'I don't believe it!'

'True as I'm standing here. I was surprised too, although,' Hazel lowered her voice, 'I think there's a good reason. She has that look about her.' She sighed. 'I hope things work out all right for her.'

Dorothea dried the rest of the dishes in silence then said: 'If I get a chance, I'll pop along and see her before we leave.'

After tea they all sat round the table and played cards for pennies. At first it was fun and Dorothea was happy to be with her parents and pleased to see Arnold comfortable with them. Then Dennis started losing and he was a bad loser. He strove to appear jovial but his eyes narrowed and the tone of his voice when he spoke to his wife became loud, almost bullying. Dorothea felt her own temper rise. The small room seemed to press in on her after spending her days in the more spacious Bonne Vista, and her mother's anxious-eyed attempts to maintain a happy atmosphere awoke in her a mixture of pity and fury. She pushed her chair back and glanced at the clock.

'We'll be catching the eight o'clock train,' she said. 'So, if you don't mind, I'll go and see if Nancy's in.'

'That's all right.' Dennis rose from the table with alacrity. 'I want to hear the news anyway.'

Dorothea left her mother talking to Arnold and went along the street to Nancy's house. Her friend opened the door.

'My God,' she said, 'Look what the wind's blown in!'

Dorothea smiled and felt reassured. Nancy looked the same as always. 'It's a quick call, Nancy. Arnold and me will be going back to York on the eight o'clock train.'

'Come on in.' Nancy opened the door wider. 'Mam and Dad are out so we have the place to ourselves. My, it's good to see you. I keep meaning to come through but,' she shrugged, 'you know how it is.' They went through the stiff, overdressed parlour into the cosy kitchen. 'This Arnold – he's the chap at the hotel, isn't he?'

'Yes.'

Nancy cocked her head on one side. 'Tell us all.'

'Nothing to tell. But what's this I hear about you?'

Nancy's face closed into a wary expression. 'What have you heard?'

'Mum says you're engaged to Bill Thomson.'

Her friend leaned back against the kitchen sink and crossed her arms. 'That's right.'

'Bit sudden, isn't it?'

'That's my business.'

Nancy's voice was cool and Dorothea felt uncomfortable. 'I'm sorry. I was just surprised, that's all.'

Nancy relented. 'Oh, what the heck? I might as well tell you, Dorrie. I'm up the spout, pregnant. Bill thinks we should get married as soon as possible.'

'Oh.' Dorothea hesitated then said, 'Is it what you want, Nancy? I mean, there are other ways.'

'Get rid of it, I suppose? No, I couldn't do that. I quite like kids.'

'No!' Dorothea was shocked. 'I didn't mean that. There's adoption, or you could just keep it yourself.'

'Oh, Dorrie.' Nancy laughed. 'It's easy to tell you're living away from here. Have you forgotten what it's like? My reputation's not too good now. If I have a kid without being married, I'll be the Scarlet Woman of the neighbourhood. And what about Mum and Dad? They'd be mortified. And who would look after the kid when I'm at work? No, I'll marry Bill.' She winked. 'I can still twist him round my little finger.'

'Is it . . . ?' Dorothea bit her lip. 'No, sorry, I shouldn't ask.'

'Is it Bill's?' Nancy asked the question for her. She raised her eyebrows so high they turned into question marks, then grinned her old grin. 'Perhaps.'

'Oh, Nancy.'

The train back to York was packed. Dorothea sat quietly in her seat watching a young woman who sat opposite with a baby on her knee. It was a plain baby, with a double chin and no hair, but then it stretched out its fat little arms towards her and grinned an engaging grin, and her heart melted. How strange it must be, she thought, to know a new life is growing within you. The train jolted and she felt Arnold's leg brush against hers. Arnold would make a good father. He would be prepared to help push the pram, perhaps read bedtime stories to a toddler. With a rush of affection she patted his hand where it lay on the upholstered armrest dividing the seats.

He smiled at her. 'I've enjoyed today, Dorrie. And I like your folks. Your dad really understands about union matters, doesn't he?'

'Yes,' she replied briefly. She remembered her father's rudeness towards her mother. Nancy came to mind again but this time Dorothea thought of her with misgivings. Quick-silver Nancy setting up home with solid old Bill. What a pity, she thought, that society decreed you couldn't have a baby without a husband.

Chapter Thirteen

Dorothea grew to love the city of York. The weathered, ancient churches and the tightly packed cluster of mediaeval streets known as The Shambles intrigued and delighted her. With Arnold, she walked the cobbled paths and tried to imagine the kind of people who had preceded them. Arnold, she discovered, lacked her imaginative interest in the past but, being a Labour man, he knew something about the guildhalls of the city. It was he who showed Dorothea the Merchant Adventurers' Hall which stood as a testimony to the days when York was the capital of Northern England.

On other days Dorothea would clip the lead on to the collar of a gambolling Jake and walk him around the walls of the city. She would pause now and again to enjoy the breathtaking views and Jake would sniff for evidence of field-mice, previous dogs and, ever hopeful, someone's discarded half-eaten sandwich.

The hotel was gaining a good reputation. The rooms were invariably booked well in advance. Reading the newspapers properly, a habit Dorothea had picked up when she travelled with Mr Spence to the shorthand exhibitions, she came to realise Norman's optimism regarding the future was well founded. It was true the shortages continued to make life difficult but things were stirring and changing. The introduction of the Health Service, for example, benefitted not only the ill and elderly.

Dorothea was aware from her study of the newspapers that a whole new welfare system was being constructed. She had read about reception centres being set up to woo tramps into what the reporter described as 'a more settled way of life'.

So she was interested when the day after reading the article, she was told by Norman that the hotel had been booked for a conference.

'To do with the Health Service, see! Lots of posh people coming: Rehabilitation Officers, Almoners, Health Visitors – God knows what they do or what they'll talk about, but who cares? It's a grand booking.'

Dorothea was delighted by Norman's news. But as soon as she was able, she left him and went to find Denise. Her employer was a lovely chap but when it came to dealing with day-to-day details, it was always advisable to talk things over with his wife. Denise confirmed the good news.

'Yes, they're coming next month. It could be a breakthrough for us, Dorrie. But,' her brow creased, 'there's so much to arrange. To tell the truth, I'm a bit worried. I wonder if we have enough space.'

'Have they set out their full requirements?'

Denise nodded, searched through the hotel filing system and produced a letter. Dorothea scanned it rapidly.

'We'll have to shift some beds around,' she commented. 'And a lot of the guests are asking for single rooms. Perhaps I'd better make inquiries next door, just in case?'

'I suppose so.' Denise sounded anxious.

'And they'll need a decent place to hold their meetings.' Dorothea thought for a moment. 'If we pull back the dividing doors between the main lounge and the small dining room, that should do.' She smiled at Denise who continued to look worried. 'It will be all right, you know. There's space for more tables in the main dining room. It's going to be exciting.'

She meant it. The news of the impending conference had worried Denise but it had challenged Dorothea. I'll make it all right, she told herself.

The conference was highly successful. The delegates, many of whom had never been to Yorkshire, fell in love with the city and the beautiful surrounding countryside. The organiser, on settling up with Norman, admitted the accommodation had been somewhat cramped but said the organisation had been excellent.

'We almost gave up in despair,' he confided to his host, 'when we found the larger hotels were unable to take us, but everything has been most satisfactory.' He lowered his voice. 'You want to hang on to that Miss Bellows. An extremely competent young woman.'

Norman was delighted. He dashed off to find Dorothea and give her a ten-pound note as a bonus. She accepted the money with a smile. She knew she had earned it.

It took her time to settle down after the departure of the conference guests. She had enjoyed the hussle and excitement. Denise, she knew, was just quietly grateful everything had gone well. Norman was even more full of plans for the future. But Dorothea was guiltily aware that her regard for him had slipped a little. He was good-humoured and kind but she was beginning to realise he had not the business acumen to turn all his grand schemes into reality. Whereas she . . . resolutely, she turned her thoughts into another direction. Arnold was taking her out for the day tomorrow. He wouldn't tell her where, it was to be a surprise. She was lucky, she thought, to have such an attentive young man interested in her and to be able to work in York, a place she loved. She decided she was perfectly content and there was nothing, nothing at all in her life that she would wish to change.

'If you intend staying more than two days, I shall need your ration book.'

Dorothea, coming down the main staircase, paused and looked towards the reception desk. Denise sounded unusually flustered. She was booking in a guest. She pushed over the book for the man to sign and saw Dorothea. She raised her hand and gave a wave. 'Dorothea, this is Mr Paige. He's an artist.'

The man turned and smiled at her. No wonder Denise sounded positively tremulous, thought Dorothea. What an absolutely gorgeous-looking man! She paused and stared down at him.

'Hello, Dorothea. Nice to meet you.' He turned his devastating smile back on Denise. 'I'll be here until Friday. Here's my ration book.' He placed it on the desk. 'I'm sure with two such charming ladies to look after me, I shall enjoy my stay.'

It was then Dorothea decided she didn't like him. He had too much of everything: good looks, charm and confidence. She studied his tall, slim frame, his perfect features and short-cut dark curly hair. She did not return his smile.

'Mr Paige was inquiring about the Castle Museum, Dorrie. You want to do some sketching there, I believe you said?'

Dorothea winced. Denise sounded positively arch. 'It's an easy place to find,' she said. She glanced at her wrist-watch. 'If you'll excuse me?' She reached the bottom of the staircase and walked swiftly past the reception desk and into her cubby hole of an office. She was conscious of the man's gaze on her retreating figure and annoyed with herself for holding her back so stiffly.

She met him again that evening when she helped serve coffee in the main lounge.

'Hello, you again? I'm sure I spotted you dashing about upstairs this afternoon. Do you do everything in this place?'

'Of course I don't. We all work as a team.'

His eyes were a curious light brown, almost the colour of amber. She found she was staring into them. Her voice became curt. 'Excuse me.'

One eyebrow rose in a curve. 'What, again?'

He was laughing at her. She pressed her lips together and hurried away from him. As she served the other guests she could sense him watching her. What an arrogant man. She'd make sure she did nothing to make him think she was interested in him or his painting! Yet, inwardly she raged at herself. Why had she noticed his nails were clipped short and kept scrupulously clean; that his pale skin already showed a bluish shadow of stubble, even though he smelt of soap and had recently shaved? Why had she noticed the tiny mole high on his right cheekbone when, she remembered guiltily, she had recently failed to notice a nasty burn on Arnold's wrist until he himself had pointed it out to her? Thankfully, she served the last guest and fled into the kitchen.

Tuesday was her day off. The weather was fine and Dorothea collected an enthusiastic Jake and went for a long walk. After going down to the river and walking round the old walls of the city, she stopped for a rest close by the ruins of Clifford's Tower. She sat down on the rough grass and raised her face to the sun, eyes closed, as Jake ran about sniffing at rabbit tracks.

'Hello.'

A shadow blocked out the rays of the sun. Dorothea opened her eyes to see Gregory Paige standing in front of her.

'I've been in the Museum. I thought it was you up here, so I walked up.' He hesitated, then taking her silence as consent, lowered himself on to the grass next to her.

'All right if I stop for a few minutes? Bit lonely when you don't know anyone.'

'I suppose so.' Her voice was cool.

He picked a blade of grass and chewed on it. When she remained silent, he spat out the grass and continued: 'Somehow, I get the impression you don't approve of me.'

'How can I disapprove? I don't know you.'

'Exactly.'

She turned and looked at him. Yesterday he had worn a suit. Today he was dressed in dark trousers and an open-necked shirt. His thick hair was ruffled by the breeze. Somehow he looked more ordinary. She allowed her stern expression to relax.

'Sorry,' she apologised.

'That's better.' He smiled at her. 'You've no idea how forbidding you looked yesterday.'

'What kind of painter are you?' she asked, curious.

'Unsuccessful.'

He grimaced when she laughed, then laughed with her. 'No, that's not strictly true. I make a decent living from book illustration. That's why I'm in York. I've been commisioned to illustrate a series of history books for children. I'm here to study mediaeval art, costume, boring stuff like that.'

'Boring?'

He shrugged. 'It's not totally boring, but I want to *paint*! There's wonderful things happening in the world of art and I want to be in on them. I'd study abstraction, constructivism, if only I had the chance.' Aware of her gaze, he stopped. 'Sorry, I get carried away.'

'Don't apologise.'

She looked at him with renewed interest. The enthusiasm with which he spoke intrigued her. The air of languid self-possession she had observed at their first meeting had disappeared. His amazing eyes, fringed she now saw with thick dark lashes, sparkled with life. Suddenly nervous, she looked away. 'It must be wonderful being so keen on your work. I'd like to hear more.'

'So I get a second chance?'

'I don't know what you mean.'

'Yesterday I wouldn't have dared ask you out but today is different. Will you come out with me tonight?'

She blushed and looked away, searching for Jake. He was wandering about near the walls of the castle and she clicked her fingers to summon him. 'Sorry, but no. You'd find me terribly boring, I'm sure, and anyway,' she swallowed, 'I already have a boy friend.'

'Pity.' Gregory put his hand on her arm. 'Still, you

could come and have tea with me in a café. Maybe I'll be able to change your mind.'

'No.' Dorothea gestured to the approaching Jake. 'That scruffy animal is mine, and not allowed in tea shops.'

'That's a shame. Hey, steady on there!' His last remark was addressed to Jake who, seeing a stranger, assumed a stiff-legged gait and bared his teeth threateningly.

'It's all right, Jake. Mr Paige is a friend.'

Still Jake growled and the suspicion of a frown clouded Dorothea's face. 'You are a friend, aren't you?'

'I'd like to be. Can you put him on a lead?'

Jake came closer. The ruff of fur about his throat stood out like a lion's mane. He growled again and Dorothea grabbed his collar. 'Sorry, he's a bit possessive.'

'I hope he's more friendly with your boy friend.' Gregory scrambled to his feet. 'My cue to depart, I think. We'll talk again when your guardian's not present.' He waved and hurried away.

Dorothea put on Jake's lead and gave him a sharp tug. 'You behave, do you hear? He's really much better than I thought.'

Jake's coat flattened down, smooth as a seal's back now. He gave her an apologetic look and then, with lofty unconcern, lifted his leg and sent a stream of urine spraying over a nearby empty paper bag.

Late that evening Dorothea came face to face with Gregory as he left the small bar of the hotel. He sketched her a clumsy bow.

'Ah, the girl with the beautiful eyes and the unfriendly dog.' From the glassy brightness of his eyes and the faint slurring of his voice, she realised he was drunk. He swayed slightly.

'Not *still* working, are you?'

'No, I've been out this evening.'

'Yes, I remember. Your boy friend.'

151

Dorothea nodded and moved to pass him.

'Good night.'

'Night.'

His hand shot out and he grasped her coat sleeve. 'My room's number twelve,' he said. 'Thought you ought to know, just in case you didn't already.' He gave her a wavering smile. Dorothea pulled her sleeve from his grasp.

'Good night, Mr Paige.' She walked upstairs, fuming. 'Conceited drunk,' she whispered. 'I was right the first time.' But once in her bedroom she leant back against the door, her heart pounding. What had he said? 'Beautiful eyes.' Despite herself, the corners of her mouth turned up in a smile.

Next day, Dorothea forgot to make up a departing guest's bill and was strangely inattentive when she and Arnold ate their midday meal in the hotel kitchen.

'I reckon Coppergate would be the ideal site for a quality restaurant,' declared Arnold. Then he stopped speaking and stared at her. 'What's the matter with you, Dorrie? You haven't heard a word I've said.'

She jumped. 'Of course I have.' She fixed her eyes on his honest dependable face and felt a wave of affection for him. Arnold didn't get drunk. He was a dear, loving man. If only he could be a little more exciting.

Chapter Fourteen

During the next three months, Gregory Paige stayed at the Bonne Vista hotel on two separate occasions but Dorothea saw little of him. She was much too busy.

Following the success of the Health Service conference, her employer had received three inquiries about the possibility of holding similar functions. Norman was simply bubbling with delight and when, once again, the chance of purchasing the next door property came along, he went immediately to see his accountant. He returned from his meeting and closeted himself in the office with his wife. Half an hour later, he asked Dorothea to join them.

'You've got business sense, Dorrie. We'd welcome your views on what to do.'

He told her what his accountant had said and spread out lists of figures and estimates.

'It's a big step, Norman. Not something to be decided in a hurry.'

Looking at Denise, Dorothea could see she was anxious about the possible expansion.

'But if we mess about, we lose the property.' Norman flung up his hands. 'We'll never have another chance like this, Dorrie.'

'Give me an hour with these accounts, Norm. Then I'll tell you what I think.'

An hour later, she gathered together the papers scattered about on the desk and went to talk to Norman. There was no doubt in her mind.

'You'd be crazy to pass up on the chance, but . . .' She stopped and laughed as her employer, a grin stretching across his face, grabbed her hand and pumped it vigorously up and down. 'Remember, I'm only your receptionist!'

'Aye, that's right, but you've a good head on your shoulders. I'd trust your judgement anywhere.' He still clasped her hand. 'What should we do now, Dorrie?'

'Reassure Denise, I should think. She's not as happy about this as you are,' she warned him.

'Oh, Denise will come round. She always does.'

'Maybe so, but remember, this is going to make a lot more work for her.'

'Not necessarily.' Norman dropped her hand to rub his own two hands together. 'We'll get more staff for a start.'

'Before you do anything, you and Denise should go and see your bank manager and find out just how much you can borrow for alterations to the property.'

'I'll go and telephone for an appointment now. Eh, Dorrie,' Norman paused in the doorway and looked back at her, 'what would we do without you?'

It was amazing how quickly financial matters were dealt with and the actual work of converting two small hotels into one large one began. Because the properties were identical, the builder commissioned by Norman to do the job assured him the work would proceed quickly.

By the time Gregory Paige paid his second visit to the Bonne Vista, Denise and Dorothea were constantly going up to their guests and apologising for the temporary inconveniences of the dust in the air and the noise levels. Part of the ground floor, to the rear of the building, had been closed off and workmen were constructing connecting doorways to the newly acquired building next door. Norman had closed down the Bonne Vista for a week, during which time the major alterations had been tackled, but he simply couldn't afford to lose any more customers.

Dorothea hadn't forgotten the impact Greg Paige had made on her during his first visit so she greeted him cautiously. On his part he was agreeable and friendly, although his eyes glinted mischievously when he inquired after her boy friend.

'He's very well, thank you,' Dorothea had replied. Arnold was indeed very well. Norman had promised him a kitchen assistant once the alterations were complete and Arnold couldn't wait to see the newly ordered kitchen equipment. Dorothea too was excited about the changes but she was also tired. Norman consulted her on so many things she began to feel worn down by the responsibility of it all. The noise of the drills and hammers, the effort to minimize the upheaval with the visitors, tiny things like not having the time to walk Jake properly, all built up in her mind and so, when she went to bed tired out, she was unable to sleep.

Late one evening, she was on her way to bed when Greg Paige came out of the Residents' Lounge and approached her.

'Hey, Dorothea.' He paused. 'I can call you that, can't I?'

'I suppose so.' She couldn't resist smiling at him. He looked so alert and lively, whereas she was exhausted. To give him his due, he had been remarkably sanguine over the small mishaps which had occurred during his stay at the hotel. That very morning the gasmen had turned off the gas for half an hour just before breakfast; several guests had been quite nasty about the late arrival of their eggs and toast.

'I was wondering if you'd have a drink with me?' Greg put his head on one side in a studiedly engaging attitude.

'Well . . .' She hesitated. The longer she stayed up, the more likelihood she had of sleeping when she finally went to bed.

'Why not?' She allowed him to lead her to the bar.

The newly appointed barman, who also doubled as porter and general handyman, raised his eyebrows as he handed her a gin and tonic. Dorothea felt annoyed. The man knew she was Arnold's girl friend, of course, but that didn't mean she couldn't have a drink with someone else.

She gave the barman a hard look and raised her glass. 'Cheers!'

'I've wanted to talk to you all week but you're obviously terribly busy with all these alterations.' Greg guided her to the rear of the bar and they sat down in two black leather chairs and put their drinks on a small table. 'I can see things are really happening in the Bonne Vista. The proprietor's wife was telling me how you are booking conferences now.'

'Yes, future prospects look good. It's just,' she sighed, 'running an hotel is very difficult when you have workmen knocking holes in walls everywhere.'

'Mrs Gill has been singing your praises. She thinks a lot of you, that's obvious.'

Dorothea looked down into her glass. 'They are nice people, good to work for.'

'Perhaps that true, but you don't want to overdo things, you know.' Greg picked up her empty glass then gestured towards the bar, asking her if she wanted another drink. When she shook her head, he sat back in his chair again. 'If you don't mind me saying so, you look whacked.'

A glint of amusement showed in Dorothea's eyes. 'Thank you for being so gallant,' she replied.

He grinned at her, unabashed. 'That boy friend of yours should look after you more.' He paused, then added, 'I would.'

'I think it's time I went to bed.' Dorothea stood up and immediately her companion leapt to his feet and stood close to her. 'What a brilliant idea,' he murmured.

Despite herself, Dorothea laughed. 'You're incorrigible!'

Greg took hold of her hand and held it in a warm grasp. 'I know,' he said. 'And I can't help it. Attractive women make me behave like that. It must be original sin. Will you come out with me tomorrow?'

'I'm sorry.' Dorothea shook her head in genuine regret. 'I'm much too busy to take time off.'

'Ah, well.' He released her hand. 'I'll be leaving tomorrow night. However,' he touched her shoulder lightly, 'I shall be back in about two months. I have a last series of sketches to do at the Museum. Remember that book I told you about?

Dorothea nodded without speaking. She was feeling that same tingle of excitement she had felt when she first met him. It bothered her. It also bothered her that she had never experienced the feeling when she was with Arnold.

'So make sure you have some free time booked for this time in two months.' Before she guessed his intention, before she could stop him, he had bent his head and dropped a swift kiss on her lips. 'Good night, Dorothea.' He walked towards the door and she stared after him.

'Oh, by the way.' Totally unruffled he turned back and said: 'Get someone else lined up to walk that damn dog of yours. He obviously doesn't like artistic people.'

'Why, you . . .' He waved at her and departed. She looked after him, caught between outrage and laughter.

At last, the alterations were completed and the modernised, larger Bonne Vista Hotel, freshly painted and refurbished, awaited its clientele. For days, Norman went about in a daze, still incredulous that his dream had come true, but also realising, perhaps for the first time, that fulfilled dreams bring with them additional responsibilities. He hung about the reception area and greeted each new guest so rapturously that Denise and Dorothea eventually banned him from the area, afraid he would frighten away any particularly timid souls.

But the fates were kind to them. The number of guests began to increase and a tentative conference booking was speedily confirmed when the person arranging the event came through to see the new, improved facilities.

157

'We're going to be OK.' Norman embraced his wife and then Dorothea in his relief. 'We're really going places, now.' A sudden thought struck him and he drew away from Dorothea and looked at her thoughtfully.

'What's the matter?' She was alarmed. It was not like Norman to look so serious.

'You and Arnold, I know you have plans. You're not planning on getting wed just yet, are you?'

Dorothea opened her mouth, but he hurried on. 'Not that we'd want to stop you or anything. I know Arnold's looking around for a good place to open his restaurant. But that's a bit in the future, isn't it?' He looked at her pleadingly. 'You see, I've just taken on three new people. I wouldn't like to have to start looking for a new chef. Not that I'd find one as good as Arnold. As for you, Dorrie, I just don't know how we would manage without you!'

'Listen to me!' At last, Dorothea managed to gain his attention. 'I'm very fond of Arnold but you really mustn't read too much into our relationship. I certainly have no plans for marriage at the moment and neither, as far as I know, has Arnold.'

Denise and Norman Gill looked unconvinced.

The next time Dorothea went out with Arnold, she tried, in a delicate manner to discuss their relationship. It didn't work. Either she was *too* delicate or perhaps it was that Arnold was in one of his 'single-minded' moods. Whatever the reason, she made no headway. They went to the local picture house and in the middle of the main feature, a western which Dorothea didn't particularly care for, she turned her head and studied Arnold's profile outlined in the dim light from the cinema projector. She was extremely fond of him, she thought. He was steady and dependable, and although reserved, he could occasionally surprise her with his unexpected understanding and thoughtfulness. Sometimes, though, he would get a particular scheme or idea in his head and then he would infuriate her by not listening to a word she said but simply forging ahead, intent on his own plan of action. He was like that at the moment. All the way to the cinema he had talked of a promising site he had seen for his proposed restaurant. She knew he would pick up on the same theme when they went to a pub for a drink after the film. Perhaps they would sort things out then.

They didn't. All Arnold wanted to talk about was the footage, the possibility of a drop in price, whether the seller would hold the offer open.

'If he won't,' Arnold sighed, 'then it's just too bad. I can't leave Norm and Denise in the lurch until they've found someone else and, anyway, I haven't enough money saved yet.'

Dorothea mouthed words of sympathy yet felt a wave of relief. 'I', he kept saying, not 'we'. Norman had got it wrong, yet again. She and Arnold were all right as they were. Perhaps their present easy-going relationship might develop. Perhaps, some time in the future, they might even marry, but not yet, certainly not yet.

She decided to widen her circle of acquaintance, not always relying on Arnold for company. She saw a note in the local paper giving details of the York Historical Society and went along one evening to see what happened there. Many of the members were elderly but they were friendly and there was one middle-aged woman Dorothea struck up a friendship with. Liz Hargreaves was Assistant Curator at the Yorkshire Museum. She was a good-humoured, lively woman with a passionate interest in the history of York, particularly the Roman history. In a very short time, the two became firm friends and in a matter of weeks, Liz proved very useful to Dorothea.

A group of holiday-makers had booked into the hotel for a weekend break. They intended exploring the city but their main interest was attending a matinée of a particular historical play showing at the Theatre Royal. On the morning of the performance Dorothea was contacted by a member of the theatre company and told that due to unforeseen circumstances, the play would not be performed.

'Oh, Lord, what are we going to do with them now?'

Denise and Dorothea looked at each other in consternation.

'Well . . .' An idea had occurred to Dorothea. 'If they were going to an historical play, then they must be interested in history.' She picked up the telephone and rang Liz's number.

At two-thirty, Dorothea collected together her party of tourists, all wearing flat shoes as she had requested, and took them to a certain point on the city walls. There she was met by Liz.

'This is a walking tour with a difference,' explained Dorothea. 'We are about to show you the various historical buildings and sites in York in which ghosts have been seen. Who knows?' She paused for effect. 'Today may be the day you will see a real live ghost.'

Her party laughed nervously, but followed her and Liz with marked enthusiasm, glancing behind from time to time.

Dorothea knew most of the reputed 'haunted' places and Liz knew all of them. On their return to the hotel the walking tour was voted a resounding success and this praise was reinforced when a few days later, Dorothea received a letter of thanks and an enlargement of a snapshot of the group, clustered closely together, on a part of the city walls where Liz assured them the ghost of a Roman soldier was seen frequently.

Following this episode, Dorothea got together with Liz and Norman and a leaflet was printed, illustrated by the photograph she had been sent, advertising a weekly tour of 'The Haunted Places of Old York' – an unusual and exciting event open only to guests booked into the Bonne Vista Hotel.

Dorothea was proud when the printer delivered a stack of the leaflets to her. When the new Bonne Vista opened, Norman had engaged another part-time receptionist. This had left Dorothea free to undertake more managerial tasks and she found she loved the responsibility and excitement of setting in hand the arrangements for the functions now held at the hotel. Her work was becoming more demanding and she loved it. In fact, she was happy with her life. She persuaded herself she had sorted out her relationship with Arnold. There really was nothing she would change, nothing at all.

And, at the back of her mind a little demon whispered, Greg Paige will be returning to the hotel soon.

Chapter Fifteen

Rob hung over the ship's rail and watched as the foaming, creamy wake of water subsided into a calm, deep blue. Just a few more hours and they would be there. But where was *there*? For over six weeks the huge ship packed with hundreds of children had sailed the ocean, and still no one had been told whereabouts in Australia they were headed for. It was wrong!

Rob spat as far as he could into the huge expanse of water. He was cross and unhappy. A group of girls dressed in white blouses and grey skirts skittered past him. They were laughing. One was saying how fantastic the trip had been. Rob stared after them and admitted to himself, morosely, that life on the ship was good. They ate well, there were classes in the morning and organised games in the afternoons. Last week there had been a slide show about the wonders of Australia showing pictures of strangely painted natives called Aborigines, kangaroos, and a brightly coloured bird that made a sound like laughter. Rob had liked that slide.

He thought about his friends and sighed. It was even hard to explain his feelings to Spider who was biding his time and waiting to see what happened. Boots, on the other hand, couldn't wait to arrive. He said he was going out into the wilderness as soon as he could to find gold and become a millionaire. Boots never worried about things. Rob envied his friend's uncomplicated attitude to life. Boots didn't hate Carlisle for sending them away from England, perhaps never to return. It had probably never even occurred to Boots that they might be separated on their arrival in Australia. Rob chewed on his thumb nail. No, that wouldn't happen! The three of them were from St Wilfred's, they were like a family. He tried to forget the other boys from the Home who had been placed on another ship.

A crewman walked past with the rolling gait of all sailors. 'Won't be long now, lad. We dock at Fremantle in five hours.'

'Yeah.' Rob straightened up. Now, at least, he knew the name of the place at which they would land.

Like a flock of sheep the children streamed down the gangplanks. The little girl directly in front of Rob was crying, whether from excitement or terror it was impossible to say. Rob glanced at his friends. Spider's face was set. The hand clutching the leather case containing his precious binoculars was rigid with tension but he forced a smile when he met Rob's gaze. Boots wore an open-mouthed grin. He clumped down the gangplank like some junior Frankenstein's monster.

'A sailor told me,' he said, 'that you sleep outside here 'cos it gets so hot in summer but you have to watch out for spiders 'cos some of them can kill you with one bite.' His grin widened. 'I reckon he was having me on. Anyway, I said we'd be OK 'cos we already have our own Spider!'

Rob stared at him then, his tension eased, he flung his arms about his two companions and laughed. The three of them shrieked with idiotic, hysterical laughter. Good old Boots! They wiped their eyes as they stepped from the gangplank and on to the soil of their new country.

Groups of adults waited for them. There were nuns in white veils and men in dark suits holding boards with lists of names. They weeded out the children, nudged them into groups and led them away. One woman came up to the boys and handed them a slice of what looked like pink fruit. Cautiously, they tasted it.

'Yuk!' Boots spat his mouthful on to the ground. 'Like eating blotting paper.'

164

'You there.' A man beckoned to them. 'What are your names?' They told him.

'You're with me.' He beckoned to Boots.

'But . . . my mates?'

'Not on this list.' The man sounded impatient.

Boot sagged like a burst balloon. 'But we're together. We came from the same place.'

'Can't help that.' The man consulted his list. 'You're down for Baralina.'

Rob looked away from his friend's face. For a horrible moment he thought Boots would burst into tears.

'But . . .'

'It's all right, Boots.' Spider pulled a notebook from his pocket. 'What's that name, mister? Will you give me the address?'

'I haven't got all day.' The man was impatient but when Spider took off his glasses and stared at him, he relented. 'It's Baralina.' He dictated the address.

'Thanks.' Spider replaced his notebook. 'We'll keep in touch, Boots. Honest.' He spat on his forefinger and held it in the air. Boots gulped back his tears and nodded. He followed the man through the crowds, constantly twisting his head for a last glimpse of his friends.

Rob and Spider watched him go. Faces sharpened by anxiety, they drew closer together for mutual comfort.

They were lucky. Two hours later they were still together, seated on a battered bus going . . . somewhere? As the bus swayed their knees touched and they drew comfort from each other but their thoughts remained their own.

Didn't think much of the finger-printing, mused Rob. Do they think we're criminals or something? He stared out of the bus window. Everything looks green, though. I thought it would be all desert. Nice to see sheep, makes it seem like England. He counted twenty other children on the bus, all boys. They were going to live in a Catholic orphanage, the man had told them,

165

Frances Anne Bond

but it was also a farm. Maybe it wouldn't be too bad.
He hoped there wouldn't be too much bowing and
Hail Marys!

He took off his sweater. It was hot, yet the bus
driver had told them it was autumn. Even the weather
was topsy-turvy in this country! They travelled a long
way before stopping for a drink, a sandwich and a
chance to go to a toilet. Before clambering back on to
the bus, the boys gathered round the driver and asked
him questions. He was a leathery-faced individual
who spoke in a lazy drawl. He grinned at some of their
queries.

'No 'roos around here, sonny. You'd need to be
further out into the Bush to see them. Plenty of
jumbucks, though.'

'What's a jumbuck?'

'Sheep, of course. Don't you poms know anything?'

Back on to the bus and more travelling. The terrain
became wilder; there were fewer cars on the roads.

'Keep your eyes peeled now,' shouted the bus
driver. 'Coming into the Bush now. Might see some
dingos or brumbies.'

Dingoes? Brumbies? The boys glanced at each
other, shrugged, then obediently looked out of the
dirty, fly-specked windows. It was late when they
arrived at their destination. Bone-tired they climbed
stiffly from the bus and said goodbye to their driver.
Then they followed the waiting black-robed priest
down a drive leading to two large stone-built houses
surrounded by smaller wooden buildings, sheds and
outhouses. The bus driver watched them go. He
sighed, leaned against his vehicle and rolled himself a
smoke.

'Poor little bastards,' he said.

The first day at the Orphanage was achingly strange
and bewildering to the newcomers. Awoken at six,
they were kitted out in khaki shorts and workshirts
and sent out to do chores before breakfast. Despite

being weary, Rob had slept badly. He had been placed in a different dormitory to Spider. It was a huge room, more than forty beds, he estimated, and his fitful sleep had been disturbed by boys snoring, muttering, and in a few cases crying. As soon as possible he found Spider.

'What do you think?' he muttered out of the corner of his mouth. A priest was moving down the line of boys allocating tasks.

Spider shook his head. 'A little lad, only about eight or nine, got a right belting this morning.'

'Why?'

'He wet the bed.'

Rob shivered but when the priest reached them, he seemed friendly enough.

'There's cows to milk or water to fetch, which is it to be?'

'Water.' The two boys spoke together.

'Very well. That direction.'

Armed with metal buckets they went to find the water pump. 'Doesn't anyone else live around here?'

Spider held the bucket as Rob pumped. 'Doesn't look like it.'

'I suppose,' Spider looked alarmed, 'we do get some schooling?'

'After the farm work is done, I expect.' Rob shrugged. 'Wonder what the grub's like?'

'I . . . Jesus!' Spider jumped back, away from the bucket.

'What is it?'

'Look in the water – there's a snake in it!'

Rob looked. 'It's only a little one,' he said after a pause. 'We're Aussie kids now, Spider. I reckon we'll have to get used to things like this.'

Some things were easy to get used to, others were not. During the next three months Rob and Spider got used to drawing water which contained frogs and snakes. They got used to the isolation, the emptiness of their surroundings. They became used to milking cows and feeding chickens. They even became used to being cuffed around the head for countless supposed rudenesses and acts of disobedience. Rob quite easily got used to irregular, if any, schooling. Spider did not.

'It's criminal,' he moaned. 'How can we learn anything if they don't teach us?'

Rob wiped the sweat from his face. They were hard at work clearing an area of scrub land. More children were expected and a new dormitory had to be built. It was taken for granted the boys would build it.

'They're not worried about us learning anything,' he said. 'We're just their labourers. Anyway, I don't think they could teach us anything. Ignorant pigs, most of them.' He spoke with feeling. Just that morning he had been belted with a leather strap for answering back.

'We'll never get a proper job when we leave here.' Spider pulled a face. 'There's not even any decent books to read, except for the bloody Bible!'

Rob raised an eyebrow at the bitterness in Spider's voice. In England, Spider had enjoyed going to church. England . . . it seemed as far away as the moon. 'Remember how we moaned about Carlisle?' he said slowly.

'Yeah.' They fell silent. St Wilfred's and Carlisle now seemed a lost paradise.

Rob spat on his hands. 'Come on, we have to clear this patch before supper, otherwise we won't get any.'

The days crawled by. The new dormitory was half built and the brothers were pleased with the progress made. Spider and Rob fell behind with school work but they learned many other things; how to make bricks by hand, how to catch rabbits. The latter accomplishment came about by accident.

One evening, Rob was overheard complaining about the food. Next morning, after prayers, he was pulled out in front of the assembled boys.

A particularly sadistic brother called Brother Doyle flicked the back of his bare legs with a bamboo cane.

'Steyart here doesn't like the food we serve. Better food in England, eh, Steyart?' Another flick of the cane. 'Well, we can't compete with England, can we, boys?' He laid on the cane a little harder. 'Perhaps Steyart should find his own food?' The strokes cut Rob's skin now and he opened his eyes wide to stop the tears. He wouldn't cry for this bastard.

Brother Doyle was smiling. He was a hunched but physically strong man with dirty fingernails. He enjoyed thoroughly the absolute power he wielded over the boys. 'So,' he continued, 'I think Steyart should go out and find something better to eat, if he's not satisfied. Find something to eat, Steyart, and we'll cook it for you.' With a final swipe of the cane, he dismissed Rob.

The boy didn't take his words seriously until he went in the dining hall for his evening meal. The servers were dishing up cabbage soup. It was watery and unappetising but he was hungry. All day long he had been hauling blocks of stone. He went to sit down, but an older boy stopped him.

'Sorry, mate. We're not allowed to serve you.'

Rob's empty stomach lurched. He turned and left the room without speaking. Outside, he wandered about aimlessly. What the hell could he find to eat in this God-forsaken place? He went to bed hungry. By the end of the second day he felt dizzy and light-headed. The boys did back-breaking labour and the sun was hot. That evening Spider gave him some bread he had smuggled out but Rob told him not to risk getting him any more. Everyone knew Spider was his friend and if he was caught, Rob knew Doyle would think up something equally unpleasant for him.

On the third day, George Harper approached him. Rob only knew George because they were in the same dormitory. George was a small boy but powerfully built with short, bandy legs and wide shoulders. He was from Devon and spoke with a slow country accent.

'Get in my work detail,' he whispered to Rob.

In the afternoon ten boys, including Rob and George, were sent out into the bushland surrounding the school to cut down trees for scaffolding. It was time to build the second storey of the new dormitory. George winked at Rob and wandered away from the main party. When they had gone a safe distance from the others, he squatted down and produced something from his pocket.

'How about us catching a rabbit?' he said.

Rob rubbed his dry lips. He found it hard to concentrate for the ache in his belly.

'Rabbits, are there any?'

George whistled. 'Use your eyes, man. There's thousands of them.'

'I've never seen any. What do we do?'

'I've made a trap. I used to catch them at home, but it will be easier here. Like I said, there's thousands of the little buggers and so tame, they'll probably give themselves up!'

Rob clapped George on the shoulder. 'I owe you, Harper.'

George grinned laconically. 'It's them or us, mate.'

After the day's work was done Rob went to find Brother Doyle. Without speaking, he held up the limp bodies of four rabbits. Doyle looked at them from beneath shaggy eyebrows.

'Well, well, you have hidden talents, Steyart. Skin them and take them to the kitchen.'

He turned on his heel and walked away from the boy. Rob grinned at his retreating back and put up two fingers.

Following this incident, the boys were actively encouraged to catch rabbits. They enjoyed it at first. It made a change from hauling rocks or clearing land, but then the rabbits became wiser and proved harder to catch. Woe betide any boy who went out with six traps and only brought three rabbits back. It gave the brothers yet another reason to beat them.

'Why do they do it, Rob? What have we done to them?'

'Maybe they hate being dumped out here as much as we do.' Rob dangled his feet in the water. They were by the swimming hole, a dammed-off part of the creek which provided them with water. 'Cheer up, Spider, not all of them are bad.'

'Enough are.' Spider's voice was listless. Rob was worried about him. When they had first arrived at the orphanage, it had been Spider who had kept up Rob's spirits. Spider had always managed to find something to distract him. He had collected strange plants to study, brightly coloured beetles and moths to draw. Then, gradually, his interest had faded. Now he sat in a dejected slump, his ribs sticking out of his skinny chest, his face burnt an angry red from the heat of the sun. Rob, on the other hand, had toughened up. His shoulders had broadened, his skin was dark brown, his hands work-hardened. He stood up and jumped into the pool. 'Come on in for a swim.'

'No. I've got to go and milk the cows in a minute.'

'OK.' Rob watched his friend wander away. He knew Spider wasn't much of a swimmer. 'There's two new brothers coming next month,' he shouted. 'Maybe they'll bring some more books.' He hoped the news might brighten up Spider. The monotony of their life was such that any change was looked on as hopeful and with more brothers, perhaps more lessons would be held. But Spider did not look back. He flapped his hand at Rob and trudged towards the milking shed. Rob sighed and submerged beneath the brackish but blessedly cool water.

Chapter Sixteen

Rob was returning from a rabbit hunt when he found Len Bevilacqua. The rabbits had proved elusive and he had travelled further away from the Orphanage than he had ever done before. Not that anyone would have noticed from the surroundings. Wherever one looked there was still the red earth, the wind-twisted scrub and dried-up salt holes. Rob was about to turn back when he spotted a rusted old pick-up truck. It had been there a long time, it looked as though it had grown from the earth. Yet he saw a wisp of smoke rising from behind it in the still air. Suddenly conscious of how quiet it was, how lonely, Rob tiptoed round to the back of the truck.

On a battered kerosene can sat an old man. He was dozing, his chin on his chest. The man's skin was as black as tar but his hair and the whiskers on his chin were milk white. Rob stood and stared. He remembered the slide show on the ship. The aborigines in the pictures had been noble savages with painted faces and proud bearing. This was just a broken-down, weary old man. A large bird flapped its wings and settled on the branches of a nearby gum tree. It threw back its head and made the sound of a crazy laugh. Both boy and man jumped. Set in a myriad of wrinkles, black eyes opened. A rusty voice croaked, 'Got a smoke, boss?'

'No.' Rob shook his head. The old man closed his eyes again. In the silence, Rob's stomach gurgled. The old man turned his gaze to the billy can slung over a small fire. Fascinated, Rob stared at his bumpy profile.

'Hungry?'

'No.' But Rob's voice was hesitant.

'Got tea.'

The aborigine threw a handful of tea leaves into the boiling billy can then, with the aid of a stick, lifted it off the fire and placed it on the ground to draw. 'Got biscuit.' He stood up and went to rummage in the cab of the truck. A sweaty old hat covered the back of his head and his too-big clothes hung on his spare frame like a sack. He came back with a tin box and gestured to Rob to sit down.

They ate and drank in silence. The aborigine seemed disinclined to talk and Rob was too awed to try. The biscuit was hard and the tea the colour of syrup and heavily sugared but Rob drank it thirstily. The old man nursed his tin mug between his hands and gazed dreamily into the distance. Finally, Rob prepared to leave.

'I have to go now. Thanks for the tea.'

The old man nodded.

Rob collected his traps and his three dead rabbits. 'Do you . . .' he hesitated. 'Do you live here?'

The old man shrugged.

'I mean, if you do – can I come and see you again?'

The aborigine spat into the fire, then looked at Rob. 'Bring smokes?'

Rob nodded. 'If I can.'

Back at the Orphanage, he rushed to find Spider and tell him about the aborigine but for once his friend's response disappointed him. Spider was much more interested in the new arrivals. 'A chap's come to take charge. A big bloke called O'Neill. He's brought loads of luggage and I think there's a chestful of books. Maybe they're for us to use at lessons.' Spider rubbed his hands together. 'Oh, and he's brought a cat with him, too. A great fluffy ginger thing. And ten more boys have arrived.'

Rob listened with interest, pleased to see Spider cheerful, but at the same time he kept thinking about the black man. He wondered how he could lay his hands on some cigarettes.

For three days the boys only saw Brother O'Neill from a distance. He strode about the place taking notes and asking questions of the anxious-looking priests who scurried in his wake. Always, by his side, paced the big, ginger cat.

'Never seen a cat do that before,' commented one boy. 'It's more like a dog, sticking with him like that.'

'I'd stick with him if he fed me pieces of chicken,' grumbled Rob. He was sick of being hungry. As more and more boys arrived, the poor meals became worse, bread and milk or cabbage soup for breakfast, toast for tea. O'Neill took most of his meals in his study and rumours were rife. It was said he had a prodigious appetite yet always saved the choicest titbits for his cat.

'You wouldn't, you know.' Sean, a fourteen year old who worked in the kitchens, was the only boy who had been close to the new Principal. 'He's a mean bastard. Look at this.' He rolled down his sock. Above his left ankle was a huge purple welt, cut and swollen in the middle. 'He did that. He has a stick with a metal piece on the bottom and if you upset him he lashes out at you. I got this because I spilt a drop of tea in the saucer when I put the cup down on his desk.' Spider sighed and looked at Rob. His eyes signalled that their hopes for improvement seemed doomed to disappointment.

One week after his arrival, Brother O'Neill addressed the boys after prayers. God, he told them, had placed them in a wild place for a reason. They would prove their love of God by creating a place of beauty within the wilderness. They must build a chapel so wonderful that people would travel there in future years to look and marvel.

Fervour made O'Neill's strong voice shake. He raised his hands, palms upwards towards Heaven. After finishing the chapel, he said, they would build a new school. Perhaps it would be possible to construct a dam to improve the water facilities and bring greenness to the land to enhance the beauty of the new buildings. He opened his arms in a gesture of embrace. With God's help, he said, they would make miracles!

He stopped speaking and looked at the assembled boys. The lack of enthusiasm on their faces must have annoyed him for the glow faded from his face and with a curt word to his second-in-command, he turned on his heel and left the platform. The boys were dismissed. They filed out of the hall in silence.

Spider removed his spectacles and polished them on his shirt. 'He's a nutter, Rob!' His grey eyes were wide with alarm.

Rob nodded soberly. 'But he's in charge,' he answered softly.

Lessons came to an abrupt halt. Building plans were put into operation. The building materials were stone and granite from the bush and the boys were the labourers. Rob sweated and pushed and pulled until his muscles cracked, and all the time he worried about Spider. Ironically, the dry, hot climate had eased the asthmatic condition suffered by his friend but this present pace of work was killing him. He never complained but Rob watched him grow thinner and thinner and he fumed as the lines of exhaustion deepened on his friend's face. Finally, he went in search of one of the more tolerant brothers and explained his fears about Spider's health. The brother listened to Rob and promised to help, if he could. Rob went away without high hopes but the next day Spider was given a new job, making bricks. This work was easier. Sand and cement were mixed together and then put into a machine that was used to press the shape of the brick. Rob continued his own back-breaking task with a lighter heart.

It was three weeks before he found an opportunity to visit the aborigine. Rob approached the area in which he had discovered the old man with foreboding. Suppose he had moved on? But luck was on his side. There he was, perched on the same kerosene can, looking as though he had not moved since Rob had left him. Self-consciously, Rob stopped in front of him and held out a cigarette.

'I could only get one,' he apologised.

With a quick movement, at odds with his

176

somnambulant appearance, the old man plucked the cigarette from Rob's fingers and nodded to the billy can. 'Tea?' he said.

Rob drank his tea seated on a rock close by the kerosene can.

After a second mug the aborigine began to talk. Len Bevilacqua was proud of his command of English. He told Rob he had white blood in him. His grandfather had been a white man. His gin, he boasted, had understood English. She had been educated at a mission school.

'Gin?' queried Rob timidly.

'My woman.' Len sighed. 'A good woman, quiet, obedient. I missed her when she died.'

'Oh.' Rob glanced at Len from beneath lowered lashes. Dare he ask questions? 'Where's your home, Len? Where do you come from?'

'Home?' The old man was puzzled.

'You know, the place where you were born?'

Len's yellow teeth showed in a smile. 'Who knows? We are all born on earth. Earth is our mother. Everywhere is home.'

'But isn't there one particular place, when you were young . . . ?' Rob's voice thickened and he turned away his face.

Len stared at the boy, his eyes bright in his wrinkled face, then he said: 'Different for us, we have Dreamtime. White men different. They ask questions, change things. They make buildings, roads.' He shook his head and threw the dregs of his tea on to the fire where it sizzled and spat.

'What's Dreamtime, Len?' Rob leant forward. 'Tell me.'

'You must go now.'

Rob's face showed dismay and the aborigine sighed, pushed back his shabby hat and scratched his head. 'Come again,' he said.

'If I can.' Rob stood up. 'You'll be here?'

'Come again,' the old man repeated. He rose, shuffled over to the cab of the pick-up, climbed inside and shut the door. Dismissed, Rob retraced his steps to the Orphanage.

For a short period of time, Spider appeared to be in better health, then he developed a racking cough which refused to leave him. He found it difficult to keep his food down, and eventually his condition became such that he was excused work and put into the Sick Bay. Rob visited him there.

'How are you feeling?'

'Much better. Look.' Spider held up a book. 'Brother Charles brought me this. He says he'll get me some more. It's almost worth being sick for.' He stopped talking and doubled up, his thin frame shaken by a bout of coughing. Rob looked away from him. The Sick Bay was a bare, four-bedded room. One other bed was occupied. A boy about ten years old was asleep, his left leg plastered and held aloft by a sling. 'Bit lonely for you.'

'It's wonderful, Rob. They're giving me better food and O'Neill looked in yesterday. He was almost decent!'

Rob stayed half an hour with his friend then left, worried. Spider *must* be ill to be treated so well.

Now the boys worked nine or ten hours a day. School work was completely abandoned. The skin sheered off Rob's hands as he hauled sugar bags full of soil to dump three or four hundred yards away from the proposed chapel. At night he would fall into bed too tired to sleep. Then he would cheer himself up by remembering that Spider was improving enough to quieten his fears yet slowly enough to miss out on the present harsh working routines. As his tired body rested, his thoughts turned towards Len Bevilacqua and he hungered to speak with the old man again. Somehow, Len's Dreamtime seemed an antidote to the world he now unwillingly inhabited. Rob's great fear was that his newfound friend, for that was how he regarded Len, would move on. He remembered the man who presented the slide show on the journey to

Australia saying aborigines never stayed long in one place. But Len was old. Surely he would stay?

Brother O'Neill went away for two weeks and to the relief of the boys and staff, work slowed down. Rob managed to slip away to see his new friend.

Len became used to Rob's company, and gradually he told the boy about the Dreamtime. Silent and intent, Rob listened. In his mind's eye, he saw Marrawuti, the sea eagle who snatches away the spirit of a man when he dies. There was Ginga, the giant crocodile, and Warramurrungundji who came from the sea in female form and created the land and gave birth to the people. Len told him that when the great spirit ancestors had ended their creation they had charged the people with the custodianship of the land and all living things.

'And so it was,' concluded Len. 'Until the white men came. But then,' he sighed, 'white men bring change for they have no Dreamtime.'

O'Neill returned and the circle of endless work recommenced. Deprived of Spider's company, often light-headed from the heat and the lack of decent meals, Rob found Len's Dreamtime becoming his Dreamtime. Slaving away at the building of the chapel, cement burns on his hands, he lost himself in thoughts of the elusive spirits Len said lived in certain secret places. In the dust and glare of the sun he imagined himself with Almudj, the rainbow serpent who inhabited a deep pool somewhere below a waterfall.

'Do we become spirits when we die?' he asked Len one day.

The old man had shaken his head. 'No. When we die, we're finished.'

Rob stared into the flickering flames of Len's fire and nodded. He preferred to believe in Len's philosophy rather than that of the brothers who talked of eternal life yet worked their charges half to death.

Spider was greatly improved. He had put on weight and looked rested and happy when Rob went next to see him. His cough had vanished. For the first time

Rob realised that Spider had the makings of a fine-looking man. His enforced bed rest had allowed the angry sunburn to fade into golden tan which made his large grey eyes look enormous. He grinned at Rob.

'I've some news. O'Neill's been in to see me. You know he's allowed me to read some of his books?' He laughed when Rob grimaced. 'I know, I don't like the man either, but he *is* better for knowing. He's a good teacher. He asked me all sorts of questions about things. He came to say,' Spider literally quivered with excitement, 'he's picked out me and two other boys. Four days each week, he's going to tutor us. Apparently there's some sort of scholarship scheme in Perth and O'Neill thinks we could stand a chance of winning a place at college. He went on about bringing credit to the school, you know what he's like. Still,' he glanced shyly at his friend, 'it's a chance to make something of myself.'

Spider, going away to college! Rob forced a smile to his lips.

'That's bloody marvellous, Spider. Always knew you had brains.'

'I'll still see you a lot, Rob, honest.'

'That's all right then.' Rob's smile was more genuine this time. 'We'll have plenty of time together but you work like mad, Spider. And if you pass the scholarship and get out of here, be sure to tell people what it's really like!'

'Too right, I will! But the scholarship exam is a year away, Rob. In the meantime, I'll be back making bricks next week.'

Rob stood up and slapped him on the shoulder. 'I'll see you on the chain gang, then.'

A bell rang, summoning the boys to their evening meal. For once, O'Neill had elected to eat in the main hall. Rob watched as the beefy, heavily built man shovelled food into his mouth. The main meal consisted of stewed rabbit. Rob reflected that he and George Harper had at least injected a little variety into the menu.

O'Neill's cat jumped up on the table beside him and the man selected a piece of meat from his plate and gave it to the animal. Rob scowled. Only last week three younger boys had been beaten for poor table manners and yet O'Neill did things like that! He might be a good teacher but Rob detested him.

When the chapel was almost completed, Rob had an accident. He was working twenty feet up on some scaffolding. He was day-dreaming as usual, but this day his dreams were not happy. Two things worried him. On his last visit to Len, the old man had been restless. He had stayed too long in one place, he said. It was time to go 'walkabout'. Rob had said nothing but had wanted to blub like a kid. What would he do without Len? And, recently, Spider had begun to act strangely.

When he first started taking lessons with Brother O'Neill, Spider had been ecstatic. Rob was pleased for him. He knew Spider hungered for knowledge the way the rest of the boys hungered for decent food. Then, slowly, things had changed. Despite their efforts to stay close, circumstances kept them apart. They were still in separate dormitories and during the two days Spider worked on the chapel project, he was kept busy making bricks. Rob, now a tough and wiry youngster, worked on construction. The four days Spider studied, he and the other two boys were not seen until bedtime and on Saturdays, the only time a reasonable period of free time was allowed, Rob usually went to see Len. Nevertheless, their bond of friendship remained strong.

Rob realised something was bothering Spider but he didn't know what, and Spider would not say. The last time they had been together they had composed a letter to send to Boots. The week before a brother had returned from town and given Rob a postcard. It had been sent from Baralina. Boots wrote he was OK but still intended to go prospecting when he left 'this pig of a place!'.

Rob showed Spider the letter. 'Sounds like Boots,' he commented. 'Do you remember that awful moment when they carted him off?'

'Of course I do.' Spider's voice was dull. 'It's a good job he went to Baralina. Any place must be better than here.'

Rob was puzzled. He stared at his friend. Was he feeling ill again? No, he had maintained his weight gain and the terrible grey look of fatigue he had worn before his illness had not reappeared, but there was something . . .

Spider must have felt his gaze for he turned his face away. 'I better go, Rob. I've a composition to finish before tomorrow.'

'But you can do it tonight,' protested Rob. 'Don't go yet.'

'Sorry.' Spider had hurried away.

From his perch on the high scaffolding, Rob looked down at the scene below. He realised he hadn't seen Spider to talk to for a week at least. He would go and find him on Saturday afternoon. Len would have to wait. Something was bugging Spider and Rob intended to find out what it was. Down below, Rob saw O'Neill approaching the building. He came every day to inspect the rate of progress. Behind him paced the cat. Bloody thing! Tail in the air, it placed its feet neatly as it followed its master.

The cat was the last thing Rob remembered. His foot slipped on something, probably a patch of wet cement, and he fell. George Harper told him later he dropped from the scaffolding like a stone. The brothers picked him up and put him in a bed in the Sick Bay. Ten hours later he was still unconscious so they took him to hospital. He was there three weeks. His body was badly bruised, he had broken a bone in his hand, but mainly the medical staff were concerned about concussion. Apparently he had raved for hours about spirits and crocodiles.

When he was finally discharged from the hospital he was collected by Brother Charles. Rob was pleased to see him. Brother Charles was a decent man who did his best in a difficult situation. Many a time he shielded a boy from the excesses of one of the more brutal members of staff. However, on the trip back, the brother barely spoke to Rob. The boy wondered why but he asked no questions. His main thought on the journey was whether Len Bevilacqua had moved on yet.

Back at the Orphanage, he became aware of a strangely tense atmosphere. Several boys that Rob regarded as friends looked away when he waved to them. He was hurt. They could at least ask him how he felt, he thought. Like a waking snake, unease uncoiled within him. He took his case up to the dormitory. George Harper awaited him.

'Better sit down, Rob.'

Numbly, he did so. He waited.

Dispassionately, he noticed George was white beneath his tan and his freckles stood out like spots across the bridge of his nose.

'It's Spider.'

'What about him?' Rob's voice was soft but inside, he was shouting, 'Don't tell me!'

'He's dead, Rob. He drowned in the swimming hole.'

Chapter Seventeen

'No!'

After that one anguished cry, Rob was silent. He pressed his hands against his stomach and rocked back and forwards on the bed. George sat beside him, staring into space. Finally, the rocking ceased. Rob scrubbed at his eyes.

'Tell me,' he whispered. 'What happened?'

George swallowed. 'They say it was an accident. Spider wasn't much of a swimmer and the creek's mucky, weeds and suchlike.'

Rob shook his head. 'It doesn't make sense. Spider hated swimming. He hardly ever went near the water-hole. Oh God, I can't believe this! I thought he was going to make it – get out of this place. Ever since O'Neill started coaching him . . .'

'*O'Neill*!' George spat out the name so venomously, Rob stopped. He stared at George.

'What is it?'

George clenched his hands on his bare knees. 'There's a lot you miss around here, Rob. Oh, I don't blame you.' He shrugged. 'You've got wrapped up with that old Abo.' He paused. 'I suppose anything that stops you thinking about this hell-hole is worth it, but . . .' He sighed, passed his hand over his eyes. 'Haven't seen that much of Spider lately, have you?'

'How could I? He's been studying with O'Neill. When I did see him he was different, hardly opened his mouth. What are you getting at, George? What about O'Neill?'

'He likes boys, Rob, *really* likes them. I mean, particularly boys with nice manners and soft skin!'

185

Rob frowned, trying to understand the enormity of what George was saying. 'But . . . Spider wasn't like that.'

'I know. We all knew. None of the boys O'Neill picked out were like that, but what could they do? Only,' and now, George's voice trembled on the verge of tears, 'Spider couldn't live with it.'

'I don't believe you. Spider never said anything. He would have told me.'

George sighed. 'If it had been *you*, would you have told him? Come on, Rob. He was ashamed.'

Rob buried his head in his hands. Another knife edge of pain pierced him. He recalled Spider's sweetness, his integrity, and bile rose in his throat. He sprang to his feet. 'I'll *kill* the bastard, I swear it!'

'Hey!' George grabbed at his arm. 'Don't be stupid, Rob. There's nothing we can do, not now.' His grip tightened. 'But we'll think of something. I promise you, Rob, we'll think of something.'

Rob was given light work for a month. He milked cows, fed the chickens and tried to keep away from Brother O'Neill. The very sight of the man made him throw up. Spider's body had been taken away. Rob couldn't even visit his grave. The day after he had arrived back at the Orphanage, Brother Charles had given him Spider's binoculars. They were the only thing that remained of his friend. It was five weeks before Rob had the heart to go and see if Len was still in the area. When he approached Len's camp, the old man was packing up. He grunted at Rob's greeting.

'Good you came. When moon is big in the sky I will go.'

He opened his hands, black and corded on the back yet pink and smooth on the palms, and gestured towards the sky. He did not mention Rob's absence but looked into the boy's face.

'You have trouble?'

When Rob nodded, Len sighed but asked no more questions. 'Same for all men,' he muttered. He stood in front of Rob and held out his hand. 'Say goodbye.'

Rob clutched the old man's hand without speaking. He went back and confided his plans to George Harper. 'I'm clearing out,' he said. 'Three or four days at the most. I can't take this place any longer.'

'Daft bugger.' George shook his head. 'How far do you think you would get? It's been tried before, you know. You'd walk a few miles towards the main road then they'd come and pick you up. Then guess what happens? Face it, Rob, you're stuck here like the rest of us.'

'Not if I go in the other direction.'

George clapped his hand to his head. 'Now I know that fall's made you crazy! There's nothing out there, mate. You wouldn't last a week! Why do you think they don't bother watching us? They know there's nowhere we can run to.' He stopped, struck by a thought. 'It's that Abo, isn't it? You're going with him.'

'Thought about it,' admitted Rob.

'Forget it, Rob. They're built for the desert, we're not. Anyway, has he said he'll take you with him?'

'No. But I think he will.'

George bit his lip. 'You're crazy, trusting an Abo. What if he leaves you somewhere to die?'

'I don't care!' Rob's voice began to shake. 'I've got to get out, George. If I don't I *will* go crazy.'

His friend's eyes bored steadily into his. Then George gave a small nod. 'OK, I'll help if I can.'

With a curious formal gesture, the boys shook hands. Rob watched George walk away, his baggy, sweat-stained shorts flapping round his bandy legs. He knew he would miss him.

Next day the whole place was in a turmoil: O'Neill's cat had disappeared. The boys were taken away from their work and dispatched to search for the animal. They met with no success. O'Neill was in a vile mood. He marched about, his cassock flying out behind him, and swore retribution on whoever had taken his pet. The boys quivered with fear but fortunately the brothers suggested other possible causes for the animal's disappearance. Perhaps it had wandered too far from the buildings and had been carried off by a dingo?

Rob barely noticed the furore. He was making preparations to leave. The following night, George slipped out of the dormitory with him. Away from the buildings they faced each other awkwardly. Finally, George grinned. 'Hope you make it, Rob.' He handed over a letter. 'If you do, post this for me somewhere.'

'Sure.' Rob pocketed the letter. 'But why? We send letters from here.'

'Rob, Rob.' George shook his head. 'Still don't get it, do you? They're all read. Any complaints and they don't get posted.'

'Pigs!' Rob spoke with feeling and George nodded. 'I almost wish I was going with you, but I've only four months to go and then I'm fifteen. Get out legal then.'

'Well, good luck.' Rob picked up Spider's binoculars.

'Just a minute.' George's teeth gleamed in the moonlight as he grinned once more. 'I've a goodbye present for you. Oh, it's nothing I can *give* you but . . .' He laughed. 'That rabbit stew we had tonight?'

'Yeah?' Rob nodded. 'O'Neill's a greedy sod, he had three helpings.'

'Good, you were watching. Well,' George's grin grew wider, 'do you know, if you skin a cat, cut off the tail and bash out the ribs, it looks exactly like a rabbit!'

He waved his hand and melted away into the gloom.

Rob panicked when he reached the old pick-up truck and couldn't see or hear Len. He had never been alone in the Bush so late at night and the faint rustlings and other sounds he couldn't identify frightened him.

'Len,' he called out quietly. A vast relief flooded through him when the old man emerged from the darkness. Rob realised he was only just in time. Len's hat was pulled low on his brow and he carried his swag. The black man frowned. 'Why you here?'

Rob took a deep breath. 'I want to go with you, please.'

Len swore. 'No. I go alone! Where I go, no use to white man.'

'I'm strong, Len. I can work hard. I've lived here over a year. I'm used to the Bush.'

Len hawked, then spat. 'This place OK. Where I go, no trees, no water sometimes. Go back, boy.'

'I won't!' To his shame, Rob's voice rose, cracked. 'I won't go back. If you won't take me, then I'll go alone.'

The old man stared at him. Rob stared back. His words sounded foolish, even to him. Then Len turned and walked away. Rob stared after him. Len *had* to take him! Hurriedly he followed the aborigine. Unbelievably he had difficulty in keeping Len's figure in view. Pottering about the wrecked truck Len had moved slowly; now he loped along, covering a lot of ground. The moon was full but as Rob blundered along he tripped over stones and whippy scrub which stung his bare legs. Len never looked back, not once. But the boy kept going and finally, as the sun came up, Len stopped. Rob saw him squat beneath the shade of a large rock and undo his swag. Rob limped towards another rock from where he could see the old man.

He was totally exhausted. His legs ached and sweat poured down his face. His mouth was parched. He sat down with a grunt and waved at the irritating cloud of flies pestering him. The shade from the rock was comforting but he dared not close his eyes for he must watch Len. The flies buzzed on and on, the old man remained motionless, and eventually, against his will, Rob's eyes closed. He awoke with a cry of alarm, jumped up then sank back when he saw Len stood over him. The aborigine's face was grim.

'Go back.'

Rob shook his head. 'No.'

Len sighed. 'Go get thistles, dead ones. We have tea, talk.'

Ignoring the stiffness in his limbs, Rob obeyed him with alacrity. Drinking tea put Len in a good mood. After his second cup, Len spoke again.

'Bad place, back there?'

Rob nodded.

'Still better than Never Never. You go back.'

'I can't.' Rob's voice was desperate.

Len's eyes closed. He appeared to sleep. Rob hugged his knees, kept silent and prayed.

Then, minutes later, Len spoke. 'OK.'

'What?'

'You come. We walk for three hours, then sleep.'

The rest of the day was silent. Rob accompanied Len without attempting conversation. He remained terrified his companion would send him back. As the miles fell away behind them his fear left him, but as the hours went by, physical exhaustion claimed him and left him with no energy for speech.

Imperceptibly, their surroundings changed. They were moving into the desert. They trudged through sandhills, past claypans and dried-up salt lakes. No trees were to be seen, only sand and spinifex. Rob wondered if Len had anything to eat. He stole a glance at the wrinkled old aborigine. Did he really know what he was doing, where they were going? The old man must have felt Rob's gaze. He felt in his bundle and pulled out a large blue-spotted handkerchief. He knotted the corners of the cloth and handed it to Rob, gesturing to him to place it on his head. Rob nodded his thanks. His confidence in his friend surged back. Len would look after him, and every step took him further and further away from the Orphanage and the hated O'Neill. Further away from Spider, too. Rob was surprised by the sting of tears in his eyes. He had thought he would be too dried-out to weep. He blinked the tears away and told himself it was merely the pain of his blisters which affected him so. The one on his left heel must have burst, he could feel the stickiness of blood inside his sock. He grasped more firmly at the strap of Spider's binoculars case and stepped out manfully.

When night fell Len became more talkative. Apparently he still felt aggrieved. He chuntered as they sat by the campfire.

'Bloody white men. No good.'

'Your grandfather was white,' Rob dared to reply.

'Him no good. He was . . . what do you say? . . . man locked up.'

Rob pondered. 'You mean, a convict?'

Len nodded. 'No bloody good.' He sighed, offered Rob some fried lizard. Rob's stomach churned but he ate it.

'We should have camel,' continued the old man. 'Camel pretty damn good animal.'

Rob thought camels lived in Africa. He wanted to ask if Len had ever owned such an animal but he dared not. He swallowed hard in an effort to get the lizard meat down his throat.

Len grinned at him. 'He carved me a toy, the old white man. When I was a little 'un. He carved me a camel.'

They finished eating and rolled up in blankets close by the fire. They fell asleep, the old man and the boy, under an ebony sky holding a thousand silvery points from the distant stars.

Chapter Eighteen

By late season, life at the Bonne Vista Hotel had settled down to normal again. As was to be expected, bookings had slowed down, but Norman Gill's bank manager expressed himself satisfied with the results so far.

'You have obviously made some sound contacts with the right government departments, Mr Gill,' he said. 'This time next year, we should really have something to celebrate.' He bid Norman farewell with a broad smile and a firm handshake.

Norman Gill danced rather than walked into the hotel. 'We've got the all-clear,' he said. He grabbed his wife and twirled her round. 'So you can stop looking worried, my pet.'

'I wasn't worried,' protested Denise.

Norman wasn't listening. He released his wife and wandered about, cheerfully prattling away. He even poured himself a large brandy, which was most unusual.

'What a team we make,' he enthused. 'You, me and Dorrie. And Arnold, of course. I was lucky when I took that young man on. You know,' he paused as a new thought struck him, 'I reckon we deserve a little treat. We've worked so damn hard these past months and things are quiet now. I know, we'll have a day away!'

'We still have some guests,' demurred Denise, but Norman swept away her objections.

'We have part-time staff on our books now, girl. I'll arrange everything. Leave it to me.'

He arranged a day in Bridlington for the four of

them. Dorothea had pointed out that Bridlington could be cold in the late autumn but Norman refused to listen.

'It's a beautiful place. Went there once when I was a kid.'

Dorothea said no more. After all, it would be a day away from the hotel. She was ready for a break. She had been feeling weary for quite some time. She assumed it was the aftermath of all the excitement over the conversion and the setting up of the conference details. She should, she told herself, be glad that things had settled down again. It would have been impossible to keep working at the pace she had set during that time, and yet . . . The thought occurred to her that her drop in spirits had coincided with the non-appearance of Greg Paige. Two months, he had said, but nothing had been heard from him since. Dorothea tossed her head and felt cross with herself for even entertaining such thoughts. Greg Paige was nothing to her.

They travelled to Bridlington packed into Norman's small car. The roads were quiet – one good thing about petrol rationing, muttered Norman – and the sun shone, although the wind was cold. The beautiful, clean beach was deserted. Denise dared Norman to paddle and, after a lot of screaming and giggling, the four of them ventured into the icy sea. Then they spied an amusement park that had stayed open because of the fine weather, so they went for a ride on the dodgem cars. It was fun. Dorothea laughed and shouted as Norman, with maniacal glee, bore down on the car she and Arnold occupied.

Later in the day, Norman and Denise slipped off to buy some fish and chips and Dorothea and Arnold returned to the beach. The blue sea was ribbed with white and a light breeze sent the high clouds racing.

'You've gone quiet, Dorrie, what are you thinking about?'

'Nothing really. It's been a lovely day, hasn't it?'

'It has.' Arnold took hold of her hand. 'It's so easy

to get bogged down with routine jobs, isn't it? Days like these make you realise there's more to life than work.'

She smiled at him. 'You're right.' She thought how well he looked and how good it was to see him relax and enjoy himself. He had sung along with Norman during the drive to the coast and she had been surprised to discover he had a good baritone voice.

A strong squall of wind buffetted them and Dorothea gasped as sharp particles of sand swirled into the air and stung her face.

'Look.' Arnold pointed to the cliff face. 'There's a sheltered spot. Can you see it? Let's go there, out of this wind.'

Laughing, they scrambled up the steep incline. Once they reached the spot and sat down they found it was warm for the bank behind them protected them from the wind.

'Oh, look Arnold – what a view!'

Before them stretched over six miles of beautiful beaches, empty at this time of the year. Out at sea, a few fishing cobles could be seen, but otherwise their only company was the sea birds.

'This place reminds me of Branswick.' Dorothea wrapped her arms about her drawn-up knees and stared out at the sea.

'You never mentioned you'd been there.'

'It was years ago, when I was a kid. Oh!' Dorothea flinched back as a gull, angry at the human invasion of his territory, swept by them screeching defiance.

'It's all right. It's a guillemot. They're always noisy.'

Arnold had slipped his arm about her shoulders. She leant against him. She felt secure, protected.

'How did you know it was a guillemot?'

'My father. He used to tell me about animals and birds.'

'You never mention your parents, do you, Arnold?'

'No.' He held her closer to him. 'It's not a happy

story. After I was born my mother never really recovered. Dad used to spend a lot of time with me, take me about with him, to give Mum a rest, I suppose. Then,' he sighed, 'when I was ten, he suddenly cleared off with another woman. Mum never got over it. She died when I was sixteen. My dad contacted me then, asked me to go and live with him.' His voice hardened. 'But I never did. I've lost touch with him now.'

'Oh, Arnold, how sad.'

He shrugged. 'It was a long time ago.'

'But don't you want to see your father again? Perhaps you should allow him to explain. He must have loved you.'

'He shouldn't have left.' Arnold's voice deepened. 'I'd like you to know, Dorrie, I would never hurt a woman like my father hurt my mother.'

'I'm sure you wouldn't, Arnold. You're too kind a man.'

'I don't always feel kind when I'm with you, Dorrie.'

Very gently, Arnold pressed Dorothea back against the chalky cliff face. Seeing the look in his eyes and hearing the desperate seriousness in his voice she shivered, feeling a warmth within her that she had never felt before in his company. When his lips met hers, she responded with ardour. It was he who pulled away from the embrace.

'You do know I love you?'

'Umm.' She had closed her eyes. She didn't want talk, she wanted him to continue kissing her.

'Dorrie, listen to me. Let's get engaged.'

She opened her eyes. 'What?'

'I want to marry you.'

She sat upright and brushed away at a spot of clay she noticed had marked her skirt.

'Marriage is such a big step, Arnold.'

'I know. But I've thought a lot about it, Dorrie. I want you to be my wife.'

She felt a mixture of emotions. Pride that he had asked her, confusion over her own feelings, and also sadness.

'Are you sure, love? I know we get on well together but,' she paused, 'I sometimes think you don't really know me very well, Arnold.'

'But I do. You're kind and loving and I want to be with you always.' He blushed bright red. 'I dream about making love to you. But it's more than that, Dorrie. We're made for each other. We both have ambitions and we would be a true partnership. We would work well together.'

Her confusion increased. In one way, he seemed so young and yet, seeing him against the backdrop of grey cliffs, she was conscious that he had within him a rugged determination, an almost implacable resolution to win her. She tried again.

'I'm not as confident as you are about this, Arnold. I'm fond of you, but . . .'

He interrupted her. 'Dorothea Bellows, please say you will marry me. I will love and look after you all the days of my life.'

He placed his fingers under her chin, tilted her face up and kissed her, softly at first and then with steadily increasing pressure. Then his fingers slid from her throat into the vee of her dress. Dorothea began to feel short of breath. This wasn't the Arnold she thought she knew so well. She liked this version. His fingers were now caressing her breasts. She realised that he, too, was breathing rapidly. His fingers trembled as he undid buttons and eased away clothes until she was naked to the waist. He groaned and she sighed as his hand stroked her body. Dear, conventional Arnold. Who would have believed he could behave so?

He seemed to have forgotten their surroundings and the fact that it was broad daylight. She hadn't, but the thought of making love in the sunshine with the sound of the sea below them excited her even more. She glanced about them and was reassured. No one would be able to see them from the cliff top and before them stretched the empty beach and ocean.

His second kiss almost crushed the life out of her.

197

He does love me, she thought. And he's right. We would be good together. I would be a fool to turn him down. He pulled her closer to him and her mind stopped reasoning as he kissed her again and again. Then reluctantly he moved away from her. He took off his jacket and spread it over the coarse grass. He reached for her again and they were side by side. She could hear the bump of his heart as well as the wash of the waves below them. Dorothea felt that wonderful weakening in her limbs as the weight of his body pressed upon hers. When the next irate gull screamed above them, they didn't even notice and when, at last, the love-making was over, they stayed close, wrapped in each other's arms.

Dorothea's euphoria lasted all of a week. Although she couldn't remember actually saying yes to Arnold's proposal of marriage, she nodded and smiled at Denise and Norman when Arnold announced to their friends that she had agreed to marry him. The Gills expressed themselves delighted with the news and said they had known all along the couple were made for each other. The journey back to York was clothed in a cloud of romantic happiness. Their news obviously made the older couple relive their own engagement day, and several times on the journey home Dorothea was touched to see Norman take hold of his wife's hand and raise it to his lips for a kiss. That's how married love should be, she thought. Norman and Denise had been married for years and most of the time they treated each other in a normal matter-of-fact way. And yet the depth of affection each felt for the other was clearly revealed at times like these.

Seated in the back of the car, her head resting on Arnold's strong shoulder, Dorothea felt at peace with the world. She had reached a safe haven. Arnold would love and look after her. She was the happiest girl in the world. She remembered their love-making, and with a sly smile shifted her hand and squeezed the top of his thigh. He tensed and looked quickly to see if either of the Gills had noticed Dorothea's gesture, but then he relaxed, and taking hold of Dorothea's errant hand, lifted it to his mouth and gently worried at her fingers. Her smile widened. She would never have thought Arnold could be such a satisfying lover. Of course, he had respected her, that was why formerly he had been rather staid. But it would be different now.

Inevitably, the beautiful romantic cloud dissipated somewhat when ordinary life resumed. Dorothea had looked forward to her next date alone with Arnold but fate conspired to keep them both too busy for several days. The new kitchen assistant gave notice and one of the large cookers recently installed in the hotel kitchen insisted on burning the meals even when the dial showed low temperatures. Arnold had to redraft all the menus and even when Dorothea wore her most expensive perfume and her sheerest blouse, he still looked harassed.

He hadn't the time to go through to Hull with Dorothea so she travelled alone to tell her parents of her engagement. They were delighted with her news. Her mother dissolved into happy tears at the thought of a wedding and her father told her she had shown some sense at last.

She stayed overnight with her parents and it was then she suffered one of her attacks. She was devastated. She was sure she had finished with those for good. Her mother comforted her.

'It didn't last for long, love. I'm sure it won't happen again. It's just the excitement. Just put it out of your mind, that's the best way.'

She tried to do that. On her journey home, she concentrated on thoughts of Arnold and of their life together. They would open the restaurant he dreamed of, and with his skills and her business acumen they would become wildly successful. Perhaps in a few years they might own a whole string of restaurants. But, of course, she closed her eyes and smiled, she would take time off when the babies arrived. She wanted two, maybe even three children. And she was quite sure Arnold would want them too.

Thinking of having children made her think of making love and she hurried back to the hotel full of anticipation. After all, they were now engaged. Arnold had promised to have a ring for her when she returned from Hull. She might have to coax him a little, she thought. He would worry about Norman finding out if they shared a room. There was no denying, Arnold was a tiny bit strait-laced but he was definitely all man, he had proved that at Bridlington. They were young, healthy and in love. She smiled to herself. He wouldn't take too much persuading.

But, somehow, it didn't work out like that. When she reached the hotel she was pleased to learn that the kitchen difficulties had been resolved, and that evening she and her fiancé went out to dinner. The meal was enjoyable, although Arnold told her the sprouts were definitely over-cooked, and over coffee he gave her a beautiful pearl and diamond ring. After dinner, they strolled by the river and Arnold held her tight and rained satisfying kisses on her face. By the time they returned to the hotel, Dorothea's body was ablaze. Fortunately, there was no one about except for the night porter. She muttered a quick good-night to him, then caught hold of Arnold's hand and pulled him towards the stairs.

'Wait a minute, love.' Arnold's face looked strained. Dorothea glanced at him inquiringly.

'I must talk to you. I need to apologise.'

He put his arm about her shoulders and directed her into a small lounge. They sat down and immediately he began to speak, swiftly and in a low voice. Dorothea listened disbelievingly.

He said he had behaved badly that day in Bridlington. He hoped she would be able to forgive him. At this point, Dorothea tried to speak but he waved her to silence. 'I have to say this, love. It's been worrying me ever since.' He said he had been selfish and he had lost control. He loved and respected her so much. Please would she forgive him? It wouldn't happen again, he promised. Not until he could claim her as his lawful wife.

'Stop this!' Finally, she got through to him. 'Arnold, I loved every minute of it. You mustn't apologise. Why,' she smiled at him mischievously, 'I was hoping we could do the same thing tonight.'

Her smile faded as his stern expression did not alter.

'You're wonderful, Dorrie. You're just saying that, aren't you? To make me feel better.'

Again, she tried to speak; this time her voice was slurred with unshed tears but he stopped her mouth with a kiss, a gentle kiss.

After a few minutes, he put his arm about her and escorted her to her bedroom. She lifted her face for another gentle good-night kiss and then dumbly trailed into her room. She undressed, climbed into bed and lay there, her body prey to a tide of conflicting emotions. He was just being the nice man she knew him to be, she told herself, but her unfulfilled craving for love made her grip her arms tightly in frustration. Then she fretted that she was abnormal in some way. Her desire seemed to her unwomanly. It made her feel tainted. It was a long time before she drifted off to sleep and her last coherent thought was one she had expressed before, on the cliffs at Bridlington.

He doesn't really know me at all!

Chapter Nineteen

Greg Paige had called one of his landscapes 'Fire and Ice'. He thought of that when he came out of the railway station at York and turned in the direction of the Bonne Vista hotel. It was winter and in the slate-coloured sky the huge flaming ball of the early setting sun was slowly descending. He paused, his artist's eye appreciating the sun's glow on the ancient stone walls of the city, then he shivered and hurried on his way. A few flakes of snow meandered in the keen air. He turned up the collar of his overcoat.

He was thankful the business with the publishing company had been sorted out and glad he had at last managed to return to York. The last couple of months had been a miserable time for him. He had always affected to feel disdain for the work he did for the Stenhouse Educational Publishing Company, but when it looked as though his contract was to be terminated he had panicked. He knew he should have got on with his 'bread and butter' work and delivered the sketches on time, but he had been to an exhibition of Japanese paintings and the way the artists had concentrated on the immediate surroundings and allowed the distance to fade into a mist, catching the imagination of the onlooker and forcing him to look further and further into the picture, had fired his own ambition. He had given himself a month off to plan his next painting and catch on canvas some of the excitement and fervour he had felt at the exhibition, but the month had stretched to two and then he had been summoned to a meeting with his editor.

Thank God his editor had been a woman. Greg had

turned on all his charm and apologised profusely. She had been initially unimpressed. There were plenty of good copyists about, she had reminded him.

The bitch! But his smile had not wavered. He had crawled to her for almost an hour, and when he left was still unsure whether or not she would save him. Ironic, he thought, the energy he had expended to keep a job in which he had no interest. Still, he had to eat! And working for the Stenhouse Company was infinitely preferable to working in an insurance company. He would never forgive his Aunt Freda for that. She was over eighty now. If only she would die! He was sure she would leave him some money. No matter how she disapproved of him, she had still helped raise him. Sometimes, when she was banging on about his unreliability, his reluctance to do some *real* work, his unsuitable friends, he felt his mask of nonchalance slip. 'Whose fault is it, Aunt Freda?' he wanted to shout. But he never did. The spidery old woman with her trembling hands and quavering voice could still inspire him with awe. Everything about her suggested gradual collapse and decay, and yet when she opened wide her faded blue eyes, they dominated Greg and he became the confused, frightened child he had been when first handed over into her care.

The hotel came into view and he switched his case over to his other hand and flexed his cold fingers. He should be wearing gloves and a hat like the other men on the street, he thought, but he never did. He was a painter, a free spirit, and so he had to act like one. Fortunately the work he was here to do could be undertaken indoors. The editor had relented. He knew she would. He had two weeks to produce a series of ten sketches, all representing facets of working-class life in Victorian England. Greg had immediately decided to do the work in York. The company would pay expenses.

Entering the hotel, he saw Dorothea was on reception. Greg was surprised at the pleasure he felt on seeing her.

'Hello there. I thought you might be married and gone by now.'

She stared at him so long he felt uncomfortable. 'You never came back when you said you would.'

'I'm sorry . . .' He searched his memory. 'Oh yes – that's right. All sorts of things happened. Problems at work.' He flashed her a winning smile. 'But I'm here now.'

'So I see.' With a gesture that was almost rude, she pushed the register over for him to sign.

'You've finally got this place sorted out then?' he said. He put down the pen and looked about him. 'It looks wonderful.'

'Oh, not *wonderful*, Mr Paige, surely? But we are pleased with it.'

She was definitely giving out unfriendly signals, but why? Greg looked at her more closely. She was thinner than he remembered but that was all to the good. He recalled she had been on the chunky side when he saw her last. Funny, he remembered he had felt quite attracted to her and yet, really, she was nothing special in the looks line. Except for those eyes. He looked into them now, and felt a tremor. Yes, he had definitely found her attractive. If he remembered rightly, the feeling had been mutual. Not that she had said anything but they had both known it was there. There had been a boy friend . . . Greg's eyes dropped to where Dorothea's left hand rested on the desk. Yes, there was the engagement ring.

Dorothea's eyes followed Greg's gaze. She flushed and withdrew her hand from the desk. 'Room seventy-four,' she said briefly, placing the key in front of him. Then she turned away.

Greg raised his eyebrows. 'Thanks,' he said. He picked up his case and went towards the newly installed lift. Once in his room, he swiftly unpacked, laid out his pens, pencils and drawing blocks on the table, had a bath, donned a dressing-gown then lay on his bed with a glass half full of whisky. He had brought his own bottle, it was cheaper.

I wonder what I've done to upset her, he reflected. He felt put out. He remembered the day they had met near that tower thing. They had got on really well there. He frowned and took a sip of whisky. They had talked about painting and she had been genuinely interested, he could tell. It was not often he met a woman he felt he could relax with, but that day he had. Of course, that ghastly little dog had been a nuisance, growling at him like that. He took another sip of whisky and felt sad. I'll never understand women, he thought. Even though three of them brought me up!

When Greg was five years old, his parents, who lived and worked abroad, had taken their only child and left him with his father's three elderly aunts. They thought they were doing the right thing. The climate in Africa was totally unsuitable for a young child. There were no other children for him to play with and no decent schools. Living with Aunt Freda and her two younger sisters, all unmarried, little Gregory could attend an exclusive day school in London, mix with the right sort of children and grow up with the spirit and attitude correct in an Englishman of the upper-middle class. Such was the reasoning of the time.

Greg never forgave his parents, particularly his mother whom he had adored. At first he cried a lot and was sullen and stubborn. The younger great-aunts twittered and fluttered about the little boy, coaxing and tempting him with treats. Aunt Freda was made of sterner stuff.

'Stop spoiling him,' she thundered at her sisters. 'He must learn to make the best of things.'

He was put on a ship once, and returned to his parents to spend the cooler, winter months with them. The visit was not a success. James and Marie Paige were dismayed to find their cuddly, smiling little infant had grown into a morose unfriendly boy. It was with relief they waved him off at the end of the visit.

Reconciled to the idea of staying with his great-aunts, determined not to return to his treacherous parents, Greg had determined to make the best of things. As he grew older, he realised he possessed one great asset. He had charm. He soon completely bewitched Aunt Mary and Aunt Ada. He was so good-natured and pleasant at school he became popular with staff and pupils. He relaxed. Life wasn't so bad. He moved to preparatory school and the pattern continued. It was there he found his purpose in life. The art teacher, a Mr Cosy, a roly-poly man who suited his name, was taken with Greg's skill with every form of artwork. He stimulated and encouraged the boy's interest and enthusiasm and eventually persuaded the formidable Miss Freda Paige to allow Greg to take private art lessons. Aunt Ada and Aunt Mary thought his pictures wonderful. Aunt Freda made no comment whatsoever. The boy was happier now he had his hobby but, of course, this art thing mustn't go too far. Painting was not a gentleman's profession . . .

Greg slept so soundly he missed dinner. Late in the evening, he ventured downstairs and humbly asked if he could have a plate of sandwiches. The girl on reception, he hadn't seen her before, obliged by bringing him a tray upon which was a pot of tea, sandwiches and a buttered teacake.

'That new chap, the one that booked in today – what a lovely smile he has,' she said to Dorothea when she met her on her way upstairs.

Dorothea gave her a blank look and walked past without speaking.

She awoke next morning to a stab of apprehension. There was something she had to remember . . . Then she remembered – Greg. Her first reaction was to wonder if she could arrange the work schedules so that she could avoid meeting him. Then the feeling of panic she was experiencing both alarmed and annoyed her. She forced herself to relax. She was being ridiculous. He had obviously forgotten all about her. He had looked so blank at the reception desk, she had been surprised he remembered her name. He recollected she had a boy friend though. Guiltily she looked down at her engagement ring. What a decent, lovely man Arnold was. He was worth two of a flirt like Greg Paige for all his winning ways.

By the time she had washed and dressed and gone down to work she had run through all Greg Paige's despicable characteristics and was therefore surprised when, coming face to face with him in the dining room, he merely smiled a little shyly and wished her good morning. Her tension eased. She was really making a great to-do about nothing at all. It was time she stopped being so silly.

She saw Greg only briefly during the next three days but on the Thursday he stopped her.

'I hope you don't mind, but . . .' He faltered when she did not return his smile, then continued. 'I've been speaking to Mr Gill and he said you might be able to help me.'

She gave him a cool look. 'In what way?'

Greg explained about his current assignment. 'Mr Gill says you have a friend who is an historian?'

'Yes, I have. Liz Hargreaves. She's curator at the Yorkshire Museum.'

'Splendid. Do you think you could introduce me? She may allow me access to certain books that would help me in my work. A personal introduction always helps – friends in high places, so to speak.'

'Yes, I suppose you would know all about things like that.'

He stared at her a moment then said: 'What is it, Dorothea – what have I done to upset you?'

'Nothing.' Colour flooded her face. 'I'm sorry. I'm just a bit jumpy at the moment.'

He touched her arm. 'Perhaps it's pre-wedding nerves?'

'Yes. No. That is, we haven't set a date yet.' She

moved away from him. 'I'll go and ring Liz now. Fix something up for you.'

She hurried away, leaving Greg staring after her.

'What do you think of him?' she asked Liz a few days later. Her friend had good-naturedly allowed Greg to use the Museum's private library.

'He's an interesting chap.'

'You think so?' Dorothea valued her friend's opinion. She knew Liz was no fool.

'Yes. Overdoes the charm a bit, but I suppose some women like that kind of thing.' Liz paused to throw a stick for Jake. They were strolling through the park at the time. 'I don't think he's as confident as he looks, though. In fact,' she paused, 'I felt there was something quite vulnerable about him.'

Dorothea was struck dumb with astonishment. Vulnerable? That was the last word she would apply to Greg. But the word remained with her, especially that evening when she called in at the bar to find him sitting there alone.

Dorothea had just finished helping Arnold pack a suitcase. The only interest Arnold had, apart from cooking and Dorothea herself, was his love of Rugby Football. He was a fine player and had recently been picked to take part in a short tour of Northern England. Norman had given him the time off and tomorrow he was away on his travels. Dorothea had seen to it he had all he needed in his case and had left him with a warm embrace. The coach was picking him up at five a.m. so he had turned in early. Dorothea knew she would miss him, but in a way his going would be a relief. He kept pressing her to decide on a date for the wedding and she was finding it increasingly difficult to find satisfactory reasons not to do so. It was a subject she found it difficult to concentrate on.

She thought Greg Paige looked somewhat tired and deflated and, remembering her friend's words and feeling some degree of guilt for the way she had behaved towards him, she bought herself a soft drink and went over to him.

'Mind if I join you?'

He looked up, then jumped to his feet. 'Good Lord, no. I could do with some company.'

Dorothea sat down. 'Work not going well?'

He shrugged. 'Well enough, I suppose. Your friend has been a great help.'

'So what's the matter? Nothing to do with the hotel, I hope.'

'Oh, no. It's just me!' He shrugged again. 'I should be feeling happy. I'm well on schedule with the sketches.' He grimaced. 'They should keep the dragon-lady I work for happy.'

She laughed. 'So why the long face?'

He raised his hands in an expressive gesture. 'Do you ever feel you don't know where you're going?'

Her smile vanished. 'Frequently.'

He continued, 'I know where I want to go. Remember, I told you once?'

'I remember,' she said softly.

'It's so damn frustrating. Time is just slipping away and I'm not getting anywhere. And I won't if I don't treat my work seriously. And yet—' he shrugged '—I have to eat.'

The obvious sincerity of his words touched her. She patted his hand in a gesture of comfort. 'I'm sure you'll make it one day,' she said. 'You just have to be patient.'

He covered her hand with his own. 'I'm not very good about being patient.' They looked at each other a moment, then Greg went on: 'I feel better already. You really are good for me. Look, I'm not working tomorrow. Liz has promised to look out some prints for me to work on the day after. Could you spare a little time to keep me company?' When she hesitated, he placed his hand on his heart. 'I promise I'll be good and not flirt with you. After all, you weren't engaged when I was here before, were you? In fact,' he pulled a comic expression, 'you can even bring your mongrel along with you, if you like, to act as chaperone.'

Inevitably, Dorothea said yes. After all, she reasoned, nothing could happen just going for a walk.

When she met him, Greg had resumed his usual high spirits. It was a crisp cold winter's afternoon, and with Jake running busily in front of them, they walked along by the river. Dorothea looked across the sparkling water. 'Isn't it lovely?' she said.

'Oh, yes. York's a beautiful city,' Greg agreed, 'but there are so many beautiful places in the world.' He spread out his arms in an expansive gesture. 'One day I'll travel to them all and paint them!'

Dorothea laughed. 'You've changed your tune,' she teased. 'What happened to last night's gloom and doom?'

'That was last night. Today, I'm happy. I'm in a lovely place with a lovely lady.' He looked slyly at Dorothea when she blushed. 'I *know* I'm going to be rich and famous some day so why should I worry?'

He looked ahead of him. 'Should that animal of yours be chasing that duck? He's very close to her tail-feathers.'

'Oh, Lord. Jake, come here!' Dorothea chased after her dog. Greg followed her, a grin of amusement on his face. When he had called her a lovely lady, he had done so out of kindness, yet watching her now, he realised he had spoken the truth. The cold air had brought colour to her face and her pale-coloured hair shone with health and vitality. She had succeeded in distracting Jake's attention and now girl and dog romped with natural grace and vitality.

Unbeknown even to himself, Greg had a romantic streak buried deep inside him. The old prints he had been working with had shown many an idealised Victorian image of motherhood. Watching Dorothea play with Jake, Greg thought her the perfect embodiment of the motherly virtues. She was, as far as he could see, entirely without artifice. She was direct and honest and yet caring. Look how she had tried to cheer him up yesterday. And yet he was quite sure she would be incredibly strong, if she had to be. Those

Victorian pictures which brought forth so much deri-
sion nowadays – the mother and babe turned out in
the snow by a cruel landlord – people forgot, those
things had happened.

Greg stared at Dorothea. She turned and waved to
him, but he didn't wave back. He could almost *see*
her, turned out in the cold night, a baby wrapped in
her shawl. She would have fought like a tiger to save
her child, he was quite sure.

He gave a wavering sigh, then smiled as she
came running back to him. 'What's the matter? He
didn't catch it, you know.' Her face held a puzzled
expression.

'Catch what? Oh, the duck! No, it's not that. I was
thinking of something else. Dorothea?'

'What?' She was busy clipping Jake's lead on to his
collar.

'I want to paint you.'

She laughed. 'Don't be silly.'

'I mean it.'

'I'm not the kind of person who gets her portrait
painted.' He could see she was embarrassed now.

'And what kind of person do you think should be
painted?'

'Well, when it's a woman, she should be elegant
and . . . beautiful.'

Ignoring the presence of Jake who still treated him
with suspicion, Greg side-stepped the dog lead and
turned Dorothea to face him. 'You are beautiful,
darling – don't you know that?'

At his words, her large, expressive eyes became
enormous and Greg's heart misgave him a little. The
word 'darling' had just slipped out. It was a word
used casually, particularly within his crowd of artistic
friends, but he knew immediately it was not a casual
word to Dorothea. To cover his confusion, he went on
hurriedly: 'Doesn't your fiancé call you beautiful? If
he doesn't, then he doesn't deserve you.' Privately,
Greg had already reached that conclusion. He had
seen Arnold a couple of times, Denise Gill had

pointed him out as Dorrie's 'intended', and in Greg's eyes he looked a grim, dour fellow.

Fortunately, Dorothea looked down then. Greg felt relieved. He noticed how her hand trembled as she held Jake's lead. It wasn't that he regretted calling her darling, because she was one, but he didn't want to mess up her life. He doubted whether he would be returning to York again. Indeed, if his plans worked out, he would soon be transferring to London, back to his old friends from art college and into an environment where he could start his *real* work.

But he meant what he said about painting Dorothea. There was an elusive quality about her which intrigued him. And he would be lying if he said he did not find her attractive. It was those damned eyes of hers!

Dorothea had started back along the riverside path and Greg, his high spirits temporarily deserting him, followed her.

Chapter Twenty

Inevitably they met again. Both doubted the wisdom of this. Dorothea wilfully misled the Gills as to where she was going in her free time. Because she was quieter than usual, they assumed she was missing Arnold and were particularly kind to her which made her feel even more guilty. Arnold deserved better than this, she thought. But Arnold had assumed a quality of unreality for Dorothea. Greg filled her every conscious thought. She showed him all her favourite places in York and it seemed to her, as they walked through the busy, picturesque streets, that life assumed a richness she had never before experienced. Colours were brighter, sounds intensified. She listened to Greg's words and explored his face with her eyes, trying to stamp his image firmly in her memory. For in two days, Arnold would return and the following day Greg would leave York, probably for ever.

The evening before Arnold's return, Greg took Dorothea out for dinner. They spoke and ate little.

'This was not the good idea I thought it was,' said Greg ruefully as he paid the presented bill and followed Dorothea out into the street.

'I'm sorry. The food was lovely, but . . .'

'I know. The last couple of days have been magic, haven't they? But now they are coming to an end. Do you feel as I do, Dorothea?' He pressed her hand as he quoted, ' "But in a fiction, in a dream of passion." '

She gasped. 'Then you *do* feel as I do?'

'Of course. I thought you realised.' His eyes were very bright as he looked at her. 'The thing is, what are we to do about it?'

215

Heedless of the passers-by, Dorothea placed her hands about his neck. She kissed him. 'Let's go back to the hotel,' she murmured.

Back at the Bonne Vista they crept up the stairs like criminals. Dorothea supposed she was one, in a way. But nothing could deter her. She ached to make love to Greg. Outside her bedroom door, she clung to him for a moment.

'Give me five minutes, darling.'

She went into her room. There was a mirror on the wall facing the door and she walked up to it and examined her reflection curiously. She was pale and her eyes looked huge. She took off her clothes and again went to the mirror. Let him find me beautiful, she thought. She put on a cotton wrap and then a frown furrowed her brow. She went to her bedside cabinet and took from a drawer a small package. Her lips twisted into a rueful smile.

During her visit to Hull, to tell her parents about her engagement, she had elicited from Nancy details of the local Family Planning Centre. Fresh from her love-making on the cliffs with Arnold, she had worried. She knew his plans did not include an accidental pregnancy. Back in York, of course, she had realised she need not have bothered. Now she closed her eyes as yet another black tide of guilt swept over her. No, she would not think of those things. Tomorrow she would sort out her life. Tomorrow Arnold would be back. But tonight was hers, hers and Greg's!

Greg paused outside Dorothea's bedroom door. Now the moment had come, he was smitten with self-doubt. He wanted this to be right. The past week, he had come to desire Dorrie more and more and he was sure the feeling was mutual, but still he hesitated.

He had experience of loving women and knew he could give a good account of himself. Indeed, many of his former lovers, usually poised, elegant women older than himself, had praised his prowess. He had greeted their praise with a modest smile. How could

216

he tell them that, for him, the true pleasure lay in the chase? When they were beneath him, moaning in pleasure, their expensive hair-styles mussed up and in disarray, there was always a moment when part of him – the artist, he supposed – drew apart. He would dispassionately notice the beads of sweat on an upper lip, the trace of lipstick on the teeth, the pulse of the throat. He never told anyone this, of course. And, inwardly, he was not displeased. It showed he was a true artist.

But this time, it was Dorothea. This time it was different. Dorothea, with her candid, almost childlike simplicity. Dorothea, with the face of the Madonna and the eyes of Salome. *She* would know. He shook his head, took a deep breath and knocked on the door.

She was wearing some kind of a house-coat and he could see there was nothing underneath it. He caught his breath. She held out her hand and drew him into the room. They stood facing each other. She smiled at him, then, without words, helped him to undress. Then she slipped off her own garment. His eyes feasted on her. She was beautiful. Then Greg realised he was observing the texture of her skin, the faint shadows on her abdomen caused by her beautifully shaped but rather heavy breasts. He swallowed.

'Dorrie, I've just realised, I haven't brought any . . . I mean . . .'

'Hush,' she said. 'I've seen to things.' She came closer to him, and resting her hands on his shoulders she ducked her head and ran her tongue along his chest, licking him. Then she caught his nipple in her teeth and gently worried at him.

He gasped. No one had done that to him before. His objectivity vanished. His body began to blaze with passion. Somehow, they were on the bed and there he entered Dorothea's willing body and in so doing also entered a world of purely erotic sensations. A world of touch, taste, smell and feeling. The sensations went on and on. With immense pleasure, Greg realised he couldn't get enough of her. Desire was a hot flame, consuming him. Eventually, exhaustion tore them apart.

In the early light of the dawn they lay side by side, not speaking, staring up at the ceiling. Then Dorothea moved. She raised herself on one elbow and looked at him.

'You're quiet, Mr Paige. Is everything to your satisfaction?' Her voice attempted humour but Greg saw anxiety in her gaze.

'Christ, yes.' He sat up and swept her into his arms again. 'Yes, yes, yes.'

She laughed, a catch in her voice. 'I'm glad.'

They were quiet for a while and then Greg asked: 'What are you going to do, Dorrie?'

When her answer came, after a short pause, he knew he had expected it. Dorothea wasn't the kind of person to live a lie.

'I shall see Arnold and break off our engagement.'

He digested the news. He felt both satisfaction, she was too good for Arnold, and a slight feeling of smugness. He had proved to be the better man. Then, quickly following these feelings, came worry.

'Dorothea, you know, you *must* know that I care for you deeply, but . . .'

'It's all right.' She put her fingers to his lips. 'You're an artist. Art is the most important thing in your life. I accept that, Greg. You made no secret of your ambitions. I don't expect anything of you.'

A welter of emotions churned within him. What a marvellous girl she was.

'But how will he take it? And what will it be like, with both of you working at the hotel?'

She sighed. 'Pretty awful, I should think. Never mind.' She smiled at him. 'If things get too desperate, I can always find another job.'

She was so brave. Greg had never met a woman before who made no demands. He hugged her to him. 'I'll keep in touch, Dorrie. I really will. And if things work out for me, I'll send for you.'

She was quiet for a moment then said, 'You don't have to make promises, Greg.'

'But I mean it, darling.' The memory of their love-making swept over him and he realised with delight he wanted her again. He kissed her closed eyelids and tasted moisture. She was crying. His passion was increased not diluted by the love and responsibility he felt for her. 'I'll start inquiries as soon as I get back to Manchester,' he said. 'And once I've found somewhere in London, I'll send for you. Don't forget, I need you for a model as well as a lover.'

'Oh, Greg.' Her voice faded into silence and there were no more words, just murmurs and sighs as they searched for each other's lips and their bodies locked together.

Greg's work at the Museum had finished and Dorothea, not without difficulty, persuaded him it would be better if he left the hotel before Arnold returned. He kissed her a passionate goodbye but she saw an unmistakable gleam of relief in his eyes as he picked up his case and left for the station. His expression did not upset her. After all, Arnold was her problem. She braced herself for the meeting.

It was traumatic, and when it was finished she hated herself.

At first, Arnold simply did not believe her. She had decided not to mention Greg Paige. She told Arnold she had been feeling unhappy about the engagement for some considerable time. She thought they were not suited and she felt sure she would not make him happy. He dismissed her whole argument with one phrase. She was 'suffering from nerves'. He said the sooner they were married the better. She tried again. She told him she thought he had created an image of her which was simply untrue and that if they did marry, they would probably end up hating each other. His face had paled at that remark and he had attempted to put his arms about her. She had backed away. In the end, she told him she had slept with another man.

His expression had made her feel like a murderess. She had mumbled something about him finding a better person to share his life with, pulled off her ring, and pressing it into his hand, had fled. The rest of the day she spent in her room. She suffered a raging headache which she fully expected to develop into one of her attacks, but mercifully it did not.

The following morning she emerged from her room into an atmosphere of stony faces and hushed voices. Arnold she did not see at all, the Gills had given him the weekend off. Denise, who was very fond of Arnold, treated Dorothea with cool off-handedness and Norman kept sending her furtive glances which she thought would drive her mad. Finally, she went to tackle them when she knew they were both working on the accounts. She said she was sorry her actions had caused disharmony and asked if they would like her to leave. Immediately, alarm showed on Norman's face and Dorothea relaxed. She knew it would not be easy staying on at the Bonne Vista but in her present turmoil she balked at the thought of applying for other jobs.

Gradually, life returned to near normal. Greg wrote to her and said he was doing all he could to sort out their life together. She kissed the letter and smiled. At the back of her mind she had thought he might find it easy to forget what had happened but she had misjudged him. She went about her tasks with a lighter mind. In view of her impending departure, she overhauled the account ledgers and the booking systems with her employers. She realised that, quite apart from the continuing pressure of seeing Arnold every day, she was ready to leave the Gills' employment and move on. She had done all she could at the Bonne Vista. Three months later, when Greg's letter arrived, she was fully prepared to make the break.

Greg met her and Jake at the barrier of King's Cross station. The packed train and dour faces of her fellow travellers had dampened her high spirits, but the beam on Greg's face sent them soaring again.

'Dorothea, you came!' He deposited a smacking kiss on her lips.

She laughed at him. 'Did you think I wouldn't?'

'No.' He picked up her case and slung his arm about her shoulders. 'You have your companion, I see.'

A shadow flitted across her face. 'I had to, Greg. I . . .'

'It's all right,' he soothed. 'I expected him. I guess we'll just have to learn to live together. Come on, we'll head back to the flat. Fortunately it's not *too* far away. Will this animal of yours behave himself on a bus?'

During the bus journey, Dorothea experienced an unexpected pang of disappointment. It was wonderful being with Greg again, but London . . . ! Through the bus window she saw unpainted shops and boarded-up, damaged buildings. The only bright property they passed was a garish amusement arcade from which issued tinny music.

'Not what you expected, eh?' Greg's face wore a half-smile. She realised that, with the quick perception which was one of the things she admired about him, he had gauged her disappointment. 'Don't worry, Dorrie. The old girl still has charm. I'll show you later.'

Greg's flat was at the top of a gently decaying Victorian residence. They climbed up four flights of uncarpeted stairs and Greg unlocked a chocolate brown door and ushered Dorothea and a panting Jake inside.

'Here we are.' Greg looked at her, then grimaced. 'Sorry, it's a tip.'

Jake sneezed, as if in agreement.

They were standing in a tiny sitting room. A threadbare carpet covered the floor, and a hideous leather settee and an ugly sideboard were covered with a confusion of clothing, old newspapers and piles of magazines. A row of dispirited yellowing plants slumped in paint-daubed pots along the mantelpiece.

Greg put down the suitcase and taking off his jacket tossed it on to a pile of papers stacked on a hard-backed chair. Immediately, everything slid off and joined the accumulated rubbish on the floor. 'I meant to tidy up but I was working and forgot the time.' He opened another door, this one liberally daubed with grimy fingermarks. 'It's better in here.'

The second room was sparsely furnished, large and airy. Along one wall stood a dresser displaying an assorted jumble of pans and crockery. A boarded-out alcove held a small oven and sink unit. A high double bed stood in one corner plumped with pillows, cush-ions and a brightly coloured patchwork quilt. There was an offcut of carpet laid in the kitchen area and a rug beside the bed. The middle of the room was empty, save for an easel and a wooden table which was covered with painting equipment. Directly overhead was a huge, uncurtained skylight.

'Oh, Greg – you really *are* a painter now!' Dorothea walked into the centre of the room and looked about her, missing the ironic lift of Greg's eyebrows. 'It's lovely.'

'Damned cold most of the time but it has the light I need.'

He went to join her and touched her shoulder lightly. 'At night, Dorrie, you can lie in bed and gaze upwards and see hundreds of stars.'

She did not move as he gently brushed his fingers backwards and forwards across the nape of her neck. 'But then,' he gave a mischievious grin. 'We don't have to wait until night-time, do we?'

For the next three days they spent their nights and mornings making love and, in the afternoons, Greg showed Dorothea the sights of London. They went to St Paul's which rose proudly above the patched-up devastation surrounding it. They walked through Hyde Park and came to Piccadilly where Dorothea's breath caught momentarily in her throat when she saw the GIs were back, lounging in gum-chewing rows on the steps below Eros.

She commented on the many foreigners hurrying along the busy streets.

'Yes, there're heaps of them. Some are displaced persons. There's a Polish ex-colonel living in the flat below us. He grows mushrooms in the cellar. Come on, Dorrie. We've seen enough for today. My feet hurt. Anyway, I want to paint you.'

Indoors again, Dorothea gave Jake a bone she had bought specially for him and Greg prepared his brushes. The dog gave her a jaundiced look when she approached him but his tail swished as she produced his present.

'You spoil him.' Greg squinted at his canvas then moved the easel fractionally.

'I know, but he's had quite an upheaval, poor old boy.' Dorothea patted Jake's head, then obediently took up her pose when she saw Greg's frown of impatience.

'That's right. Hold it there.' As Greg painted, he told Dorothea how he had managed to get the flat. 'I made some good friends at art college, Dorrie. Some of them are doing well.' He pulled a face. 'If I'd had more help . . .' He sighed. 'Anyway, one chap, Hugh, has landed a decent job writing art reviews. Then an art gallery fixed him up with some useful contacts and he now works a few hours each week teaching drawing at the local Poly. He knew how desperately I wanted to come to London so he wrote and offered me this flat. He's moved on to better things. I think he might swing it for me to teach at the Poly next term!'

'That's marvellous.'

'Yes.' Greg's eyes narrowed. 'Don't move, Dorrie, there's a love.'

Dorothea did as he asked. He was working on a head and shoulders study of her. She sat quietly and watched him work.

As Greg worked, he put on concentration like a

coat. The languid, teasing style disappeared and he grew more and more intense, frowning and muttering away to himself as he feverishly tried to capture the effect he was aiming for. He had already told Dorothea she was a difficult subject. 'You're an enigma, Dorothea. There's something elusive about you.' After half an hour she moved, surreptitiously, to ease her stiffness. Nevertheless, Greg saw her movement. He put down the brush.

'I'm a pig, aren't I? Here, does this help?' He came over to her and massaged the back of her neck.

'Umm . . . lovely.' Dorothea closed her eyes. How glad she was she had come to Greg.

She could smell the turpentine he had spilled on the old shirt he wore for painting, and hear outside the muted sounds of traffic. She was enchanted with the flat. On the first morning she had tackled the disorder. She had washed paintwork, disposed of months of accumulated fluff from beneath the bed, and polished windows. Greg had been impressed with her efforts. So long as she left his painting area alone, he told her, she could do anything she liked.

Now the flat seemed like home, particularly this large, strange room in which they spent all their time. She had even become used to going down two flights of stairs to use the communal toilet. To her enchanted eyes the other people in the house were interesting characters: the old lady who had worked the music halls and who dyed her grey hair red, and the colonel with his clipped accent and courtly bows.

If she opened her eyes slightly she could see splashes of paint on Greg's shirt, cerulean blue and viridian green. He had told her the proper names and they sounded as strong and vibrant as the actual colours; strong and vibrant as their love-making. She shivered. He gave her a hug.

'You're cold. What a pig I am. Look, go and wrap the quilt around you and I'll make us a drink.' But seeing her curled up beneath the quilt, he forgot the tea and instead came to join her.

The following day he took her to the National Portrait Gallery. She listened as he talked about colour and technique but the only impression she took away with her was that Henry VIII looked incredibly mean. She was more interested in the faces she saw on the streets, strange, dark faces. Immigrants, said Greg, from the West Indies.

Fleetingly, Dorothea thought of Rob Steyart, sent away to another country, and yet now people from all over the world seemed to be flooding into England. But she was charmed by the new arrivals' flashing eyes and sing-song voices. Their presence on the grey streets of London brought a hint of spice and distant sunshine.

When Dorothea had been with him for a week, Greg decided to have a party. 'I haven't the cash to take you anywhere special, Dorrie, but I can run to a few beers and a plate of sandwiches. And I want you to meet my friends.'

She protested. 'I'm happy just being with you, Greg. And you shouldn't spend *any* money you don't have to. If only I could get a job,' she worried.

'You'll get a job easily enough.' He was rummaging about in a drawer, looking for an address book. 'There's always jobs in London for someone with your skills. Also,' he paused, produced the book and waved it in triumph above his head, 'they're building a huge festival site on the South Bank of the river. Lots and lots of hotels will be full up with foreign visitors before long. They'll need more staff. Oh, you'll get a job all right. But let's discuss jobs next week. Tomorrow,' he grinned, 'we'll have a party!'

An hour before the guests were due to arrive, Dorothea felt nervous. 'Shall I dress up, Greg?'

He gave her a puzzled look. 'Good Lord, no. It's not that kind of a party.' Dorothea went and put on a straight black skirt and her prettiest blouse. She still felt nervous.

'Where are the other women?' she inquired later that evening as the door opened to admit yet another young man with paint beneath his fingernails. Greg dropped a kiss on the end of her nose. 'Who needs other women when you're here?'

Hugh and Ralph, Kenny and Ben, poured out the beer and sprawled on cushions on the floor. Initially, Dorothea felt awkward, particularly when she saw the surprise on their faces, but they were so friendly and natural with her that she soon relaxed. She was also pleased to see Jake sneak out of his basket and sit himself next to the young man called Kenny.

'Hello, who's this then?' Kenny dropped a heavy hand on Jake's head and scratched his ears.

'Dorothea's best friend. Next to me, of course.' Greg pulled a face. 'It was a job lot, see. I couldn't get one without the other.'

'He's great, aren't you, old boy?' Kenny crouched down and gazed into Jake's eyes. The dog wagged his tail. 'Look at that face, full of character.'

'He's a bit down in the dumps at the moment,' volunteered Dorothea. 'I don't think he cares too much for London.'

She didn't say that neither did he care for Greg and made it patently obvious every time Greg approached him.

'He looks perky enough now. It must be the smell of the food.'

She had made a huge pan of spaghetti and when she handed round the plates they complimented her on the food and on cleaning up Greg's 'pig-sty'. They courteously tried to include her in their conversation but as the glasses emptied and their faces became flushed, they spoke of people and methods of painting she had never heard of. Dorothea didn't mind. Their enthusiasm interested her. She sat back in her chair, content to watch them. How they talked! Their faces were animated and their hands wove pictures in the lamplit room. She looked across at Greg and felt her heart burst with love and contentment.

Later, she cleared away their empty plates and the full ashtrays and they helped her tidy up with exaggerated, drunken courtesy. Then Greg, with tipsy charm, pulled her on to his knee and kissed her. She turned peony-red. He kissed her again, lingeringly.

'What's the matter, Dorrie? You're my girl, aren't you?'

She lay back against his arm and let the inhibitions, the rigid conventions of her working-class background, fade away. 'You know I am,' she replied, and smiled.

Greg's friends stopped talking and stared at her.

'I see what you mean, Greg,' said the young man called Kenny. 'Yes, indeed – eminently paintable.'

In the early hours of the morning, their guests departed. Dorothea moved about collecting glasses. Greg yawned. 'Leave those, Dorrie. We'll see to them in the morning. Come to bed.' Dorothea followed him gladly, first spending a couple of minutes fussing Jake. She was so happy herself she wanted everyone to feel the same. For once, Greg went straight to sleep. Dorothea put her arms about his sleeping form and looked up at the stars showing through the skylight. Life was absolutely perfect, she decided.

Chapter Twenty-One

I did the right thing, thought Dorothea as she hurried along Steadman Street on her way to work. She smiled to see the new green growth, soft as spring itself, showing on the trees fringing the pavement. Optimism, hope for the future, flooded through her. Last week had been hard. Greg had been sunk in gloom, sour and sharp as old vinegar, and two more bills had arrived in the post. Dorothea had never felt low enough to regret moving to London but Greg was so unpredictable sometimes it made her nervous. She told herself it was because he was an artist, and wasn't it his mercurial temperament that had attracted her to him in the first place? Yesterday she had walked down this street on the verge of tears. She had overslept and was in a frantic rush to get ready for work. Greg, slumped beneath the patchwork quilt, had issued a stream of acid and uncalled-for comments. She had thrown her hairbrush at him, screamed at him that he was a bastard, and rushed out. But when she returned to the flat in the evening, he had prepared a beautiful supper for her and there were fresh flowers by her plate.

A passer-by stopped her and asked for directions and Dorothea's smile broadened. She felt like a proper Londoner with each day that passed. She reached Waterloo Bridge and paused to study the progress of the Festival of Britain site. When she had commenced working at the Doran Hotel as a receptionist, she had daily passed a strange collection of skeletal shapes but now the view in front of her made her catch her breath.

Across the river, walls of glass and aluminium sparkled in the spring sunshine. The Skylon floated upon its cradle, spectacularly outlined against the clear sky. Dorothea shaded her eyes to stare at it. How exciting it all was! She wondered if she could persuade her mother to come and see the Festival when it opened? But Dennis wouldn't allow it. He had little time for his daughter now.

Dorothea took a last look then hurried onwards. At least, she reflected, her mother wrote to her. Hazel's letters were now the only link with Dorothea's old life. Since the day she had stepped into the taxi outside the Bonne Vista, her suitcase in the trunk of the cab, Jake pulling and panting on his lead and evincing strong disapproval at the thought of a car ride, her links with York had been broken. Arnold she had not expected to hear from, she could only hope he had now recovered from his disappointment. But the fact the Gills had not replied to her letter to them had hurt her. But her mother wrote every fortnight and kept her up to date with news from Hull. It was from Hazel she had learned that Nancy had produced twin boys. A wry smile twisted Dorothea's lips when she read that piece of information. Trust Nancy not to do things by half!

She reached the hotel and ran up the steps leading to the entrance. As she pushed at the revolving door and went into the foyer, she spotted a thin, white-haired gentleman checking in at the desk and her face broke into a welcoming smile. He was one of her favourite guests.

'Mr Whitney, how nice to see you again.'

The man smiled back. 'Hello, my dear.'

'Will you be staying long this time?'

'A week, possibly eight days.'

'Then, I'll order the *Financial Times* for you, shall I?'

'Thank you.' The elderly man inclined his head courteously. He picked up his keys, turned towards the lift, then paused. 'The flowers look beautiful.'

The Doran Hotel boasted one hundred and twenty rooms and held a four star classification. Initially Dorothea had been awed by the place. However, the awe had rapidly disappeared when she became more closely acquainted with the hotel. The carpets were thick and kind to the feet and a chandelier hung in reception but service and discipline was slack. Newspapers in the reading room went unchanged for days, coffee cups remained on tables unless staff were prodded, and fluff could be found behind every wardrobe. But the money was good and money was what Dorothea needed.

After powdering her nose, Dorothea took her place at the Reception Desk. As she pulled the book detailing arrivals and departures towards her, she gave a secret smile and remembered her varied duties at the Bonne Vista. There was no peeling of potatoes and setting up breakfast tables for the receptionists at the Doran. She often wished there were *more* duties she could take over. When her routine tasks were accomplished, she checked to see that the ashtrays in the reception lounge had been emptied and cleaned, and gave the flower display fresh water. She was speaking to one of the porters when Mr Whitney returned to the desk.

'Right away, Albert, before you do anything else. I distinctly remember asking you yesterday to replace that burned-out light bulb. It may seem a small matter to you, but someone could easily trip up in that dark area.' Dorothea dismissed the man with a curt nod and turned to the waiting guest.

'Yes, Mr Whitney?'

'Will you book me a taxi for two o'clock, please, and do you have any writing paper and envelopes?'

'Of course.' Dorothea opened a drawer. 'I'll book the taxi immediately. Writing paper and envelopes are in the oak desk in the corner of the reading room and there are some postage stamps here if you wish.' She proffered the stamps.

'Thank you.' He accepted them with a twinkle in

his eyes. 'Do I detect your hand in these improvements, Miss Bellows?'

She blushed and made a non-committal reply. He wandered off to the reading room and she watched him and wondered why he used the Doran. On the surface he seemed a benevolent elderly gentleman but she had observed before how sharp he was, how little he missed. And he was obviously wealthy. His luggage and the clothes he wore were of the highest quality. She shrugged. It was nothing to do with her.

After work, she went shopping. She had suggested to Greg that he buy some essential groceries today but she doubted that he had even heard her. He was finishing off a painting and had retreated into his own private world. The fickle sunshine had fled and when the bus carrying her homewards lurched to a stop, grey leaden clouds were pressing down the London sky like a lid on a box. Dorothea struggled through the crowd of tired travellers and alighted thankfully on the pavement. Her feet hurt and the journey had been more unpleasant than usual for she had been pressed up against a man suffering from halitosis. The newspaper hoarding near the bus stop further depressed her. Bold, black headlines screamed of increased English involvement in the Korean War. Dorothea grasped her bags of shopping and plodded towards the flat. Any day now, Greg could be called up! Not for the first time she marvelled at his seeming insouciance at the prospect. To spend two years in the Army would be bad enough, but if he should be sent to Korea . . . She pushed the thought away. Perhaps, she thought, the painting will be finished. Perhaps supper will be set out on a tray on the table by the bed. She smiled.

The flat door was locked. She had to fumble in her handbag for a key. Inside, the lights were off and the gloom carried the smell of cheap wine and cigarettes. She flicked on the light and discovered Greg and his friend, Hugh Conley, prone on the carpet. There were cushions beneath their heads and glasses in their hands. From his bed in the corner, Jake raised his head and thumped his tail in greeting.

'Ha, the little woman.' Hugh levered himself up and waved his glass at her. 'Greetings.'

Dorothea stepped over him. She deposited the shopping on the draining board and hung up her coat. Of all Greg's friends, Hugh was the only one she disliked. He was well mannered and scrupulously polite to her, but when she was with him, she sensed an undercurrent of distaste which confused her. When she turned back to them, they were seated cross-legged on the cushions. They grinned at her. Jake came to Dorothea and pressed against her leg, as if offering support. When she spoke, there was an edge to her voice.

'You said you were going to work on your painting, Greg.'

'I have. It's finished. We were celebrating.'

'Best he's done yet.' Hugh nodded sagely.

Greg looked at her under his lashes. 'Want to see it?'

'Later.' She felt a spurt of temper as she glanced round the room. 'Has Jake been out?'

'Dorrie, I've been *working*!' Seeing the look on her face, Greg added hurriedly: 'He was out for a run this morning. I gave the kid in the flat below a bob to take him.'

'Good.' Her tension eased and she rubbed Jake's ears. She worried about him. He slept a lot and much of his hitherto cheeky aggression had disappeared. He didn't think much of London. Of course, he was getting old. He had been fully grown when Dorothea had found him.

'I'm starving, Dorrie. Did you bring some grub in with you?'

Her irritation returned. 'As a matter of fact, I have. But if you remember, Greg, *you* were supposed to do the shopping today.'

She saw the grin fade from his face and his eyes darken but her sense of grievance made her continue.

233

'I know your painting's important, Greg, but you could have tidied up a bit. Why, even the breakfast things are unwashed!'

He sprang to his feet. A nerve twitched at the side of his jaw but his voice remained calm. 'Things like that don't matter, Dorrie, but you'll never understand that, will you? I'm afraid you have the typical house-wife's mentality.'

She flinched. She hated it when Greg became sar-castic. But she wouldn't let him know she was hurt. She kept her own voice calm. 'Yes, I know it's all trivia to you but I'm tired. I've worked hard all day and I'm damned if I'm going to come home and wait on you.'

For a moment Greg's face remained impassive, then he sighed and ran his hand through his hair. 'I'm sorry, love. Please don't be cross. I want us to be happy.' He held out his hand to her. 'It really is a good painting.'

'Well, I think she's right.' Hugh's drawl made them both jump. When Dorothea looked across at him, she frowned. His eyes held a disturbing brightness.

'After all, Dorrie's keeping you. The least you can do to repay her is to keep the love-nest clean and tidy.'

'That's a bloody stupid remark. She's not keeping . . .'

Dorothea put her hand on Greg's arm to restrain him as he moved towards Hugh.

'We have a mutual agreement, Hugh. We share. Anyway,' her voice was icy, 'I can't think what our living arrangements have to do with you.'

'Point taken, my dear.' Hugh's face retained a faint smile. He looked up and stared into her eyes. 'I was taking your side, you know.'

A dark shadow seemed to loom between them. She stepped back. 'I'll unpack the shopping, not that there's much of it. Not nearly enough for three,' she added.

Hugh merely smiled.

With one of his disconcerting switches of mood,

Greg followed her into the kitchen alcove, encircled her waist with his hands and nuzzled the back of her neck.

'I'm sorry, love. Let me help you. Tell you what, I'll do a few potatoes and then poor old Hugh can stay and eat with us.'

They ate a scratch meal then Dorothea stacked the dirty plates. 'No pudding – but there's some biscuits in the cupboard.'

'That was great.' Greg smiled at her. 'Leave the washing-up. I'll do it.' He didn't, of course. When Dorothea had put away the last of the crockery, she curled up in the shabby armchair and listened to them talk.

'How can you possibly compare Lowry with Maurice Utrillo?'

'Then there's the related groups of ovoid shapes, the curvilinear characters . . .'

She slept and awoke at one-thirty in the morning with a crick in her neck, and still they talked.

'What about Giacomo Balla's impression of continuous movement?'

'And Calder's *The Circus*.'

'Greg.' She left the chair and padded over to him. 'It's terribly late.'

He looked at her impatiently. 'So?'

'I have to be up early tomorrow.'

'Well, go to bed. No one's stopping you.'

She bit her lip. She took a cover off the bed and went into the cold, virtually unused sitting-room to undress. Draped in the cover she crept into the kitchen area to clean her teeth then hurried towards the bed. She hated the thought of Hugh seeing her undressed. And yet it was silly. He painted unclothed men and women all the time. Safe in the downy feather bed she sneaked a look at them. They hadn't even glanced her way, absorbed as they were in serious discussion. She could never understand their world but, she comforted herself, Hugh rarely came to the flat. She snuggled down, listening to their voices rising and falling like the wash of the waves.

As dawn filtered into the room she heard the flat door

close and felt Greg's naked body slide into bed next to her. He was cold and initially she drew away from him. Then, even in her state of sleep, she felt the awakening of desire and put her arms about him. He kissed her ear then yawned.

'God, how Hugh goes on,' he muttered. He flung a heavy arm across her body. Already his breathing was thickening into sleep.

'Greg?'

'Sorry, darling. Too knackered.' He slept.

On 3 May, the King, speaking into a microphone from the west steps of St Paul's, declared the Festival of Britain well and truly open. The following Tuesday, Dorothea's fellow receptionist at the Doran chattered away, telling her all about it. It had poured down, the bright umbrellas of the Festival's many open-air cafés becoming sodden in minutes. But it was all wonderful and Dorrie must go and see everything soon. Of course, sighed Vida, she wouldn't see the King. Vida had stood for hours on Ludgate Hill to see the Royal Family.

Dorothea only half listened. She had seen the close-up photographs of the King in the newspapers and had thought how ill and drawn he looked, but perhaps it was just the newsprint. Perhaps it was just her. She was feeling pessimistic. Greg was working like a slave on his new painting, a gas bill had arrived, and that morning she had received a letter from her mother. Hazel wrote to say she wouldn't be coming to London after all. Her letter was typical, determinedly cheerful but evasive. It was written in a way to cheer up Dorothea but instead it depressed her. Between the lines of gossip she could sense her mother's loneliness and that made her feel guilty. She missed Hazel more than she had ever imagined she would. She wondered how long her father would maintain his disapproval.

However, when she arrived home from work she found Greg excited and happy. The afternoon post had brought him a cheque. An art dealer in the district had taken a few of his canvases to display in his shop and one had been sold.

'Forty-five pounds, Dorrie! That head and shoulders study I did of you, remember? I told you that you were good for me.' He picked her up and swung her round.

'That's marvellous, Greg.'

'I know it's not much, I pulled in much more money with my book illustrations, but it's the first *real* painting I've sold, Dorrie. And it's only the beginning.'

He was bubbling with excitement and his euphoria lifted her spirits. They celebrated with fish and chips from the corner chippy. Greg had suggested going out to a restaurant but, gently, Dorothea reminded him of the outstanding gas bill.

Later that night, when they were in bed, Greg took hold of Dorothea's hand and kissed it, tentatively. 'You had a letter today, didn't you, from your mother?'

'Yes.'

Greg waited. The flat was silent except for the faint snoring noise coming from Jake's basket.

'I knew something had upset you. What is it?'

'She can't come to visit after all.'

'Oh, I'm sorry. I know how much you were looking forward to seeing her. Look,' he raised himself on one elbow, 'would you like to go through to Hull? You've got some days leave due from the hotel and we could scrape up the money.'

'Thanks, but no. I'd like to, but it wouldn't work. Dad would be bloody-minded and that would make things difficult for Mum.'

He sighed. 'I've mucked things up for you, haven't I?'

'No.' She turned towards him. 'Things have always been difficult between Dad and me. And yet,' she was silent for a moment, 'I miss them both.'

'I envy you that, you know.'

Her brow wrinkled. 'What do you mean?'

'Family feelings, even uncomfortable ones. And missing people.'

'But you have relatives.'

Dorothea knew very little of Greg's background but she had learnt that his parents lived and worked abroad and that his only remaining aunt was incredibly old and quite rich.

'Not really. Oh, when I'm absolutely on the breadline, I go – cap in hand – to Aunt Freda and receive an hour-long lecture and a tiny cheque. She's disgusted by the way I've turned out.'

'But your parents?'

His laugh was bitter. 'You can't have feelings for strangers, Dorrie. Mother and Father are busy people. My birth really inconvenienced them. They packed me off to the aunts as soon as they possibly could. God!' Dorothea felt his body tense beside her. 'Can you imagine it, a poor snotty-nosed kid of five being dumped on a trio of twittering elderly spinsters?'

Dorothea pressed herself closer to him. 'Oh, Greg.'

'It's all right.' He patted her stomach, stroked her. 'I survived. Where do you think I learned how to be charming to ladies? By the time I reached twelve, I had perfected the art of pleasing. I could twist them round my little finger, all except my Aunt Freda. Of course, she had to be the one who outlived the other two!'

'And your parents?'

His hand stilled. 'Oh, *they're* still alive. We exchange Christmas cards.' At her shocked exclamation, he laughed, moved his hand. 'It doesn't matter. I've sold a painting, a *real* painting! And I have you now. I'm sorry about your folks but we don't need anyone else, do we? We have each other. Say you'll never leave me, Dorrie. Go on, say it!'

As he spoke, the movement of his hand increased and her breathing quickened. 'Say it!'

She put her hands on his shoulders. 'I'll never leave you, Greg.'

238

Chapter Twenty-Two

One morning in July two envelopes lay in the postbox addressed to Greg. He opened them, read the contents then gazed into space for a moment. Then he went quietly up the stairs back to the flat. He kicked off his slippers and padded bare-foot through to Dorothea who was still in bed. The bedsprings groaned as he sat down beside her.

'Wake up, Dorrie. Look – money!' Greg fluttered one of the letters in front of her face. She groaned.

He tut-tutted. 'So blasé already!'

'Sorry.' She sat up and rubbed her eyes. 'Tell me?'

'Cheque for thirty pounds; for the pen and ink sketch of the toddler in St James's Park.'

She beamed. 'Greg, that's wonderful!'

'Not bad, is it? And Hugh's landed a job writing for the *Art Today* monthly. He's bound to give me a plug, so things should start happening there.' Unaware of Dorothea's lack of response, he bent down and scrabbled under the bed. 'Seen my blue shoes?'

'No. Why?'

'Why, why! It's your day off, isn't it?'

'Yes, but . . .'

'Well, get up then! That is, if you want to go and see the Festival.'

She caught her breath. 'We're going today?'

'Why not? You're off work, the sun's shining, and—' he flourished the cheque in the air '—we have the wherewithal.'

*　　*　　*

They jostled their way across the Bailey bridge in the middle of a crowd of people.

Greg whispered, 'Why does everyone get the same idea at the same time?'

'It's always crowded.' Dorothea linked her arm through his. 'I'm glad. It's like a party. Just look at those colours, Greg. Oh, let's see everything!'

They worked their way through the many pavilions. They sat in strange chairs made from wire and ate ice-cream and they donned 3-D polaroid spectacles in the Telecinema. Then they went to see the water mobile splashing away outside the Ships and Sea Pavilion. Dorothea could never remember feeling so alive and happy before. There were so many new and exciting things to exclaim over. Greg was similarly affected.

'See the clean lines of that furniture, Dorrie? It's called "Contemporary Style". When we're rich, we'll buy that, get rid of the old rubbish we have at the moment.' Oblivious of the thronging crowd, he laughed and pulled her close to him, kissing her.

'Greg!' Dorothea pushed him away.

'What? No one's bothered. Look around you.'

She glanced round and saw that he was right. There was a peculiar 'un-English' feeling about the crowds massed in the Festival grounds. It was as if the open air cafés, the murals, sculptures, the zinging colours and the atmosphere of space had provoked a heady excitement in a people formerly dulled and saddened by the years of war.

When darkness fell and the lights were switched on they still did not want to leave. They decided to treat themselves to a meal in one of the restaurants in the Festival Hall. They were looking about for a free table when a voice hailed them:

'Greg, over here!'

Kenny Moorhead waved to them. He was with a group of young people seated at a table by a huge glass wall overlooking the dark glistening waters of the Thames.

Greg hesitated. 'What do you want to do?'

'Let's join them.'

Kenny had been one of the young men who had attended Greg's party on Dorothea's arrival in London and she liked him. He jumped up at their approach.

'I'll grab another couple of chairs.'

He introduced his friends, and enthusiastically, they all discussed the Festival.

'Isn't it wonderful? Have you seen the 3-D film? Have you seen Ceri Richards's composition of Trafalgar Square yet?'

'No, Kenny.' Dorothea frowned at him. 'No painting talk tonight, please!'

He laughed. 'You're right. Have I introduced you to Steve? He's from the North, too. And this is Clara. Isn't she beautiful?'

Clara was indeed beautiful. She had long red-gold hair and deeply blue eyes, and Dorothea noticed how immediately and intently those eyes focused on Greg. Kenny also noticed. He patted Dorothea's hand in the manner of an elder brother and whispered, 'No need to worry. Greg finds classical beauty boring.'

Dorothea gave him a quizzical look and he clapped his hand over his mouth. 'Sorry, I've done it again, haven't I?'

She grinned. 'It's all right, Kenny. But what about you? Isn't Clara your girl friend?'

'Sort of.' Kenny's eyebrows rose into comical peaks. 'But then, I'm not the perfect escort for a beautiful creature like that, am I?'

She looked at his blunt features. His brown curly hair was already receding from his high forehead and his nose took a definite slope to the right. She remembered his mentioning it had been broken in a rugger match when he was at school.

'Anyone with any sense at all would love you to be their escort,' she told him. He blushed and they both felt a little awkward. It was a relief when conversation turned to more general matters.

After the meal Dorothea sat back and enjoyed the

view. Through the glass, she could see the lights of the
river boats coming and going, carrying visitors to the
Festival Pleasure Gardens at Battersea. She suddenly
realised how content and happy she was. Opposite
her, Steve and a girl called Sally were laughing over
the latest Ealing comedy film they had both seen,
Kenny was listening to them and smiling, and Clara
. . . She was still sending out strong signals to Greg.
Dorothea didn't care. Greg had pulled his chair closer
to hers. His arm was draped around her shoulder and
every so often he sent her his secret smile and trailed
his fingers loosely across the nape of her neck. She
shivered with pleasure. At that moment she wouldn't
have changed places with anyone.

The following morning, Greg took his second letter
out of his pocket and gave it to Dorothea. He watched
as she read it.

She looked up. 'Oh, Greg, what shall we do?'

He shrugged his shoulders. 'Nothing. I'll turn up
for the medical, of course.'

'Maybe you could ask to be deferred?'

'I'm a painter, Dorrie, not a coal miner or a trainee
doctor. Just an artist. God!' Despite his calm expression his voice wavered as he continued, 'Can you
imagine their reaction when I tell them? They'll probably tell me army life will be the makings of me, turn
me into a real man!'

'Don't, Greg.' She went to him and put her arms
about his unresponsive figure. 'Maybe it won't be so
bad. Think. There'll be lots of new experiences you'll
be able to use later in your work.'

'Good old Dorrie.' His voice was flat, his arms
hanging heavily by his side. 'I knew *you'd* try and find
a bright side to this mess.'

She bit her lip. 'Why not? There's nothing else we
can do.'

'There might be. I've been thinking.' He retrieved
the letter from Dorothea and gazed down at it.
'There's Hugh. He knows a lot, has contacts.'

'Oh, yes, he would have!'

Greg stared at her. 'Why do you resent him so much? He's been a good friend to me.'

'I don't know,' she answered quietly. 'There's something about him. And,' she stared down at her hands, 'he certainly doesn't like me. He patronises me.'

'For Christsakes!' His angry reaction made her jump. 'He's the only one who might be able to get me out of this mess and you're concerned because he patronises you! Hugh's an artistic snob, everyone knows that, but he has influential friends.'

Greg pushed the letter into his pocket. 'I've not said much, Dorrie, but I dread National Service. It's such a bloody waste of time, for one thing. And *now* – just when my work's taking off! It's so unfair. I'm going round to Hugh's, see if he's in.' He pushed his hand through his hair and gave a mirthless grin. 'Of course,' he continued, 'we can always hope the medical shows I've got an incurable disease. That way, I'll get out of National Service, and when I die, my paintings will be worth a fortune!'

The door slammed shut behind him.

Greg passed his medical A1 and Hugh promised to ask around. The six weeks' period between the medical examination and the letter telling him where to report were hard on both Greg and Dorothea. Greg stopped painting and alternated between foolish high spirits and dark depression. He drank too much. Dorothea tried to be cheerful but inwardly she felt aggrieved. Not once had Greg mentioned the fact he would miss her or asked how she felt about his possible long absence. The spectre of Korea haunted her. She found it inconceivable that Greg, however absorbed he was in painting, hadn't realised he might actually end up fighting in a war.

One Wednesday morning Greg received notification of his draft, a railway warrant and information as to where to report. The same day Hugh came to see him. He rushed into the flat, ignored Dorothea but slapped Greg on the back.

'Think I've got it, Greg. Told you I would!'

'Too late, old man.' Greg produced his documents. 'These came today.'

'It doesn't matter.' Hugh chuckled and threw himself into a chair. 'What you have to do,' he paused, savouring the look of impatience on his friend's face, 'is to sign on for *three* years.'

'What!' Greg and Dorothea spoke together.

'True.' Hugh laughed again. 'It's beautiful in its simplicity. If you sign on for three years, you can buy yourself out in a few months.'

There was silence. Greg thought about it. Then he said, 'You're sure about this?'

'Yes. Found two chaps who did it. You'll need money, of course.'

'How much?' Dorothea spoke quietly.

'Not sure yet. I'll find out. Shouldn't be *too* drastic.' Hugh stretched out his legs. 'Get me a drink, Greg. I deserve one, don't you think?'

'We're out of beer. I'll go down to the corner shop in a minute.' Greg was lost in thought. 'What does "nothing too drastic" mean?'

'Few hundred. If you're really stuck, I could help out. You could call it an investment, Greg. I have faith in your work.'

'No!' Greg and Dorothea spoke the word at the same time but Dorothea's voice drowned out Greg's. He frowned at her before continuing: 'You've done enough for me. I know,' an expression of relief spread over his face, 'Aunt Freda! She'll moan but she'll pay up.' He grinned, the lines of tension already leaving his face. 'I'll go and buy some booze. You can tell me more and we'll celebrate. I can't thank you enough, Hugh.'

After his departure the silence in the room weighed heavy. Dorothea called Jake to her side, obscurely glad of his company. Hugh stared at her for a moment, then said, 'Look a little happier, Dorrie. You're not losing your sweetheart after all. A few months and he'll be back with you. And no overseas drafting, either. Aren't you grateful to your old pal, Hugh?'

Dorothea managed to mumble a few words in reply then they waited for Greg's return in silence, the old feeling of antagonism alive in the air surrounding them.

Greg tried hard to be cheerful before he left. 'See the pay book, love? At least I'll be earning money whilst I'm peeling spuds and square-bashing.'

During the weeks that followed Dorothea missed him, yet in many ways she enjoyed herself. With Greg away, she was able to tackle the disorder of the flat. She cleared away mountains of his clutter, stacking unused canvases away in a cupboard, picking up countless half-finished pen sketches scattered about the floor, smoothing them out and placing them in a drawer. The core of his painting area she left untouched, knowing how sacred it was to him. But she painted the walls of the flat pale green and made new cushions for the two sagging yet comfortable armchairs.

After the departure of the initial influx of foreign visitors to the Festival of Britain, things slackened off at the hotel but then various trade organisations came to visit the site in order to set up business deals. Many of these parties booked in at the Doran and, once again, Dorothea found her organisational skills being called upon. Her name became known to the visiting groups and invariably it was she to whom the letter and telephone calls were addressed.

Guests at the Doran sang her praises so loudly the Manager gave her a bonus. With Greg away, she found the time to take Jake for long walks and was delighted to see some of his old vitality return. He even chased a ginger cat one day, although he came nowhere near to catching it. When he returned to her side, tail wagging, tongue lolling, she laughed and hugged him with a catch in her throat. What a pity her beloved pet and her beloved man didn't like each other!

Summer warmth cooled into autumn crispness.

Dorothea was profoundly grateful Hugh Conley kept away from her. Kenny Moorhead called in to see her a couple of times, sweeping her off to the local pub for a drink to stop her 'moping', as he put it. Kenny was always good company. She learnt that he had known Greg for many years, they had attended the same school. He told her he was convinced Greg was a great painter.

'You're good for him, you know,' he said. 'You look after him and keep him on an even keel. He needs that.' He asked how Greg was surviving army life.

'Not too badly, I think,' she replied. 'His letters don't really say much.'

'So stupid, forcing him into the army. Pure waste of time and talent.'

He looked so miserable, Dorothea tried to cheer him up. 'And what about your work, Kenny?'

He ducked his head, looking embarrassed. 'I've packed it in, Dorrie. Oh, I'll keep painting as a hobby, don't you worry.' He forced a smile when he saw her concerned expression. 'Deep down I've always known, I suppose. I'm good, but not good enough. I could probably make a living on the fringes of the art world, but I don't want that. I've always been good at figure-work. My father's prepared to support me while I do an accountancy course. I'm lucky really. I've even got out of National Service because I've got a dodgy foot. Come on, cheer up.'

He patted her hand then took her glass. 'Fancy another drink?' He stood up, turned to go to the public bar, then hesitated: 'Don't tell Greg, will you? I want to do that myself.'

Poor Kenny! What a hard decision it must have been for him. Dorothea resolved to ask him round to the flat when Greg came on leave. Kenny's decision to change his career must not jeopardise the friendship they had with him. Anyway, she smiled at him over her replenished glass, it would be good to have a friend who was *not* an artist.

At Ch   reg came home on leave. Dorothea

hardly recognised him. His beautiful hair cropped close to his head, dressed in an ill-fitting uniform, he seemed broader, more substantial, harder-edged in some indefinable way. She stared at him and felt shy, unsure of how to behave. Then he stepped through the doorway of the flat and gave her a bearhug. Jake barked, raced across the room and sank his teeth into Greg's left ankle. He swayed, tried to kick Jake away, and the three of them ended up in a rumpled heap on the floor.

Greg swore. 'Bloody fine welcome.' He kicked out again at the unrepentant dog. 'Clear off, you ugly mutt!'

Jake retreated to his basket from which he gave Greg a bellicose stare. Caught between laughter and tears, Dorothea stared at Greg. 'I'm sorry, love.'

'It's all right. Good job I'm wearing thick socks.' He rubbed his ankle and struggled to a sitting position on the floor. 'You've bought a new rug?'

'Yes, it's in a Contemporary style, like those at the Festival. Do you like it?'

'Mmm. You've painted the place, too.' He glanced about him, noting the holly decorating the pictures on the wall and the tiny Christmas tree in the corner. 'It's good to be home, Dorrie. My sketches, the other stuff – they're safely packed away, are they?'

She shook her head. 'You don't have to ask that, Greg.'

'No.'

After a brief look around him, Greg's amazing amber-coloured eyes focused upon Dorothea. Immediately, she was aware of his physical magnetism; aware, too, that in their undignified tumble, her skirt had ridden up her body, showing her long, shapely legs, the pale blue cami-knickers she wore. Her breathing suddenly accelerated. She marvelled at the effect Greg had on her. For the past three months she had never thought once of love-making. Now, staring back at him, she felt her bones melt and warmth spread into her hips and belly. Greg's eyes narrowed and he held out his hand. 'Come here,' he said. 'I want my Christmas present now.'

The army *had* changed Greg. He seemed older, more responsible. He helped Dorothea with domestic chores, joking that Forces life had made him into a cook. His interests had widened for he now read the whole of the newspaper not just the art pages and spoke soberly about the crisis in Egypt. Dorothea had worried he might be angry about the tidying away of his work but he merely shrugged when she mentioned it. He seemed reluctant even to talk about painting and she came to realise he had locked away his ambitions until he was free to take up his proper life again. He told her little about army life. It was boring, he said.

After their initial, wild passion on the day of his arrival, Dorothea found that during their love-making, Greg was more gentle, considerate of her needs. Paradoxically, this confused her. For the first time ever, she thought, he was offering what seemed like a commitment to the future. She felt secure in his love. Indeed, she allowed herself to consider marriage, perhaps a child. And yet . . . to be honest, she missed the intensity, the sexual excitement they had shared after one of their hitherto unholy rows. She fretted, lying awake at night. Will I ever know what I really want? she thought.

Chapter Twenty-Three

Two weeks after waving goodbye to Greg at the railway station, Dorothea caught a train herself, to Hull. Hazel had written and asked her to visit.

'Your dad wants to see you, Dorrie. Please come! He says he won't row with you. You're old enough to live your own life, now.'

As always with Hazel's letters, Dorothea read between the lines. During the past months she had detected a determination within her mother to see her again. To Dorothea it was obvious, Hazel had delivered an ultimatum: either Dorrie was to be welcomed back into the family home or she, Hazel, would travel to London and stay some considerable time. Dorothea's lips had curved into a bitter-sweet smile. Her father liked coming home to a neat and tidy home. He liked freshly ironed shirts in the wardrobe and hot meals on his table. Faced with a choice between high-flown principles and home comforts, the principles had lost out! Dorothea faced her home-coming with mixed feelings.

Hull hadn't changed. The sweetish, cloying smell from the fishmeal factory hung over the rows of terraced houses and old ladies still sat on their doorsteps to watch the world go by. Carrying her suitcase, Dorothea used the short-cut through West Dock schoolyard to reach Harrow Street. A small boy ran up to her and asked if she had 'a penny for two halfpennies, please'. She put down her case, delved in her pocket and produced a penny, telling the lad to keep his half-pennies. A few moments later, she looked back to see him repeating his money-making operation.

In Harrow Street two small girls were holding a jumble sale outside their home. On a pile of upturned fish boxes were set out discarded toys and shabby books. Dorothea stopped and bought two cloth books depicting farm animals which she might or might not give to Nancy for her twin boys. She was looking forward to seeing her friend. She grinned at the little girls and gave them sixpence. She had run her own jumble sales in days gone by. She looked round the drab street and felt the warmth of home-coming. No, Hull didn't change; it possessed a gritty energy and community of spirit that London, for all its bustle and glamour, did not. She put the books in her hand-bag and turned towards home.

The changes in her parents were infinitesimal but Dorothea's eyes, sharpened by separation, noticed that Hazel's skin now stretched too tightly across her cheek bones and tiny lines showed at the corners of her mouth. Still, she was lovely and seeing the look in her eyes, a sudden rush of dampness to her own clouded Dorothea's vision. She dropped her suitcase.

'Mum,' she said.

Hazel flung her arms about her taller daughter and the two women clung to each other for a moment. Then the sound of a cough separated them. Dorothea braced herself. Would there be harsh words, despite his promise? No. Her father placed his hand awkwardly on her arm and spoke.

'Hello, Dorrie. It's been a long time. It's good to see you.'

His short hair was greyer than she remembered. She mumbled something and dropped a kiss on his cheek. She caught a wisp of aftershave and felt her eyes pricking again. He had spruced himself up for her arrival.

They ate ham salad for tea and talked of unimportant things. Hazel was glad to hear Jake, who was being looked after by Vida, was keeping well. Her father told Dorothea about the terrible dockside blaze that had caused thousands of pounds' worth of damage. Greg was not mentioned. Initially tense, Dorothea gradually relaxed. After tea she went upstairs to unpack and Hazel, reluctant to let her daughter out of her sight, followed her.

'Such good clothes you have, Dorrie.' She fingered a tweed skirt. She looked at Dorothea shyly. 'Your chap must be earning good money from his painting, after all?'

'I buy my own clothes, Mum.' Dorothea regretted the hard edge to her voice but couldn't repress it. 'Greg's doing National Service at the moment. I told you in my letters. I pay my own way. I always have.'

'Why, yes. I didn't mean . . .'

Seeing Hazel's lips tremble, Dorothea felt the old mixture of love and irritation. No, nothing changed.

Her father's attitude was also hard to take. Dorothea had expected pointed remarks, even a full-scale lecture on her wicked behaviour, but Dennis acted as though nothing had happened. Instead, he addressed her as if she was still a schoolgirl, reminding her to watch the roads and to turn the lights off at bedtime. She realised he had refused to think about the facets of her life that distressed him. She was relieved but also annoyed. How wonderful, she thought, how painless, if we could all do that!

The most enjoyable part of her visit was seeing Nancy again. Hazel gave her Nancy's new address. Nancy, Bill and the twins had moved, but only two streets away from the Dempsters.

'Well!' Nancy poured out a huge mug of tea for Dorothea. 'They offered us one of them new council houses, all mod-cons, but it's bleeding miles away from town. I would have gone cuckoo.' She sat down with a sigh. 'Now, tell me everything.'

They talked for hours. Dorothea unloaded her hopes and fears and Nancy nodded her head sagely but offered no advice. 'Don't believe in it, see.'

Then she talked to Dorothea. 'Bill's becoming a real drag, but I should have known. Always take a woman for granted once they've got you. Still,' she winked, 'he's away on a trawler four weeks at a time so it could be worse. And I've got my mam close by, and these two.' She swept the twins on to her lap and offered them proudly for Dorothea's approval. They were adorable. Just looking at them gave her a queer pain. They had plump sturdy bodies, round heads, large round eyes and flat noses. Dorothea played with them and afterwards helped Nancy bath them.

'You might as well get in some practice. Might be your turn next,' said Nancy.

Dorothea made no reply but she had to answer her father when he said goodbye to her on the last day of her visit.

'I'm glad you came, Dorrie.' Dennis had on his overalls. He was on an early shift so would be at work when Dorothea went for her train. He shifted his feet awkwardly. 'I promised your mother I wouldn't say nowt, but . . .' He paused, then his words came out in a rush.

'Why the hell don't you get married? Your mam says you're happy with this chap. You've been with him a long time now. I just don't understand. It's not right, Dorrie. And what about kids? Your mum and me, we're not getting any younger. I tell you straight, I'd like to be a grandfather. Chap I work with, Ernie Wright, he's got four grandsons and he's younger than me. Don't you want kids?'

'One day, perhaps,' Dorothea looked away from her father's red face. 'But if I do, it will be because *I* want a child, Dad, not because *you* think it's time you had a grandchild!'

The silence went on so long she eventually looked back, with some trepidation, at her father. She was relieved to see no anger in his face. He stared at her then gave a tight nod.

'Fair enough. But just bear in mind, if you do decide to have a kid, make things proper first. If only for the bairn's sake.'

'Oh, Dad.' A rush of affection swept through Dorothea. Dennis was a difficult, cantankerous man but he worked long and hard to provide a home for his family and he was honest in his beliefs and ideals. 'I'll remember. Only, sometimes, life's not as simple as you seem to think.' She kissed him.

When she said goodbye to Hazel, her mother was determinedly cheerful.

'Now you've been home, it will be easier next time Dorrie, I promise.'

'It's been lovely, Mum. You must come to me, next visit.'

'I'll try. Oh, I almost forgot this.'

Hazel handed Dorothea an envelope. 'It's a late Christmas card. It was addressed to me but I knew you'd like to see it. It's from Rob Steyart. I was ever so surprised when it arrived.'

The envelope sported an Australian stamp. Inside, instead of the traditional Christmas scene, the card showed a picture of a kangaroo. There was no long message, just a scrawled, 'Love, Rob'.

Dorothea stared down at it. 'Can I keep it, Mum?'

'Of course you can. You were his best friend.'

Dorothea gazed out of the train window, watching the scenery slip by, becoming undefined in the quickly gathering darkness of the wintry afternoon. She thought about her visit, of her mother's face, her father's words and strongly chiselled features. She smiled, remembering Nancy's twins, and stirred restlessly. Her monthly period hadn't started yet. She thought travelling might have got things moving but it hadn't. But there was nothing to worry about. Her monthly flow was always erratic and she took precautions. A voice whispered inside her, 'What about the night Greg came home?'

She frowned, then smiled. She was being silly. She mustn't have a baby. Greg would go crazy at the very idea. It was seeing the twins that made her think such things. To distract her thoughts she took Rob's card from her handbag and looked at it.

Rob, where are you now? What are you now? Surely not a farmer?

She sighed and closed her eyes. The only certainty about life, she thought, is its uncertainty. So why worry about things? Unbidden, the sound of the twins' chuckling laughter sounded in her memory. She smiled.

Chapter Twenty-Four

Dorothea had been told to rest but there was a large bluebottle buzzing around her small, high-ceilinged hospital room, and outside she could hear a group of nurses in fits of giggles over something a doctor had said. She raised her ungainly body to a sitting position and punched viciously at the hard pillow, releasing some of her pent-up irritation. Rest, that's all they went on about. How *could* she rest with disjointed thoughts bumbling about in her head like that blasted bluebottle? She made herself breathe deeply. The Sister would no doubt bob back into her room soon and take her blood pressure again.

'Relax, Miss Bellows. We must relax – don't want to hurt baby, do we?' Sister's face was a mask of bland professionalism but Dorothea had caught the slight emphasis on the word 'Miss'. She obviously disapproved of unmarried mothers. Well, that was her problem!

Dorothea brooded. She supposed she *could* have pretended. She could have bought a cheap wedding ring and when Greg visited her, which he did at irregular intervals, invariably late with his hands empty of gifts, she could have pretended he was her husband. But why should she? She had no feeling of shame. A brief smile flickered across her face. And married or not, the younger nurses envied her. She had seen it in their eyes and in the way they lingered when Greg's loose-limbed figure appeared, his worn cords and checked shirt moulded to his slim form, his hair now grown long, flopping over his wide brow.

Dorothea sighed. At least the continuing rise of her

blood pressure had brought her the refuge of a single room. For five weeks she had lain in the large maternity ward surrounded by newly delivered mothers. Five weeks she had been told to stay flat in bed and rest, allowed to move only as far as the toilet. The other women moved about, sat on their beds perfumed and lipsticked, awaiting visits from husbands and relatives. Though they were superficially friendly, she had caught their whispers: 'Not married, living with an artist!'

She caught their sideways glances, imagined the thoughts clicking away in their heads like beads on an abacus. What on earth did he see in her? Puffy face, nondescript features, stringy hair! No wonder he hadn't married her.

Thank God the bluebottle had stopped its frantic flight. She could see it, motionless, on the patch of sunlight which spread like hot butter across the opposite wall. She must ask a nurse to move the vase of roses out of the sun. How kind of Mr Whitney to buy them for her. Vida had delivered them, coming into the room solemn-eyed, clutching them to her breast like a shield. Vida didn't like hospitals. Well, neither did she! Vida had sat at the extreme edge of her chair and tried to ignore the bulge of Dorothea's stomach. Yet Dorothea caught her constantly glancing at it. Dorothea knew Vida was desperate to marry and have children and yet was fearful of childbirth. She tried to set her at ease.

'What lovely roses. Did the Manager of the hotel . . . ?'

'No. It was Mr Whitney. He sends you his best wishes and this card.'

Vida handed the card to Dorothea. It bore an address in Mayfair and the message 'If you need a friend'.

'He must think a lot of you. He delayed his departure in order to give me the flowers.'

Dorothea tucked the card safely into her purse. Apart from his courteous exchanges at the Doran she knew nothing about Mr Whitney, yet she felt he was a man she could trust.

It might have been better if the roses *had* been sent to her by the management of the Doran Hotel. On learning of her pregnancy and her enquiry as to whether they would hold her job, the Manager had been disapproving but not totally dismissive. If she could guarantee a return to work six weeks after the child was born, they would consider the matter. Dorothea had been relieved but not surprised. She knew she was the best receptionist they had. But things hadn't worked out. She had been off work for seven weeks now and she was still only six months pregnant.

A bell sounded somewhere. That meant visiting time was over and Greg had not come. She didn't mind. She felt drowsy now and whenever Greg visited there was always so much tension, she could never sleep afterwards. It was her fault things had gone so wrong. She should have waited, given him more time. Instead she had blurted out the fact she was pregnant the first day he had left the army and come home for good. What a fool she had been sitting alone in the flat building up cosy little pictures of how he would take the news. Of course, it would be a shock, but when he became accustomed to the idea he'd be proud, perhaps even suggest marriage . . . Maybe pregnancy did that to you, made you believe in fairy tales? When she had told him, the look on his face . . . No, she would not think about that, because she was drifting off to sleep and sleep was good for the baby.

'Right! Time for a blood pressure check, Miss Bellows.'

Sister was back with a clanking, noisy trolley. Dorothea opened her eyes. 'I was just going to sleep,' she protested.

'Sorry, but hospital timetables must be kept to.'

The cuff was already on her upper arm. She watched as Sister consulted the dial. 'How is it?'

'Nothing for you to bother about.'

'Before you go, could you move the flowers, please? The sun . . .'

'Of course. I'll put them in the corridor. It's cool there.'

She marched to the window and drew the curtains. 'Now, you get some sleep.'

'There's a bluebottle . . .'

But Sister had collected the flowers and gone. Dorothea lay back on her pillow and shut her eyes. The bluebottle, trapped between curtains and glass, battered itself noisily and mercilessly against the window.

The next day brought Greg. He tip-toed in, placed a bottle of orange juice on the bedside cabinet and sat down. Like Vida, he consciously avoided looking at her shrouded body. Watching him, she felt a spurt of pure venom. 'Look at me,' she felt like shouting. 'It's really happening, you know. You can't wish it away. And it's your child as well as mine!' But she didn't because they'd played that scene before and all it had brought her was high blood pressure and hospitalisation.

Keep calm, she told herself. It *will* work out in time, it has to. When he sees the child, things will be different. And she crossed her fingers beneath the bedclothes and forced a smile.

'Everything all right?'

He shrugged. 'I suppose so. There's a letter from your mum.' He dropped it on to the bed. Can't he even bear to touch my hand? she thought.

'Go on, read it now if you like. I'll look at the evening paper.'

Hazel's letter was full of motherly cluckings. 'Take care,' she ended. 'I'm sure Greg will look after you. P.S. I'm knitting in lemon wool so it will suit either boy or girl.'

Dorothea folded the letter. Was her mother really so blind? Of course the week she had visited them Greg had been charming to her and when Greg was charming few could resist, certainly not her mother. She studied his face as he read the newspaper. He was thinner than ever and looked tired. This pregnancy was taking it out of him as well as her. She sighed. The change she had thought she saw in him last Christmas, the veneer of maturity, had evaporated like morning mist. He now looked every inch the nervy, talented young artist. He would be painting himself to death in her absence, she supposed, and not eating properly.

She felt a strong kick under her heart and, startled, sat up. She had never felt the baby's presence so strongly before. It was as if it was saying: 'Hey, remember me. I'm important too, you know.'

Greg must have seen her start. He said, 'What's the matter? You all right?'

'It was the baby. He's really kicking.' Boldly, she dared him: 'Want to feel?'

'No.' He shrank back into his chair and changed the subject. 'Kenny sends you his love. I saw him yesterday in the market.'

Dorothea rested her hand on her stomach and stared hard at him.

'Don't worry.' Silently, she addressed her child. 'He will love you, really.' But what if he didn't? She faced the choice and made it. 'Whatever happens, we'll be OK.' Impossibly, laughter bubbled up within her. She forced her face into straightness. 'Your granny's knitting in lemon for you.'

The silence was becoming heavy. She broke it. 'How's Jake?'

'A bloody nuisance.' Greg put down the paper. 'He messed on the floor yesterday.'

'Never!'

'He did. I'd walked through it before I noticed.' He pulled a face of disgust.

'Oh, Greg, I can't believe it. He's always been so clean.'

'He isn't now! You have to face it, Dorrie. He's old and becoming incontinent. He wets all the time.'

'I don't believe you. And if he does, it must be because you don't take him out.'

'God!' Greg clenched his fist and hit his forehead, a theatrical gesture. 'Haven't I enough to do? I come here, I see to the flat, do the cooking – now it's that bloody dog. He never liked me! I should be *painting*, Dorrie – can't you understand? There's a gallery interested in exhibiting my work but they want more canvases. It's hard enough concentrating with you in here. And if I don't work, I don't sell and what do we live on?'

'Sorry – I'm sorry.' Tears of weakness sprang to Dorothea's eyes. The muzzy feeling was back in her head. That was bad. She had felt like that before her last black-out, the one that put her in the hospital. She breathed slowly and deeply. Think about the baby.

'Perhaps,' she whispered, 'the boy downstairs could give Jake a run every day?'

'I'll try and arrange something.' Greg replaced his chair neatly by the wall, shuffling his feet like a child in disgrace. 'I really will have to go. Hugh said he might call round about this gallery business. Anyway, the nurse said I shouldn't stay too long and you do look tired.' Before he left the room he bent over her and kissed her on the lips.

She forced herself into serenity. It was the least she could do for her child. She thought of it as *her* child now. She pushed away worries about money. Slowly but surely Greg's work was becoming known, and anyway they were used to being short of cash. And Greg could be kind and gentle. He would love his own child when he saw it.

As for her distrust of Hugh, it was irrational. Pregnant women could be so. He could help Greg, that was all. But Jake – she remembered her last glimpse of the dog, the day she was rushed into hospital. He looked so miserable, a crumpled heap in his basket. Tears pricked her eyes. He couldn't understand. She blew her nose. She was being ridiculous. Greg wasn't a monster, he would look after the dog. Anyway, much as she loved Jake, he was an animal and all her energy must be concentrated on the coming child. Would it have Greg's looks? She hoped so. She touched her lips where he had kissed them. When she was home again, when they were together, they would be happy. She slept.

She dreamed she was a child again and standing in the bombed-out ruins of Jack Lombard's house in Hull. There were gaping holes in the floor and about her ominous creaks and groans from the unsafe masonry. Far off she could hear a dog bark and although she was frightened she knew she must find him. She moved forward. The floorboards beneath her feet shuddered then gave way and she only just managed to stop herself from falling down into a black void. There were clouds of dust everywhere which clogged her eyes and mouth. Behind her, she could hear voices and looking back saw Nancy and her father, staring at her with faces fixed in horror. Nancy was grown-up with her two little boys in a pushchair. The toddlers were rocking the pushchair. It was going to topple over and Dorothea tried to shout to Nancy, to warn her, but the dust clogged her mouth. And still a dog barked.

She awoke into darkness. She coughed to clear the dust from her mouth, but how could it be dust? She was in hospital. There was a throbbing sensation in her head and black circles whirled before her eyes. She moaned and felt her limbs becoming rigid. She tried again to clear her throat then realised, with horror, that her mouth was full of blood. Her tongue hurt. She must have bitten it. With one huge, last effort she pressed the attention button by her bed before hurtling down into oblivion.

She floated in a calm grey mist in which faces came and went. Mouths opened and closed but she heard nothing. It was pain-free and peaceful and she felt resentment when, one morning, she opened her eyes to find a white-coated doctor sitting by her bed. He patted her hand and said: 'That's better, Dorothea. You're back with us.'

It was the young doctor, the one who made the nurses giggle. He looked serious now. She turned her head and looked round. She was in the same bed, the same room. 'But I haven't been anywhere,' she wanted to say. Before she could open her mouth, she was asleep. The next day she awoke and they told her something but before she could consider it they made her swallow a pill which put her to sleep again. The next time she awoke she refused their pills. Pills would make her sleep and she had done nothing but sleep for weeks and weeks. She had done it for the baby but now there was no baby. She would not sleep and she would not cry. Her grief was too private to show to strangers. No one had wanted the baby except her. She hugged her grief to her as she would now never hug her baby. She had never even seen it.

No visitors were allowed for three days. She had been so ill. The Sister whom she had thought disapproving was kind to her. When duty rota allowed she came to sit by Dorothea's bed. 'Your blood pressure suddenly soared; we couldn't control it. You went into fits. It's called Eclampsia.' She hesitated. 'Your child was a girl, perfect in every way, just born too soon.' She took Dorothea's hand. 'We nearly lost you too. It will be no comfort now, but it's nearly always first pregnancies when this happens. You'll probably go on to have several children.'

Greg was allowed to visit then, and he came every day and brought her flowers. He was kind and attempted to comfort her but it was as if he stood behind a pane of glass. Every time she looked at him, she thought: Are you glad?

But Greg was patient. He willed her to get better. He brought her books, told her funny stories about the people who worked in the gallery, and Dorothea became interested in life again. She was young and strong and wounds heal, although they leave scars. After two more weeks, she was allowed to leave hospital. She dressed herself in a blue two-piece suit and looked in a mirror. She looked different. She had lost a lot of weight, not just the baby. She thought her legs were too thin but Greg said she looked marvellous. He came to collect her in a taxi.

'I've a treat for you.'

They went to a small Italian restaurant, the first one Dorothea had ever visited. The owner, dressed in a striped shirt, his black trousers covered with a long white apron, awaited them at the door. He ushered them to a corner table decorated with flowers and red candles stuck in wine bottles.

'Greg – it's lovely!'

They ate spaghetti bolognese and drank a carafe of red wine, and Dorothea pronounced it the best meal she had ever eaten.

'Anything would taste good after hospital food,' Greg replied, then frowned. 'Sorry, I didn't mean to remind you.'

'It's all right.' She raised her glass to him. 'It's in the past. Now, how's your work going?'

Greg insisted on another taxi home. 'No buses tonight, my love. This is a very special day.'

The wine had made Dorothea feel happy and relaxed. In the cab she rested her head upon Greg's shoulder, but suddenly he seemed tense, his conversation monosyllabic. She thought she understood. The past months had been a trying period and, she smiled to herself, the flat was probably a complete tip! When the taxi pulled up she jumped out before Greg had finished paying the driver.

'Oh, I can't wait to see Jake. Hurry up with the key, Greg.'

'Dorrie, I . . .'

But she had already taken the key from his hand, unlocked the door and rushed up the stairs. The flat smelt of lavender furniture polish and everywhere looked clean – and empty. She rushed through the sitting room, in which they never sat, and into the studio-cum-bedroom. He was not there. She swung

round to where Greg stood. He had followed her
upstairs and now he watched her from the doorway,
his face grim.

'Where is he?'

'Dorrie . . .'

'Where is he?' She caught the note of hysteria in her
own voice and strove to remain calm.

Watching her face turn pale, Greg wondered if she
was about to faint. 'Look, sit down and I'll tell you.'
He crossed to her and pushed her, unresisting, into a
chair.

'I'm sorry, love, but he's gone.'

'I don't understand.'

Greg sighed and averted his gaze from her mask-
like face. 'The boy who used to take him out, remember?' He threw her an anxious glance but she simply
stared at him. 'Well, Jake bit him, quite badly.' He
ignored her sound of dissent and continued: 'His
mother was livid. Talked about reporting it to the
police. There was nothing else for it. I had him put
down.' He stopped, jarred by the shudder he saw pass
through her body. 'I know it's sad, Dorrie, but he was
old and his temper was very uncertain.'

She whispered through pale lips: 'When?'

'Just a few days after you lost the baby.' Greg's
shoulders drooped. 'So I couldn't discuss it with you.
I'm sorry.'

'Liar. You always hated him!' She shivered. 'Why
did you wait until now to tell me?'

'I don't know, I just couldn't . . .' He ran his fingers through his hair. 'I wanted things to be good
between us, Dorrie, and I knew . . .' He made as if to
come to her but the look on her face warned him not
to. 'It's true, all true. Ask the boy's mother.'

Tiredness suddenly roared through her. She could
barely keep her eyes open. She bent her head. 'Greg,
all I want to do at this minute is sleep – by myself. Do
you mind?'

'No. Of course not.' He gestured to the hide settee
behind him. 'I'll collect a blanket and sleep there. If

you hear a bump in the night, you'll know I've slipped off.' His smile, feeble enough at his weak joke, disappeared as she stood up, turned her back on him and walked towards the bed.

She went to sleep immediately, running into the welcoming darkness. But in the dawn light which filtered palely through the skylight window, she awoke. She was used to waking to a feeling of loss, it was part of her life now, but then she remembered. She had lost Jake, too. Despair flooded her body and she cried. Tears she had been unable to shed for her child flooded down her face when she remembered the ugly little dog that had shared her green years. And as she cried, emotions swirled in her mind like pieces in a kaleidoscope, but all the colours were dark. Guilt predominated. Her child had died because of her stupid high blood pressure and Jake had died because she had not protected him. Had he gone willingly to his death, feeling lost and lonely? *Would* Jake have bitten a child? He had always liked children, played with them in the parks. But if she did not believe Greg . . . ? She brushed away her tears but new ones came, sliding down her face and wetting her pillow. What kind of person was she, when she cried for a dog and had not cried for her baby? But when she shut her eyes she could see only Jake. Her daughter had been buried before she, Dorothea, could see her.

She lay until the storm of weeping abated then tossed back the bedclothes and blundered over to the small chest of drawers in which Greg kept his meagre possessions. She opened the top drawer and searched for a handkerchief. As always, the drawer's contents were in complete confusion. Her fingers touched something wrapped in tissue paper, something hard and strangely shaped. She drew it from its hiding place and unwrapped the paper. It was a mobile, hand-carved and painted, made to hang over a child's cot. She held it up. It was a flock of tiny birds. She recognised Greg's deft touch in the graceful span of wings. The figures stirred and spun slowly round and she looked at the meticulously painted beaks and feathers, the bright dabs of eyes. And as she looked the terrible knot inside her unravelled.

She re-wrapped the mobile and replaced it at the back of the drawer. Then she went into the sitting room and looked down at Greg. Incredibly, he was asleep, his neck twisted at an impossible angle, his feet hanging over the end of the hideously uncomfortable settee. She touched his big toe. It was cold. She mopped her face with her arm then touched him on the shoulder.

'Greg.'

'What!' He jumped and opened his eyes. 'Dorrie? What is it? Is everything all right?'

'It will be,' she replied. 'Look, you might as well come to bed. You can't possibly stay on that thing.'

Chapter Twenty-Five

Bookings were up again. Dorothea filed away the latest batch of arrivals slips in the correct index slots then looked up at the clock with a frown. Vida was late. It was a nuisance because Dorothea had promised to leave a few minutes early and take some urgent summary sheets to their accountants in Cavendish Square. She also had an appointment of her own.

Dorothea always enjoyed walking in the city, particularly now, for there was a buzz of excitement in the air. One month to Coronation Day and everywhere decorations were going up. In Kensington Gardens a complete tented town had sprouted, especially erected to house the thousands of Commonwealth troops visiting London. In the West End the buildings had disappeared beneath a forest of scaffolding. Dorothea looked up when the entrance door opened and a crowd of people swept into the foyer. She smiled when she saw a tall, dark man in brilliant red robes. Vida had told her he was a tribal chief from Tanganyika. Ah, here she came now.

'Sorry.' Her face was flushed and excited. 'I've been with Mum to buy a television. It's lovely, fourteen inches. We'll see everything clearly on that.'

'I thought you and your family would be camping out in The Mall?' Dorothea knew what an ardent royalist Vida was.

'No. Mum says we'll see more on the box.' Vida's expression sobered. She was obviously struck with compunction. 'You're quite *sure* you don't mind working that day?'

'Quite sure,' Dorothea reassured her. 'I'll probably

267

see as much as you. There's a TV set in the lounge and everyone will be glued to that. There'll be nothing for me to do. I can slip in and watch everything there. Still,' she put down her pen and stood up, 'I must go now. I have an appointment.'

'See you tomorrow.'

Vida put on her reading glasses and began to hum the latest Donald Peers hit, 'In a Golden Coach'.

Dorothea made her way to Cavendish Square where the pavements were thronged with sightseers and on the road cars lined up, bumper to bumper. She delivered the papers to the accountants then hurried down Harley Street. She spotted the lanky figure of a man waiting for her, and waved.

'Kenny, thanks for agreeing to meet me.'

'Pleasure.' He pumped her hand up and down. 'Come on, I know a decent place which will be quiet enough for us to talk.' He glanced round. 'Bloody people everywhere.'

'I didn't know you were a grouch, Kenny. I think it's all very exciting.'

Dorothea followed as he turned into a narrow back street and went towards a brightly painted coffee bar. 'However did you spot this place?'

'I work not far from here. I often call in at lunchtimes. Now, what can I get you?'

When they were seated in the new lightweight modern chairs, frothy coffee in front of them, Dorothea asked Kenny about his work.

'It's going well. I've taken exams and my fingers are crossed. Actually,' he laughed, 'I think I've done OK. Maybe I was meant to be an accountant all the time.' He took a sip of coffee. 'How are things with you?'

'So-so.' She drew lines in her froth with the edge of a teaspoon. 'You haven't been round, Kenny. We haven't seen you for ages.'

'Sorry, but what with the exams and,' he paused, 'other things.'

She wondered if at last he had a steady girl friend. 'Sorry, I didn't mean to pry.'

'Of course not.' His hand closed lightly around her wrist, stopped her from tracing her meaningless patterns. 'Come on, love. What's the matter?'

'I don't *know* what's the matter.' Her voice trembled. 'That's the trouble.'

He stayed silent, waiting for her to continue.

'I knew things would be hard, after losing the baby,' Dorothea's voice was hesitant, 'but I thought they'd work out eventually.

'We still *cared* and financially things became easier. I was given my job back at the hotel and then Greg's paintings started to take off. I suppose you know about that?'

He nodded. 'Yes, I've seen various items about him in the papers.'

'But he's changed so much, Kenny. He never relaxes. He seems *driven*. He doesn't laugh any more. He's shut me out of his life. I came to ask if you would come round and see him. It might do some good.'

Kenny released her hand, reached in his pocket and brought out a packet of cigarettes. He offered the packet to Dorothea but she shook her head, watching him all the time. 'Will you, Kenny?'

'What makes you think I could help him?' His voice was sombre.

'Because he trusts you – knows you're a *real* friend! The people around him now are hangers-on who mean nothing to him. He goes out with them most nights and drinks too much, then comes home, collapses on the bed, goes out like a light. Wakes up late, paints all day, doesn't bother to eat . . .' She stopped abruptly.

'Does he still see Hugh Conley?'

'Not so much lately, thank God!'

He looked at her curiously. 'Never liked him, did you?'

'No. I think he's bad for Greg.'

Kenny sighed. 'You might be right. But what about *you*, Dorrie? Where do you fit in?'

Colour tinged her face, but she answered him

bravely. 'I still love Greg and I'm sure he loves me, but there's some kind of invisible wall between us now. Most of the time he's carefully kind with me; occasionally he's vile.' She bit her lip. 'He screams and shouts at me when I . . . We rarely sleep together now. Perhaps he thinks I'll trick him into another baby! I wouldn't do that.' She fumbled in her bag for a handkerchief as her eyes glistened. 'Sorry,' she apologised.

'No need.' His eyes had grown dark. He moved closer to her. The metal leg of his chair made a harsh grating noise on the tiled floor. 'You have to talk to someone. I'll call round, Dorrie, but whether I can be of any help . . .' He shrugged. 'Hang on to the thought that Greg loves you. I'm sure he does. You should have seen the state he was in when you were so ill. But you must remember, he's a gifted artist. People like Greg don't react to stress like ordinary people. All I can suggest is that you be patient.'

'I know.' Dorothea took a handkerchief out of her bag and blew her nose vigorously. 'Now, tell me when you will come and visit us? How about Sunday?'

'Well, I don't . . .'

'Kenny!'

He capitulated. 'Oh, all right. What time?'

'Any time at all, you know that.' She pushed back her chair. 'I'll have to go. You will come, won't you, Kenny? You've stayed away too long. Don't worry. Greg understands about your decision to give up painting. He told me it took a lot of guts to face the truth like you did. We've both missed you.'

She stopped talking and a faint frown wrinkled her brow. A strange expression had flitted across Kenny's face, a compound of longing yet reluctance, almost self-loathing. She blinked and looked at him again. She was imagining things. He lounged in his chair and grinned at her, his lazy relaxed grin. She smiled back. Idiot, she chided herself. She was getting as jumpy as Greg.

Kenny's visit delighted Greg. As Dorothea cleared

away the remnants of their meal, the two men sprawled on the floor and talked painting. It was the old days recreated. Seeing Greg looking so relaxed, Dorothea hugged herself. Her plan had worked. Kenny and Greg talked and talked, finally reminiscing about a Ruskin Spear exhibition they had visited in 1951.

'Lucky devil's gone to Prague, do you know?' Kenny yawned. 'Something to do with kids' paintings and the British Czech Friendship League.'

'Still keep up with news of the art world, do you?' Greg shook his head. 'You needn't have packed it in, Kenny. You could have made a decent living.'

Embarrassed, Kenny rose to his feet. 'I don't like being second best, Greg. You must realise how I feel. Anyway, signs are I shall be a first-rate accountant.' He prodded Greg with his foot. 'On your feet, genius. I want to see the latest fruits of your labour.'

In her kitchen cubby-hole where she was washing up, Dorothea listened to the rise and fall of their voices. Then Greg popped his head around the partition.

'I'm taking this accountant chappie to the pub for an hour, love. We won't be long.'

He blew her a kiss before they left the flat. She finished the dishes, dried her hands then walked over to the covered easel, removed the cloth and stared at Greg's latest painting. She could never really understand what all the fuss was about. It was days since she had really studied the work. Once again, it was a portrait of her. Greg had said it was almost finished but to her eyes there still seemed a lot of work to do. She sighed. It was a good job Greg never minded that she knew nothing about art. She pulled up a stool, sat down in front of the portrait and looked at it again. The background was indistinct and a mixture of subtle colours, mainly lilac and blue. She sat in a relaxed pose, her head inclined, gazing out at the beholders. Her attitude suggested restfulness but, staring at the picture of herself, Dorothea thought she could see tension in the clasped hands and an ironic twist to her mouth. She didn't think her eyes were right, they were too dreamy. She felt uneasy and took the cloth and covered up the painting. When Greg returned home she was curled up in an armchair deep in the adventures of *Forever Amber*.

Because Dorothea had to work on Coronation Day, Greg sacrificed precious painting hours to take her out on Coronation Eve. They had a meal in a decent restaurant, Greg had more money now, and then they mixed with the crowds thronging the capital. When evening approached they went along with a mass of people to marvel at the huge glittering crowns suspended in the Mall. The weather was terrible yet despite the rain pouring down hundreds of people were preparing to bed down in the streets for the night.

'Look, over there.' Dorothea pointed to a family of two adults and three children settling down on the wet pavement surrounded by blankets, tinned food and a spirit stove.

'They must be mad!' Greg shivered and turned up the collar of his coat. 'Can we go home now? It's freezing.'

'I suppose so.' The tremendous atmosphere had affected Dorothea. She almost wished she could wrap old newspapers around her legs and stay with the expectant, shivering crowd.

But they went back to the flat. They drank cocoa to warm themselves up and then they went to bed. When Dorothea tentatively put her arms about Greg, he turned to her. Their love-making, like their behaviour towards each other, was uncertain, lacking in passion. But later, when Greg slept, Dorothea remained awake. Things would get better, she told herself. After what they had been through, they had to.

She was early to work the next morning so she was already at the hotel when the news broke of the conquest of Everest. Dorothea cheered along with the rest of the staff and listened eagerly to the news on the radio. Later, she managed to slip into the main lounge of the hotel and watch the Coronation ceremony.

When the Queen entered Westminster Abbey to the cries of 'Vivat, Vivat' from the boys of Westminster School, she shed a few tears. Elizabeth looked so small and young to be the centre of such mediaeval magnificence. Once the main ceremony was concluded, Dorothea was kept busy. There were individual parties, telephone calls, demands for sandwiches and queries of all kinds. By the time she returned to the flat she was almost asleep on her feet. The buses and underground trains were packed, there were drunks everywhere. Greg was working. No, he said, he hadn't seen the Coronation.

'Why not? You could have gone downstairs. Surely you haven't been stuck up here by yourself all day?' Dorothea regretted the sharpness in her voice when she saw Greg's eyebrows rise but she couldn't control her irritation. She wanted to discuss the day with him, share her thoughts, but there he was, stuck in front of his damned easel.

'Don't get snappy just because I'm not caught up in this present madness over the Royal Family, Dorrie.' His eyes studied her face then he looked back at his painting. 'I should pop into bed if I were you. You look tired.'

She said a rude word and left the flat, slamming the door behind her. She went downstairs to the family who lived below them to exclaim over and discuss the details of Elizabeth's dress and all the other magical events of the wonderful day.

Chapter Twenty-Six

In the October following the Coronation Dorothea travelled North to visit her parents. She needed a rest and a change of scene. Although her relationship with Greg was less stressed than it had been it was still far from perfect. Much of the joy and excitement of their life together had mysteriously vanished. It was worry over that, not physical work, that had drained Dorothea, made her so tired. She was sick of playing the role of peacemaker, soothing Greg's injured feelings, making allowances for his artistic temperament, repressing her feelings of rejection when he made it plain that at times he had no desire for her. Oh God, she thought suddenly, after all my brave words I'm turning into a woman like my mother after all!

Yet, paradoxically, when she arrived home she found her mother and father happy together. Dennis's abrasive manner had softened and Dorothea found he was spending much more time with his wife. Hazel was so content she was becoming plump.

'Your dad's come off the committee at the Labour Club, Dorrie,' she whispered. 'And he comes shopping with me now.'

Dorothea was pleased to see her mother's happiness but she felt a nagging regret when she looked at her father. Dennis had changed. His shoulders were stooped and his former caustic comments on life had, in general, mellowed. Only when he spoke of the Labour Party did some of his former fire return.

'Socialists! They're all turning into bloody Conservatives now!'

Meeting her father again had been difficult for

Dorothea. On her last visit she had thought they had drawn closer together but when Dennis had heard she was pregnant the old antagonism had flared up. In her letters, Hazel had glossed over his disapproval of his daughter's way of life, but Dorothea had known how outraged and angry he was. Accordingly, her own reaction had been to harden her heart towards him. Even when she had lost her child, Dennis had not come to London to see her. He had written to her, a one-page letter saying he hoped she would soon be well again, but she knew he would never come to the flat, agree to meet Greg. She had not replied to his letter.

Months later, he had written a postscript to one of Hazel's letters, telling her she would be welcome at home should she ever wish to visit. Journeying to Hull, Dorothea had viewed the prospect of seeing Hazel with pleasure but felt reserve and uncertainty when she thought of her father. However, on greeting her, he had taken her hand and avoided her eyes. She saw a small man, bereft of his former convictions, sliding into old age with carpet-slippered feet and passive resignation. As before, Dennis made no reference to her life in London. He told her she was welcome and padded off to make the tea, leaving the two women to talk. Hazel had bought a television set so she could watch the Coronation. Although months had passed she was still enchanted by memories of it. 'Did you see the Queen of Tonga, Dorothea? Wasn't she a wonderful-looking woman?'

Dorothea agreed. The two women chatted for hours and Dennis read his paper. Then Hazel announced with a yawn she was going to bed. 'It's grand to see you, Dorrie. We'll go to town and do some shopping tomorrow, shall we?'

'I'd like that.'

There was silence after she left the room, then Dennis stirred. 'I'm glad you came, Dorrie. She's right glad to see you.'

'It's lovely to be back, Dad.'

He put down his paper and, for the first time since she arrived, looked directly at her. 'I'm glad, too.'

Dorothea felt a sudden lump in her throat.

'Since Hazel told me you were coming, I've been thinking and,' her father's eyes remained steady, 'I reckon I owe you an apology, lass. I should have come when you lost the baby.'

'Oh, Dad.' Dorothea paused, cleared her throat.

'I'm not saying I've changed my mind about the life you're leading but,' he sighed, 'you're my daughter and I should have come.'

'Well, Mum came to see me in the hospital, and really there was nothing anyone could do.'

'No, you had rotten luck.' He sighed.

Dorothea tried to think of something to change the subject, release the tension.

'What's this I hear about you leaving the Committee?'

He shrugged. 'Don't like the way things are going, lass. All those promises but when it came to it, they didn't have the guts to press on with nationalisation. And now everything seems to be changing. Youngsters nowadays are more interested in televisions and washing machines than they are in moral principles. It's a funny old world.'

He stood up, came across to her and patted her hand. 'You'll come to the Club with your mother and me tomorrow night, won't you?'

'I'd like to.'

At the Working Men's Club he introduced her to his drinking pals with pride. 'This is my daughter. She works in London. She has a smashing job in a posh hotel – earned it through her own efforts too. Went to night classes, she did, after days working in a factory. Got all sorts of qualifications.'

His mellowed attitude made it a serene visit and Dorothea relaxed, enjoying the change. Never once did Dennis mention Greg or bring up the possibility and desirability of his daughter marrying.

When Dorothea went to visit Nancy she found that

her friend had also changed. She was pregnant again, and despite long and loud protests on her part had been rehoused on a new estate on the outskirts of the town. Dorothea had to catch two buses to get to her new house.

'Something went wrong with the drains at the old place,' Nancy explained. 'The landlord said he couldn't afford to fix them so now we're stuck out here.'

'What are your neighbours like?'

'Bloody awful! All they talk about are knitting patterns and recipes. I hate being stuck with a load of women. Still,' she stared out of her kitchen window, 'we have a garden.'

She turned back to Dorothea with a trace of her old grin. 'Pity I hate gardening, isn't it?'

'You look well,' Dorothea lied.

Nancy wore a grubby overall which strained over her prominent stomach. Her hair was stringy and needed a wash.

'Don't lie. I know I look terrible.' Nancy bent, with difficulty, to scoop up one of her youngsters who was busily engaged in kicking his brother's head as he sprawled on the floor. 'I don't get much time to bother with myself, what with these two and their dad away at sea most of the time.'

'Shall I take them out for a few hours?' offered Dorothea bravely. 'Then you could have a rest.'

The formerly angelic toddlers had changed. They now resembled miniature heavy-weight boxers with cropped hair, bruised knees and malevolent expressions.

'No, it's all right. Mam will come up later. She comes twice a week to give me a hand. I'll snatch a couple of hours on the bed later today.'

With an absent-minded gesture, Nancy wiped her son's nose and deposited him back on the floor. Then she stretched, her hand to the small of her back. She pushed back her hair and smiled across at Dorothea with a total lack of envy.

'I'm right glad you got out of here, Dorrie. I think of you in London sometimes, working in a posh hotel and having a good time with that bloke you're not married to. You had more sense than I had.' She indicated Dorothea's suit. 'Look at the clothes you wear, you're real quality now!'

Chapter Twenty-Seven

Dorothea was still thinking about Nancy when her train approached King's Cross. Poor Nancy, she deserved better. During Dorothea's visit, Nancy had hardly mentioned her husband. Apparently he returned home one week in four, split his wage packet with her, then went back to sea again. Remembering Bill's earlier adoration of Nancy, Dorothea sighed. Maybe it was also 'poor Bill'? To cheer herself up, Dorothea turned her thoughts towards the Gills. During her visit home, she had plucked up courage and travelled to York for a day. Business was booming at the Bonne Vista and Denise and Norman had been surprised, then genuinely pleased to see Dorothea. They had spent a pleasant couple of hours reminiscing.

They heard without comment that Dorothea was still with Greg Paige. Denise had flicked a quick glance over Dorothea's ringless left hand, then reached over and poured out another cup of tea. Arnold, they told her, had opened his own restaurant nine months ago. He was married and a baby was expected in the spring.

So many new babies. Dorothea closed her eyes then opened them again as the train jolted to a halt. She left the station and headed down the Underground. She had returned a day earlier than originally planned. After her visit to the Gills, she had felt restless, overcome with a sudden desire to return to London and Greg. The weeklong separation had made her realise how much she loved him. She wanted to be with him, at the flat.

She knew he would be there. He was working on the last stages of his latest painting which meant his present existence would be virtually hermitlike. She would buy something good for their evening meal, surprise him.

Trains on the District Line were packed. Dorothea put down her case and counted herself fortunate to find a corner seat where she could keep an eye on her luggage. At the next stop four young men jostled their way into the compartment. They were about seventeen years of age and full of boisterous high spirits, laughing and pushing at each other. Several middle-aged travellers tut-tutted and rustled their newspapers expressing disgust, but Dorothea watched the boys and smiled. There was no harm in them, they were just young. Two of them were dressed in extraordinary clothes. Their trousers were narrow, their jackets had velvet collars and their shoes boasted two-inch crepe soles. When Dorothea's neighbour muttered a sour comment about their dress, she frowned at him. What vitality they had! With a pang she realised she had left her youth behind her. She looked despondently across the carriage and an old man winked at her. That made her feel better. Age was relative, she thought. Mr Whitney now, he would have smiled at these strangely dressed youngsters. She wondered how the old gentleman was; he had not visited the Doran Hotel recently. She still had his card somewhere. Ah, it was her station.

She left the Underground and walked up the stairs into the daylight, appreciating the warmth in the air. The afternoon streets were comparatively quiet, the weather gentle. She had become soft living in London, she thought. The cold northern winds which she had once taken for granted now caused her to shiver, brought goosepimples up on her skin.

She was pleased to find the front door unlocked. It saved her dumping down her case to search for her key. She walked up the stairs quietly and stopped at the top, surprised to hear a rumble of voices coming from the flat. Who could it be? She opened the door, put down her case in the sitting-room then went through the half-opened door into the studio.

Maybe the voices ceased or perhaps it was the roaring in her head that drowned out the sound of them. She stopped, stared, then blinked. But before she blinked, the scene before her was frozen forever upon her consciousness. Years later, she could recall every detail of the naked couple on the bed. Her first realisation was the total relaxation of the figures, an obvious sign of complete, sexual satisfaction. Then the smaller details intruded; the two heads so close on the pillow, Greg's left leg sprawled over that of his companion, his beautiful high-arched foot hanging over the side of the bed. Then, the dissolving of the frozen tableau – awareness, the audible intake of breath, the look of shock and the pathetic fumbling for clothes.

She would never forget, though she tried to, the icy coldness that swept through her body. She really thought she was inwardly bleeding to death. That her life's blood was leaving her head, her heart, and dropping from her body. She even glanced down at the floor, expecting to see pools of her blood collecting there. Later, much later, she became adept at blanking out the remainder of the scene. Yet sometimes, when she was in a self-flagellatory mood, of her own volition she would recall Greg's stricken face, the way he pulled the sheet to his chin. Then his companion, sitting up, holding out his hand, saying words she refused to hear . . . God, how she hated him!

'You!'

'Dorrie, please. Let me . . .'

Her tongue was too large. Her words sounded slurred. *'You were my friend!'*

Somehow, she forced her legs to move. She backed away, snatched up her case and fled down the stairs. Beneath the shock a seething volcano of fury threatened, giving her the strength to slam the front door behind her. She would never go back. She had caught the man she loved and the man she trusted engaged in a grotesque parody of the act of love. And she had been suspicious of Hugh!

A woman passing by stopped, stared at Dorothea's face, hesitated then hurried on. Like a baby duckling seeking a surrogate mother, Dorothea found her feet following the woman. She crossed the road and Dorothea followed. A taxi driver sounded his horn when he narrowly avoided hitting her. She looked round and then, when she looked back, the woman had disappeared. She wandered along aimlessly and finally came face to face with a pair of high ornamental gates. She stared at them, then nodded. Of course. She was at the small, unassuming park in which she used to exercise Jake. She remembered there was a bench just inside the gates, near a bank of rhododendron bushes. Coloured lights were floating in front of her eyes now and her hand couldn't feel the case she was still, presumably, carrying. She opened the gates. Thank God the park was deserted. The grass had been recently cut. She breathed in the scent but underlying the sweetness was another smell, one she hoped never to experience again. She put her hand towards the bench and then there was darkness.

How untidy she looked, slumped on the ground. Her skirt was above her knees and her arms and head were resting on the wooden seat of the garden bench. No wonder the park keeper had a dismayed look on his face. Dorothea raised her hand to her head. With distaste she saw there were flecks of vomit on her suit.

'I'm not drunk,' she said indistinctly.

'Bless you, I never thought you were.' The old man was stronger than he looked. He hoisted her on to the seat and steadied her. 'Your clothes are much too good.'

She closed her eyes and a macabre echo of laughter sounded inside her head. First Nancy, and now this man.

'My case?'

'It's here. You dropped it a few yards away. Look, have you any medicine you should take?'

She shook her head. 'I'll be all right if I can rest here for a few minutes.' She tried to smile but her face felt stiff. 'You're very kind.' He continued to be kind. He shooed away two inquisitive small boys and waited with her until she felt well enough to try and walk. Then he escorted her to a tobacconist's shop outside the park gates and waited as the owner rang a cab for her. When it arrived he helped her into the back seat and placed her suitcase close by her.

'Still think you should go to your doctor or a hospital,' he said.

'No, thank you.' She shook his work-hardened hand. 'I just need to go home and rest.'

But she had no home!

She directed the taxi driver to the Doran Hotel. She was relieved Vida was not at reception. She told the girl on duty not to take any messages for her then took down the key to a small room at the top of the building which she knew was rarely used. She climbed the back staircase, entered her temporary refuge and locked the door behind her. The smell from her spoiled clothes nauseated her. She stripped off, washed in cold water then sat on the bed, her head in her hands. She still felt totally detached from her situation and her surroundings. A constant noise outside the bedroom distracted her, yet it took her ten minutes to realise it came from a vacuum cleaner. A maid was hoovering the corridor carpet.

Then, slowly, the numbness dissipated and she began to shake. Like a wound when the anaesthetic wears off, the pain began. Beneath it lay the corrosive emotion of self-disgust. Did they laugh at her? she wondered. Her lover and the man she went to for help. She closed her eyes in shame when she remembered her conversation with Kenny. She had brought him back into their life. And how could Greg, formerly such an ardent and wonderful lover, turn to another man? Was it her fault? She rocked backwards and forwards. Yet beneath her self-doubt, her pain and fury remained and acted as catalysts. They would *not* destroy her! Always, she had pandered to Greg's needs. Because he was the artist she had given in to him over everything. Well, never again. From now on she would look after herself.

She would have to leave her job. Greg could come to the Doran and find her there and she never wanted to set eyes upon him again. She would find another, better job! She remembered her feeling of discomfort when Dennis had boasted about her at his Club. His friends had nodded and smiled but she had felt a fraud, knowing she was merely a receptionist in an ordinary hotel. Her love, she realised, her *obsession* with Greg had stunted her original ambitions. But she was still in her twenties, there was plenty of time. She must make plans.

She jumped up from the bed and reached for her handbag. If only she had more money! Despite the recent acclaim of Greg, it was still her wages which paid for the rent of the flat. She pressed her lips together, and opening her purse shook the contents on to the bed. She counted the cash and checked her bankbook. So little! She zipped open the compartment at the back of her purse and felt inside. The sharp corner of a card caught her finger. She drew it forth.

'If you need a friend.'

Chapter Twenty-Eight

Rob rode slowly down the main street of the small outback town. It was identical to the other towns he had passed through during the last few years – shabby, dusty and short on people. Still, he thought, the inhabitants were doing their best. There were foaming umbrellas of jacaranda softening several of the corrugated iron bungalows, and outside the General Stores a spindly young tree drooped in a green-painted tub. His eyes brightened. Glory be! He had spotted a pub sign. Rob had been on the road for hours and his parched mouth felt as bad as he and his battered old motorcycle looked. Outside the pub, he cut the bike's engine and dismounted stiffly from the saddle. He took off the dust coat he wore, stuffed it into his saddle bag, pushed open the swing door and walked into the bar.

The bartender was lazily pushing a damp cloth backwards and forwards over the counter. He looked up, his expression visibly brightening at the sight of a customer. Rob asked for a beer. The bartender served him and watched with interest as he downed the drink in one long pull. Rob asked for another then, as an afterthought, requested a pack of small cigars.

'Knew it!' The bartender slapped the top of his bar with delight. 'Knew you were different. You're a pom, aren't you?'

Rob's face relaxed into a faint grin. 'Strewth,' he said, in an exaggerated Aussie accent, 'is it *that* obvious?'

'Naw. It was when you asked for the ''smokes''.' Abandoning all pretence at work, the bartender drew

287

himself a glass of beer then waited. His expression begged for conversation. Rob lit a cigar and took a long, satisfying pull. He didn't want to talk, his nomadic, lonely life had made him sparing with words, but looking round the empty bar, he relented.

'Been here since I was a kid,' he said. 'I was schooled in the Bush.' His mouth twisted into a bitter grin. 'I've drifted since then, worked in lots of places. I've thought about heading for the coast but,' he shrugged, 'what would I do there? Maybe I'll make Adelaide some day.' He took another swig of beer, savouring the cool, bitter taste. 'Decent little place you have here.'

'It's OK. Quiet now but the railway's close by. We get busy sometimes.' The bartender's face brightened. 'Pub's packed then. We get the stockmen and the buyers, and then at the end of summer the miners come through, heading for Andamooka and the other fields. You been mining?'

Rob shook his head. 'Never fancied it.'

'Thought you might have. Another pom came through here a couple of months back. He was heading for Coober Pedy.'

Rob stubbed out his cigar. 'I'm just passing through. Know a good place to eat? I could do with some tucker.'

'Well now.' The bartender's brow furrowed in thought. 'There's Ma Bennett, a good cook but she's been a bit queer since her old man lit out with a young sheila. Then there's the Greek place, but you'd have to clean up before you go in there.' The man frowned. 'They moved in here nine months ago – bloody foreigners! Stiff-necked lot. Got a peach of a daughter, too, but no chance – you know what I mean.' He winked at Rob then blinked when he saw how the young man was staring at him. The stranger was no more than a kid really, but his physique was impressive and his eyes held a cold gleam.

'Didn't mean you, of course.' The bartender stepped back. 'Poms are OK, but there are all sorts flooding into the country now: Germans, Poles, Chinese.' He gave an uneasy laugh as he watched Rob look down into his glass. 'Bloody Government's on about land rights for the Boongs now. Before you know it, they'll be running the place!'

'You can't call the Boongs foreigners, my friend.' Rob's voice was gentle but the bartender remained silent as his customer drained his glass and put it on the bar. 'I'll have another beer before I go to eat. Out there, on the veranda.'

Rob went outside and sat upon a creaky old chair. He nodded his thanks to the bartender when he brought out his drink but did not speak. He put the glass on the veranda ledge and stared out at the deserted street. There was silence except for a beat-up old truck that rattled by and snuffles from a couple of mangy mongrels who lay in a patch of shade and chased their fleas. What would the bartender think, Rob reflected, if he knew his customer's dearest friend had been a despised Boong? And yet, he sighed and swallowed a mouthful of beer, in part he understood the white man's disdain for the Aborigine.

For two years he and Len had travelled together. Rob still remembered how often he had been terrified during the first few weeks. He had been terrified of the wilderness, terrified Len would get tired of him and abandon him, and terrified O'Neill would come after him. With a wry smile, Rob remembered . . .

Len had been a wily old stick. He had kept Rob far enough away from civilisation to avoid questions, trouble, yet not far enough into the outback for it to destroy him. Len looked after Rob. He calmed his fears over fearsome-looking spiders and snakes that appeared dangerous but pointed out the redback spider, no bigger than a little fingernail, whose bite was fatal. He taught Rob how to cook snake, passing it over the heat of a fire to throw back the juices into the flesh, then cutting incisions along both sides close to the backbone and rolling and tying with string, before covering with red hot ashes to cook. Rob had almost thrown up when presented with his first snake meal but taking a mouthful he had found the flesh white and firm as chicken. He had eaten many snake meals since then.

Len had taught him survival. He had also pointed out other things. Emus skittering along on long, thin legs; a goanna catching a rabbit and swallowing it whole. Rob had learnt how to walk over desert sand and dirt-track roads caked hard and lumpy with sun-baked mud. After six weeks spent travelling without seeing another human being, they arrived at a sheep station where they were given work and no questions asked. They spent months travelling round the lonely boundaries of the spread, putting up fences. The work was monotonous, but again, Rob learnt many things: how to cook chops wrapped in gum leaves over an open fire of twigs; how to ride. One night a wild black stallion came close to court Rob's mare. He had watched entranced as the brumbie showed off his long mane and sweeping tail, strutting and arrogant before the placid female. Then Rob had moved, a twig had cracked, and the stallion, sensing his presence, had raced away. Rob told Len about him.

'If you have a good stock horse, you can catch 'em sometimes,' Len had replied. 'After a hard winter when the feed's been poor.'

They moved on again, found a few weeks' work in a woodyard. The owner had looked hard at the old Aborigine and the young white boy but asked no questions. In the Bush, people minded their own business. As the months slipped by Rob's affection for Len grew. He was so old but he could work harder and longer than Rob. When each job ended, they travelled until they found another one. No more did Len talk of leaving Rob. They were partners.

They came to an area the old-timers called Heartbreak Plains. Abandoned shells of stone homesteads recalled the despair of early farmers, but there were also new buildings and men hopeful of wresting a living from the hard, dry earth.

They took a job poisoning rabbits for a wheat farmer. They were a terrible problem despite the building of fine mesh fences to keep them out of the crops. Whatever the farmer did, the rabbits found a way in to destroy the pastures and the crops. Len did not like the job. His people relied on the rabbits for their food but the farmer offered good money so he agreed. There would always be something else to eat. The Spirits would provide.

In the beginning Rob was an object of curiosity to the white men they met. What was a white kid doing in the company of an old Abo? But he became a man quickly and eventually there were times when he would be invited to join their company. He would sit with a group of sheep-shearers, eating their bread, cold meat and pickles and listening to their tales. He clumsily learnt to roll his own smokes and his eyes would widen when they talked of their adventures with women. And, always, would come the question: 'What are you doing hanging around with a Boong?'

When Rob's ears turned red and he stuttered out some reply, they shook their heads.

'You should stick to your own kind, sonny. No good came from an Abo.'

Then he would fall silent, seething with mixed emotions. When he thought of the treatment he had received from 'his own kind' he knew his first loyalty would be to his friend, yet part of him yearned for the camaraderie of these lean, laconic men.

Len never asked about his meeting with the sheepshearers or drovers. When Rob went to sit with them, Len simply faded away into the darkness. If they went into a town, things were also difficult. The first time Rob went to town with Len he was surprised to see how the old man changed. He actually seemed to shrink. His black skin seemed to acquire a yellowish glow and his eyes flickered.

'You look round, Rob. I see you later.'

'You got family here, Len?'

The old man had brushed his hand over his mouth.

Then, without replying to Rob's question, he had set off down the street, almost running. Rob stared after him and shrugged. He looked round and felt a twinge of excitement. It was a poor kind of town, not like the ones he remembered in England, but after months in the bush it was exciting. There was a church, a bottle shop, a Mission Hall and a couple of shops.

Rob spent time in the General Store. He was fascinated at the variety of goods on display. There were mops and meatsafes, bolts of cloth, bags of potatoes, and minor items such as cards of buttons, jars of sweets, belts and boots. He counted the money in his pockets and deliberated whether or not to buy himself a new, wide-brimmed hat. He decided against it and wandered out again into the dusty street. Three hours passed and darkness was gathering. Rob was bored. He went to look for Len. He wanted to know whether the old man intended them to camp outside the town for the night or whether they should spend a few bob on a flop-house. And Len had their money. It was black night before he found his friend.

He fell over him. Len was in a shady corner near the bottle shop, flat on his back and snoring. Amongst the litter of broken beer bottles lay other black men and women. Rob shook Len by the shoulder but the Aborigine merely groaned. Rob stared down at his friend, then left. He spent the night on a patch of wild ground behind a lean-to but he chose the place because it was near to a house which, amazingly, had a garden. Whoever lived in the house must have done a heap of humping water to keep the plants alive, Rob thought. When he slept, he breathed in the flower scents carried by the night breeze and dreamed of England.

The following morning Len came up to him. He looked dazed and ashamed. He avoided Rob's eyes and his wrinkled hands shook. A truck had been laid on to take the men back to the sheep station and Len's voice was low when he confessed, beneath the rumbling noise of the truck wheels, that he had spent all their money.

'Town no good for this old Abo, Boss. Next trip, I stay behind.'

Rob coughed to clear the lump in his throat. Len hadn't called him 'Boss' since their first meeting. He looked and saw how stooped the old man was. Where was the old warrior who had taught him about the Dreamtime? Without speaking, Rob held out the chewing tobacco he had bought for Len instead of buying the new hat.

Their partnership lasted another eight months. In that time Rob grew to his full height of five feet seven inches, but his shoulders were broad, his frame compact and muscular. His skin was tanned and his gaze steady and direct. He was fifteen and looked twenty. Len grew more stooped, more wrinkled but he was as tough as ever. He went on three more benders and after the last one he was sick for a week. After that, he stayed away from the towns. Their last job together lasted longer than any other and Len became restless. He was sick of staying in one place. He was sick of work. He wanted to go 'Walkabout'. Rob too was restless. He didn't know what he wanted. Some nights he would stay in the bunk house with the other drovers, sometimes he would camp out with Len. He always accepted lifts into town. He liked to watch the girls walk down the street. They were mysterious creatures to him, with their red lips and swaying hips. One day, a man told him about a place where you could sleep with a woman for a price. He took his savings and begged a lift into town. For two hours he hung about outside the clapboard house with its discreetly veiled curtains but his courage failed him. He slept rough and next day, when he returned to the station, Len had gone.

Sitting on the veranda at Dryton, Rob finished his beer and reflected upon his feelings at that time. Relief, he remembered, mixed with a sense of enormous loss. Len had left him a present. It was a drawing on a piece of stringbark. Len had painted a goanna in red and yellow ochre. The work was crude but to Rob it was a painting to be treasured. He still had it, safely rolled up and stored in the case that held Spider's binoculars. Perhaps that's my fate, he thought drearily, to lose all my friends but end up with their belongings. A puff of dust rose from the wooden planks of the veranda as he pushed back his chair. He was tired and hungry. He would feel better when he had eaten.

Further down the street was a two-storey building which boasted a sign reading 'Beacon Hotel'. The desk clerk had his ear glued to a local radio programme. When Rob tapped the desk, he stood up with a sigh. He took Rob's money and handed him a key.

'Extra for a bath,' he said. He looked at Rob with distaste. 'If you want, you can leave your dirty duds outside the bedroom door. The black girl will wash them for you. Be ready tomorrow morning.'

'Thanks.' Rob reached in his pocket for another note.

An hour later, clean and refreshed, he left the hotel and went looking for the Greek restaurant the bartender had spoken about. From the outside it looked good. There were cheerful red chintz curtains at the windows and inside the gentle glow of lamps. He pushed open the door. The smell of food made his stomach groan in anticipation. He sat down and looked about him. He was glad he had made the effort to clean up. A well-dressed elderly couple was seated at the next table and beyond them a young couple with a child. By the window sat two old-timers. One chewed tobacco but he did so decently, neither hawking nor spitting. Rob noticed the proper cotton table cloth and smiled with pleasure.

'Like the menu?'

A soft voice caused him to look up. The dark-haired girl smiled and handed him a card. 'Lamb's good, or there's steak.'

He mumbled something and stared. She laughed. 'I'll come back later.' He looked at the card but saw only the girl's black eyes and the way her skirt swirled about her slim legs as she walked away. The life Rob led brought him long periods of loneliness, and most of the time he never thought about women. He worked hard and the few women on the stations were invariably married, middle-aged and looked at him with strictly maternal eyes. They invited him into their family to share a home-cooked meal and sometimes pressed into his hands home-made jam or a pair of knitted socks.

Rob was young and his blood rose strong. There had been a woman in Kitandra, a blue-eyed woman some ten years older than himself. She had a bold smile and a generous nature and Rob remembered her with affection but he was under no illusions. Two days out of the town and he would be replaced in her affections. This girl was different. When she came back to his table, he ordered something, he couldn't remember what, then watched her as she walked over to the huge juke box in the corner of the room and bent over to make her choice of record. He knew she was aware of his gaze. She pressed a button on the machine, pushed back her hair which hung long and glossy, dimpled a smile at Rob and disappeared through the curtains leading to the kitchen. He rubbed his hands together beneath the crisp white tablecloth. They were sweating.

After ten minutes, she brought him his meal. 'Hope you enjoy it.'

He was pretty sure the fragrance that hung about her had been freshly applied. He felt a surge of confidence. She liked him.

'Thanks.'

He looked deep into those black, black eyes and was rewarded with a blush of pink across her high cheekbones. She had brought him steak. It was good. He followed with apple pie and cream and then ordered coffee. The restaurant was now empty except for the two old men.

She carried the coffee to his table then slipped into

the seat opposite his. She cupped her face in her hands and watched as he sugared the cup. 'You just arrived?'

He nodded, gulped a mouthful of coffee then drew in a sharp breath as the scalding liquid exploded in his mouth. Her eyes twinkled.

'Thought so. Not often we get strangers this time of year.' She paused. 'I'm Irene Botetsios. My pa owns this place.'

He cleared his throat. 'Rob. Rob Steyart.'

'Robert. Rob.' She tried the name experimentally then smiled. 'You just passing through?'

'Yes.'

Mesmerised, he saw her full lips pout.

'Well, I might just hang around for a while. See what turns up.'

'Oh.' She reached out and touched his hand. 'I do hope so. It's such a boring town. Just old farmers and their wives.'

'Same everywhere, I guess.' Rob finished his coffee. 'Sometimes I think I'll make my way to Adelaide. See what a real city's like.'

She sighed. 'I'd love to go there. See all the lovely shops, the Gulf of St Vincent . . .'

They stared at each other then started as one of the old men spoke. 'Adelaide's no great shakes. Wowserville, that's what folk call it. Bunch of killjoys there.' Malicious old eyes glittered at the two youngsters from a seamed, weatherbeaten face. 'Never satisfied, some people. Allus want to be where they ain't.'

The girl tossed back her hair. 'See what I mean,' she whispered. She stood up. 'I'd best get back, otherwise Pa will be out here giving you the third-degree.'

She went away and then came back with the bill. Rob paid her. 'You'll come in again, won't you, before you leave?'

He nodded. Outside in the street he recreated the sweet curves of her body and the half-hidden invitation in her eyes. His tiredness had evaporated. He drew in a great lungful of the blessedly cool evening air. Jeez, he thought, as he reluctantly turned in the direction of the hotel, one of Len's kindly spirits, the Mimis, must have directed him towards the town of Dryton.

Chapter Twenty-Nine

Two months later Rob was still there. A dairy farmer, Mr Hancock, had been ready and eager to give him work. Hancock was expanding his dairy herd and there was plenty of work around his spread. He even offered Rob the use of a tiny one-roomed cottage on his land which an earlier settler had once occupied. Rob accepted the offer with pleasure; the cottage was snug and weatherproofed, but as he went about his work he often looked at Mr Hancock's home. The Hancock family lived in a low rambling cream-painted bungalow with a high-pitched roof. The surrounding land was laid out in gardens, and white-edged paths and a chain-wire fence enclosed the whole. One day . . . thought Rob. He realised his views on life were changing. For years he had been his own man, taking off when he felt like it, but suddenly he was visited by visions of a home of his own, meals taken at his own fireside, and a wife, even kids. He knew where all these thoughts originated.

Irene . . . she would make a wonderful wife. So slim, so vivacious, yet the swaying hips beneath her trim waist were built for child-bearing. He liked to imagine himself in bed with Irene with a lovable toddler possessed of her beautiful eyes in a room next door.

Irene enchanted him; she was fire and laughter. 'Faster,' she would call, and cling with her arms about his waist as they tore about the countryside on his motorbike. She loved the sensation of speed. 'Faster!' And she laughed when the machine wobbled as he trembled with the smell and the feel of her. Not that he had actually managed to feel very much.

Rob scowled as he went about his task of feeding the herd. Her eyes promised so much but as a good Greek Orthodox girl she permitted few liberties. Another girl he would have quarrelled with, called a tease and worse, but he could not be angry with Irene. Instead he would pull away from her kisses and ride back to his lonely cottage to toss and turn the night away on his hard, narrow mattress.

Irene had introduced Rob to her parents. After an initial period of coolness, Mr and Mrs Botetsios treated him with punctilious courtesy and barely concealed alarm. Rob understood their fears. To them he was a roustabout, a nobody. Yet with old-fashioned good manners they welcomed him to their house. He was Irene's friend. They showed him yellowing photographs of long-dead aunts and uncles in the 'old country', and plied him with food and wine. He appreciated their graciousness. After a few glasses of wine, Mr Botetsios began to relax in Rob's company. One evening, when Irene went to help her mother in the kitchen, he explained to Rob: 'Irene is our only child, our treasure. We have spoilt her, of course, and she is a little wilful but,' he stared somewhat hazily at Rob, 'she is still so young, barely seventeen.'

Rob wondered what his host would say if he knew that he himself was only two years older.

'She enjoys your company. There are so few young people in this place. Yet I should tell you,' Mr Botetsios paused delicately, 'in one year, when Irene is eighteen, the son of a good friend of mine who lives in Queensland will visit us. There is an arrangement, you see.'

Rob saw.

Mr Botetsios rolled his eyes. 'A beautiful daughter is a great responsibility but we know Irene is a good girl and I was greatly relieved to hear you are English. Everyone knows Englishmen are gentlemen.'

Irene re-entered the room which spared Rob from

replying. Listening to Mr Botetsios, Rob wondered how a parent could be so blind. True, Irene was young but she was also as old as Eve. Every movement, every sideward glance at him, told Rob she was a restless, passionate woman. His face reddened just thinking about her.

But when Mr Botetsios beckoned to his daughter and she came and sat on the arm of his chair, Rob saw how dutiful was her pose. Her lace blouse was closed primly about her throat and her beautiful hair, which flowed loose and free when they rode the motorbike, was coiled neatly at the back of her small head. Rob swallowed and shifted in his chair. He wondered if there was ever a man who truly understood a woman.

For a week after that visit, Rob stayed away from Irene. He was building his house of dreams on shifting sand. She was promised to another. She was merely teasing him, she didn't love him. But the next time he visited town she came running from the restaurant. Her small white hands clutched at his shirt like dancing moths.

'What have I done, Robbie? Don't you like me any more?'

He covered her hands with his own. 'Of course I do, but it's better I stop seeing you so much, Irene. I shall be moving on soon and—' he paused '—I don't think your parents are happy about our friendship.'

'But it's silly, we haven't done anything wrong.' She smiled up at him like an artless child. He was obscurely glad she was so small; it made him feel taller. 'It's Christmas soon. Surely you won't leave before Christmas? You must stay until then. I am making you a present.'

He felt a mixture of love and irritation. Surely she couldn't be *so* innocent. She must know what she was doing to him?

Weakly, he said, 'I can come and see you Saturday.'

'Lovely.' She stood on tiptoe to kiss him, a friendly kiss which lasted a fraction too long and set the blood pulsing in his veins. His hands pulled her closer to him. She gave a breathless laugh and pulled away. He released her.

'We'd better be careful,' she whispered. 'There is always someone to watch, to gossip.' She sighed. 'I hate this place. What a pity we can't go to Adelaide, Rob, just you and me.' She blew him a kiss and hurried away. He watched her go, his senses twanging like a badly played violin.

The day before Christmas Eve, Rob rode into town. First, he called at the pub. He talked desultorily to the few men in the bar and swatted irritably at the persistent flies. It was so bloody hot, unnatural. With sudden nostalgia he thought of England which he still mentally called home. As clear as yesterday he remembered the day he had bought earrings for Dorothea Bellows. Remembering Dorrie reminded him of Jake. He spoke to the bartender.

'Bob, where's that old yellow mongrel? The one that beds down just outside, under the veranda? I've got some scraps for it in my saddle bag.'

'Oh, him. He's a goner, Rob. He was hit by a pick-up two days ago. Johnson buried him.'

'Oh.' Rob took a swallow of beer and tried to hide his unreasonable feeling of distress. 'Poor old mutt. Didn't have much of a life, did he?'

Irene was sulky when he met her.

'My parents, they are so . . .' She pouted. 'Work, work, work, that is all they live for. We should do something different at Christmas. But, no, there is always the work.'

Rob hated to see her usually vivacious face downcast. He slipped his arm around her. 'There's a New Year's Eve Dance on over at Belmont. Do you think they would allow me to take you?'

'Would you?' Her lips turned up in a smile. 'I think Pa would agree. He likes you. And I have a new dress to wear.'

'Mr Hancock would let me have one of the trucks.'

They discussed ways of gaining her parents' permission, then Irene sighed. 'I wish you could spend

Christmas Day with us but Pa says no. It is a religious day, he says, and you are not really religious.'

'Never mind. We can look forward to going to the dance.'

'But what will you do, Rob?'

'On Christmas Day? I'll be all right. Mrs Hancock has arranged a picnic for everyone. We're going to Hartz Reach. It still seems funny to me to have a picnic on Christmas Day. If we tried that in England, we'd all freeze to death!'

'You don't talk about England much, do you? Tell me, Rob – tell me about England.'

'Tell me about England.'

Rob had told Irene about England and on Christmas Day, seated on sun-parched grass, eating cold turkey and potato salad, the scent of wattle in the air, he told the same things to the Hancocks' fourteen-year-old son Richard, who was fascinated about anything to do with the old country.

'My great-grandad came from Kent,' the lad boasted. His eyes rounded. 'He was a convict. I think he was a highwayman but Dad says he probably just stole a loaf of bread. Do you know Kent?'

Rob shook his head. He thought how strange it was that Australians vied with each other to find convict skeletons in respectable family cupboards. Returning from the picnic he unearthed writing paper and an envelope and started a letter to Dorothea. It was a long time since he had written to her and she had no address to contact him, but the death of the nameless mongrel and the talk of England had revived memories. He addressed the letter care of Dorothea's parents then went to bed to dream of a picnic on the dockside in Hull and a naked Irene dancing for him in the snow. He awoke at two in the morning lathered in sweat and spent the remaining hours of darkness lying on top of his rough blanket staring at the walls of the lonely cottage.

Rob was proud to be Irene's escort to the New

Year's Eve Dance. The other guys' eyes popped almost out of their heads when they saw her. Her new dress was demure in style but the soft material clung to her figure and her freshly washed hair hung thick and fragrant down her back. Rob tightened his grip around her small waist as they danced. It was one of those moments when he was sure he loved her. There were other times, he was not so sure. Things she said, her little-girl voice, could confuse him. And when he was away from her, he resented the way she could tease him into uncontrollable passion merely to turn him off, like switching off a lamp. Why did she do it? Was she playing games with him? The thought slipped into his mind that she was merely testing out her powers; maybe thinking of him as a way out of boring old Dryton. No! He shook his head. What about his Christmas present? She had given him a finely stitched linen shirt. It must have taken her hours and hours to make yet she had been shy at his praise. She brushed away his astonished thanks. All Greek girls knew how to sew, she had told him. Rob had been thankful that, on impulse, he had earlier bought her a string of crystal beads to accompany the bottle of perfume, her original Christmas present.

Re-entering the hall, decorated with coloured paper chains and a painted mural incongruously depicting Father Christmas on his sleigh, Rob saw Irene smilingly shake her head in refusal at a tall, red-headed young stockman asking for a dance. Suddenly, he felt happy. She *did* care for him. He went to claim the next dance.

Christmas had long been forgotten one Saturday when Rob cut the engine of his motorbike and went into the Three Bells pub for a drink. As he pushed open the door, there came a mighty roar: 'My God, it *is* you! Over here, Rob Steyart. Christ, you're still a little bastard, aren't you?'

A huge man dressed in denims and checked shirt bore down on Rob. He stood in front of him and beamed. 'Know me, don't you?'

'Boots!' He staggered when the big man clapped

him on the shoulder then his face lit up in a smile. 'I can't believe this! It's really you?'

'Thought you'd got rid of me, did you? I received those letters you and Spider wrote to me and I wrote back but then . . . nothing. Couldn't be bothered to write any more, I suppose.'

Rob's face darkened. 'No, it wasn't that. Other things happened.'

Boots stared down at Rob then shouted over to the bartender. 'Two schooners at that corner table, mate. And,' he waved his arm towards the three strangers standing at the bar, 'give them a drink too. It's my shout.'

Rob followed Boots to the corner table. He sat down and stared at his friend.

Boots was massive, but without a spare ounce of fat. His hair was cropped short as a convict's and his huge hands were heavily scarred yet his light blue eyes were clear and steady and his smile guileless and generous. Rob's own eyes filled with tears, tears he was not ashamed of.

'Boots, I can't . . .' he choked.

Boots took the brimming glasses of beer from the barman. He pushed Rob's drink towards him. 'Now,' he said, 'tell me. What about Spider? Is he here with you?'

Rob looked down and shook his head. Boots's face clouded.

'Tell me,' he said again, but now his voice was quiet.

When Rob finished speaking Boots said nothing for a moment. He twisted the beer glass in his strong, hard hands. Then he sighed.

'Poor little bastard.' His eyes as they met Rob's gaze were moist. He raised his glass. 'To Spider,' he said. They both drained their glasses and Boots shouted for a refill.

'I went much the same way as you,' he continued, turning to Rob. 'They didn't keep me penned up for long. Who wants to learn to be a bloody cockie?

Mind, no one messed with me.' A bleak grin flitted across his features. 'I was too much of a handful, I suppose.' He leaned back in his chair. 'I've done most things since those days, Rob. I worked as a jackeroo for a while but horses and me never got on. Then I tried the city but somehow,' he shook his head, 'after life in the Bush, city life's like being shut in a box; so many people, so much noise, smells, everybody rushing. It wasn't for me. So,' he grinned, 'I became a miner.'

Light dawned on Rob. 'So you're the guy Bob told me about when I first landed up here. The pom who mined for opals?'

'Could be, although there's a few more English at Coober Pedy. Mind you, I've been around. I've worked iron in the Pilbara region and silver in Broken Hill. I tell you, mate, I've seen more of Australia than the natural Aussies. Anyway, enough about me, what are you doing?'

'Not too much, really. Working for a dairy farmer right now. He's a good enough bloke.'

Boots clapped him on the shoulder again. 'Right! Well, that's enough talking for now. Come on to the bar and meet my mates. We sure have something to celebrate.'

Rob was introduced to Boots's companions and more drinks were bought. What followed became a blur. Rob vaguely remembered staggering from the pub and collapsing beneath the veranda with the rest of the group. In the morning he awoke with a burning thirst and a head that seemed to contain a steamhammer yet still he felt good inside. He felt even better when Boots informed him he would be staying in Dryton for a few days before turning to Coober Pedy.

'I'm not letting go of you yet, old mate. We have too much to talk about.'

Boots and his friends were booked into the hotel. After a bath and a change of clothes they looked respectable. When evening came Boots accompanied Rob to the Greek restaurant for a meal. His companions had taken the pick-up and gone looking for girls but Boots had declined their invitation to join them. He had another surprise for Rob. 'I'm married, see. She's a fine lady.' He had blushed at Rob's look of surprise. 'We're expecting a nipper in four months' time.'

Rob congratulated him but found it hard to imagine Boots with a wife and family. 'Where's your wife now?'

'Kate, she's called Kate. She's been with her parents for a while. Too damn hot at Coober Pedy in the summer months but she'll be back home now. We've a nice little dugout and there's female company nearby.'

'Dugout?'

'Sure, haven't you heard? Most folk live underground at CP. It's a lot cooler.' Boots laughed at the expression on Rob's face. 'Why don't you come and see the place for yourself?' he suggested impulsively. 'There's nowhere on earth like it. It suits me. Maybe it would suit you. Opal mining's hard work but the money's OK and there's always the chance that one day you'll strike it rich.'

'I don't think so, Boots. I've never fancied mining.'

'Well,' Boots shrugged his massive shoulders, 'it's up to you. Now, I'm hungry and I want to see this gorgeous girl you've been telling me about.'

'I like your friend.'

Irene lay back against the bark of a red gum tree and smiled at Rob. It was a beautiful day, fine and warm with the added benefit of a soft breeze. They had taken a picnic, climbed on Rob's motorbike and ridden out, away from the town. Now they were alone, and except for the occasional hoot from an unseen bird, it was quiet.

'At first I thought him big and rough but he speaks of his wife with much love and he is so fond of you, Rob.' She patted the ground next to her. 'Come and sit down.'

Rob hesitated. She looked lovely. The square-necked blouse she wore emphasised the richness of her breasts and his eyes lingered on a thin strip of pearly white skin at its neckline which contrasted strongly with her lightly tanned face and neck. She had kicked off her sandals and the sight of her slim, bare legs set off his old, familiar hunger. Almost reluctantly, he went to her.

'Did your parents mind you coming out here with me?' Rob had noted Mr and Mrs Botetsios's courtesy was becoming more and more strained.

'No.' Irene chuckled. 'I said Rosie Grant and her brother were coming with us.' She snuggled closer to Rob, slipping her arm through his and resting her hand on his knee. 'Your friend also told me about the opals. So beautiful, he says, and valuable and they are just lying there.'

'I don't think it's that easy.' Rob could feel the warmth from her hand on his leg. 'Mining's damn hard work, particularly in the desert heat.'

'Yes, but Boots says you might find one big stone, and then you are rich.'

'Hey, what is this?' Rob turned to face her. 'Are you trying to get rid of me?'

'No.' She pouted. 'But we'll never get away from here if you stay with Mr Hancock. And,' she blinked, 'I know you will get sick of this place and leave and my parents will force me to marry a complete stranger!'

'Nonsense, Irene. Your parents would never force you, they love you.'

'Nevertheless, it is our custom.'

Suddenly she threw herself into Rob's arms. 'I never thought about it really, never worried until I met you, Rob. But now . . . I think of you all the time. They will never let us marry. I am so afraid you will leave. Please, you do love me, don't you?'

She drew his face down towards her and they kissed, again and again. Her lips parted and as Rob's tongue explored her mouth she moaned, clinging to him tightly. Clumsily, he began to undo the buttons on her blouse. Excitement knifed through him when he realised she was helping him. God, this was for real! When they were both naked, he realised *how* real. Suddenly, all Irene's previous inhibitions had evaporated and she was brazen in her desire for gratification. Rob forgot Mr Botetsios's words to him. He forgot he was an 'English gentleman'. He forgot his previous experience with the woman in Kitandra. He was just nineteen years old and this wonderful, desirable girl who had kept him at arm's length for months was beneath him, her body soft and welcoming, her fingernails scoring his back with the urgency of her need. He entered her gently although his wanting was a physical pain, then, as she shuddered and clawed at his back they became wild things, overwhelmed by sensations neither of them had experienced before.

Afterwards, she asked again if he loved her. He looked at the shadows below her eyes, the droop of her full lips, and felt strong, protective and wise. He felt truly a man. He put his arms around her. 'Yes,' he said.

He would speak to her parents, he told her. They must allow a marriage. She made a sound of dissent. They would never agree.

'Then,' he said, 'I will make enough money to take you away from here.'

The next day he found Boots and told him he would be with them when they set off for Coober Pedy.

Chapter Thirty

Outside Dryton the road was dusty and pitted with pot-holes. The men in the back groaned as the utility truck backfired, checked, then careered along again.

'He's in a bloody hurry,' said one man laconically, clutching the tailboard as the truck bounced and rattled along the road, often throwing the travellers in the back into a confused heap.

'He's mad we didn't start on time,' replied the man next to him.

'It's a long ride to Coober Pedy. He wants to get back to his missis!' The speaker looked across at Rob. 'Want a smoke, mate?'

Rob shook his head and gazed at the road behind them. He was disinclined for conversation. He was worried about Irene. After the picnic they had returned to Dryton to find her father waiting for them. The friends who had supposedly accompanied them had been seen in town. Mr Botetsios had ordered Irene into the house and then spoken to Rob. He had been quiet but firm. Rob was not to see Irene again. Mr Botetsios was to write to their friends in Queensland immediately. He suggested, again firmly, that Rob consider moving on. The memory of recent love-making had turned Rob dumb. He felt as guilty as hell. He was sure Mr Botetsios could read in his eyes what had happened. He had hung his head, walked away without speaking. That was three days ago and now he was going with Boots to mine for opals. At least Mr Botetsios had agreed to give Irene his letter. She would know he loved her and was planning a future for them both.

'What the hell!'

There was a screech of brakes, a grinding of gears as the truck suddenly lurched to a halt. The men swore, sorted themselves out from the tangle of arms and legs and leaned over the side to see what was going on. Rob also looked and caught his breath as a small figure, which presumably had been standing in the centre of the road, walked round to the driver's cab. It could have been a slight young boy, dressed in work-manlike pants and boots, wearing a cap pulled down low on the brow, but Rob knew it was no boy. He would have recognised that pert profile anywhere. He jumped down from the back of the trunk.

'Christ! What are you doing out here, Irene?'

Her face was serious. 'Don't be mad, Rob. I had to come.'

Boots climbed out of the driver's seat and slammed shut the door. His face was grim. 'I don't know what you two are planning but we're not hanging about here, Rob. Take her over there,' he gestured to the side of the road, 'and sort things out. In five minutes from now,' he looked at his watch, 'we're moving on. Whether or not you're coming with us is up to you.'

Rob caught hold of Irene's hand and took her aside. 'Did you get my letter?'

'Yes, that's why I'm here.' Tears glittered in her eyes. 'You know Pa's arranging for George Zaleski to come and visit. He'll make me marry him, Rob.'

'No, Irene. He . . .'

'He *will*. You think Pa's reasonable, but he's not. He guessed we made love. He made me tell him. He says I've disgraced his name and the sooner I'm married the better. But not to you. Even if you come back he won't let us be together. How can I marry George, Rob? I love you.'

'Don't cry.' He touched her cheek where a tear had slid down, leaving a dirty mark. 'You shouldn't have to marry anyone yet. You're still so young.'

She pulled away from him. 'My mother was sixteen when she married, younger than me. Don't you *want* to marry me? I thought . . . the other day . . .'

Another tear slipped down her face. Rob thought how defenceless she looked, dressed in the over-large trousers and jacket.

'Where did you get those clothes?'

'Rosie gave them to me, but,' a smile trembled on her lips, 'they're much too big. And her brother brought me out here, on his motorbike, so I could go with you.'

Boots tooted the car horn. He had climbed back into the cab and was looking in their direction.

'I have to come with you now, Rob. I can't go back!'

'But your parents . . .'

'It's all right. I left them a message. I told them we are going to be married.'

'Married!' But . . .' Rob looked at her and saw the doubt creep across her face. 'What if you don't like Coober Pedy?' he said, lamely. 'You hate Dryton and Coober Pedy may be much worse. It's right out in the Bush.'

'But I'll be with you, Rob. And maybe we'll be lucky. You might find a big stone, worth lots of money.'

'That's just a dream.' He shook his head then jumped and looked across at Boots who stuck his head out of the truck window and shouted: 'Come on, you two.'

They went towards him. Irene slipped her hand in Rob's. It felt soft and warm. He felt a sudden rush of love.

'Can I come, Rob?'

'Sure you can.' He looked at Boots. 'Is that OK, Boots?'

'Suppose so.' Boots's face cracked in a grin. 'Bit like the Aussie version of Gretna Green, isn't it, Rob?' He opened the door for Irene and waited as she scrambled in. 'You'll be company for my Kate, Irene.'

She beamed at him. 'There's a church in Coober Pedy, isn't there, Boots?'

'Not exactly, love. But we'll sort something out, even if we have to kidnap a pastor!' He wound up the window.

When the truck rattled down the main street of a town called Kingoonya it was mid-afternoon. Boots cut the engine, leaned back in his seat and wiped his sweaty face with a grimy handkerchief. Then he leaned over and opened the door for Irene.

'Right, boys,' he shouted. 'Everyone out, then it's the last lap, only another one hundred and eighty miles of dirt road to go!' He grinned. The men climbed down, banging their clothes to shift some of the dust. Boots walked creakily round the back of the truck and beckoned to Rob. 'Like a word, old son.'

Avoiding Irene's anxious gaze Rob followed him a little distance from the vehicle.

'It's really serious, then?' Boots nodded in Irene's direction.

'Yes.'

'Well, if you're sure.' Boots pulled at his bottom lip. 'She's certainly got spirit, not just a looker.' He thought for a moment. 'You both seem set on marriage but there's no church at Coober Pedy yet. Still, if you want things legal I know where I can contact a pastor. He lives just outside Kingoonya.'

'That would be great, Boots. I'm not sure though.' Rob's brow creased. 'Nominally, as you know, I'm Catholic and Irene's Greek Orthodox. Do you think . . . ?'

'Listen, Rob.' Boots smote him on his shoulder. 'We're in the Bush now. A pastor is a pastor – you'll be legally married all right!'

So, with Boots and a quiet, lean miner called Ray Eckerman standing as witnesses, the marriage took place.

There was no time for a honeymoon, just a quick beer and a meal at a nearby pub then they were back on the road.

Rob never forgot his first sight of Coober Pedy. Boots had told him many of the miners and their families would be returning to the fields during the next couple of weeks. It was early May, a time when the searing heat of the summer was cooling, making work possible. Yet, when the truck jolted to a halt, Rob saw before them an empty wilderness.

'Where is it?' he asked.

'This is it, mate. This is what you get!'

'Jesus!'

They got out of the vehicle and Rob took Irene's hand. A bare, flat landscape stretched out before them; an old, old, landscape, wrinkled and worn from endless ages. The only buildings to be seen were a store with the name Brewster's painted on it and another building, Marks and Fields Opal Store, on the right. Dotted about were a few patches of what looked like rough gorse but there were no trees, not a single tree. Rob gulped. He had passed through areas like this before but Irene, what about her? He squeezed her fingers but dared not look at her. 'Where is everyone?' he asked.

Ray Eckerman pointed towards the flat-topped hills around them. Then Rob saw there were doorways cut into the side of the slopes. He swallowed. Were these the dugouts Boots had mentioned? It was, he thought, like being in *Alice in Wonderland*. Any minute he expected a door to open and a large rabbit to hurry out, carrying his pocket watch!

'Come on, you two.' Boots loomed over them. 'Come and meet my old lady.'

As they followed him Rob risked a glance at Irene. She looked shell-shocked. They turned to wave goodbye to their travelling companions and Rob came to a sudden halt.

'Come on.' Boots looked back at him. 'What is it?'

'Over there.' Rob pointed.

Walking sedately along the empty, dusty track came two camels.

'Oh, them. They bring the water in. Why, what's the matter?' Boots looked on in amazement as Rob doubled over and began to laugh. 'Come on, you silly bugger, what's so funny?'

'Nothing.' Rob mopped his eyes with his sleeve, grinned at Irene and gave her a swift kiss, before hurrying after Boots. The laughter still bubbled away inside him but it felt good. He knew it was almost an hysterical reaction but it had served to release his tension. They were going to be all right. He took a last backwards look at the camels. What a pity, he thought, that Len wasn't here.

Kate Gillan looked a good match for her husband. She was tall, strongly made, with wide shoulders and a heavy frame but she was also a bonny woman. Her features were even and her hair thick, dark brown and glossy. Her wide blue eyes lit up at the sight of her husband. Oblivious of his companions she rushed forward and hugged Boots, then deposited a smacking kiss on his lips. Then, recalling her manners, she blushed, stepped back and waited to be introduced.

'Kate, this is an old mate of mine, Rob Steyart, and his brand-new wife, Irene.'

'Pleased to meet you.' She shook Rob's hand and gave Irene a broad, welcoming smile.

'Rob and me go back a long way, Kate.' Boots yawned. 'Tell you all about it later, but we want a rest and a wash first. Been a hell of a dusty trip.'

An hour later, clean and refreshed, they sat down for a home-cooked meal. Rob had expressed doubts about intruding on Boots's home-coming but Kate had laughed.

'This is a friendly place, Rob. It has to be, everyone living here relies on his mates. As for the meal, I always cook a lot of food when Boots is expected.'

Rob smiled his thanks. He liked Kate. He looked at Irene. She was quiet and he was worried. He wondered what was going through her head. But he was pleased to see she was regarding their surroundings with interest. His spirits rose. She was not unhappy, merely tired and curious. Boots and Kate were exchanging loving looks and a few quiet words so Rob also examined the room in which they were eating. So this was a dugout!

The room had been hacked out of the natural sandstone and the first thing Rob had been aware of was just how beautifully cool it felt. The surface of the walls and roof was rough yet curiously attractive. The roof was stippled in natural colours, cream and ochre and red-brown. The place was cosy, furnished just like a normal house with sideboard, chairs, a dresser and a table. Lighting was provided by hurricane lamps. They did not give a strong light but bathed the domestic scene with a rosy glow. Rob was impressed. Everything below ground, he thought, was much better than he had expected. He wondered how they managed for food and water but he was too tired to ask tonight. And the meal Kate had served up had been delicious. He stifled a yawn. God, he was tired. Boots was explaining the situation to Kate.

'Rob's coming in on our claim. He's got a small grub-stake and we picked up extra equipment in Dryton.'

'You don't mind, Kate?' Rob was anxious. He was a stranger to Boots's wife. Perhaps she would resent his sudden appearance.

His anxiety was dispelled by her warm smile.

'Boots knows what he's doing, Rob. I can see how pleased he is to have met up with you again. That's good enough for me.'

Irene gave a yawn so huge it cracked her jaw. Kate laughed and stood up. 'Poor kid's wore out, Boots.' She addressed Irene. 'Boots will take you over to Mrs Brewster's for the night. You *could* stay here, but you'd be a bit cramped and,' she blushed, 'I gather you're newly married. You'll want to be alone. We can catch up on the talking tomorrow.'

Boots also rose to his feet. He put his hand on Kate's softly rounded stomach. 'They're not the only ones who want to be alone. I need to catch up with my wife and junior here.'

Kate coloured. 'Sorry, you two. My husband!'

'Don't be sorry . . .'

'No need . . .'

317

Rob and Irene spoke together. They laughed and stood up.

'We'll sort out somewhere for you to live tomorrow,' said Boots. 'Now, we all need sleep.' He grinned at Rob and poked him in the ribs as he shepherded them out of the dugout. 'Or something,' he whispered.

Mrs Brewster's place was above ground and the bedroom she showed them to was over-warm, the atmosphere dry and with a trace of dust in the air which made Rob want to cough. He pulled a face; already he was beginning to appreciate the advantages of living underground. However, there were compensations. They had a window and a view.

'I'm so tired, Rob.' Irene put her arm around his waist. She had washed again and brushed out her luxuriant hair. Rob smiled when he looked down at her. From the one small, canvas bag she had brought with her, she had extracted a silky, clinging nightdress in a cream-coloured material. His heartbeat quickened when he saw how it moulded to her breasts and belly but then he also saw the patches of tiredness shadowed beneath her eyes.

'It's all right, love. I'm tired too.'

'But it's our wedding night!' She pressed her head against his chest. He folded his arms about her. Again, he felt glad she was a small woman. Tonight she made him feel ten feet tall. Silently, he made a vow to treasure and protect her.

'We'll have lots of other nights, Irene. The rest of our lives.' Doubt punctured his happiness when she did not reply, merely pressed closer to him.

'Please don't worry, love. Don't let this place get to you. I'll work hard. We'll get some money. Even if we don't make a lucky strike, we can move on if you hate it here. I'll always look after you, I promise.'

'It's all right, Rob.' Now she looked up at him and smiled. 'I like Kate, I think we shall be friends. And I'll make a good wife. I can cook and sew.'

'Sure.' Rob's voice teased her. 'Why else do you think I agreed to marry you?'

They fell silent and looked out of the window at the strange landscape. They moved closer together. The red earth road they had travelled earlier stretched out into the distance, now coloured a greyish-green by the moonlight. In the distance stood high, conical structures. They looked like giant anthills. Rob supposed they were debris from the mining shafts. Would he make a good miner? He shivered. The sky above them was huge, star-pricked. He was glad of the warmth of Irene next to him. Irene, his wife. He turned and kissed her and her mouth became alive beneath his. They turned away from the window, towards the bed.

'I guess,' he murmured, 'we're not so tired, after all.'

Chapter Thirty-One

Next morning, Boots dropped Irene off at his home to talk women's talk with Kate and then he took Rob on a tour of the minefields. 'Some lucky lad found opal here in 1915 and the fields have been extending ever since. I gather during the forties opal production almost ceased but then the Eight Mile Field was discovered and things picked up again. Now, prices are rising. I tell you, Rob, it's a good time to come in.'

'I just hope I don't let you down, mate.' Rob pointed to the conical mounds he had noticed the night before. 'What are they?'

'Mullock heaps, waste material from the mines.'

'But there's so many of them.'

'There's lots of mines. Under the law, it's one claim per person, one hundred and fifty feet by one hundred and fifty feet. We have to dig the shafts by hand.' Boots grinned. 'You can see why I really do need a partner, but it has to be someone you trust. Come on.' He stopped the truck. 'I'll show you my,' he corrected himself, '*our* claim.'

They descended the shaft, using holes in the wall which acted as steps. At the bottom, Boots lit candles. 'I must get some more carbide lamps,' he said. 'They're no great shakes but a damn sight better than candles.'

Rob said nothing. He felt apprehensive. He was glad to find it was cool in the passage-way. There was a good draught of air; it must be moving through some other shaft. Boots set off, his bulky figure brushing against the sides of the narrow tunnel, and Rob hurried after him. He held up the candle Boots had given to him. He had no desire to be left alone.

The light from the candle flickered on the sandstone walls of the tunnel. Suddenly, he caught his breath. He had spotted a vein of creamy white colour in the dull sandstone. He called to Boots to come back.

'What is it?' Rob pointed to the vein of colour. 'Is it opal?'

His friend's rumbling laugh disappointed him. 'No, mate. It's not as easy as that. That's "potch". It has no value except that it's a pointer to the fact real opal is somewhere about. When you see your first real lump of opal, you'll remember it, I promise you. Now, I'll explain a few more things then we'll go back and find somewhere for you and your lady to live.'

Before nightfall Rob and Irene had a home. A discontented miner had lit out after last year's disappointing season leaving instructions to his neighbours that anyone who came along with twenty pounds to spare could have his dugout and any furniture remaining.

'It's not like Kate's home, of course, but it will do for a start, won't it? Boots has promised to help me dig out another room before long and there's a table and chairs. We can buy a new mattress from the store.'

Rob looked anxiously at Irene. She was again dressed in her over-large trousers and jacket. She looked like a deliciously desirable female version of Charlie Chaplin. She wrinkled her nose at Rob, enhancing the likeness to the little clown. 'Our first home, Rob. We'll certainly remember it!'

She sighed and ran her hand over the dusty table. 'Will Kate lend me a scrubbing brush, do you think?'

'Irene!' Rob picked her up and whirled her round. 'You're marvellous. Let's go over to the store, see what they have there and what we can afford. Then we'll come back and clean this place up. We're going to be happy here, I just know it!'

Rob knelt in the tunnel, one hip pressed against the sandstone. He rested his pick and wiped the sweat from his face. God, it was hot! Boots had packed in an hour ago but only because it was his turn to cook a meal. The women had gone away for the hot season. So had many of the miners but Boots and Rob had decided to keep working, even though present conditions were atrocious. The past months had been unlucky for them. The opals they had found had been low grade and the German buyer who visited Coober Pedy had offered poor prices. All he had really wanted was 'crystal' opal.

'Stupid Kraut!' Boots had snarled; their dismal results had affected even his good temper. 'Does he think we just pick the stuff up off the floor?'

Rob's shoulder muscles were screaming in protest and he debated whether to call it a day. He decided to give it another half hour. He moved his lamp so the light fell fully on the rock face where he was working. It was essential to have the light, you never knew when colour was going to spark out at you. He grinned, his teeth shining whitely against his dusty, sweat-streaked face. Opals had got to him and he knew it. In many ways, Coober Pedy was a bloody awful place. It was lonely, heat-ridden and home to millions of flies but it also had something special.

A strange variety of people lived together in harmony. Aussies, Poles, Italians, English and Czechs were joined together in a common bond. The awesome isolation, the constant battle against the harsh climate united them and they all knew and shared in the continuing excitement, the hope of making a lucky strike. Rob swung his pick. The line of potch was still strong, maybe it was a lucky omen. He broke away some fragments of sandstone, then he caught his breath. In the dim light of the lamp, pinwheels of colour flashed. There were splashes of blue and orange. He sat back on his heels as excitement caught his throat. He put down his pick and took hold of a scraper. He gouged out the piece of opal and his excitement faded. It was just a small piece and he could find no more. But then, as he turned and twisted the opal, holding it beneath the lamp to bring

323

out the colours, his pleasure returned. It was a piece of opalised fossil shell and the most beautiful piece he had ever found. He stared down at the dancing colours. It was so old, millions of years old, and yet age and the pressure of the earth had made it more beautiful. And it was his. He had found it. At that moment, he knew he wanted to stay at Coober Pedy, whatever the future brought. But would Irene feel the same? As he put the opal safely in his pocket, then shovelled away the pile of mullock at his feet, he thought about his wife.

Throughout the past months he had watched Irene's initial enthusiasm fade away. He had watched and grieved that, as he grew more comfortable, flourished in this bleak environment, Irene grew more and more weary of the constant heat, dust and loneliness. He understood her feelings and, in his heart, applauded her efforts to make the best of things.

The other women living in and around Coober Pedy were used to the Outback. Indeed, Rob had heard one woman praising the place. How lovely, she had said, it was to be able to go visiting, have female company. That woman had grown up on an isolated cattle spread, hundreds of miles away from any human habitation. But Irene was different. Rob frowned. She had tried so hard. She kept their dugout clean and as free from dust as possible. She cooked surprisingly good meals with the tinned goods available and she went visiting the other women, mainly with Kate as her companion. But she was not happy. Rob pushed away his thoughts. They raised questions for which he had no answers. His fingers closed over his latest find. Tomorrow he might find something even better. He climbed the shaft leading out of the mine. Boots should have a meal ready by now.

It was late afternoon. A good day with not too much dust in the air. The sun brought out the colours of the land, the ochre and brown of the roads, the smoke-blue haze of the far distance. The cooler temperature above ground reminded Rob the hot season was ending. The womenfolk would return soon.

Boots had prepared 'floaters', meat pies in pea soup. 'This is bonzer,' joked Rob. 'With Kate away, you're turning into a cook.'

'Maybe, but I can't wait for next week when we head for Kingoonya railway depot to pick them up.'

'Me, too.' Rob took another mouthful of pie. He thought about Boots and Kate. They had something special. It wasn't just the sex thing. In fact, it was rare anyone saw the couple embrace but sometimes, seeing the look that passed between them, Rob felt . . . wistful. And Boots was crazy about his baby son.

Rob pushed his plate away. Well, every marriage was different. Irene now . . . he smiled when he thought of her. No doubt she would come back laden with parcels, things they couldn't really afford, and she'd be full of excitement and chatter. Then, later, they would go to bed. He felt the heat rise in his body. Abruptly, he pushed back his chair and took out his find.

'What do you think of this, Boots?' He put the opalised fossil shell on the table.

'Jeez, that's pretty.' Boots turned the piece over and over in his thick fingers. 'It could be worth quite a bit. It's mostly red-fire opal and because it's a fossil shell, that will put up the price. Whereabouts did you find it?'

Rob explained and the next day they marked out the area and worked for hours but with no luck. Finally, the line of potch ran out.

'Ah, well.' Boots flung down his pick. 'There's a good horizontal level further on.' He wiped his forehead. 'Always another day, eh?' Rob was silent as they returned home but Boots remained cheerful. His wife and baby would be home soon. Nothing could spoil that.

There was a small crowd of men assembled at the Kingoonya rail depot. When the train drew in Rob spotted Kate and Irene hanging out of a window and waving vigorously.

'There they are!'

He went forward with Boots to meet them. Kate

tenderly handed down the baby then jumped down and into Boots's bearhug. Irene followed her off the train. Rob hugged his wife.

'You've put on weight,' he said, smiling down at her. 'It suits you.'

'Oh, I've missed you.' She clung to him in a long kiss which was wonderful but which turned the tips of his ears red for he knew they had an interested audience.

There were scraps of information exchanged, waves to friends and wonderment over how baby Peter had grown before the two couples went to the Kingoonya hotel for a meal.

'I've bought a new radio, Rob, and a teaset. Oh, I hope it isn't broken. It shouldn't be, the shop assistant packed it well. And I've brought some seeds back with me. I'm going to have a garden.'

'You're an optimist, Irene.' Boots grinned at her. 'Rob's been busy too. Just wait until you reach home.' He stopped speaking when Rob shot him a warning frown.

'What is it? What have you done, Rob?' Irene clasped her hands like a small girl. 'You haven't had a lucky strike, have you?'

'Nothing brilliant.' Rob saw disappointment cloud her face. 'Tell me, how did you get on with your folks?'

After many weeks and an exchange of letters the rift with Irene's parents had been partially healed. They were still unhappy about the way things had worked out but Irene was their only child and they stopped short of breaking off contact with the young couple.

'Pa says next time I visit you must go too.' Irene dimpled. 'He says we must marry in their church. He doesn't really believe our marriage was legal.'

Her words caused an awkward pause. Rob scratched his nose. There were times when he wondered the same thing.

Boots broke the silence. 'Let's get moving, folks. It's a long road home.'

At Coober Pedy they said goodbye and went to their

own dugouts. Irene's face, pale with dust and fatigue, blushed rosily when she saw their home.

'Rob, how clever of you.'

He had fixed up wind lights by mounting a generator on a high tower next to the dugout which charged a bank of batteries.

'It's wonderful.' Irene stared round the dugout. 'What a difference it makes.'

'That's not all.' Rob pointed proudly to the corner of the room. 'It's a kero fridge. It's really good, Irene. It only needs a weekly fill of kerosene and an occasional trim of the wick and it keeps food really well. Do you like it?'

'It's marvellous.' Irene flung her arms around him. 'What a clever husband I have,' she murmured. 'And how I have missed you.'

The wind generator and the fridge were forgotten. Rob picked her up and carried her through to the small bedroom Boots and he had gouged out of the sandstone. How had he ever thought he could live without missing her?

Irene's happiness lasted four weeks. She cleaned the dugout thoroughly, set out her new teaset and invited all the women who lived in easy travelling distance to visit her. She planted her seeds which quickly died. The improved lighting enabled her to set up an old sewing machine she had begged from her mother. She cut and sewed herself three new dresses and then she flagged.

She began to nag. 'It's so boring here, Rob. There's nothing to do and nowhere to go. I don't even see you as much as I used to.'

'We have to work hard right now, Irene. There's a new buyer coming here in a couple of weeks.'

Her face brightened. 'Oh. Maybe you could ask him here for a meal. I'd give anything to see a new face.'

Rob felt a twinge of irritation. 'You haven't been back five minutes. Surely it's not that bad!'

'I'm sorry.' With one of her impetuous changes of mood she stood on tiptoes to kiss him. 'I can't help being like I am, Rob.'

'I know.' He kissed her back. 'If the buyer takes our stock, Boots thinks we can buy an air-operated jack hammer, maybe even a motorised winch. If we do, Irene, we'll be able to work much quicker. Then, when we make a good strike, we could have a holiday, go somewhere really nice.'

'Oh, I do hope we do.' Irene shuddered theatrically. 'I love you, Rob, and you're a good husband, but there are so many boring people living here. I'm frightened *we'll* get like that. Promise me we won't.'

'I promise.' He held her close and rested his chin on the top of her head. He didn't think his companions were boring. They worked hard and played hard. Why, when the truck which carried mail and stores arrived every Saturday the whole town turned out to meet and celebrate. They would laugh and talk, drink and dance. One of the Italians was organising a bowling league and several of the miners played musical instruments. Rob thought it was great. After years travelling alone, moving from one station to another, he revelled in the company, whether it be an oldtimer talking about days gone by or a younger immigrant speaking of his life in another country. Why didn't Irene find these people interesting? He sighed. He supposed women looked for different things in life.

Three months later, Irene whispered to him that she was pregnant.

'What?'

'Pregnant – you know.' She stared at him seriously then her face broke into a smile. 'Don't look like that. You're glad, aren't you?'

'If you are.'

'Of course I am. It is natural for a woman to have a baby. You know,' she lowered her voice, 'I'm sure our baby will be much prettier than Kate's Peter. I mean, with you and me as parents . . .'

For the first three months she bloomed. Her face rounded and her hair shone with vitality. She kept busy stitching tiny garments and embroidering exquisite motifs on the front of them. She made herself maternity dresses and took to wearing them much too early.

Kate warned her, 'You'll be sick of the sight of them before the baby arrives, Irene.'

'Pooh, that is nonsense. Greek women know how to have babies, how to be good mothers.'

Initially, Rob felt proud and happy but as he watched Irene, he began to experience a feeling of unease. She was showing the same excitement she had felt when they arrived at Coober Pedy. Then she had announced she would be the best housewife in the world. She had dusted and polished like a child playing house but now the dugout was becoming increasingly dingy and uncared for. Irene spent hours resting on the bed and reading and re-reading articles about baby-care contained in the tattered magazines she begged from the other women. Did she really want a baby or was she playing a new game called 'motherhood'? He was looking forward to being a father but even he, unused to children of any kind, knew it wasn't all smiling cherubs in spotless white gowns. He tried to talk to her about his worries but she smilingly dismissed him.

'Men know nothing about babies.'

He went to see Kate and talked to her, feeling disloyal and unhappy.

'I shouldn't worry.' Kate smiled at him. 'I understand what you're saying. Irene *is* very childlike in many ways but when the baby arrives she'll cope, I'm sure. Nature has a way of working things out.' Rob hoped she was right. He realised his feelings for Irene were changing. He still loved her, he thought he always would, but she was like a swift flowing stream that dazzled you with its brightness but which ran restlessly. There was no depth, no stillness in her.

Worry remained with him as he worked. Returning home one evening he stubbed his toe on a large rock littering the path. He was tired and the pain in his toe provoked an outburst of cursing. Rob rarely swore.

Feeling ashamed of himself he glanced round but fortunately there was no one near him. To cheer himself up he took his pouch from his pocket and looked at the latest pieces of opal he had unearthed. They were pretty good. He juggled the stones in his hand and they flashed their magic fire. With the money he would receive from this little lot he would be able to put more money into the partnership, thereby becoming equal partners with Boots. The flash of the stones reminded him of the earrings he had bought years ago for Dorothea Bellows. The woman in the shop had said they were opals. His face serious, he replaced the stones in the pouch. Dorothea Bellows! She'd be married now, he supposed. Probably had kids. He rather thought Dorothea would have grown into a similar kind of woman to Kate.

He sighed, then smiled as he patted his other pocket. One of the Italians had given him a new magazine for Irene. On the front cover was a picture of a baby about six months old. It was all gummy smiles, blowing bubbles. For the first time, Rob thought of his coming child as a *real* baby. A few more months and he would have a son or a daughter. Lost in thought, he again stumbled on the rough path but this time, he smiled. He took his foot and booted the offending lump of shale off the pathway and into the surrounding scrubland.

Chapter Thirty-Two

As Irene's pregnancy progressed she remained in remarkably good health but her early euphoria vanished. She wasn't sick once but as her figure blurred her temper deteriorated. She stopped going out.

'There's nowhere to go,' she told Rob when he remonstrated with her.

'But you need exercise. It can't be good for you, Irene, shut up in here all day. Shall I borrow the pick-up and run you over to see Olive Kenyon?'

Olive lived at Bolshevik Gully and was also expecting a baby.

Irene shook her head. 'I don't want to be jolted around in a truck, eaten by flies, just to see someone as fat as me.'

'You're not fat.' Rob put his arm around her. 'You look smashing and you know it. You're not six months yet and the baby hardly shows. And even when you're big, you know I'll still love you.'

Irene pushed him away. 'It's all right for you,' she said. 'You don't know what it feels like. It's already moving around and I can't sleep properly. And it will be ages before it's born. Rob—' Her eyes filled with tears as she looked at him.

'What?'

'I want to go home.'

He sighed, feeling guilty and miserable. 'Dryton, you mean?

'Yes. I'll have company there and my mother will look after me. If anything should go wrong, the doctor's just at the end of the street.'

'But nothing should go wrong. And you've just

admitted there's ages to go yet.' Rob hesitated. 'I could take you there but I couldn't stay, it wouldn't be fair to Boots. No, it's not possible, Irene. Not yet. After all, the flying doctor calls regularly and gives you a check-up. Look, if something's worrying you, let's call him up on the radio.'

Irene wouldn't look at him. 'It's not the same, Rob.'

He forced down a flash of temper. 'I expected you to want to be with your mother when the baby's born but I didn't expect this, Irene. The other women here seem to manage OK – why can't you?'

At last she raised her head and Rob was shocked at the expression of rigid obstinacy she wore.

'I've made up my mind. If you won't take me, I'll go on my own. I'm leaving next week.'

Of course, he took her back to her parents. He stayed in Dryton for three weeks, time away from the mine he could ill afford. Because she had won, Irene was soft and smiling again. She told her parents how much she loved Rob and how they were looking forward to the birth of their child. Rob was received with strained courtesy into the Botetsios household. Four days after their arrival, Mr Botetsios took him on one side and told him arrangements had been made for a 'proper' marriage ceremony, quiet of course, in view of the circumstances. Rob nodded and smiled and wondered at the empty feeling inside him.

The Greek Church was small but richly ornate with pearl-inlaid icons and a heavy scent of incense. Rob watched the priest dressed in sky blue vestments trimmed with cloth of silver bow and sway, and dutifully responded in accordance with Mr Botetsios's coaching but at the high point of the ceremony his inner thoughts flew back to the earth spirits described by Len and he smiled ruefully. He would always be a pagan at heart, he thought.

Irene saw him smile and beamed back at him. She looked beautiful in a dress her mother had especially made for her. It was cut on flowing lines to disguise the bulge beginning to show beneath her still slim waist.

Rob took hold of his wife's hand and squeezed it. 'Love you,' he whispered to her.

Rob left Irene with her parents and returned to Coober Pedy. He went to see Boots and found him making 'sausages' with gelignite.

'I've sussed a good area, Rob. It's promising, really promising.'

His hunch proved right. During the next few months the partners mined good milky-white opal. The 'once in a lifetime' find didn't materialise but their savings began to grow.

'Keep this up,' joked Boots, 'and we'll be sending our youngsters to public schools!'

Rob grinned without replying. He was more absent-minded than usual. The time for Irene's confinement drew closer and he thought of her constantly. He wrote to her regularly but her replies were spasmodic. He thought of her small frame and fretted at the thought of what she must go through. A week before the expected date he couldn't stay away any longer and he took the truck and drove to Dryton. He arrived very late at night to be met by a smiling Mrs Botetsios.

'You are too late by seven hours,' she told him. 'Irene had a baby boy at five o'clock.'

'How is she?' Rob's face was tight with tension.

'She's fine. Everything went well.'

Irene looked fine. When he entered her bedroom she sat up in bed and held out her arms. It was several minutes before he looked round for the baby.

'He's there.' She pointed to a wicker cradle in the corner of the room. His son had a pointed head, no hair and cloudy blue eyes. Rob thought he was wonderful.

'I'd like,' he said cautiously, 'to call him Alexander, after my father.'

Irene pulled a face. 'Maybe . . . My father is called Nicholas. A fine name, don't you think?'

Two weeks later, Rob took Irene and Nicholas Alexander Steyart back home, to Coober Pedy.

By the time Boots and Rob had unloaded the forty-four gallon drum of water from the utility truck they were sweating profusely. Rob pushed his hat to the back of his head and wiped his forehead with a grimy handkerchief.

'Thanks, mate. Jeez, I never knew us to get through so much water before.'

'Babies,' Boots answered succinctly. He waved his hand at Rob, jumped into the ute and drove away. A cloud of dust marked his departure.

Rob went indoors. Nine-month-old Nicky dropped the ball he was playing with and shuffled on his bottom towards his father. Rob picked him up and swung him high in the air. Nicky laughed and banged his hands on his father's head. He was a beautiful child with Irene's large, dark eyes and Rob's strong frame and well-shaped limbs.

'How's things?'

'All right.' Irene's voice was listless. She took plates from a shelf on the wall, carried them to the table and banged them down with unnecessary vehemence. Then she pushed her hair back with an irritable gesture. Rob suppressed a sigh and placed Nicky gently back upon the floor.

'We passed Steve's masterpiece on the way home,' he said, and squinted at his wife. 'It's coming on beaut.'

Steve Matusiac was one of the colourful characters living at Coober Pedy. He had a place in Crowder's Gully and was in the process of constructing an Australian coat-of-arms out of beer bottles. 'He says we have to drink more beer to help him get the thing finished.'

'Really.'

Irene was clearly disinclined for conversation. Nevertheless, he persisted. 'Oh, and Kate sent a message. It's Peter's birthday party next week. Will you take Nicky along about two o'clock?'

Irene was opening a tin of peas. She paused. 'Perhaps.' She tipped the contents of the tin into a saucepan. 'We might not be here.'

Rob frowned. 'What?'

She put the pan on the stove then turned to face him. 'I went down to meet the mail truck this morning. I needed some fresh stores and,' she paused, 'there was a letter from Mother.'

'Oh!' Rob's voice was heavy. 'She's on the same tack, I suppose?' He mimicked his mother-in-law's voice with wry humour. 'Coober Pedy's no place for a baby. Why don't you all come back and live in Dryton?'

'Well?' Irene challenged him. 'Why don't we?'

The expression in his eyes was bleak. 'We've been through it again and again.' He sighed. 'We're doing all right here. And what would I do in Dryton, for God's sake? Live off your father? Wait on tables in his restaurant?'

'Don't be ridiculous!' Irene's black eyes flashed sparks of anger. 'Of course you wouldn't. You found work there before.'

'True. And the money I earned barely kept *me*! Now I have you and Nicky to support, and before you say anything else, I will *not* live on handouts from your father. Please, love.' His voice softened. 'See sense. Life's not so bad here. We've got this place nice now, haven't we?'

When Irene had stayed with her parents, before Nicky had been born, Rob had gouged another room from the sandstone. They now had a sitting room. There were shelves on the wall filled with books and ornaments. There was a colourful carpet on the floor and easy chairs. In the kitchen stood a green-painted food cabinet and along one wall Rob had fitted a breakfast bar.

'Yes, you've worked hard but it doesn't alter the fact that when we step outside, there's nothing; nothing but flies, dust and heat.'

'You make it sound terrible, Irene. It's not that bad.'

335

'It is to me! I'm sick of it, Rob.' She was shouting now. 'Sick of it.'

Rob went and picked up Nicky. The shouting had caused the baby's grin to fade away and now he looked from his father to his mother with a solemn expression on his little face. Rob jogged him up and down in his arms.

'You're upsetting him,' he said. In contrast to Irene's, his voice was quiet.

'I'm sorry, but I must make you understand, Rob. I can't stay here any longer. I'm taking Nicky and going home.'

Rob's voice remained quiet but his face darkened. 'So Dryton's wonderful now, is it? I seem to remember you hated the place. And no one forced you to come here, you know. It was you who decided we'd dig up a fortune.'

'I know – you needn't remind me! But what about you? You promised, Rob. Just a few months, you said, and then we'd move on. Remember, we used to talk about going to Adelaide? Now it looks as though we'll be stuck in this dump for the rest of our lives.'

The hiss of a pan boiling over made them both start. Irene averted her face from Rob. Without further conversation, she dished up and put Nicky in his high chair but half-way through the silent meal she put down her knife and fork and pushed her plate away.

'I'm sorry, Rob, I really am, but I've had enough. I'll go and stay with my parents, probably for quite a while. Perhaps then you'll really think about things. Decide which is more important to you – your family or the damned opals!'

Rob drove his wife and baby to Dryton and his in-laws' house and stayed there for two days before bidding them a miserable farewell. The atmosphere in the house was strained. Rob, despite his unhappiness, tried to act normally but resentment lurked beneath his politeness when he watched Mrs Botetsios. He blamed much of Irene's restlessness on her mother's letters to her and he fumed when he saw his mother-in-law treating her daughter as if she was still a little girl. Irene, he also saw, revelled in such treatment. Haltingly, he tried to explain his feelings to Nicholas Botetsios.

'I just feel that if Irene gave it a chance, she'd come to appreciate the advantages of living at Coober Pedy. There's some good people living there, some nice women. It's a community with a good spirit.' His smile was embarrassed. 'I *do* listen to her, but I can't explain. After years of knocking about doing odd jobs, I've found something I can do well in a place I like. I'm a good miner, I have a feel for opals. Of course,' he sighed and scratched his head, 'maybe I'm just struck with the gambling fever and my partner and I will never find a lucky strike. At times I think I'm being selfish and she's right. But we've a nice little home there and if we leave, what shall I do for a living?' He looked earnestly at his father-in-law. 'I do want our marriage to work.'

'I know you do.' Mr Botetsios poured them both another glass of wine. 'And I'm sure my daughter loves you but—' He looked uncomfortable. 'I guess Irene is too used to getting her own way. My wife's very maternal and with only having one child . . .' He shrugged. 'Also this Coober Pedy, it does sound uncomfortable. A hard life for a woman?'

Moodily Rob swallowed his wine. 'It is,' he admitted.

Leave-taking was difficult. Irene burst into tears, Nicky copied his mother and Rob's own eyes were moist.

'We'll sort something out,' he promised his wife. He put his arms about her and Nicky and hugged them both. 'I promise.'

'And I'll come back when the weather cools down, Rob.' Irene's voice was husky with tears. She put her cheek against Nicky's dark hair. 'Wave bye-bye to your daddy, Nicky.'

Rob's throat felt strained, and he wavered. What

the hell did it matter what he did for a living, so long as they could be together? Then, behind Irene, he saw his mother-in-law's closed face and he knew it wouldn't work. He couldn't come back to Dryton and live in Irene's parents' home without money or prospects. Mrs Botetsios rested her hand protectively on Irene's shoulder and Rob forced a last smile then walked away. As he opened the door of the pick-up truck, an edge of resentment tempered his feeling of loss. The resentment was against Irene as much as her mother.

Weeks passed and Rob adapted, more quickly than he had anticipated, to living on his own. His experience as a boy in the Bush stood him in good stead and there were always Boots and Kate when he craved company. Boots had become like a brother to Rob and Kate was always there, ready to listen without offering advice or taking sides.

A few more miners drifted into the little town. One family had three small children and there was talk of building a school. The newcomers brought with them news of the outside world. They also said that prices for opal were rising. Then, one day, a Chinese buyer arrived and, to the amazement of the miners, offered twenty pounds per ounce for good crystal opal.

Rob and Boots worked longer hours and harder than ever.

'Found anything good?'

'Could be.' Rob was tumbling the rough opals in water to remove the sandstone. The partners were preparing a parcel of gems to offer to a visiting buyer. He handed some pieces to Boots who waited with a pair of tile snips to chip off the opals from the rough in order to expose the colour of the stones.

'Look at this.' He passed another piece to Boots who examined it, worked with the snips then held the remaining section up to the light. 'It's a beaut, Rob.' He gave it back.

The gem flashed a tangle of sparkling colours, yet

when Rob held it up to the light, he could see straight
through it. The familiar excitement stirred inside him.
'Fantastic,' he breathed.

'Yeah, pity it's the only one that's first-rate.'

A 'parcel' comprised a packet of different graded
stones. The grading was made on colour and quality
and only a small portion of excellent material was
found in most parcels. The prices paid reflected this.

'Well, that's it.' Boots packed up his belongings.
'Kate told me to invite you for a meal tonight.'

'Thanks, that would be great. If you're sure it's no
bother?'

'Don't be stupid, man.' Boots clapped his hat on
his head. 'You're family. You ought to know it by
now. Young Pete's always on about his uncle Rob.'

'He's a grand kid. We're good mates.'

Rob fell silent, feeling a sudden hunger to see his
own son.

With unusual perception, Boots tuned in to his
thoughts. 'Thinking about visiting Irene? Can spare
you if you want, now that we've got this lot sorted.'

'Maybe. In a couple of weeks.'

Nothing more was said. Boots knew the situation.

It was late when Rob left their dugout and went
back to his own lonely home. He lit a lamp, the wind
lights were on the blink again, and sat down to consider his position. Things couldn't go on like this; one
of them had to give, and he was beginning to realise it
would have to be him. If he was honest, he could
sympathise with Irene's point of view yet a stubborn
streak in him resisted the thought. Deep down, he
really believed they could make a good life in Coober
Pedy. He sighed and, unusually for him, took down a
bottle of whisky and poured out a generous measure.
He considered his marriage.

Wasn't that the real trouble? Be honest, *really* honest, he told himself. He had to admit he didn't miss
Irene too much. Nicky yes, Irene no. Oh, when he
went to Dryton feelings flared but – he took another
swallow of whisky – wasn't that mostly because he

just wanted to sleep with her? The sexual chemistry was there, strong as ever, but they sure had nothing to talk about! The things that interested her, shopping and clothes, left him cold. And he was damn sure he bored her. He gave a humourless smile. What a pity you couldn't spend your whole life in bed. But there was Nicky . . .

He rose from his chair and went outside. The night was silent. The dark sky above made him feel as insignificant as a scurrying ant. Yet he had a son. He stared up at the sky and remembered the ache of his own childhood. How he could never accept his father's disappearance. He decided he would go to Dryton and patch things up with Irene. Three months, that's all he would ask. Three months to sort things out with Boots, and then he would leave Coober Pedy. He sighed, yet felt more relaxed as he went back indoors to finish off the bottle.

Chapter Thirty-Three

Rob set off to visit Irene in a spirit of optimism. He had his own utility truck now and he decided to make the journey by road. The train was less boneshaking but there was still the problem of getting from the railway depot to the town. He made good time and as he jolted his way down Dryton's main street he smiled, a trifle grimly. Irene, since living in Coober Pedy, had begun to talk about Dryton as though it was a high point of civilisation but really, thought Rob, there wasn't much difference between the two places, give or take a few shops and the restaurant.

It was mid-afternoon and an air of somnolence hung about the place. Two women strolled along the sidewalk and an old dog was stretched out in the middle of the road. Rob slowed down and sounded his horn. The dog didn't even twitch an ear. Rob swore under his breath and manoeuvred his vehicle around the animal. For the umpteenth time a fly settled on his nose. He swatted it away. He could swear the same fly had travelled the last one hundred miles with him!

Mrs Botetsios answered his knock on the door. He was disconcerted to see surprise on her face.

'You got my letter, didn't you, telling you I was coming?'

'Yes, and I wrote straight back.'

They stared at each other then Rob said, 'Can I come in?'

Recollecting her manners, Irene's mother stepped back. 'Of course.' She watched him enter the house. 'Didn't you get my letter?'

'No.' Rob put down his bag and glanced round. 'Where's Irene?'

'I posted it last Monday.'

'Ah,' Rob looked round at her, 'mail only comes once a week.'

'Oh dear, that's a pity. You see, Irene's not here at present.'

Rob's brow creased. 'Where is she?'

'Come into the kitchen. I'll make us a drink.' Mrs Botetsios's movements were flurried. She went to fill the kettle. 'Nicky's here.' Rob's bewilderment increased. 'You mean, she's gone off somewhere and left Nicky behind?'

'She's having a short holiday.' Mrs Botetsios sounded defensive. 'Do you remember Rosie Grant, Irene's friend? Well, she's married now and her husband's taken her to live in Adelaide.'

She paused at the expression on Rob's face.

'I believe I can guess the rest,' he said slowly. 'Adelaide always did figure in Irene's scheme of things, didn't it?'

'She's not doing anything wrong.' With some force, his mother-in-law placed a cup of tea before him. 'My daughter has been extremely tense and unhappy lately.' She didn't add the words 'thanks to you' but she paused and Rob could almost see them, hanging in the air like a cloud. 'I became concerned about her and suggested she drop a line to Rosie. They were good friends. When Rosie replied and invited her for a short visit, both Nicholas and myself thought it a good idea. We helped her with the fare, of course.'

'Of course.' Rob pushed away the tea so violently some of the liquid slopped into the saucer. 'She didn't let me know. And what about Nicky?'

'He's fine. My husband has him out at the moment but they will be back shortly.'

'How long does Irene intend to stay in Adelaide?'

'Not too long.' Mrs Botetsios glanced at the clock. 'I must prepare Nicky's tea. Nicholas and I will have to go to the restaurant soon.' She anticipated Rob's next question. 'We have everything organised. A good little woman comes and babysits for Nicky when we're working.'

'Well, you'll be able to cancel her for a start.'

Rob's voice was sarcastic and his mother-in-law coloured but she answered him smoothly: 'Yes, of course. You'll want to spend time with your son, now you're here.' She waited and Rob wondered if she expected him to say thank you. He did not do so.

Nicky was a revelation to Rob. He had loved his son as a baby in a protective responsible way but now he delighted in the alert, responsive toddler his child had become. During the three days of his visit he determined more and more to patch things up with Irene. When the time for his departure came, he could hardly tear himself away from the boy.

'Ask Irene to write as soon as she gets back,' he requested of his father-in-law. 'Tell her it's time the Steyarts were a proper family again.'

Nicholas Botetsios nodded his head. 'I will, Rob. Depend upon it.'

Back at Coober Pedy Rob flung himself into work. If he had to leave the place, he wanted to make as much money as he possibly could. He discussed business arrangements with Boots and they set up meetings with bank officials to decide how their mining assets could be split. Then he waited for Irene's letter. Two weeks went by then three and still she had not written. He wrote to his father-in-law and fretted when he received no reply. He wanted to return to Dryton but knew that was impossible. Boots had carried more than his share of the burden of work at the mine during the last few months. Then his friend fell down one of the many unmarked shafts. Fortunately, help was at hand and he was hauled up and found to be without serious injury but he was cut and bruised and his left ankle was sprained. He was put to bed and told to stay there for a week.

'What a bloody stupid thing to do,' he grumbled to Rob. 'I thought I knew all the danger spots.'

'At the rate they're digging now, mate,' replied Rob, 'it's a wonder half the population of Coober Pedy haven't broken their necks.'

Boots had almost recovered when Irene's letter finally arrived. Rob had congregated with the usual crowd on mail day. Norman Angus, the mail man, knew Rob was hoping for a letter and his sun-reddened face was grinning as he handed over the envelope.

'Here you are, mate. Hope it's good news.'

Rob took the letter back to his dugout. The envelope was addressed in his father-in-law's handwriting but once opened, another, smaller envelope fell out. This was addressed in Irene's hand. With a tightening of his stomach, Rob opened it.

Rob,
This is a hard letter to write but before you get mad, think for a moment. You'll know that I am speaking the truth. There is no way we can be happy together. You like your way of life and I hate it. I didn't realise just how much until I came to visit Rosie.

Oh, Rob – please understand. Adelaide is all that I imagined. I'm sorry, but I am going to stay here. I feel truly alive for the first time in my life! I'm still with Rosie and her husband but I have been offered a job. I'm going to be an usherette at a theatre. The money's good so I shall be able to get a place of my own before too long.

I have explained things to my mother and she has agreed to keep Nicky until I get things sorted out. Don't worry about him. He loves being with his grandparents. I think he is happier with them than with me, you know how short-tempered I can be. When things settle down, we'll fix up for you to see him from time to time. Don't hate me

too much, Rob. You know you want to stay in
that awful place, goodness knows why!
Yours, Irene

A terrible anger filled him. He crumpled the letter in
his hand. Here he was, willing to change his whole life
for Irene, and now she had dismissed him! It was half
an hour before he had calmed down enough to go and
see his friends.

'What are you going to do, Rob?' Kate's face was
sombre.

'I'm going to sort things out!'

He turned his set, unhappy face towards Boots.
'I'm sorry, mate. But I promise you, this is the last
time I'll be chasing about. I'm going to find Irene and
settle things. If she decides to stay in Adelaide, she
can, but one thing I promise you – if I return to
Coober Pedy, I'll have my son with me!'

By the time Rob reached the outskirts of Adelaide, he
was totally exhausted. The journey had been gruelling
and his body demanded sleep. He kept a watch for
somewhere to stop; a place to eat a decent meal, have
a bath and a rest, but he was almost into the city
before he spotted a small hotel. He turned his truck
into the driveway with a sigh of relief. Yet once in his
hotel room he couldn't sleep. He forced himself to
rest quietly on the bed but when he tried to relax,
endless pictures flickered behind his closed eyes.

The guilt and confusion on his in-laws' faces when
he disclosed to them the contents of Irene's letter;
Nicky's small hand waving goodbye to him; and
scenes from the journey itself. Rob had tramped
many a road in his early days but he had never been as
far as Adelaide. In happier circumstances he would
have enjoyed the experience. He had travelled
through plains pearl-grey with saltbush, seen twisted,
stunted trees, mulga and gidyea, ironwood and
corkwood. Always an observer of nature, and despite
his preoccupation, he had marvelled at the way this

hardiest of growth adapted to a meagre rainfall. Then had come the sight of the Flinders Ranges, starkly eroded red peaks soaring above the sombre plains.

He sighed and sat up, swung his legs down from the bed and supported his head in his hands. It had been a waste of time and money stopping at the hotel. He couldn't rest. He might as well push on, find Irene and confront her.

The Adelaide Hills made an idyllic approach to the city but he was not looking at the scenery now. All the times they had discussed coming to Adelaide! His mouth stretched into a mirthless grin. He slowed down and checked the road signs. Then he glanced at the piece of paper on the dashboard which showed Rosie Bell's, Rosie Grant's that was, present address.

Once in the city he had to concentrate on his driving. He had never known so much traffic. Rob reckoned he was a good driver and used to hazards. But in the Bush the hazards were 'roos or emus dashing across the road in front of you, potholes or the occasional 'willy-willy', the roaring winds that could spring up so quickly. If you got caught in one of those you could be stuck in the outback for a couple of days for the ferocious winds blew the red grit high into the sky then allowed it to fall again into every crack and crevice of the vehicles, totally immobilising them. These were things Rob could cope with, but the way the Adelaide folk drove had him grasping the wheel of his truck nervously. He did see, however, that he was driving through a gracious city. On the western slopes terraced high above the buildings were vineyards and the properties he drove past were solid and well built. Trees lined the wide streets and there were lots of shops. No wonder, thought Rob, and his heart softened a little towards his wife, no wonder Irene was loath to leave.

He found the street he was looking for and parked the truck. He wiped his hands on his pants before pressing the doorbell. A big girl with wispy brown hair opened the door. Immediately, Rob recognised

Rosie. When he introduced himself, she bit her lip, stared at him a moment then invited him in.

'We rent the upstairs flat,' she explained, leading the way up a flight of stairs. 'But we're hoping to buy our own place soon. Clive works for a meat-packer.'

She asked him to enter a sparsely furnished, white-painted room, gestured to him to sit down and perched herself uneasily on the edge of a chair opposite him.

'I knew someone would turn up,' she said, a nervous quiver in her voice, 'but I didn't know who.'

Rob stared at her and a cold feeling started in his stomach. 'She isn't here any more, is she?'

Rosie shook her head. Her sandy eyelashes blinked rapidly. 'This is awful,' she whispered. 'I feel it's partly my fault.'

'You mustn't feel that.' Rob dropped his gaze from her face and looked down at his hands instead. 'But please, tell me . . .'

She nodded, straightened in her chair. 'I was surprised to get her letter,' she said. 'But we were friends so I asked Clive if she could visit and he said "OK, invite her". She arrived and it was great, at first. Irene just loved it here and she was such good company, you know how bubbly she can be.' Rosie shot a look at Rob and hurriedly continued: 'We went shopping and at the weekend Clive got the car out and we showed her the sights. But then,' she clasped her hands together, 'it got a bit difficult. She stayed ten days before Clive sort of hinted . . . well, you know. He thought she ought to go home. After all, there was her little boy.'

Again she looked at Rob, and again he said nothing.

'Eventually,' Rosie continued, 'he told her straight out, she'd have to go home. She was sleeping on the couch, you see, and there's not much room in the flat. We only have the one bedroom. Anyway, I could see she was upset and I felt terrible. She went out early next day and when she came back she told me she had got a job! I was astonished. I had no idea she meant to stay in Adelaide. What about Nicky? I asked her, and what about you, of course.' Rosie blushed and ducked her head. 'Then Irene began to cry and it all came out; about your difficulties, I mean.' She stopped.

'Go on, please.' Rob turned away and looked out of the window. A wind must be getting up, he thought. The green boughs of the tree outside were swaying from side to side. It must be nice, living so high you can see the tree tops.

'She'd got a job at a theatre. She said the pay was pretty good. She had all kinds of plans. She would find a place to rent and bring Nicky here. She said she was determined he would grow up in a proper place, a civilised place. I asked her who would look after Nicky when she was at work but she wouldn't listen. She was all lit up and excited, the way she always is when she gets a new idea.'

Rob's throat was dry. He wished Rosie would offer him a cup of tea. 'Then she said, could she stay for just a few more days, until she found somewhere to live.' Rosie's voice stumbled to a halt.

'I see.' Rob rubbed his hand over his face. 'So she's in a boarding-house now, is she? If you can just let me have her address?'

'I can't.' Rosie plucked at her dress. She sniffed. 'I'd better tell you the rest.'

'You mean, there's more?'

She nodded, fixed her eyes on his face and launched into a rapid speech which Rob, listening to her, guessed she had rehearsed in her mind for this very occasion.

'Irene fixed up a place to live but then the day before she was due to move in, she came home looking absolutely radiant. She kept on and on about this couple she had met at the theatre, become friendly with. She'd mentioned them before, and a couple of nights she'd gone out with them for a drink.'

An embarrassed look crept across Rosie's face. 'To be honest, we hadn't paid too much attention. Things were a bit difficult between Clive and me. We were just glad to have a few hours together on our own. Anyway, she said this couple had a little boy Nicky's age. They were in theatre work and were going to travel the country. I didn't catch the details, but she said they had asked her to go with them. I thought it sounded peculiar but she said, no, she would look after the two boys and live with them so she wouldn't need a flat after all.'

Rob's brow wrinkled. 'That's crazy! Let's get this straight – she's gone off with strangers, you don't know who? My God!' He sprang to his feet. 'Anything could have happened to her! She never collected Nicky.' Rosie stayed quietly in her seat. Her eyes were clouded. He glared at her. 'You should have stopped her.'

'We tried to talk to her, Rob, but she wouldn't listen. To be honest, it was a relief when she left.'

'I knew nothing of all this. She wrote to tell me she had found a job as an usherette, but this . .' He walked over to Rosie and glared down at her. 'You must have a forwarding address, something.'

'No. But . . .' Rosie hesitated. 'Please don't worry so much. I'm sure she's all right.'

'How can you say that?'

'Because I saw Irene before she left. She . . .' Rosie cleared her throat. 'She *said* it was a family she'd met but it was just one name she used all the time. It was Bruce. Bruce said this and Bruce did that . . . and then, the last time I saw her,' Rosie's voice sank into a whisper, 'I heard a car stop outside and I looked out. It was a beautiful car, looked really expensive. A tall, fair-haired man got out and opened the door for her. She came into the house and rushed into the flat. She was dancing on air. She collected the remainder of her stuff and I noticed she had a thick silver bangle on her wrist. I'd never seen it before. I commented on it because it was so beautiful and she blushed and said it was a present.

'I'm sorry, Mr Steyart, but you mustn't worry about Irene, because I'm pretty sure it wasn't a family she went away with.' Rob turned on her so abruptly Rosie jumped but she met his gaze bravely. 'I know it's hard, but remember – Irene always wanted the best.'

The room was warm but a cold finger reached out and touched Rob's spine. His jaw muscles felt stiff.

'Thanks, Rosie, for telling me the truth. But,' he sighed, 'it's the truth as you see it. I know Irene has her faults but I can't believe she would go away and leave Nicky without a good reason.'

Rosie stood up. 'I'm sorry. Look, shall I make some tea? You look as though you could use a drink.'

Now that she had offered, Rob no longer wanted to stay. He had to get away and think.

'No thanks. I'll be off now.'

She accompanied him down the stairs. 'If you'll leave your address, I'll contact you immediately if I hear anything.'

Rob wrote down his address on the back of an envelope, gave it to her, thanked her, then went and sat in his truck.

He stayed there a long time. He was deeply shocked. Surely Rosie had misinterpreted Irene's actions? His wife was impulsive, childish at times, but she wouldn't, couldn't, just go away like that, leaving Nicky behind. Yet a little voice whispered to him that she had been willing enough to leave her son in Dryton. No, that was different. She had only intended staying in Adelaide for a short holiday. Rob shook his head. He must *do* something. He must find his wife. He took a deep breath then twisted the key in the ignition. But as he drove away, Rosie's words echoed in his mind and they held the ring of truth.

He checked the addresses Rosie had given him. First, he went to the theatre. Yes, the Manager confirmed, Irene had worked there for a short period of time.

'A bright, attractive young woman.' He shook his head. 'I was most disappointed when she just walked out and never came back. You never can tell, can you?'

Rob asked more questions but the Manager knew no one involved with his theatre with the Christian name of Bruce. Rob left the theatre and toured the nearby bars, asking his questions. Again, he had no luck. Finally, he went to the local newspaper office. He arranged for regular notices to be placed over the next three months asking for information regarding the whereabouts of Irene Steyart, née Botetsios. He paid in advance. Then he parked the truck in a side-street, went into the nearest bar and quietly and systematically got blind drunk.

Chapter Thirty-Four

The lift glided smoothly up to the fifth floor of the business headquarters of Slater, Curzon & Whitney Enterprises. Dorothea got out, walked along the richly carpeted, softly lit corridor and pushed open the door at the end.

'Morning, Jenny.' She nodded to the slim, middle-aged woman seated behind the desk facing the door. 'I've an appointment with Mr Whitney at 10.30.' She glanced at her watch. 'I'm just a few minutes early.'

Adam Whitney's secretary smiled at her. 'There's someone with him right now. Would you like a coffee while you wait?'

'No thanks.' Dorothea picked up a newspaper from a side table and moved across the room to sit by the window. 'Isn't it a glorious day?'

'Um, beautiful. But then,' Jenny Laker turned back to her typing, 'May's always been my favourite month.'

Dorothea opened the newspaper. Glaring headlines announced: CONSERVATIVES WIN 1955 ELECTION! The result had been expected but she grimaced when she read that less than one and a half million Labour supporters had bothered to vote. Her father's prediction that the Labour Party would lose its way seemed to have come true. Because of Dennis's political views, Dorothea had followed the Election with interest. She knew the result would disappoint and infuriate him. When Aneurin Bevan, the ex-coal miner, had been defeated by a young economist-administrator educated at Winchester, Dennis had said the party had lost its sense of mission. Perhaps he was right. Yet for the young and politically disinterested, the future seemed bright.

She folded her newspaper and again glanced at her watch. Dorothea looked forward to her meeting with her employer. It had been nine months since she was last in this office and almost two years since she had first entered the building. Her mind drifted back to that day.

On her first visit, she had been too immersed in her own misery to appreciate the distinction of her surroundings. Dorothea gave a rueful smile. Jenny must have wondered who on earth this person with the haunted face was! Thank God Adam Whitney had agreed to see her. When Jenny had shown her into his office, he had given her a keen look, risen from his seat and poured her a large brandy. He had told her to drink it down then busied himself with his papers until she recovered her composure. Finally he had looked up.

'How can I help, Dorothea?'

She had fumbled in her bag, produced his card and pushed it across the desk towards him. He had picked it up.

'You need a job, is that it?'

She had nodded, finally found her voice. 'Yes, if you have anything. Something's happened. I . . .' She steadied herself. 'I need to move, as quickly as possible. I hate to ask favours, but . . .'

He had studied her face then pressed the intercom on his desk and issued instructions to his secretary. Moments later, Jenny had entered and handed him a buff-coloured folder. He had thanked her. Without looking in Dorothea's direction, Jenny had left the room, closing the door softly behind her. Adam Whitney had studied the contents of the folder and Dorothea had watched him. The brandy had revived her, driven away the deathly chill inside her.

She had thought of Mr Whitney as a frail old gentleman but now she began to revise her opinion. It was true that he was elderly and his form was slight but she now saw that his frame was wiry rather than frail. As an occasional guest at the Doran he had given the impression of being a typical retired gentleman but now he seemed completely different. Dressed in banker's black, a thin gold chain showing across his waistcoat, his every movement showed decisiveness and authority. She jumped as he abruptly pushed away the file and looked at her.

'There's a vacancy at the Menzies Hotel in Paddington. It's not one of our top-liners but you would be able to handle the work without difficulty and you can live in, if you wish. The salary's fair.' He stopped speaking and she realised he was awaiting her reply.

'That would be wonderful,' she stammered. 'I can't thank . . .' To her horror, her voice broke. Then relief overwhelmed her.

'Don't be humble, Dorothea.' Mr Whitney sighed. He transferred his gaze to a point over her head. 'I'm not doing you a favour. You're a damn good receptionist and I'm happy to employ you. It's my job to find people with potential. You show promise. I can use you.' He shrugged. 'The Menzies job is merely a stopgap, but until you sort yourself out . . .'

He hesitated, then went on: 'I won't ask what kind of trouble you're in. It's obvious you are deeply distressed.' He gave a dry cough. 'I was also sorry to hear you lost the child you were expecting. However,' he took a fountain pen from his breast pocket and scribbled a note on a sheet of paper, 'we must all find our own salvation.' He gave the note to her. 'Give this to Jenny and she'll give you the information you need.' For the first time he smiled. 'If you can get your private life under control and work damn hard, I can promise you that you won't always be a receptionist.'

'Thank you.' Aware her interview was at an end, Dorothea stood up. Impulsively, she stuck out her hand across the desk. 'I won't let you down,' she said.

Mr Whitney put out his own hand. 'I know that,' he replied. 'That's why I'm giving you a job.'

She had kept her word. After six months at the

Menzies, she had been moved on to another, finer
hotel. The Ogmore had been close by the National
Postal Museum. Dorothea had been astonished to
find how many philately enthusiasts came to London
just to visit the museum in King Edward Street. As
always, she took it upon herself to find out a little
about the place so she could converse intelligently
with the guests. After two months she could hold her
own in a conversation about the philatelic corre-
spondence archives of Thomas de la Rue and Company who had furnished stamps to over one hundred
and fifty countries since 1855, or discuss the RM Collection. She also undertook to furnish details of the
special exhibitions held at the museum.

Then she moved to the Kenilworth Hotel where she
realised just how many Americans were coming to
visit the Old Country. She found out they wanted to
experience the historical aspects of England – except
when it came to the bathroom and toilet facilities!
Every day she dealt with some irate couple from Texas
or New Jersey who couldn't understand why hot
water suddenly ran cold and why they had bathrooms
and not showers. She had earned her money at the
Kenilworth.

From time to time she would receive a brief memo
from Mr Whitney's secretary requesting her atten-
dance at seminars. On the first occasion she had gone
to the address given wondering what to expect. She
soon realised that her employer demanded his
employees learn every facet of the hotel trade.
Dorothea, in company with other hopefuls, had spent
a day in the kitchens of one of the largest hotels in
London, observing their procedures, and on other
trips she had been instructed in how refuse was collected or how paperwork relating to long-stay visitors
from the Middle East was collated to answer the Foreign Office's requirements.

Now she was Head Receptionist at the
Wellingborough, one of the most important hotels in
the city. She had learned so much during the past two

years, including the fact that the unassuming gentleman who had used the Doran was actually a highly respected entrepreneur who had built up a business empire with assiduity and dedication. Dorothea smoothed her skirt with her hands. She was looking forward to seeing Mr Whitney. She had something of interest to tell him.

The buzz of the intercom broke into her thoughts. She jumped, then stood up as Jenny nodded to her. 'He'll see you now.'

When she reached the door, it opened suddenly and a tall man with dark brushed-back hair hurried out. Dorothea saw an expression of suppressed annoyance on his face but when he noticed her, he stood to one side politely enough, to allow her to enter Adam Whitney's office. She caught an impression of thin, attractive features before he turned away and closed the door behind her.

'Come in, Dorothea.' Mr Whitney rose to greet her. He shook her hand warmly and offered her a sherry.

'No, thanks.' She sat down in the chair he indicated and watched as he poured himself a drink.

'Surely you haven't dressed yourself up so attractively just for an old man like me?' Adam returned to sit behind his desk.

'But of course.' Dorothea smiled. She knew her employer liked to see well-groomed women and she had made a special effort with her appearance. She was wearing a mint green tailored suit with a straight skirt which showed her long, slim legs to advantage. The favourable effect was further enhanced by her plain calf court shoes and matching handbag.

'May I return your compliment with one of my own? I must say, you look very well.'

'You may indeed.' There was colour in Adam Whitney's usually pale cheeks and his eyes sparkled. 'That's because I have just concluded a spirited conversation, or should I say argument, with my nephew. I enjoyed it. Life gets boring, you know, when people are afraid to say what they really think. At least there are still a few in this organisation who are prepared to disagree with "the old man". Charles knows my way is to pick people who can do the things I want in the way I want things doing, but he says that's old-fashioned paternalism and I should relinquish some of my responsibilities. What do you think, Dorothea?'

'I think,' she replied cautiously, 'that you would have to be very sure of the person to whom you are considering passing on these responsibilities. I also think employees respond positively to being valued and cared for, even if it is in a paternalistic way, but they also like to know what's going on.'

'That's interesting.' Adam twisted the stem of his sherry glass. 'I . . .' He broke off as the telephone shrilled. 'Excuse me, Dorothea.'

He lifted the receiver and she waited a little impatiently as he talked of ground rents and back-leasing arrangements. Normally, she would have found such conversation interesting but today she wanted to tell him her news. Finally, he replaced the receiver.

'Now,' he began, 'as you know, this appointment was set up to discuss your next move. I have a proposition.'

'So have I,' Dorothea interrupted him, then paused. 'I'm sorry, I didn't mean to be rude but I wanted to show you this.' She passed Adam a large manila envelope then sat back in her chair. He opened the envelope and stared down at the contents. She waited for him to speak and when he did not, she went on: 'It came through last week. I can't believe it. I came top – out of one hundred students.'

Finally, her employer looked up and she was surprised to see a stern expression on his face.

'Why didn't you tell me you were studying accountancy, Dorothea?'

'I wanted to be able to produce something solid,' she replied. 'You know I've always enjoyed working with figures and so I enrolled for this course. It was difficult to fit in the studying but as I was working shifts, I managed it. I knew you were considering me for a new post . . .'

Her words trailed away as the expected congratulations were not forthcoming.

'You must have worked extremely hard.' Adam Whitney replaced the certificate in the envelope and passed it back to her. 'But you should have told me. You see, I have totally different plans for you.'

'Oh!' She said no more but her colour heightened and there was defiance in her suddenly upright figure. Her employer tapped a pencil on the blotter on his desk and his voice sharpened.

'I'm sorry if you're disappointed, but listen to me. Dorothea, I have dozens of accountants within the company's framework, I have dozens of financial advisers – and they all have better qualifications than you! I'm sorry, but that's the truth. However,' he stole a glance at her set profile, 'you possess something else I can use.'

He pulled some papers towards him. 'I've been reading your file. You have the facility to get on with people. You are good at smoothing down awkward characters, you keep things running smoothly, you make people feel good.'

'And they are useful assets, are they?' Dorothea's expression was sardonic.

'Indeed they are.' Adam leaned back in his chair. 'There's a vacancy in my Publicity Department. You'd find the work varied and interesting. Publicity release notices to the Press, they co-ordinate personnel work. They do lots of things.' He smiled at her. 'Much more interesting than reception work.'

She did not smile back. 'I don't know anything at all about publicity.'

'Then it's time you learned.' Adam's voice developed a sharp edge. 'If you want to rise in this company, Dorothea, you need to know something about everything. Of course, if you prefer to remain a receptionist,' he stood up, 'there are plenty of other hotels.'

Dorothea rose to her feet. She felt let down and upset at the dismissal of her hopes but she met her employer's eyes steadily. 'I'm sorry, Mr Whitney, I should have let you know about the accountancy course.'

'Yes, you should, but nothing is ever wasted.' Adam's voice was abstracted. She knew he was still annoyed. She moved towards the door. 'Jenny has the details.' He waved his hand in farewell.

The old devil! He always got his own way. Dorothea's liking for the old man was momentarily swamped by anger. True, he had been her saviour but she had worked damned hard for his company over the last two years and the way he had dismissed her achievement at coming top of her year at the Economics and Accountancy College aroused her resentment.

She closed the door behind her with the suspicion of a bang and said aloud: 'Devious old sod!'

She heard a shocked exclamation. She turned and blenched. Jenny was staring at her with rounded eyes and next to her was the man who had brushed past Dorothea on her way into Adam Whitney's office. The man who was Adam Whitney's nephew. The exclamation had come from Jenny; that was obvious from the amused expression on the tall man's face.

'My sentiments exactly,' he said genially.

Dorothea blushed. 'I shouldn't have said that. I have a high regard for Mr Whitney, it's just that . . .' She paused.

'He *is* a devious old sod.' The man had been sitting on the edge of Jenny's desk, obviously passing the time of day. Now he stood up. 'It must be lunchtime. As we are both employees of Slater, Curzon & Whitney, and we both know and love our employer, let's have a bite to eat together? There's a good coffee shop on the corner.'

'Oh, thank you but no.' Then Dorothea paused. The spat with Adam Whitney had sent adrenalin coursing through her and this stranger, she thought, was most attractive. For a long time, she had lived in a sort of limbo as far as personal relationships had been concerned. Time had passed and the shock of Greg's betrayal had become less acute but she had never felt the slightest interest in any of the men she had met at work. Also, she had spent all her free time studying, and to what avail? She squared her shoulders and smiled. 'On second thoughts, that would be very nice,' she said.

Chapter Thirty-Five

Dorothea went off to her first day's work in the Publicity department still feeling rebellious. As Head Receptionist at the Wellingborough, she had managed a team of three junior receptionists and enjoyed the facilities of her own comfortable office. In Publicity she shared a desk with a Mr Sanders, an elderly man who incessantly smoked strong-smelling cigars and leered at her through heavy-lensed, horn-rimmed glasses. The department was situated in an adjacent building to the head offices of Slater, Curzon & Whitney but whereas Mr Whitney's surroundings were luxurious, Publicity's arena of work was positively spartan. Windows were badly fitted and draughts whistled through the rooms on windy days. Dorothea forsook her smart suits and went to work in sweaters and trousers. Not only did she feel warmer, but she hoped the veiling of her legs might dissuade Mr Sanders from continually groping for her knees beneath the desk.

The only advantage, she thought, was the increase in salary. Mr Whitney had always dealt fairly with her in that regard but within hotel structures of pay, reception work was notoriously poorly rewarded. Perhaps, thought Dorothea, I can save now, start to look round for a place of my own. She was sick of living in hotels.

Her immediate superior was a man called Cecil Buchman. Their first meeting was not auspicious. His first words to her, after a brief handshake were, 'Ah, Miss Bellows – Mr Whitney's protégée, I believe?'

'Am I?' She had looked up at him, startled.

He had shrugged. 'What experience have you had in publicity, Miss Bellows?'

'Why, none.'

'That's a pity. Most of my team have spent two or three years working in Publicity departments in the provinces before coming here.' He paused. 'Still, Mr Whitney usually knows what he's doing.' He had looked down at his papers. 'I'll leave you to shake down on your own for a couple of days, then we'll see what you are capable of.'

'Thank you, Mr Buchman. Thank you very much,' she had replied, her voice matching his in coolness.

She returned to her half-share of the desk and sat down. She noticed the buzz of conversation in the main office died away as soon as she entered. She looked about her defiantly. Mr Sanders pushed across a pile of newspapers. 'The boss told me to give you these,' he said. 'They'll give you a feel for the work.'

He smiled his thick-lipped smile and, sliding his hand under the desk, gave her thigh a squeeze. Dorothea took a deep breath. She reached for her bag and brought out a packet of cigarettes and a box of matches.

'Anyone object?' she asked with a sweet smile. No one did. Mr Sanders continued to caress her leg, a stupid smile on his face. Dorothea smoked rarely, only in times of stress. She lit a cigarette, drew deeply upon it then placed the glowing tip on the back of Mr Sanders's hand. He sat back in his chair with a muffled yelp. Dorothea felt better, particularly when she saw two of the women in the room suppressing smiles. She pulled the papers towards her and began to study them. She'd show them how good she was!

In Publicity, Dorothea found the hours long and often hectic. There were always deadlines looming. Every morning a welter of newspapers came into the department and the staff took turns to go through them all, looking for references to the businesses operating under the banner of Slater, Curzon & Whitney. The department did not place advertisements

themselves, that would have been vulgar, but Dorothea
learned as she became more friendly with her colleag-
ues that great importance was attached to keeping
good news items before the public. If a famous actor
or politician booked into one of their hotels, or if a
particularly prestigious event was staged, then Publicity arranged for photographs to be released and all the
leading newspapers were contacted and invited to
come to a press reception. Alternatively, if a strike at
one of their establishments occurred or a guest died of
a heart attack, it was Publicity who found a way to
stop the news leaking out.

On her second day at work, two of the women
who worked in the office asked Dorothea if she would
like to have lunch with them. Seated in a nearby café,
they congratulated her on her treatment of Mr
Sanders.

'I've been wanting that pig to get his come-uppance
for years,' said one of them.

It took longer to win the approval of the other
members of the publicity team, and after working in
the department six weeks, Dorothea appreciated their
point of view. The work *was* specialised and she realised she had a lot to learn. Many a night she returned
to her room at the Wellingborough feeling depressed
and lonely. If only she could get a place of her own!
Once she had ceased working at the hotel, her links
with the hotel staff had broken. She could hardly, she
thought, go down to reception and distract the girls
from their work simply to talk to her. And yet her new
workmates could hardly be called friendly. When she
was working for the accountancy examinations, she
hadn't bothered about her lack of friends, but now
her life seemed completely made up of work. She was
in this mood one evening when she received a telephone call. The caller was Charles Richardson.

'Sorry, who did you say?'

'Don't tell me you don't remember me?'

The voice sounded genuinely put-out and Dorothea
felt a spurt of amusement when she finally realised

who was speaking. She didn't suppose many women forgot a man like Charles Richardson.

'No, of course I remember you. I was thinking of something else, that was all. But I am surprised to hear from you. And how did you know where to find me?'

'Jenny, old Adam's secretary, let me have the telephone number. You don't mind, do you?'

'No.' But Adam Whitney might, thought Dorothea. She was surprised that Jenny had passed on information to Adam's nephew, even if he did work for the company. Yet, remembering his charm on the day he had taken her to the coffee shop, perhaps it wasn't so surprising.

'So, what can I do for you, Mr Richardson?'

'It was Charles when we lunched together – why so formal now? Particularly as I rang to invite you out to dinner.'

There was a long pause and then Dorothea said slowly, 'Your uncle didn't put you up to this, did he?'

'Good God, no! What on earth made you say that?'

She didn't know. Perhaps the continued insinuations of Mr Buchman that Adam Whitney played too large a part in Dorothea's life were starting to affect her. But if not because of Adam Whitney, then why? She hadn't seen Charles since the meal in the coffee shop, nor had she expected to.

'Are you still there, Dorothea. Look – I might as well come clean.' He sounded a touch embarrassed. 'I was taking a certain lady out tonight. Booked a super meal at a new place in the West End. But the fact is . . . we had a row. It seemed a pity to waste the evening. It took me ages to get a table. The restaurant's *the* place at the moment, and then I thought . . .'

'I'd do for second choice.' She finished his sentence for him.

'Oh dear, it sounds dreadful, doesn't it? Are you offended? But I remembered, you see. We got on well together, didn't we?'

Yes, thought Dorothea, they had. Charles had been fun to be with and he had treated her as though she had some intelligence which she had appreciated.

'I'd love to come,' she said. 'What time do you want me to be ready?'

Over the next six months Dorothea's life improved enormously. The evening out with Charles had been a huge success. He had a bubbling sense of fun and in his company she found herself regaining a sense of humour which she realised she had lost over the last two years. Scarred by her experience with Greg, she had been in danger of becoming a dour workaholic.

After that first date, she and Charles kept in touch and from time to time they met up and went out together. Initially, Dorothea couldn't understand why he kept ringing her but then she came to realise that he, too, enjoyed their relationship. It was surprising, she thought, that she liked him so much, for he was a charmer and Dorothea had had enough charm to last her all her life. She was honest enough to admit it gave her pleasure to be seen out with such a presentable escort, but also, because their relationship stayed strictly platonic, she could relax with him and simply enjoy his company.

Charles led a hectic romantic life and his name was often in the society columns, linked with various good-looking, usually wealthy girls with blue blood in their veins.

Dorothea would hear nothing from him for a period of three or four weeks when a new affair was being conducted. Then he would appear outside her door with a huge bunch of flowers and, on being invited in, would collapse into a chair and kick off his shoes. 'Bloody hard work, all this socialising,' he would groan. Loosening his tie, he would lean back and ask: 'How's the job going, then?'

He was, she thought, genuinely interested in her career. He recognised her ambition and applauded it. He himself worked as hard as he played and Dorothea thought Adam Whitney must be secretly well pleased with his nephew.

At work she was making progress, except with Mr Buchman. Her co-workers had come to realise Dorothea was a hard worker and keen to learn. They also came to appreciate her special skills in accountancy. A percentage of their tasks was bound up with essential but boring figurework. Dorothea overhauled the outdated systems they were using and considerably lessened their work load. Her ability to do excellent shorthand also came in useful. But Mr Buchman still insisted on treating her as Adam Whitney's pet. Dorothea regretted his attitude, particularly when she came to realise he was a good man at his job, quick thinking but usually overworked. The creative, inventive side of publicity work interested Dorothea more and more and she ached to be allowed to tackle more serious jobs.

One day when she arrived at the office, she found the place in pandemonium. Buchman had been off ill with 'flu for three days, half the staff were similarly affected, and a man called Mr Black, standing in for Mr Buchman, was a nervous wreck.

'There's been a robbery in the Ewart Hotel,' he told Dorothea hoarsely, 'and we mustn't let *that* leak out. And now Janet's rang in to say she's ill in bed.'

'Oh, dear.' Dorothea shrugged off her coat, then wished she could keep it on. The wind was howling through the ill-fitting windows. 'What shall I do first?'

'I don't know.' Mr Black raised his hands in despair. 'There's the opening of the Clarmount in three weeks,' he wailed. 'No one's even considered that but I just haven't had the time!'

'Shall I see if I can come up with an idea?'

Mr Black pulled at his lip nervously. 'It needs someone with a lot of experience really, but . . .' He eyed Dorothea and she gave him what she hoped was a confident smile. A chance, she thought exultantly, a chance to show what I'm really worth!

'OK.' Mr Black gave up the struggle. 'After all, there's no one else!'

The Clarmount was a hotel recently acquired by the Whitney Group. It had been a run-down, seedy place but it was on a prime site. The building had been completely renovated and a date fixed for a grand re-opening. A considerable budget had been allocated for the event but nothing else really considered. Dorothea read the papers carefully and felt her spirits fall. There was no angle, nothing on which to build a really spectacular feature. After hours of cogitation she still had not come up with an idea. When the others left at the end of the day, she stayed in the office. Then, at last, an idea began to form in her mind. She took out a comprehensive map of the area and began to smile.

Next day, she presented a draft of her conclusions to Mr Black. He read it then gave her the go-ahead.

'Damned original idea, Dorrie. Well done!'

Dorothea's interest in history had stayed with her and during her time as a receptionist at the Kenilworth and the Wellingborough she had spent some of her spare time tramping around the London streets, learning all she could about the interesting old tales associated with various districts. All the time she had been studying the information on the Clarmount something had been niggling away in her memory. Then it came to her. In the seventeenth century a princess of France had come to England to be married and had lodged for over a month in a house where the hotel now stood. Apparently she had been a vivacious young woman and had won the hearts of the Cockneys – so much so that, in local slang of the time, they had re-christened the district in her honour. Unfortunately, the young princess had succumbed to fever and died just before the wedding but her title could still be found in local street names in that area, although corrupted by time into something more English-sounding.

Dorothea's plan was that the story be revived and a

search be made for any French families living reasonably close to the hotel. 'It's a wealthy area,' she explained to Mr Black. 'I've rung round and made inquiries, and apart from some rich industrialists there are at least two genuine French families there with claims to blue blood. We could also contact the French Embassy and invite them to attend the Reception. It would be different, wouldn't it? I think the Press would be interested enough to cover the event fairly comprehensively if we put on a good enough show.'

'Yes, it's a nice fresh angle. You can put it to Mr Buchman yourself – he should be back in two days.'

But when Mr Buchman came back, Dorothea herself was down with 'flu. She was in bed three days. As soon as she felt better she went home.

Although the worse aspects of the 'flu had left her – the fever and the bouts of shivering – she still felt weak and depressed. And her illness couldn't have come at a worse time. Buchman was back at work and, thinking of Mr Black's total panic at being left in charge of the depleted staff, she felt sure he would pass her ideas on the opening of the Clarmount off as his own. Henry Black was not a bad man but he was timid and careful of his own job. He would seize on anything which would reassure his superior that he had coped well in an emergency. Dorothea didn't feel well enough to engage in a battle, and knowing Mr Buchman's reservations about her decided she couldn't win – not this time. She rang in to say she was taking the three days' leave she was entitled to and packed her bag.

Home was now a haven to her. For many months after she had walked out on Greg she had not been able to tell her parents the truth. To explain her change of address she had concocted an elaborate tale, half truth, half lies. She wrote that she had another job. And that she had to live in at the hotel to undertake certain training. She also wrote that Greg was visiting his old auntie who had been ill. She didn't

370

like lying but her shame and horror was too deep to be revealed to others. Time passed and her mother's letters became full of careful inquiries. Dorothea realised they would have to be told that she and Greg had parted, even though she still had no desire to tell them the whole story.

On the journey to Hull the old sense of rebellion stirred. Why did they have to know about her personal life? Would she never be free of the ties of family? How insidious were the threads between parents and children, how stubborn and strong, even though they were woven from something as fragile as love.

Having determined not to tell them the whole truth, Dorothea alighted from the train to be met by her mother. Hazel gave her a hug and they went home. Her father was there to greet her and, unusually for someone not given to outward signs of affection, he also hugged her closely to him. Hazel had prepared tea and there was hot water for her bath. It felt good to be back in her own little bedroom, snuggled down in the sagging bed in which she had dreamed her childish dreams. The next day, she came to realise that Hazel had no intention of asking any questions. Used from childhood to combating her mother's delicate but pointed questions, Dorothea felt enormous relief. Somehow, she didn't know how or why, her mother and father had come to terms with the fact their daughter was now an adult.

Feeling a rush of love she waited until she and Hazel were alone in the kitchen, then made a pot of tea, sat down and told her mother everything. When she had finished, she felt as if she had been absolved of some crime. Merely speaking about the whole, horrific episode in some way cauterised her wound. When she finished speaking, her mother had come to her, held her close and shared in her desolation.

Hazel asked Dorothea if she should tell Dennis. She had hesitated. 'I suppose so,' she said eventually. 'I don't want any more lies, Mum.' Nothing more was said on the subject, but when Dorothea was leaving to go back to London, Dennis went to the station with her. He gave her a massive bearhug before she boarded the train and told her in a husky voice to take care of herself. Then he stepped back and said: 'You'll be all right, Dorrie. You're better without a bastard like that.'

Chapter Thirty-Six

On her first morning back at work Dorothea was told to report to Mr Buchman.

'Hope you're over the 'flu now, young woman.' He looked at her over his glasses. 'Lucky you could take the extra days off.'

'They were due to me,' she replied. Her voice sounded defensive.

'True.' He sat back in his chair and stared at her. She shifted uncomfortably.

'Damn good idea you had regarding the Clarmount opening.'

She gaped at him.

'As you can imagine, I'm up to my eyes in it right now so . . .' he held out a document file for her to take ' . . . it's all yours. I've double-checked everything. Better get on to it right away.'

When she did not move, he raised his eyebrows. 'Of course, if you think you can't handle it . . . ?'

'Oh, I can!' She held the file to her chest in a protective gesture. 'Thank you.'

She moved back to her desk in a dream. She even smiled at Mr Sanders. She sat down, opened the file and reached for the telephone. She worked harder that day than she had ever worked in her life, but she took time off to go down to the cake shop at the corner of the street and buy Mr Black a cream cake to have with his afternoon tea.

Ten months after joining the Publicity department, Dorothea received a summons to Adam Whitney's office. As usual, he came straight to the point of the meeting.

'Cecil Buchman's leaving the company. He's going to Canada in two months. Think you can handle his job?'

Dorothea gulped. For a moment she felt blind panic. It was too much, too soon . . . but then she took a deep breath and nodded. 'Yes, I can.'

Adam flashed her a brief smile. 'Good girl,' he said approvingly. 'If it's any interest, Cecil recommended you. He reckons you have instinctive flair and that's something which can't be taught, no matter how long you work in Publicity. He admitted he was wrong about you at the beginning, but he said the way you salvaged that Melton débâcle was nothing short of miraculous.'

Dorothea nodded without comment. The Melton affair was something that only happened once in a lifetime. At least, one fervently hoped so! One of their top hotels had been booked for a spectacular charity event. Celebrities from stage and screen, business tycoons and minor royals, had bought tickets. At the last minute, it had been discovered the whole thing was a con. By some whim of the Devil, Buchman had been on holiday at the time. He was fulfilling a lifetime's ambition to visit Africa.

When they had been unable to contact him no one knew what to do. Mr Black had wanted personally to involve Mr Whitney but then Dorothea had come up with an idea. It was a long shot, but the rest of the Publicity staff had agreed to go along with her. In a burst of feverish activity they researched the background of the con-artist and found he had tenuous links with two of the film stars due to attend the function and three members of the Cabinet. These people were immediately contacted. Of course, Dorothea pointed out to them, they themselves were in no way suspected of being implicated in the sorry business, but . . . Hastily, they agreed to help. The villain involved was quietly taken into custody, the politicians and stars who baled out the occasion were thanked for their additional generous-hearted funding, without too many details being revealed, and the whole evening was a huge success. The following day, Dorothea slept for sixteen hours.

'Mind you,' she brought her attention back to what her employer was saying, 'you wouldn't have been offered the position if I didn't know you had a damn good back-up team to support you.'

Dorothea thought of Mr Black, Mr Sanders and all the others. How would they react? Adam Whitney read her expression.

'I've already spoken to Black,' he said. 'He has expressed his willingness to work with you.' Adam chuckled. 'Nice old boy, Henry. Wise, too. He knows his own limitations. Would have a nervous breakdown if he had to run the show, but a good conscientious worker all the same. As for the others, they seem happy enough. Not everyone wants the long hours and the responsibility the job entails.' He looked at her searchingly. 'Sure about this, Dorrie?'

She gulped. It was a big promotion and carried a lot of responsibility. 'Of course I am,' she replied.

'Good girl. I thought that would be your answer.' Adam beamed at her and handed her a cheque. 'Your salary will be adjusted accordingly but take this in the meantime. Jenny tells me you are moving into your own flat.'

'Yes. It's small but central. I'm looking forward to a place of my own.' Dorothea looked at the cheque then gasped.

'Don't thank me.' Adam waved his hand. 'I like to give my promising employees a bonus from time to time. It keeps them on their toes.'

'Thank you.' She folded the cheque and put it carefully in her bag.

'I was right, wasn't I?'

'Sorry?'

'About the publicity job.'

She laughed. 'Yes, you were right.'

375

'That's good.'

Her employer looked at her a moment, then said: 'During the next twelve months the Publicity department will carry a heavy load. It's not general knowledge yet, but William Summers has decided to sell his chain of hotels. I've called a special meeting of the Board and suggested we bid for them. I think we can negotiate a reasonable price. They are damn fine hotels and well run but William has suddenly decided he's getting too old to manage them. He wants to retire.'

Adam stopped talking at the expression on Dorothea's face. 'What's the matter? Oh, I see.' He laughed. 'I know, I know – I'm a couple of years older than Summers but damn it, it's too good an opportunity to miss.

'Anyway,' his wrinkled face creased into a smile, 'I'm taking my nephew's advice. I'm beginning to delegate. I always have really, but Charles doesn't see it that way. If he thought about it more, he would realise that. Every Head of Administration has been hand-picked by me; I have made sure that every senior executive has absorbed and applied the company's philosophy and methods. I have also insisted that they, in turn, educate the staff below them, and so on. Therefore, I can, if I wish, sit back now and allow most of the work to be done by other people. But they are people *I* have picked! It works, Dorothea. My judgement is based on instinct as well as experience and common sense, and it works. I wasn't wrong with you, was I? I know I can trust you, otherwise I wouldn't have told you about Summers.'

'I appreciate that, Mr Whitney.'

'Well, I'm fond of you, my dear. You know,' Adam's face grew serious, 'I have many associates and I trust most of them but there are very few I actually feel a fondness for.' He deliberated. 'Perhaps it's because you're a northern lass, Dorothea. I come from the north myself, you know.' He saw the look of surprise on her face. 'You didn't know that, did you? Oh, yes, my father had a butcher's shop in Halifax.' He paused, lost in thought, then bestirred himself. 'And because I am fond of you, I hope you won't take exception at what I am going to say next.'

A certain wariness came over Dorothea's features. She waited.

'I understand you are meeting my nephew socially?'

She parried his question with one of her own. 'Is there some unwritten rule that I may not do so?'

'No, but . . .' Adam stopped when he saw her eyes narrow. 'Don't jump to conclusions, my dear,' he continued. 'Charles is my nephew, but it is *you* I am thinking of.'

'Indeed.'

The emphasis on that one word was ironic.

Adam Whitney sighed. 'Do you remember our first meeting, Dorothea, in the Doran?'

'Yes.'

He sighed again. 'I noticed you straight away. I noticed your efficiency, your friendly manner. I saw how good you were at your job. Since you've worked for me, I have seen you develop other skills. You can communicate and you have a rare capacity to stand back and take an overall view. And yet . . .' He fell silent.

Dorothea leaned forward in her chair. 'And yet?' she prompted.

He shrugged. 'You seem to make a habit of picking the wrong man.'

The colour flared in Dorothea's face. She stiffened. 'You have no right . . .' She struggled for composure. 'My private life is my own, Mr Whitney. If it affected my working life, *then* would be the time for you to comment. But not *once*—' again she strove to keep her voice even '—not once have I been absent from work unjustifiably. Not once has my private life interfered with my work for the company. Frankly, I'm amazed and disappointed by your comment.' She paused, and when she spoke again her voice was composed and cool. 'When Charles,' she emphasised the name, 'suggested that you were too paternalistic, it seems he was right.'

Her employer's eyebrows rose but his attitude remained relaxed. 'I apologise,' he said. 'My words were ill-chosen. But Dorothea,' he rose and went to stand by the window, 'listen to me, please.

'I have known Charles all his life. He is a good businessman, charming and amusing, but he is also manipulative and extremely selfish. He has an eye for the main chance and at times can be positively heartless. In business deals, such characteristics can be an asset. Privately,' the old man stared out of the window, 'they are not so good. I know you have been unhappy in the past, Dorothea. I would hate to see you make another mistake. You're doing so well, don't mess things up.' He shook his head. 'For a cool-headed woman I'm inclined to think your emotions run wild sometimes.'

When Dorothea laughed, he swung round to face her, a look of astonishment on his face.

'I'm sorry.' The anger had faded from her face. She looked positively mischievous. 'You really *do* have my welfare at heart, don't you?'

'Of course.'

'Then you needn't worry. It's not like you think. There's no romance involved in my relationship with Charles. It's purely friendship. As you say, he's good company and he makes me laugh. He talks to me about his latest girlfriends, for goodness' sake! Oh, I know he's all the things you mentioned. He's a snob, too. One evening we met some of his friends unexpectedly and he actually wouldn't introduce me properly because he said Bellows for a surname was just *too* much.' She laughed again. 'If it had been anyone else I would have been furious but, somehow, Charles gets away with murder.'

'Well, that's all right then.' Adam Whitney looked unconvinced.

'Please believe me, there's nothing whatsoever to be concerned about.'

They talked a little longer then Dorothea left. But

after her departure Adam's face resumed its serious expression. As far as he knew, Dorothea had no boy friend. She was such an attractive, vibrant woman, he thought. Would she stay content with mere friendship? Well, it was none of his business. Reluctantly, his lips curved into a smile. Paternalistic, eh! He returned to his seat behind the desk, picked up the Advisory Committee's Report on room occupancy rates at the Summers chain of hotels, and thoughts of Dorothea and Charles fled from his mind.

'Dorrie, it's lovely!'

Hazel Bellows looked with delight round the high-ceilinged, white-painted room. Dorothea had decorated her new flat herself, often working until the early hours of the morning. Her new home was on the first floor of a narrow brick-built house which, in company with its neighbours, curved in a gracious crescent around a small green park. Because it was within walking distance of Covent Garden, she had been able to scour the neighbourhood seeking bits and pieces of furniture which she felt would enhance her property. From the flea markets she had picked up a polished mahogany table, a Victorian sofa bed and a Persian carpet. The carpet was faded in the middle but still displayed muted, beautiful colours.

'There's plenty to do yet, but it's beginning to take shape. There's no rush. I would rather take my time furnishing the place than buy things I don't like.'

'Of course.' Hazel darted about opening doors. 'Oh, you have your own little bathroom, how lovely. Much better than having to share.'

Dorothea was glad of her mother's approval. Hazel had come to visit especially to view Dorothea's new home. She waited until Hazel returned to the living room, then said, 'Only the one bed, Mum. Do you mind sharing?'

'Not in the least. You know,' Hazel touched the polished table, 'I think you've done marvels, Dorrie.

When I think, only two years ago all you had were the clothes you stood up in.'

The flat seemed suddenly quiet and Hazel looked anxious. 'I'm sorry, I shouldn't have said that. I don't want to bring back bad memories for you.'

'It's all right, Mum. Anyway, it's nearly three years since Greg and I parted. I'm over that now.' She changed the subject. 'I think I'll have some bookshelves built in that alcove, and I may buy a picture for over the fireplace. You could help me choose . . .'

Dorothea made sure Hazel enjoyed her visit to London. Due to her contacts with the Press she was able to obtain tickets for a top London show which Hazel loved. Then, another day, they visited Hampton Court. The next day, they went for tea at the Savoy. At first, Hazel was nervous in the opulent surroundings but then she relaxed. Dorothea smiled to see her mother playing the grand lady. She was glad she was now in a position to provide treats. Dennis had no interest in anything outside Hull but Hazel had always hankered for a little of the 'high life'.

'Dare I have another cake, do you think?' Hazel eyed the cake trolley longingly.

'Why not? You're lucky, Mum. You'll always be slim.' Dorothea pulled a face. 'Why couldn't I take after your side of the family?'

The comment was not strictly true. Hazel was rounding with age but, conversely, the extra weight filled out her face, making her appear younger than her years.

She selected a cream slice. 'Well, it is a special occasion.' She looked at her daughter. 'And you're talking silly. I've never seen you look so well. In fact, if you lose any more weight you'll look positively skinny! Of course,' she licked her fingers daintily, 'that new hair style makes your face look thinner.'

'Does it really?'

'Yes.' Hazel paused. 'You look very much like Ingrid Bergman now.'

Dorothea laughed but was inwardly gratified. Someone else had told her that. And it was Charles she had to thank for her transformation. Over the last six months he had tactfully taken her in hand. The new hairstyle had been his idea. He had also suggested changes in her dress. During the past two years Dorothea had evolved her own way of dressing for work. She now wore well-cut slacks or skirts with neat blouses or sweaters. Charles had approved but pointed out to her that she didn't always have to look so businesslike. Leisure dressing, he said, should be different, more fun. He had shown her that muted, glowing colours suited her; he had introduced her to softer, silkier fabrics. Once she had realised he knew what he was talking about, she had followed his advice gratefully and her confidence had grown when she saw how good she looked.

For her trip to the Savoy Dorothea wore a full-skirted dress in a bronze colour. With a thin dark-green leather belt cinching her slim waist and wearing toning court shoes – she had finally found the courage to wear high heels – she was pleasantly aware she was attracting the right kind of attention. Dorothea realised she liked clothes and it was good to feel that men found her desirable. She remembered too well her plump, painful adolescence and beneath that remembrance, pushed deep down, was the festering knowledge that, eventually, Greg had preferred to go to bed with a man rather than her.

'I forgot to tell you, Dorrie. You don't know about Nancy, do you?'

Dorothea's attention returned to her mother. 'No, what about her?'

'She's run off – with a brush salesman!'

'What!'

'It's true.' Hazel nodded sagely. 'There's been a terrible to-do.'

'I wondered why she never answered my last letter.' Dorothea stared at her mother. 'What happened? And what about the children?'

'She took them with her.' A small, guilty grin crept across Hazel's face. She hastily suppressed it. 'I'm sorry,' she apologised. 'I know it's certainly nothing to smile about but,' she dimpled again, 'I can't help wondering what that poor man will do with those awful children?'

Dorothea's own lips quirked at Hazel's expression. She guessed her mother would carry a bit of the child in her until the day she died. 'Tell me,' she urged.

'Well, poor Nancy was very unhappy, you know.' Hazel shook her head. 'Her mother used to tell me things. And Bill Thomson turned out to be a sullen sort of man. Nancy was always a bit wild, of course, but she was a very good mother. Spoilt them, but I suppose she had to lavish her affection on someone. Personally, I don't blame the girl.' Hazel sipped at her tea and Dorothea waited impatiently.

'The chap was called Marsey or Massie, I'm not sure which. He used to come to our house. He sold good stuff. I bought a mop off him, I remember. It lasted . . .'

'*Mother*, tell me what happened!'

'What? Oh, sorry.' Hazel mentally marshalled her thoughts. 'It appears he visited Nancy for a long time; when Bill was at sea, of course. Then Bill found out about him. He went mad, quite understandably. But he blacked Nancy's eye, then slammed out of the house threatening to find out where this chap lived and kill him! As soon as he left, Nancy packed her bags and went to her mother. Poor Mrs Dempsey, she didn't know what to do.

'I think she advised Nancy to go home again but Nancy wouldn't. She told her mum that this chap was crazy for her and he wasn't married. He had been on at her for ages to leave Bill but there were the children. Anyway, to cut a long story short, Nancy went out to a phone box and called him. Three hours later he was on the doorstep. She loaded the kids and their luggage into his car and off they went!

'She's written to her mother and told her things are

all right and she's not to worry, but of course she does. All mothers worry.' Hazel finished her tea and sat back in her chair, bright-eyed. 'But you know, Dorrie, I think Nancy will be all right. I *liked* that salesman. His eyes were kind. It's only when I remember . . . he was a bachelor, Nancy told her mother, and those three lads!'

Two days later, Hazel returned home. She never stayed longer than a week. Dennis was having increasing difficulty walking and had been forced to retire from work. The family doctor said there was little to be done. Dennis had emphysema. He had been quite happy about Hazel's visit, but she didn't like to leave him alone for long.

The flat was quiet after her departure. Too quiet for Dorothea. Ever since Mr Whitney had employed her she had lived in hotels. She was used to noise and bustle. She had dreamed about her own little place for so long but now she had achieved her ambition she realised it would take her time to adjust to living on her own.

Hazel had brought down with her a small case. She had collected together some of Dorothea's bits and pieces she thought she might like to keep in London. Dorothea took the case and unpacked it. The first item that came into view was a shabby old teddy bear. She gave a smile of pleasure on seeing it and gave it a cuddle before placing it on her chest of drawers. It had been her first friend. There were also some of her favourite childhood books and a framed photograph of her parents. Then she found a cushion she had embroidered and a musical box which had been given to her by a family friend. She sat down on the bed and lifted the lid. She had, she remembered, kept small treasures in there. Inside were the earrings Rob Steyart has sent her just before he went to Australia. Dear Rob. She took them out and held them in the palm of her hand. The light was fading so she rose and switched on a lamp. The earrings sparkled in the light.

They really were most attractive. She wondered how he had ever managed to save up the money to buy them.

On impulse she put them on and went into the bathroom her mother had so much admired to see how they looked. Her new haircut was in the urchin style. Wisps of hair fell across her forehead and on to her cheeks but the earrings showed up clearly. She noticed how the mingled blue-green of the stones emphasised the colour of her eyes. She remembered she had recently bought a new green dress. She went to find it. Half an hour later she surveyed her appearance in the mirror and decided she looked good. She looked across at her recently installed telephone and on impulse walked across and dialled Charles's number. As she waited for him to answer she thought of Adam Whitney's concern, and smiled. Poor Adam! He was old. He didn't realise men and women were now more equal. As an equal, she felt no qualms about ringing Charles instead of waiting patiently until he got in touch with her. In the event he was delighted by her call.

'It's been too long since I saw you,' he said. 'Let's go out.'

Two hours later they were halfway through a meal at the Lanterna Club. Dorothea looked at their table, laden with flowers, candles and wine.

'You're doing me proud this evening, Charles,' she said. 'Why the big occasion?'

'I could do nothing less. I'm so pleased you rang me.'

He refilled her wine glass. 'Also I remembered we have a celebration. You've just moved into your flat, haven't you? And then,' he raised his glass and grinned at her, 'I must confess, last week I wined and dined a certain young woman here. She was absolutely gorgeous to look at and I spent a lot of money but, to tell the truth, she bored me to tears. I decided then to bring someone who would truly appreciate the place and also match me in good conversation.'

'Am I supposed to be flattered?' Dorothea's voice mocked him. 'You really are conceited, Charles. But . . .' she reached forward to touch his hand ' . . . it is sweet of you to treat me.' She smiled. 'If any of your friends come in, I'll try not to embarrass you.'

'You'd never do that.' Charles's voice remained light but his expression became serious. 'Anyone with any sense at all would be proud to be your escort.'

He saw her look at him curiously and he continued, his voice matter-of-fact, 'I'm glad to see you're continuing to follow my advice on clothes. You look terrific tonight.'

She put the increased heat in her face down to the wine. They finished their meal and lingered over coffee and brandy. Dorothea told Charles about her latest buys for the flat and news of the Publicity department. He told her about his business trip to France. The restaurant had a small dance floor and they danced a quick-step, matching each other's steps perfectly. Then the band played a foxtrot. Charles held her close to him and Dorothea's face was glowing when they returned to their table. Charles was being particularly attentive this evening. It was lovely but she sensed it pointed to a change in their hitherto easy relationship and she wasn't sure whether she wanted it to change. She picked up her evening purse.

'I think I'd better go and powder my nose,' she said. 'I won't be long.'

'I'll miss you. Hurry back.' He smiled his slow lazy smile. She gave him a curt nod of her head. She didn't know whether the flutter of feeling she felt was excitement or irritation.

As she left the ladies' room she heard a familiar voice. For a moment she froze, then looked round for a way of escape. There was no way to hide. She swallowed hard, then turned round.

'Dorothea!' Kenny stood before her. He held out his hand. He looked just the same. Even his expression was the same, kindly, concerned.

'How are you?'

She felt sick. 'Please let me pass,' she said.

His eyes flickered. 'Please, Dorrie, just give me a moment. So often I've wanted to explain, make you understand . . .'

'*No!*' She practically screamed. A couple passing by looked at her in alarm. 'Don't explain! I don't want to hear. Just leave me alone.'

'But . . .'

'I know what I saw. I want to forget.'

'But Greg and I . . .'

Her heart missed another beat. 'Is he here?'

'We're leaving. He went on ahead of me.'

Thank God, she thought. She wouldn't have to see him.

'Leave me alone, Kenny. Please.'

She rushed past him and stumbled into the restaurant. She took a deep breath and went back to her table.

'You all right, Dorothea?'

'Of course.' She slipped into her seat and forced her stiff face into a smile. Charles gave her a thoughtful look then lit a cigar and began to talk of inconsequential things. She began to relax, grateful to him for his understanding. She knew he was much too astute not to realise something had upset her but he asked no more questions.

She drank her brandy quickly and he immediately ordered two more from the waiter. He exerted himself to make her laugh. He paid her outrageous compliments and was cruelly witty about the other dinner guests. By the time he persuaded her to dance again, he had succeeded in his object. She rested her hand on his shoulder as they danced a samba.

'You are an idiot, Charles.'

'I know, but a lovable one surely?'

He drove her home in the early hours of the morning. He walked her to the door of her flat, where he hesitated. Then he placed his hands on her shoulders and lightly kissed the tip of her nose.

'You are OK, Dorothea?'

She felt real affection for him. 'Yes,' she said. 'Thanks to you.'

'Do you know what I would like most in all the world at this moment?' He waited, and when she didn't reply he went on, 'To see your flat.'

She hesitated. 'I don't know, Charles.'

He touched her cheek. 'I've been a perfect escort, haven't I?'

'Yes, but . . .'

He pulled a face. 'A coffee, pet. All I want is a coffee.'

Dorothea felt she wanted to laugh and to cry at the same time. 'Are you sure?' She looked up at him. She didn't know it, but mirrored in her eyes were all her churning emotions – anger, loss, pain, and a need for comfort.

His brows drew together. He looked down at her in surprise. Then he countered her question with one of his own.

'What do *you* want, Dorothea? Whatever it is, it's OK with me.'

She rested her head on his shoulder for a brief moment then she turned and unlocked the door.

'You'd better come in,' she said.

Chapter Thirty-Seven

When Rob recovered from his blinder, he made his weary way back to talk to Mr and Mrs Botetsios. As he told his tale, he saw them visibly age. He had to some extent directed his anger towards them. It had been easier to do that rather than dwell on thoughts of Irene. Yet, seeing Nicholas's hands begin to shake and the stricken look in his mother-in-law's eyes, he tempered his harsh judgement. Nicholas and Teresa Botetsios had loved their daughter not wisely but too well and now they were reaping the harvest.

He too felt a sense of guilt. He admitted to them he had known how much Irene had hated the Outback. He had been selfish, he said. He should have found another way of living.

'No, Rob.' Teresa Botetsios's voice held unaccustomed humility. 'I know you tried to be a good husband. And although Irene was young, too young perhaps for marriage, you were young also. Much of the blame lies with us. We made her believe life was easy. We protected her too much and now we must suffer the consequences, as indeed, must Irene.' Her voice broke on a sob. She turned to her husband. 'Oh, Nicholas, what will happen to our baby?'

Rob's throat tightened as he looked at the couple. 'Perhaps the newspaper ads will come up with something?'

Teresa sighed. 'She was always so headstrong, but this . . .' She straightened her back and her voice strengthened. 'But what about Nicky?'

Rob met her eyes squarely. 'He goes with me.'

'But . . . he needs a woman to look after him, Rob.

And he is growing so fast, soon he will need schooling . . .'

Nicholas Botetsios held up his hand. 'Be quiet, Teresa. Do you never learn? Nicky is Rob's son, he must be with his father.'

He turned to Rob. 'I am sorry, but the shock – and she loves him so much.'

'I know.' Rob tried to smile but failed dismally. 'I shall bring him to visit you as often as I can.'

Nicky's chatter kept Rob from brooding on the trip back to Coober Pedy. The small boy asked endless questions and the discomforts of the journey seemed to bother him not one wit.

'What's that?' he queried as Rob's truck approached a line of cars queuing up just outside the town.

'They've come to collect water,' explained Rob. 'There's an underground water tank here.'

'What's that man doing?'

Rob grinned for the first time in ages. A man called Matthew Jenks was jigging around at the side of the cars, stripped down to his underpants. 'I guess the shower's working today.'

'Shower?'

Once told, nothing would deter Nicky from his demand for a shower. Rob grunted and turned the truck round. The shower was a powdered milk tin punched with pin holes. Each person was allowed five minutes beneath the spray. Watching his son standing beneath the water, an ear-splitting grin on his face, Rob felt happy for the first time since leaving Coober Pedy. He had a grand kid, he mused, as he hauled him from the shower, roughly dried him and helped him into his clothes. One thing Rob had noticed at Dryton was that Teresa frequently used Greek when talking to her grandson. That must stop. Nicky was Australian born and Rob experienced a warm glow as he anticipated watching his boy grow up a true Aussie. Impulsively he hugged Nicky's wriggling body.

The child submitted to his embrace gracefully, then asked: 'Is Mummy coming back here?'

Rob's good feeling disappeared. 'Perhaps,' he replied. He started up the truck for the last leg of the journey. He glanced across and saw Nicky's solemn expression as he gazed out of the window. Rob began to tell him stories about the Dreamtime.

Late in 1961 a two-roomed school opened in Coober Pedy and Peter Gillan was one of the first pupils. A year later, Nicholas Steyart was delighted when he was old enough to join his friend. Rob took his son to school on his first day. He watched with mixed feelings as, with a cheery wave, Nicky ran into the building without a second glance. Rob climbed back into his ute wondering where the years had gone. The toddler he had brought back to Coober Pedy was now a confident six year old. But then, he reflected, many other things had changed – except the condition of the roads. Carefully, he guided his truck over a particularly rough piece of terrain.

The mining community town had spread in all directions. The Government had set aside five thousand acres of land outside the town which was now an Aborigine Reserve and more fields were being opened up every day. There was even talk of establishing an air link between Coober Pedy and Adelaide. If Irene ever returned, Rob's lips flattened into a bitter smile, perhaps she might like the place a little better now! He pushed that thought away. His wife would never return. It was better not to think of her.

It was a calm hot day. Rob changed gear and steered the ute in the direction of the Seven Mile. He swore and wound up the window as clouds of brown-yellow dust swirled into the truck. Things were changing on the fields too.

Everywhere, motor-driven hoists stood above shafts and the air was filled with the sound of compressors. Yet, paradoxically, opal mining did not change. The run of opal, the nature of the land, still meant that partnerships must remain small; two or three men who trusted each other working together. Rob and Boots had recently pegged a new claim where the ground was so hard it was necessary to sink with the use of hammer and chisel, yet both of them tackled the job with enthusiasm. They had a feeling about the place. Rob knew that opal could be found as veins in horizontal levels or in steeply dipping 'verticals'. The gems were always in front of faults in the earth which could run for only a few feet or up to half a mile. Sinking a new shaft was always a gamble. Perhaps, he thought, that was the attraction. He reached his destination and stopped the truck. He waved at Boots.

'How's it going?'

'Bloody hard!' Boots's vest was sweat-stained. He paused and wiped his face. 'When I was a little kid,' he reminisced, 'I was always on about finding gold, remember?'

Rob nodded. He took his own tools from the back of the ute and started work.

'I was an idiot,' continued Boots. 'I really thought all you had to do was find the stuff and pick it up off the ground.'

'No such luck.' Rob grimaced. Already his shirt was clinging to his back.

'Nicky go into school OK?' queried his partner.

'Couldn't wait.'

'That's good.' Boots wiped his forehead. 'Our Peter will look out for him.'

'Yes, I know. They're good mates.'

Both men fell silent and concentrated on their work. As Rob slogged away, his mind wandered. Next month, he thought, I must take Nicky to see his grandparents. Poor devils, they had never fully recovered from Irene's defection. He wondered if they had heard anything of her. He knew that not long after he had returned to Coober Pedy they had received a letter. They had given it to him to read.

Irene had written that they were not to worry. She

was very well. She was sorry to have hurt everyone. Everyone! Rob's mouth thinned. She hadn't even mentioned his name, or Nicky's. He wondered yet again how she could possibly have cast aside her own child. He remembered how excited she had been when she became pregnant. Lots of women left their husbands, and maybe he had given her reason to leave him, but to leave your child! He shook his head. He would never understand. The envelope had been postmarked Melbourne but she had given no address. Since then there had been odd postcards. God knew where she was now. Rob no longer cared. He would never forgive her for leaving Nicky. Teresa Botetsios was of a like mind. She never mentioned her daughter's name. But Irene's father was always pathetically excited when a communication arrived. The old man suffered from heart trouble now and his health was frail. Rob stopped work for a moment and stretched to ease his back. Yes, he must take Nicky soon. They lived for their grandson.

Nicky – how was his day going? Rob anticipated no problems. He had been right to bring the boy to Coober Pedy. Sure, it was a hot and dusty place but there was room for a child to grow, to run wild and learn about mankind and nature. From the beginning Rob had schooled his son in the particular dangers of the place and set strict rules and Nicky had never betrayed his trust. He had plenty of playmates now and Kate to act as surrogate mother. Rob grinned. She would be missing Nicky like hell today.

When he had arrived in Coober Pedy with Nicky in tow, Kate had immediately set about mothering the boy. Initially, Rob had worried he was taking advantage of her kindly nature but as he saw Kate knit woollies for Nicky, bake cakes for them both and tell stories to his son, he came to understand that Nicky was giving something to Kate. Unfortunately, no brothers or sisters had arrived for Peter and Kate was a maternal sort of woman. She loved seeing to Nicky and, indeed, insisted that at regular intervals Rob leave his son with her and take a few hours off from being a single parent. Rob appreciated the break. Much as he loved the boy he spent too many hours sitting alone outside his dugout, staring at the sky and reflecting upon what might have been whilst Nicky slumbered in his bed inside. The evenings he was free to wander down to the bar, shoot a little pool and chat with other men had provided him with a safety valve. He had a lot to thank Kate for.

He sighed and stretched again. He noticed Boots was taking a break. He had opened a flask. He handed Rob a cup of cold tea. 'Going pretty well.'

'Yeah.' Rob accepted the cup with a nod of thanks. 'Still got a feeling about this one, Boots?'

'Sure have.'

Rob drank his tea and gazed about him. The bright sun brought out the colours in the area surrounding them. The strips of road gleamed and the strong light glinted off the galvanised tanks and light-coloured mullock heaps surrounding them. The immediate view was harsh yet curiously exhilarating. Further away he could see dark violet shadows on the hill slopes, entrances to dugouts, and above them all curved the brilliant blue sky. This place had really got to him, he thought. He swallowed the last of his tea and started work again.

Two weeks later they bottomed out on the level and there it was. 'Jeez,' said Boots, 'we've struck gold!'

Rob's laugh was loud with amazement. 'Not gold, Boots – opal!'

The floor of the shaft was a solid sheet of opal. The two men stared in disbelief. They had never seen so much of the stuff collected together like that. They moved their lamps and the colours sprang out at them; red and blue, pink, violet and orange. Every time a lamp moved the colours changed, patterns mingling into breathtaking creations. For several seconds the friends were struck dumb. They stood and wondered if they were dreaming. Then Boots crouched down and examined the gems closely. When he looked up at Rob his face held an awed expression.

'It looks good, Rob, all of it! It looks really good stuff!'

Then the excitement hit them and they laughed, slapped each other on the back and danced about like schoolboys. When Rob stopped jigging he rested his hand on Boots's shoulder.

'Everything's going to change, Boots. We're rich, really rich.'

Boots frowned. 'Let's get out of here. Think what we're going to do.'

After a last, lingering look around they climbed back up the shaft and into the sunlight.

'We must be careful.' Boots's face fell in solemn lines. 'Eighty per cent of the miners are good blokes but there's always the "ratters"!'

Rob nodded. 'We'll have to put a watch on the place and keep our mouths shut.'

'Ratters', he knew, were characters who preferred to pick over other men's claims after the owners had gone home for the night.

'We'll tell Kate, of course, and bring her along to see but—' he looked at Boots '—better not say anything to the boys yet.'

'Agreed.' Boots's solemnity cracked and a wide grin spread across his broad face. 'Come on, let's go and tell the wife.'

Their run of luck held. They kept their secret and mined the opal. Buyers were contacted and came up especially to grade and assess their find. By the time their strike became general knowledge they were on their way to becoming rich men. Feeling shell-shocked, they discussed what to do next.

'A wonderful holiday?' Boots turned to stare at his wife.

'I thought you were stuck on this place? Now you tell me you want to go away.'

'A *holiday*, I said.'

Kate pulled his hair, an affectionate gesture. 'I

don't think I want to leave this place permanently although we could, I suppose. Maybe we can still live here but go somewhere nice every year in the hot season?'

'I know why you want to stay.' Boots winked at Rob. 'Getting to be an important lady, my Kate. Chairwoman of the PTA, arranges the school sports day, on the committee agitating for the formation of a medical centre – she'll be standing for Mayor next!'

'Oh, you!' Kate boxed his ears. 'I've always wanted to see the Great Barrier Reef,' she confessed.

'Then you shall, my darling.' Boots patted her bottom.

Kate looked across at Rob. 'What about you, Rob?' She hesitated. 'Will you try and find Irene?'

'No.' He shook his head. 'That part of my life's over, Kate.' He smiled to allay her worried look. 'But there's lots of things for us to think about. The money is going to change our lives, whether or not we want it to. There's the boys' future to consider.

'Perhaps a holiday is a good idea. The kids would love it too, I'm sure.' He looked suddenly abashed. 'Sorry, I'm jumping to conclusions. I'm sure you, Boots and Peter will have a great time.'

'But you're coming too?' Kate frowned.

'I don't think so. You deserve some time on your own.'

'Don't be daft, mate.' Boots sounded annoyed and Kate shook her head reproachfully. 'Oh, Rob, don't you know it yet? You and Nicky – you're *family*!'

Chapter Thirty-Eight

Feeling like millionaires they flew to Cairns. They found it to be a bright city with public buildings of white stone fronting trim tropical parks. They climbed the tortuous Gillies Highway and looked down on emerald rectangles of cane growing in the red-brown earth. Kate enjoyed shopping in the fine new stores with their large plate-glass windows. After a week sampling city life they went down to the Docks and hired a boat and an experienced sailor to take them to the Reef.

Neither Kate nor the boys had ever seen the sea and they found their first sight of it inspiring and rather frightening. Then they fell in love with it. They spent two weeks moving about in the one thousand two hundred mile long string of coral cays and islands lying off the coast of Queensland. Both Rob and Boots could swim so they donned goggles and flippers and swam about marvelling at the diversity of nature. Kate and the boys had to see the coral through a glass-bottomed boat but they pestered the menfolk to teach them how to swim so that they too could see the wonders at first hand. Try as they might, they made a poor job of it and Rob and Boots promised them they would return another year.

Other days they spent exploring the sandy islets of the Reef and tried their hand at fishing for black marlin. Then they flew to Sydney.

Now totally enraptured by the sea, Peter and Nicky voted each day for Bondi Beach but Rob found he liked wandering about Sydney Harbour the best. Several days, when the rest of them went to the beach, he went alone to the waterside suburbs.

He followed crooked streets that ran narrowly uphill. He walked past quaint stone houses that recalled windjammer and whaling days and climbed up long flights of sandstone steps. He sat on bedraggled jetties and watched fishermen cast their lines and a feeling of nostalgic sadness gathered and grew inside him.

He didn't really know why. The holiday had been wonderful. He knew the boys had enjoyed every minute and so had Boots and Kate. But he needed time away from them. He knew that Kate in particular wanted him to have a good time, worried about him, but inevitably there were times when he had felt an intruder. In the almost honeymoon atmosphere of the Reef he had seen them exchange that smiling look which only happily married couples can share. He had seen the way their hands would touch, then cling together. When it happened, he always averted his eyes. If only he and Irene . . . There had been a moment, just before they left on the holiday, when he had considered re-advertising, but he had decided against it. His resentment was still too strong. Why should Irene share in their good fortune? If she returned he would never know if it was simply because of the money. And Nicky had stopped mentioning his mother. It seemed that he had forgotten her. If only, thought Rob, I could do the same.

After two weeks in Sydney, Boots suggested they return home. It had been wonderful, he said, but he could do with some peace. The people and the traffic were getting him down. Rob smiled and neglected to point out that the compressors on the field were equally noisy. At first the boys grumbled then brightened up when they realised how they could boast about their travels to their schoolmates. Kate too was not averse to the thought of returning home, but she glanced at Rob.

'What do you think?'

'A good idea.' He forced a grin. 'Perhaps in a few more days.'

The next day he left the hotel and went off on his own again. He was in a strange mood. He walked the busy streets through crowds of hurrying people and didn't know what he wanted. He wandered aimlessly, glancing in the shop windows, and then came to a halt outside a gracious old building, tastefully renovated. Above the doorway was a sign, 'Halycon Gallery'. A poster was pinned to the door showing photographs of what were presumably paintings on show inside the building. It was the poster which caught Rob's attention.

One of the photographs was of a painting showing a girl sitting in a hard-backed chair. She was looking directly out of the canvas, her hands clasped in her lap. Rob peered at the photograph then stood back and looked at it again. There was a strange feeling in the pit of his stomach. He was absolutely certain the girl in the painting was Dorothea Bellows. He stood still for a minute then he stirred and his eyes moved to a metal plate attached to the door. Good, the gallery was open. He went inside.

The poster had said the paintings were by a promising new artist from England. His work was displayed on the second floor of the gallery. Rob climbed the curving staircase and found the room. The sun streamed through the large windows and gilded the polished wooden floor. About twenty paintings hung on the walls.

The larger pieces of work were of the modern school, large swirling masses of brilliant colour, but Rob ignored these. He went directly to stand in front of the small painting on the far side of the room. It *was* Dorothea! His hands clenched at his side. She was just as he remembered. A huge wave of home-sickness crashed down on him. Vividly, he remembered their walks with Jake, the gentle pooling of light from street lamps upon damp pavements, the smell from the fish and chip shop. He almost heard the gruff voices of the men working on the Fish Dock. He closed his eyes. He was a small boy again, hearing the squeak of chalk upon the school blackboard, smelling the strange odour of the swimming baths. He opened his eyes. There must be an assistant somewhere, a curator? A girl with long blonde hair stood before a picture near the doorway of the room. Rob went up to her.

'The picture over there.' He waved his hand. 'Can you tell me something about it?'

'I'm sorry.' The girl gave a timid smile. 'I'm like you. I've just come in to see the paintings but,' she nodded towards the far corner of the room, 'there's a bell on that desk.'

'Thanks, I never noticed.' Rob hurried to the desk and pressed the bell. A minute later a tall man with a bald head appeared in the doorway.

'Yes?'

'Are you the curator?'

'No. He's at lunch actually. But perhaps I can help you?'

Rob led the man to the picture. 'If it's for sale as I presume it is, I want to buy it.'

'I'm sorry.' The bald-headed man hesitated. 'I see you haven't bought a catalogue. If you had you would have seen that the pictures with a small blue seal on the corner of the frame are for sale. This painting has no such seal.'

'So I can't buy it?'

'No, I'm afraid not.'

'Look,' Rob bit his lip, 'I'll pay over the odds.'

'It's not the money, it's . . .'

'Could I see the artist? I have a special reason for buying the picture, you see. Will he see me?'

The man he had interrupted gave him a curious look. 'I'm sorry you're disappointed but it's not a question of the price. Mr Paige, he's the painter, is not in Sydney. I'm his business manager. I'm in charge of this collection. Only four of the pictures are for sale. We need the other exhibits, we're showing them in other cities, you see. Also,' he paused, 'I'm certain Mr Paige would not sell that particular work.'

'Oh.' Rob stared at the painting. He felt a dull ache of disappointment. 'Well, I'll have a catalogue then.'

The tall man handed him a catalogue and waved away the money Rob offered. 'Take it with my compliments.' He looked over Rob's shoulder. 'It is a wonderful painting, isn't it?'

Rob nodded.

He walked slowly back towards the hotel, clutching the catalogue in his hand. And as he walked the dullness, his feeling of indecision, departed. By the time he had reached the hotel, washed and changed his shirt, he had made up his mind. At dinner, over a starter of melon cocktail, he told the others: 'I'm taking a trip to England.'

'Good God!' Boots dropped his spoon. 'Why?'

Rob shrugged. 'I want to, that's why.'

'I think you've gone mad.' Boots ignored the warning looks Kate was semaphoring to him with her eyebrows. 'You've no family over there. Anyway, what did England do for us?'

'I know – but I still need to go.' Rob brooded, hurt by Boots's disapproval. 'I don't know how to explain. It's just something I have to do.' He forced a smile to his face. 'You'll come with me, won't you, Nicky?'

'*Me*!' Dismay filled his son's face. 'But I'll miss the start of the new term! I've got a new teacher and we're going to study geology. Do I have to go, Dad? It's ages since we were at home and Pete and me have planned heaps of things to do.'

'But, Nicky—' Rob heard the plea in his voice and coloured. 'You'd like it there. It's a marvellous opportunity.'

His son stared at him then dropped his head and moodily spooned pieces of melon into his mouth. Looking at him, Rob could see only the double crown in his thick, dark hair.

He sighed. 'OK, if school's that important to you, then I won't go.'

Kate studied his face. 'You're really keen on this idea, Rob?' she asked.

'I was,' he admitted.

'Then you go. Nicky can move in with us until you get back.' Her quiet voice held reassurance. 'You know he'll be OK with us.'

'That's good of you, Kate, but if I went I'd be away about six weeks. It will cost a hell of a lot of money. It wouldn't be worth travelling all that way just for a couple of weeks.'

'That doesn't make any difference. You know we love Nicky. I think you should go, Rob. There's something you have to get out of your system. Perhaps a trip home will do it.'

He hesitated, torn by doubts. 'What about it, Nick? What do you think. Would you miss me?'

'Of course.' Nicky's head came up. He thought a moment then grinned. 'You'd write often, wouldn't you? Remember to put lots of stamps on the envelopes.'

Nicky and Peter had recently developed a craze for stamp collecting.

'No, I don't think I'll go.' Looking at his son, Rob thought he loved him too much to leave him, even if Nicky himself didn't seem to mind the idea.

'Aw, go on, Dad. I don't mind, honest.' Nicky's grin grew wilder. 'Aunt Kate's cooking is a lot better than yours anyway.'

Rob's hand went to the pocket of his jacket. He could feel the catalogue through the material. He had been away so long – what would he find in England if he returned? Nicky had picked up the menu from the table and was looking to see what was the main course. He certainly didn't seem worried or upset. Rob made up his mind. He would do it – he would go to England!

He turned in his seat and beckoned to a nearby waiter. 'We'll have a bottle of champagne, please.'

PART III
HOMING

Chapter Thirty-Nine

Rob looked down at the landing lights winking in the blackness and was overwhelmed with excitement. They had arrived! He was back in the country of his birth. The woman in the seat next to him gave a nervous cough and he turned and smiled at her. She was in her mid-forties and her face held a frightened expression. Rob noticed that the knuckles on her hands gleamed whitely as she clutched at the armrests of her seat.

'We're almost there,' he comforted her.

She forced a sickly smile. 'Stupid, I know, but I hate this part. I'm all right when we're in the air.'

He nodded.

'You seem perfectly relaxed, young man. Do you travel by plane often?'

'No. This is my first trip.'

'Young man!' Rob supposed to her he did seem a young man but he was twenty-eight years of age now and hadn't really felt young for years. He grimaced. The last time he felt young was the day he married Irene, in Kingoonya. The plane flew lower. He looked out of the window again but it was too dark to see anything. There were only the friendly lights, showing the way. He felt another surge of excitement.

Damn it! At this moment he did feel young, scared-young, uncertain, yet full of hopes and anticipation. It felt good! He had started his journey filled with a deep sense of guilt but as the hours had slipped away that had departed. Frustrating thoughts about his problems, his marriage to Irene, what to do next with his life, even – God forgive him – Nicky, had receded into the background. He was on his way home!

So this was London. Rob stopped walking and shook his head in bewilderment. A man carrying a briefcase bumped into him, tipped his bowler hat in apology and hurried on. Then a white-faced young woman wearing startling black eye-make up jostled his arm. Rob mumbled an apology but she had already disappeared. He stepped into the temporary refuge of a shop doorway and took out his notebook.

When the idea of coming to London had first struck him he had contacted a firm of Sydney travel agents. They had been most helpful. They had first suggested that he try and establish some link in England before travelling there. At first, he had refused. He was impatient to put his plan into action. But then he had seen the sense of their advice. So he had returned to Coober Pedy. He had seen Nicky settle into his new form and had written letters. Waiting had been difficult. At one time, he had almost decided not to bother! The whole idea was crazy. But there were so many unresolved feelings within him, and there was resentment too. Why had he been so summarily dispatched to Australia? Had anything come to light regarding the disappearance of his father? At other times he told himself he was just running away from his present unsatisfactory way of living.

The first communication he had received from England was a formal letter telling him that St Wilfred's School for Boys had been closed five years ago. Rob's file had been transferred to the Records Department situated in London. Rob was given the address and told that if he telephoned for an appointment he would be at liberty to study the papers. Then an airmail letter from Hazel Bellows had arrived.

Rob's hands had trembled as they handled the flimsy paper. Thank God, he thought, they were still at the old address. Hazel's letter was kindly. She was surprised, she wrote, that Rob still remembered them. She was in good health but her husband was poorly. Dorothea now lived in London. She was not married. She was one of the new career girls and had a wonderful job. Mrs Bellows enclosed her daughter's address and said she knew Dorothea would be pleased to see him. She ended her letter by saying she had often thought of the little lad who had taken their dog for walks, and who had been whisked off so swiftly to the other side of the world. Rob had worn a grim smile on his face as he carefully refolded the letter. At long last, that little lad was about to return.

London was a totally different world. Rob was thankful the money he had made from mining opal had allowed him to visit cities in Australia, otherwise, he thought, he couldn't have coped. He had read newspapers, of course, and seen newsreels but his main perception of England's capital city had been shaped by a couple of musty books he had read. On one of the sheep stations, a friend had been an avid fan of Dickens and he had lent Rob his books. They had been tattered old copies with illustrations by Phiz. With nothing else to do, Rob had read them eagerly and soon fallen victim to Dickens's magic, his colourful descriptions and wonderful, odd characters. Thereafter, Rob had seen London as a city of historic state buildings, houses inhabited by the rich and dark twisting streets teeming with the poor. Reality was different.

The palaces and parks were as impressive as he had imagined, and the Houses of Parliament by the side of the silver water of the River Thames enchanted him, but so much of the city, old London, was being swallowed up by rebuilding. Rob saw the famous Golden Lane Flats, seventeen storeys high, and the new Thorn House, towering over the Victorian frontages of the Charing Cross area. He spotted special shops called delicatessens which sold exotic foodstuffs he had never heard of. He was surprised by the number of foreign nationalities thronging the streets. He saw loose-limbed Jamaicans, groups of young people chattering in foreign languages. They were, he surmised, overseas students. One morning a beautiful Indian woman glided passed him with a flutter of her silken sari.

Drinking in a pub, he heard a Cockney voice lamenting the disappearance of the frosted glass partitions and mahogany fittings. Glancing about him, Rob saw red metal funnel lamps and perforated hardboard, and realised that even for the inhabitants of the city, times were changing fast. He watched and listened and found everything fascinating. He had been in London for three days. He was adapting to the accent, the time change and his surroundings.

He left the pub. Outside, he shivered. Pity about the weather, he thought. But he knew it wasn't just the change in temperature that was affecting him. He was going to try and find Dorothea.

Dorothea laid down her pen, stretched and then yawned. Last night she had not gone to bed at all, merely snatched a couple of hours' rest on the couch in the corner of her office. But now she could relax. The final arrangements for the Oxford and Cambridge function had been completed.

After an upset with his usual venue, Lord Berkeley had contacted the Coleridge Hotel and said he would like to hold the annual event there. It had fallen to Dorothea to co-ordinate the arrangements. She checked off her list again. It had been a rush but she had done it, even to that special touch of specifying that the flower arrangements on the tables be in the appropriate two tones of blue. She collected up her notes, her books, and the list of telephone numbers and threw them into the top drawer of her desk. Then she sat back in her chair and looked about her.

As always, the sight of the beautiful room in which she worked brought her pleasure. The room was large, the floor carpeted with thick, mushroom-coloured broadloom which added to the feeling of space. On the pale green walls hung signed photographs of celebrities Dorothea had met. Two years ago Adam Whitney had appointed her Press Officer and Functions Director of the Coleridge Hotel. The appointment had surprised her. She had thought she had found her niche heading the Publicity department. The staff there had grown due to a much increased workload because of the take-over of the Summers' Group. Two ambitious young men had joined her team, Simon Leckonby and Ian Turner. Mr Sanders had retired. Dorothea had delighted in her work. The pressure of responsibility, the long hours, had not troubled her. She loved the challenge of solving immediate problems and the hurly-burly of the life. Then Adam had moved her to the Coleridge.

'If you remember, you didn't want to go to Publicity,' he reminded her when she protested.

'But that was different. I didn't know anything about Publicity then,' she replied.

'The same thing applies to your new appointment, Dorothea.' Adam was wearing that look on his face which meant he would brook no argument. 'I'm appointing Leckonby to your old job. I think he's up to it. I need you at the Coleridge.'

A month later she had walked into the beautiful office she now occupied.

In monetary terms, her present position was a definite promotion. For the first time in her life, Dorothea did not have to worry about paying bills. She could afford to buy beautiful clothes and fripperies for her home. And in many ways, her Press work was similar to that conducted in the Company's Publicity department. But now she handled Press Relations for the nobility, the blue-blooded descendants of the proudest names in England. She organised grand functions for people who were used to grandeur. Her clients were people who went to Venice to buy their glassware, who popped over to Longchamps to see their 'gee-gees' run.

Dorothea gritted her teeth and set out to learn new

lessons in life. In time she came to know and like many of the people she worked for but at other times, when someone bewailed a temporary lull in fortune, told her they had been forced to sell their third car, her smile became forced. She thought of her father and how he had worked so hard all his life. Now he was in the last stages of emphysema, coughing out his lungs in the little council house in Hull. Dennis had never been abroad in his life.

A gleam of humour lightened Dorothea's sombre thoughts. Come to think of it, neither had she! When she was little Dorrie Bellows, back home, going abroad had been one of her ambitions but now she was Miss Bellows, Thea to her friends, she had the money but not the time.

It had been Charles Richardson who had first started to call her 'Thea'. When she had protested, he had laughed.

'Come off it, darling. Here I am escorting an attractive, intelligent woman about town, a woman who knows lots of important people . . . how can she *not* want to change your name? I mean *Dorrie*! Anyway, Thea isn't a proper change, merely a derivative.'

The conversation had taken place at Dorothea's flat. Charles had been waiting for her to change. He was to take her out to dinner. He looked up and smiled when she marched out of her bedroom and glared at him.

'That's a typically "Charles" remark! You've always hated my name, haven't you? What a pity you can't introduce me as Cynthia Chomley-Walters or some other double-barrelled mouthful!'

'Ouch!' He had winced. Watching his eyes crinkle at the corners, Dorothea wished, not for the first time, that he wasn't so damned attractive.

On the night she had invited him in for coffee and he had stayed with her until daybreak, he had done much to soothe the still raw wound of Greg's defection. He had sensed her need for comfort and reassurance and with few words but great skill he had taken her to bed and made love to her.

Afterwards she had fallen immediately into sleep but awoke to a hot flush of embarrassment when she saw him tip-toeing about the bedroom collecting his clothes. She had started to speak but he had shook his head.

'If a pale grey sock turns up, love,' he had said. 'Stick it in an envelope and send it to me, will you?'

Then he had bent over her and kissed the tip of her nose. 'You were absolutely lovely but I can't help feeling you might be regretting things this morning. Please don't. I'll never refer to what happened last night unless you do first. But don't give up on our friendship, will you? I'll ring you next week.' He had flipped his fingers at her and departed.

Remembering, Dorothea unconsciously softened her tone.

'I'm not ashamed of my name, Charles. You must stop trying to make me over. I shall never be one of your fluffy blondes, you know.'

'Thank God for that!' He stood up. 'I don't want to make you over, darling. It's just that Dorrie no longer suits the woman you have become, and Thea *does*. Look!' He caught hold of her hand and swung her round to face the mirror. 'Tell me I'm wrong!'

Dorothea gazed at her reflection. She had taken particular pains with her appearance this evening for she knew her occasional outings with Charles always attracted attention. It amused her that the Society circles in which he moved couldn't quite work out their precise relationship. How amused they would be, she pondered, if they knew that she felt equally confused. She did not love Charles, he did not love her, and yet . . .

She shivered as she felt his hand caress her neck. She thought of their shared moments of laughter, the times their business lives crossed and they solved problems together or took part in animated arguments. A long time ago she had told Adam Whitney they were friends. They were still friends but there also existed between them an exciting unspoken tension. A tension, she admitted, which was entirely due to sexual attraction. Most times she fought against that attraction, she had no desire to become one of the string of his girl friends, but occasionally she succumbed. She moved away from his touch.

'You approve of my new outfit, do you?'

'You look fantastic.'

She wore a short black crepe dress with a gently flaring skirt which stopped at the knee. The lines of the dress were deceptively simple and the high plain neckline emphasised the purity of the creamy complexion above. Over the dress she wore a dramatic evening jacket of beetle green moiré silk which drew attention to her unusually coloured eyes. She took a last glance in the mirror and conceded that Charles had a point.

She shrugged. 'Thea it is, then – but don't invent any titled parents for me!'

Charles laughed and hugged her as they went towards the door. 'I wouldn't dare.'

Now, seated behind her desk, Dorothea realised how rarely she actually had the time just to sit and think. For the last three years her life-style had been hectic, but recently it felt as if she was on a merry-go-round that was whirling out of control. She picked up a pencil and played with it. Perhaps she ought to take a holiday? Her neck muscles were tense and her eyes felt tired. But she found it hard to relax nowadays. She realised she was gripping the pencil tightly between her fingers and laid it down on the desk.

She glanced around her office again in an effort to reassure herself. So many years, she thought suddenly. So many years since she had gone off to that draughty classroom in Hull to practise her shorthand. But she'd done it, hadn't she? She'd fulfilled her ambitions, all of them. Dear Mr Spence. She sighed. She supposed he had died long ago. How the years hurried by. She wished she had been able to keep in touch with Nancy. It seemed like yesterday when they had walked home together from the factory. Was she living happily with her brush salesman? She frowned suddenly and tried to switch her mind from the thought of Nancy in a little house somewhere with a smiling brush salesman and her three boys. They had probably grown up to be holy terrors, she thought. And maybe Nancy had more children now, quarrelling and fighting. That's what most of the households had been like in the Hessle Road area of Hull. Dorothea thought of her own beautiful flat full of pictures and was comforted.

She wondered when Charles would ring. He had been on an extended trip to America but, if her memory served her, he had been due to return to England a week ago.

Thank God her relationship with him had survived. Not only survived but developed into a friendship which enhanced her life. Without Charles, her experience with Greg might totally have fouled her up. Many attractive men had asked Dorothea to go out with them over the past years but she had always refused. She had never felt the slightest inclination to get embroiled in an affair. Some of her suitors had felt affronted. One man, in particular, had refused to accept her indifference to him. He had bombarded her with small gifts, flowers, telephone calls. In the end, he had become a nuisance and she had told him so. He had retaliated by calling her a cold bitch. She had shrugged, unmoved. The truth was romance held a low priority in her life. She preferred the excitement of her career.

She wondered how the American trip had gone. On impulse, she decided to see if Charles was in. She picked up her telephone, paused, then put it down again. He would ring her when he was ready. She would not chase after him. She read a report then signed some letters. With sudden resolve she picked up the telephone again. Why shouldn't she ring him? He was a business colleague as well as a friend and occasional lover.

'Hello.' His voice sounded thick with sleep.

'It's me, Thea.' She was amused. 'God, Charles, you can't still be asleep at this hour?'

'Why not? I worked damn hard in the States, Thea, and I don't have to meet with the Board until tomorrow.' Charles's voice sharpened, became alert. 'Things all right with you?'

'OK. A sudden request from Lord Berkeley set up a panic here but I've cleared my desk now. In fact, I was just thinking, I need a break. Do you fancy meeting me this evening. You could tell me about America?'

'I'm not sure.' Charles's voice was hesitant. 'Thing is, it's a bit difficult right now.'

'Oh?' She frowned, suddenly realising. 'I'm sorry. You're not alone, are you?'

'No. I'll ring you later, shall I? We could meet tomorrow?'

'Fine.' Cursing the flatness in her voice, Dorothea forced herself to sound animated. 'Don't rush. Leave it until next week. Hope things go well with the Board.'

She replaced the phone, and taking a pack of cigarettes from her desk drawer, lit one with jerky movements. Her own feelings infuriated her. She drew deeply on her cigarette. Why did such episodes throw her so much? She knew he saw other women. It was no secret. Was it because she saw only Charles and he knew it? To hell with it all! She stubbed out the cigarette. What she needed was some sleep.

There was a soft knock on her door. Her secretary entered.

'What is it, Frances?'

'There's a gentleman outside. His name is Steyart. He hasn't an appointment but he says he's sure you will see him.'

'I'm just on my way home. I'm not seeing anyone . . .' She stopped. '*What* name did you say?'

'Steyart.' The secretary paused, curious at the expression of disbelief on Dorothea's face. 'He has a funny accent,' she said helpfully. 'I think he's Australian.'

'Good grief!' Dorothea stared into space for a moment, then recollected herself. 'Show him in, please.'

Frances disappeared and a moment later a man of stocky build and medium height stood in her place. In silence, Dorothea stared at his sun-tanned face, strong features; at his firm jaw line and the resolute curve of his lips.

'My God, it *is* you!'

'It is.' Rob's face broke into a huge grin.

'But . . . you're in Australia.'

'Not now. I arrived here a couple of days ago.'

'I can't believe this.' Dorothea gestured helplessly. 'Do sit down. Tell me, how did you find me? Are you staying in London?'

The words tumbled from her mouth. She kept her eyes fixed on Rob. Throughout the years she had never completely forgotten him but in her thoughts he had remained the shock-headed schoolboy of ten years old. Seeing the stranger before her, she felt almost shy, and yet, looking into his deep-set eyes, she felt a sense of recognition stir inside her. She stood up and came from behind her desk, holding out her hands. He seized them and squeezed them in his own hard, strong fingers.

'I wrote to your mother. Didn't she tell you?'

Dorothea cast her mind back. 'I don't think so. No, I'm sure she didn't.' She smiled at Rob and gently tugged her hands free. She moved to the door, opened it, called to Frances to bring coffee then came back into the room, talking all the time. 'Mum's had a lot of worries over Dad recently. He's in and out of hospital. I suppose she just forgot. Oh, Rob, you've no idea how pleased I am to see you.'

'I'm glad. I didn't know whether to come here. I've been ringing your home telephone number for the last two days but there was no reply, so I thought I'd try you at work. Do you mind?'

'Of course not.'

Frances came in with the coffee. She placed the tray

on a table near the couch then departed, throwing a curious look in Rob's direction.

'Come on, make yourself comfortable.' Dorothea led the way to the couch and poured out the coffee. They sat down and smiled into each other's eyes until Dorothea became embarrassed by Rob's intent gaze and looked away.

'Sorry about the phone. I've been terribly busy these past few days so I've stayed over at the hotel.'

'It doesn't matter. Your mum said you had a fantastic job.' Rob looked round the office. 'You've certainly done well for yourself, Dorrie.'

'Yes.' She grinned at him. Her tiredness had evaporated. 'But what about you?'

Rob told her about his partnership with Boots and their lucky strike of opals. 'I've had some difficulties at home. Suddenly I just decided to take a trip to the Old Country. Silly of me, perhaps.' He shrugged his shoulders defensively.

Dorothea saw the lines around his eyes and mouth. He was several years younger than she was but looked older. She remembered the young boy she had known and the way he had been shipped off overseas and felt sympathy for the man he had become. She touched his hand.

'I rang the Home, you know. After your letter letting me know you were being sent to Australia.'

'Who did you speak to – Carlisle?' Rob's smile was mirthless. 'Got short change from him, I bet. Still,' he looked down, 'there's a lot worse than him in the world.'

Such bitterness! Dorothea made a decision.

'Come on, let's get out of the hotel. We can go back to my place. We have a lot of years to catch up on.'

She spoke briefly to her secretary, then they left the office. They took the lift down and she smiled as she watched him silently take in the magnificence of the entrance hall where crystal chandeliers hung above dark red carpeting and page boys in white gloves scurried about delivering messages. He stopped

before the huge vases of cool white lilies rising from
banks of rowan berries which were displayed in
alcoves each side of the sweeping staircase.

'My goodness, Kate would love those.'

'Kate? Is she your wife?'

Again his brow furrowed. 'No,' he answered
shortly. 'Just a friend.'

Their conversation during the journey to the flat
was spasmodic. Rob seemed unnerved by the number
of people travelling on the Underground.

'How do you bear it?'

'What?'

'These crowds.'

'You get used to it. Haven't you been down here
before?'

'God, no. I used taxis.'

'I see. I do, too. But it's easier on the Tube, as long
as it isn't rush hour, of course.'

'Isn't this rush hour?'

'Oh, no. It gets much worse than this.'

'My God!'

Dorothea smiled as Rob lapsed into silence. Their
lives had certainly followed different paths. How
strange that he should come looking for her. She was
glad he had. She realised she was interested to know
about his life.

Inside Dorothea's flat he collapsed into an easy
chair with a sigh of relief. 'That's better.'

She took off her coat. 'Want something to eat?'

'No. That's all I seem to do all day – eat. If you
don't mind, can we just talk? Catch up on old times?'

'All right.'

Feeling awkward, now that they were on their own,
Dorothea perched on the arm of a chair opposite.
'Where do we start?'

Rob ruffled his hair, a self-conscious gesture. 'I'm
not sure. Do you mind if I take off my jacket? I'm not
used to wearing one in the house.'

'Help yourself.' She watched as he stood up. He's
muscular for his height, she thought, remembering

417

again the skinny schoolboy. She couldn't stop looking at him. One minute he seemed a perfect stranger then she thought she could detect traces of the boy he had been. It was intriguing.

'That's better.' He sat down and suddenly sent her a heart-warming whole-hearted smile. 'It's not easy, is it? Over the years, I've dreamed of this moment but now that it's here . . .' He shrugged. 'I was remembering a plump girl with a hot temper who worked at the Tinworks and was kind to me and an ugly mutt of a dog. Of course—' remembering the painting he paused. 'I knew you must have changed but now . . .' He rubbed his chin and grinned again, but this time the grin held confused admiration and embarrassment. 'I hardly recognise you, Dorrie.'

She blushed.

'It's more of a shock for me,' she protested. 'I didn't know you were coming. And look at you! What happened to the scrawny little lad who used to serenade me?'

'Jeez!' Rob clapped his hand to his head. 'I'd forgotten about that.'

They both laughed, and from then on it was easier. They talked and talked but avoided personal issues. Dorothea told Rob about her work in York and how she rose to her present position. Rob told her about life in Australia. Finally, he caught her concealing a yawn. Immediately, he stood up.

'I mustn't outstay my welcome,' he said. 'I forgot, if you've had to stay over at work these past days, you must be very tired. I'd like to meet you again, though, if that's all right with you?'

'I'd like that.' Dorothea gave him a warm smile. She had caught the slight hesitation in his voice. 'After all these years, I don't want you just to disappear again. In fact,' she deliberated, 'I think I'll try and book a few days' leave. It's certainly due to me and there's nothing urgent on at work now.'

'That would be beaut.' He gave her a serious look.

'But I wouldn't want you to get into trouble. Will it be OK with your boss?'

Dorothea smiled. 'Quite OK.'

He still hasn't realised, she thought. He doesn't know I *am* the boss.

'Ring me tomorrow and we'll make plans.' She stood up. 'How are you getting back to your hotel? On the Underground?'

'Hell, no.' He collected his jacket. 'Will you ring me a taxi?'

She waved from the window as the cab pulled away, then glanced at the clock. They had talked for three hours. Perhaps, she mused, they could travel up to Hull for a couple of days. He was bound to want to visit the place and she could see her mum and dad. She smiled and went to run herself a bath.

Chapter Forty

Two days after the unexpected appearance of Rob Steyart in her office, Dorothea insisted on taking him out to dinner. She chose a small, intimate Italian restaurant to which Charles had occasionally taken her. The food, she knew, was excellent and the atmosphere relaxed. As yet, she realised, she knew so little of Rob and she would hate to intimidate him by taking him somewhere he would be uncomfortable. God knows, if he had lived in the Outback for most of his life, perhaps he had never before visited a decent restaurant!

By the time the main course arrived at their table, she was able to laugh at her fears, even feel a little ashamed. Rob Steyart was certainly no savage. He seemed perfectly at home and surprised her when he spoke a few words in Italian to their waiter.

'What did you say?' she asked.

'I told him the pasta was superb and I hoped he would bring me a generous portion of zabaglione.' He laughed at her expression. 'Where I live,' he explained, 'it's like the United Nations. One of my best friends is Dino Fabrasi. He came over from Naples four years ago.'

'Tell me about them all, Rob. I'd love to hear.'

They ordered more wine and then talked. Dorothea was fascinated by his tales. Her admiration for him grew. Somehow, despite his hard times, he had managed to learn so much, gain positive things from his experiences. His knowledge of Italian, for instance. How many other men, she thought, would have taken the trouble to learn a friend's language?

She was amused to see the only time he was embarrassed was when she insisted on paying the bill.

'It just doesn't feel right, Dorrie. What sort of chap allows a woman to pay for his meal?'

It was a remark her father would have made! She patted his hand. 'It was my invitation, Rob, and it is my pleasure to pay.'

He submitted with bad grace, and only 'if you come out with me very soon'.

Two days later he arrived in a taxi and swept her off to a superior dinner at a plush restaurant whose large windows overlooked the River Thames.

'How did you know about this place? It only opened a month ago,' Dorothea asked.

He grinned cheerfully. 'I soon find my way about,' he replied. 'I'm a fast learner.'

You certainly are, thought Dorothea. The more she found out about Rob, the more she wanted to know.

'You still keen to go up north?' she asked him.

'Too true.'

'Right. I'll fix up those days off work.'

They were on their way to the north. Rob was driving and Dorothea held the map on her lap. She looked across at him and smiled.

'You're enjoying this, aren't you?'

'You bet I am. The surface is fantastic. Certainly beats most of the roads I've driven on in Australia.'

'We're making good time. We'll stop for a drink soon, shall we? Then press on to Hull.'

He nodded then concentrated on the road in front of him. As the traffic thinned, he relaxed. It felt good to be driving a car again. He admired an elegant, modern bridge they passed beneath, then, as the scenery unfolded around them like a reel of cinema tape, he thought about Dorothea.

His first sight of her, the sheer style of the woman seated behind the large desk, had petrified him. Finding the hotel, waiting to see her, he had imagined all sorts of images yet had not produced anything close to the reality. His first reaction had been dismay. Then she had raised her eyelashes, which were thick and long and flecked with gold, and he had known it would be all right. Initially, her expression had been wary but then she had smiled and her straight gaze had held pleasure and warmth. He knew then that the girl he remembered was still there, however expensively packaged in smart clothes and good grooming. And today, he decided, she looked even more wonderful, dressed in slim black trousers, a sweater which was a funny burnt-orange sort of colour and wearing no make-up. Her short hair was ruffled in the breeze coming through the partly opened window and the sun had brought freckles out on her nose. He sighed contentedly.

'I'm glad you don't wear that thick black stuff around your eyes, Dorrie. I got a shock when I saw the girls in London. Some of them look like pandas!'

He glanced at her in time to see her eyebrows lift and wondered if he had spoken out of turn. But then she gave a short laugh.

'That black stuff, as you call it, Rob, is peel-off eyeliner and it's the height of fashion for the kids. It's hardly my scene. I'm over thirty now, you know.'

'So you are. I'd quite forgotten.' He drove in silence for a few minutes then commented: 'It's strange, but now that I'm back in England and in your company I sometimes feel that I've never been away. Australia seems a dream.' He sighed. 'Except for Nicky, of course.'

'Your son, yes.' Her voice was quiet. 'You must miss him a lot.'

'I do.' He peered ahead. 'We come off this road soon, don't we?'

'About five minutes' more driving, I think.' She checked the map.

'I had my first letter from him yesterday,' he went on. 'He sounded fine. Doesn't seem to be missing me at all!'

'But that's good.' Dorothea sat forward, watching

for the next signpost. 'From what you've told me, he's an independent little boy. And he's sent you a letter, he must be thinking about you sometimes.'

'Yes, you're right. You know, Dorrie – I thought you would have children by now. You'd be good with them. You certainly were with me.'

He saw darkness gather on her face and his reminiscent smile faded. 'I'm sorry. I never meant . . .'

'It's all right.' She turned her head away. 'It was a long time ago.' She pointed. 'There, we turn off there.'

They continued their journey, sometimes talking, sometimes sitting in silence, but it was an unstrained silence. During the past days they had renewed their bond of friendship. They had talked of many things but left out the private areas. Dorothea knew that Rob was separated from his wife but had custody of his son. Rob knew that Dorothea had lived a long time with someone but that the relationship had not worked out. Now she concentrated on her career. That was all. For the moment it was enough that they had slipped so easily into acceptance of each other's company.

It was two in the afternoon when they reached the outskirts of Hull. Dorothea looked up in surprise when Rob suddenly stopped the car.

'What is it?'

'Nothing.' His voice was abstracted. 'Just wanted to stretch my legs.'

'But we're nearly there.'

He did not reply, just opened the door, got out and walked to the front of the vehicle. He leaned against the bumper of the car, put his hands in his pockets and gazed into space. Dorothea frowned, then followed him. A chill breeze had sprung up. It made her shiver.

'You can tell we're back in the north,' she commented.

'Maybe that's it.' Rob's face as he looked at her was pale beneath his tan. 'I was fine in London, but coming here . . .' He sighed.

'What is it, Rob?' Dorothea laid her hand on his arm. 'What do you expect to find here?'

'Haven't a clue, Dorrie, that's the trouble. Maybe I was mad to come back to England. I don't know what I'm looking for, but I *need* to find something!' He gave a rueful grin. 'Everything is such a mess.'

She patted his arm. 'Everyone feels like that at times, Rob. God knows, I have! I'm glad you came back. It's interesting to see how you've turned out.' She poked him in the ribs. 'Come on, stop feeling sorry for yourself. You've got your son and from what you've told me, quite a bit of money. Life can be exciting! You could do whatever you want, now.'

He straightened up. 'Sorry – didn't mean to pull a blue.' He noticed her shiver again. 'Come on, back in the car. You look frozen.'

'I feel the cold. Goodness, the chilblains I used to get when I was a kid!'

Rob opened the car door for her. 'And it's your spring,' he commented. 'You ought to visit Australia, Dorrie. Warm enough there for you.'

'Maybe one day I will.' Her answer was light but her brows drew together when she noticed the intent expression in his eyes.

Rob's mood changed to one of anticipation as he began to recognise familiar landmarks. 'Look,' he gestured, 'the Fisherman's Memorial – and there, that's my old school. Oh, just a minute.' He jammed on the brakes.

'What now?' Dorothea turned to see him smiling.

'That fish and chip shop's open. Let's buy some.'

'No, Rob. You know my mum, she'll have a meal waiting for us.'

'Please, Dorrie. You've no idea how often I've dreamt of eating some fish and chips straight out of the newspaper.'

And so they arrived at Warren Street with a huge parcel of fish and chips on the back seat of the car.

'The car hire people will love this,' murmured Dorothea as she got out. 'That smell will linger for ages.' But she smiled when the house door opened and Hazel appeared to greet them.

Dorothea had told her parents that Rob would be driving her to Hull but she had been concerned in case his presence might cause problems. She knew her father was too ill to be upset by strangers in his home. As it happened, everything went well. The excitement of the arrival, the soothing down of Hazel who had, as predicted by Dorothea, a roast in the oven, the rush to warm plates and produce salt and vinegar for the fish and chips, dispelled any stiffness over Rob's presence.

As the meal finished, Dorothea pushed aside the knowledge that she was bound to suffer from indigestion, she *never* ate fish and chips now, and looked round the circle of faces. She was glad to see Rob looked perfectly relaxed. He was eating the last of the chips with relish and chattering to Hazel about Australia. She was listening to him, her rosy face animated and happy.

'Mum,' she said suddenly, 'why didn't you tell me Rob was coming back to England?'

'I did, love.' Hazel looked puzzled. 'I wrote you all about it in the letter I sent with your Easter card.'

'I didn't get an Easter card!'

'Oh!' Hazel was upset. 'That's a shame. It was a lovely card. It had violets and lilies of the valley on it.'

'Never mind. At least Rob received his letter from you and knew where to find me.'

Dorothea looked at her father. Then her glance slid away. She didn't want him to notice the shock she was afraid might show on her face. It was over eight months since she had seen him last and his rapid deterioration distressed her.

Dennis's best jacket hung on his wasted frame. His cheeks had fallen in, giving him a skeletal appearance, and his skin had a sickly, yellowish cast. Nevertheless, he smiled at her and patted the place next to him on the settee.

'Come and sit here, Dorrie. Tell me what you've been up to.'

As Dorothea sat down she took hold of his hand and felt sad as she felt the frailty of his thin fingers. What had happened to the strong-willed, hard-bodied father who had dominated her childhood? She began to talk, in an animated manner, of her life in London. She told him about the Oxford and Cambridge function she had arranged, and the American film star she had met two weeks ago. She knew Dennis was inordinately proud not of the salary she now received but the fact she had attained a position of power and influence.

When she stopped, he patted her hand. 'You're doing well, lass,' he commented. He sighed. 'That was a bad business, you were a fool over that painter chappie, but you see, you've got over it! I always knew you would get on in life.'

'Dad!' Dorothea flushed and darted a look at Rob, hoping he had not heard. It was all right. He was deep in conversation with her mother.

'Now what have I said?' Dennis's voice sounded injured but his eyes twinkled. 'Always fire and water, aren't we, Dorrie? But I am proud of you. You must know that.'

Dorothea lowered her head and felt a lump in her throat.

He patted her hand again then sat back. 'Did you go to the Rally, in Trafalgar Square?'

She turned a puzzled face towards him. 'Pardon?'

'The "Ban the Bomb" Rally, during the Easter holiday? Don't look so daft, lass. I'm only asking a question.'

Comprehension dawned. 'Oh, that. No. I didn't.'

'Pity. If I'd have been in London, I would have gone.' Dennis chuckled at the look on her face. 'Don't worry, I'm not senile. My lungs and my legs are packing up but there's nowt wrong with my brain. I read the papers.' He peered at her from beneath eyebrows like wire wool. 'Don't you?'

'Of course I do. When I have time.'

She caught the defensive note in her voice and

inwardly cursed. He's doing it again, she thought. Putting me in the wrong.

'Read the papers, Dorrie. Read as many of them as you can.' Dennis coughed. 'They all put their own bloody point of view, of course, but still, read them. Like I said, I'm proud of what you've achieved, but don't you go getting cocky. There's more to life than making money, you know. A lot of things are changing. You need to keep your eyes open.'

His voice thinned and he wheezed, then coughed again. Hazel jumped to her feet.

'Oh, Dennis, you've overdone things. You know you shouldn't talk so much. Let me help you upstairs for a rest.'

'Could I help you, sir?' Rob came across to Dennis and bent over him.

'No, no.' Dennis waved him away. 'Dorrie can help me. You two get on with your conversation. As for me, the day I can't talk will be the day I pop my clogs. Still,' he sighed, 'I think I will have a rest.'

Assisted by Dorothea, he made the slow climb up the stairs. On each third step, he had to stop to fight for breath.

'They're too much for you, Dad. Why doesn't Mum bring a bed downstairs?' Dorothea's voice was fierce.

'No, I won't let her.' He clung on to her arm. 'We're nearly there.'

In the bedroom, she unlaced his shoes for him and eased them off his feet. She helped him lie on the bed then covered him with a quilted bedspread. When she finished she was biting back her tears.

'Surely the doctors can do more for you?'

'No.' Dennis had closed his eyes.

Looking at his bleached and beaky profile Dorothea thought that if it wasn't for the pulse racing in his throat, he could have been dead already. She jumped when he suddenly turned his face towards her and looked at her. 'I'm just worn out, Dorrie. Can't blame the doctors for that, can we?'

When she did not reply a smile flickered around his pale lips. He gestured for her to sit on the side of the bed. She did so.

'Good girl. Knew you wouldn't talk a lot of rubbish about me getting better. We all have to die, now it's my turn.' He breathed noisily, sucking the air for breath. 'I suppose I should say something to you, something important, but I'm damned if I can think of anything.' He smiled at her. 'We understand each other, don't we?'

'Yes, Dad.' Dorothea's voice was almost inaudible.

'Sorry you haven't got a chap but, you know,' Dennis paused, 'there's a lot of nonsense talked about love. There's two kinds of people, Dorrie. There's the "takers" and the "givers". That Greg, he was a "taker". That would have been all right but,' he paused again and through his half-opened eyes a malicious twinkle showed, 'you're a "taker" as well.'

Dorothea bit her lip and resisted a strong inclination to withdraw her hand from her father's grip. Nevertheless, Dennis must have felt her slight recoil.

'Now don't get annoyed. There's nothing wrong with being a "taker". I'm one! Your mum's a "giver" and although you may not believe this, we've had a happy marriage. And don't go thinking "givers" are weak, because they're not. In some ways they're stronger than we are. Still,' he sighed. 'I don't know why I'm telling you all this. You'll go your own way, thank God. You're strong-willed and you need a strong chap. Greg was weak. But don't put all your energies into work, Dorrie. That would be a waste of a good woman . . .'

Dennis's voice was trailing away now. He was drifting off to sleep. Dorothea stood up to go but her father roused himself.

'You'll keep your eye on your mother, won't you, love? Although,' his voice faded and Dorothea had to lean over him to catch his next words, 'Hazel might surprise you. I'd like to think so . . .'

His words ceased. Dorothea straightened up and

tiptoed to the bedroom door. She looked back at the pitifully shrunken body on the bed and felt once more the disturbing mixture of hostility, admiration and love she always felt in the presence of her father.

Downstairs, Rob was preparing to leave.

'I'm sorry we can't put you up, dear.' Hazel's face was anxious. 'We've only the two bedrooms, see, and with Dennis's illness . . .'

'It's no bother, honestly,' Rob reassured her. 'I'm booked into a hotel not far from here. And I'll see you tomorrow. Dorothea is going to take me round some of the old haunts.'

'Come about two o'clock,' she said. 'That will give Mum and me the morning to have a natter.' She smiled at Hazel.

'I'll do that.' Rob shook hands with Hazel, hesitated, then finally dropped a shy kiss on her cheek before leaving.

'He seems to have grown into a nice chap, Dorrie.' Hazel smiled at her daughter after Rob had left.

'Yes,' replied Dorothea. 'It's good to see him again.'

'Better bring your top coat, it's cold again.' Rob grinned as Dorothea pulled a face at him. She had slept well and now she felt happier, confident about the future. It was a Sunday and the streets were quiet when Rob parked the car in the centre of Hull. They began to walk and Dorothea pointed out to him the many changes that had occurred over the past seventeen years. There were high rise flats and new businesses everywhere. In Hedon Road Dorothea paused and gestured to the Imperial Typewriter factory which had opened during the fifties.

'That reminds me of my night-classes,' she said.

'Just a minute.' Rob stopped walking. He fumbled in his pocket and brought out an old envelope and a pencil, then he thought for a moment and drew something on the paper. He showed it to Dorothea. 'There!'

Dorothea looked down at the tiny symbol, the thin upward stroke, the thick downward line. 'I remember that,' she cried. 'Your name in shorthand – fancy you remembering!'

'It's being back in Hull with you,' he replied.

They passed the ABC Cinema in Ferensway. 'At least this cinema has stayed open.' Dorothea slipped her arm companionably through his. 'Mum was saying how many of them have shut since television's arrived.'

'Didn't this one do all kinds of things? Live entertainment, dances, things like that? Maybe that's why it's survived. Look, there's a poster outside now. Let's go and see what it says.'

They crossed the road and went to read the billboard.

'There's a dance on Wednesday night, Dorothea. Let's go. It might be fun.'

'I don't know.' She sounded dubious. 'I haven't been to a dance for ages.'

'All the more reason. Go on, say you will. Let's pretend we're eighteen again!'

The thought crossed Dorothea's mind that if she was eighteen again, Rob was therefore much too young to go dancing, but she smiled and agreed.

They explored further but the Sunday quietness and the bleak weather had a subduing effect on them and by mutual consent they retraced their path to the car and drove back to Hessle Road.

'Sorry,' Dorothea apologised. 'There's not a lot to do in Hull on a Sunday.'

'You should spend a Sunday in Coober Pedy!' Rob sounded as though he was suppressing a chuckle and Dorothea looked at him curiously. They were passing the Victorian frontage of West Dock Avenue School when the sun came out.

'That's an omen. Let's get out here.' Without waiting for Dorothea's response, Rob stepped on the brake. 'Now this place *does* bring back memories.'

Why does he have this obsession? wondered

Dorothea as she dutifully trailed after Rob as he hurried to the school gates. She came back only to see her parents. The one thing she remembered feeling about Hull when she was young was her eagerness to leave the place. If her memory was correct, Rob had been miserable living with his gran and miserable at school. Why did he insist on painting the past in rosy colours? Something to do with his sudden emigration, she concluded.

She jumped as Rob, who had been peering through a window, swung round to face her.

'Come on, Dorrie. We'll walk down to the Dock.'

He slung his arm about her shoulders and imperceptibly manoeuvred her along the Avenue. Annoyed, she opened her mouth to protest. She had no desire to walk along a smelly dock! Then she paused. The sun's rays were sending down welcome warmth, the grey sky was deepening to blue, and Rob's usually serious face was lively with pleasure. She shrugged. The weight of his arm about her shoulder disturbed her. She didn't really like being touched. And Rob was taking charge. She didn't like that, either. She moved away from him delicately and was relieved when he did not appear to notice, simply chattered on excitedly.

'The deckhands used to cut through the schoolyard sometimes and when they had been to the pub they used to throw pennies to us kids, do you remember? The teachers didn't like it. And, sometimes, if a trawler had just arrived home, a dad would come into school to see his kid; disrupt the classes and everything.' He sighed. 'I always felt jealous when that happened.'

They reached St Andrew's Dock. They wandered along, pitching stones into the quietly lapping water. Now both of them were reminiscing.

'I was always glad my dad worked on the railways,' Dorothea said. 'Nancy's dad smelt horrible when he came home from work.'

'Nancy? She was your best friend, wasn't she? What happened to her?'

Dorothea told him. 'I'm afraid I've lost touch with

432

her now,' she said. 'But her mum tells my mum things and I think she's happy with this traveller chap.'

'Good for her.' Rob stopped walking and sat down on a wooden trolley used for transporting fish baskets. Dorothea hesitated then sat down gingerly beside him. She was glad she wasn't wearing her usual Sunday clothes.

'It must have taken some guts for her to leave her husband.'

'Yes.' Dorothea's mouth quirked into a grin. 'The brush salesman must have had some guts, too.'

'Still, there's times when you have to stop drifting and make decisions, change things.'

'If you're unhappy, then I agree.'

'Are you happy?' Rob did not look at her.

'Yes, I think so. Although "content" might be. a better word.'

'I'm not – so I'm going to do something about it.'

'Good for you.' Dorothea looked at him curiously. 'You've already started, haven't you? I mean, you came over here.'

'Yes. But now I'm planning what to do when I go back.'

'Oh.'

Dorothea was surprised at her surprise. Of course, he would go back to Australia. It was his home now.

'I just wondered – I thought perhaps, now you have money, you might decide to stay here?'

'No.' Rob threw another stone into the Dock. They both stared at the widening ripples of water. 'It may sound stupid, but it's as if I had to come home to sort myself out. I needed to distance myself from my problems. I'm glad I came. It's been great, particularly seeing you again.' He smiled at her. 'But I don't belong in England any more. And I have Nicky to think of. There will be more opportunities for him in Australia. No, I'm working out what I will do when I get back, but I won't bore you with the details.'

'I'm not bored.'

Ignoring her protest, he stood up. Taking her hands, he pulled her to her feet.

'It was worth the trip over to see you again and know you've made a success of your life. I'm glad you're content, Dorrie.'

Impulsively, he dropped a quick kiss on her mouth. They were both the same height, standing close together, and it happened so quickly Dorothea had no time to be startled. Nevertheless, she shivered.

'Come on, it's time we went.' Rob pulled her arm through his and marched her back along the Dock.

'Stop acting like an elder brother, Rob.' Dorothea's voice sounded more tart than she had intended but he took no offence, merely grinned at her. Reluctantly, she grinned back. It was strange, she thought, but she could still feel the warmth of his kiss on her lips.

Chapter Forty-One

Rob had been aware of Dorothea's shock on seeing Dennis, so he was careful not to intrude too often on the family. He went off in the hired car and explored the area. He drove to Holderness and Spurn Head. He also walked the four miles to the end of Spurn Point to see the lighthouse and the Humber Lifeboat. As always, the sight of the sea turned his thoughts towards his father. He sighed, hoping that Dorothea would cope well with *her* father's impending death. It was obvious the old man couldn't go on much longer.

Another day Rob explored the banks of the Humber and gasped to see the thousands of sea birds nesting on the mud flats. An elderly bird watcher, seeing his interest, came over to talk to him. Rob grinned to himself as he was lectured on the different species. He tried to remember all the names in order to impress Dorothea with his knowledge. She may be a high class lady now, but he bet she didn't know about turnstones, dunlins, shelducks and redshanks!

He had persuaded her to go to the dance on Wednesday night and he looked forward to the evening with anticipation. He dressed carefully in dark trousers, a new blazer and a white shirt with thin stripes of blue. When Dorothea opened the door to him he was glad he had taken pains with his appearance. She wore a swirly-skirted, powder blue dress and was wearing earrings that looked like white flowers. She laughed when he complimented her on her appearance.

'This dress has been in the back of the wardrobe

for at least four years. I had nothing with me that would
be suitable for a dance and, anyway, who knows what
they wear for a night out in Hull?' She noticed his
discomfiture and added, kindly, 'I'm glad you like it,
though.'

Hazel came to say hello to Rob. 'I told her she looked
nice.' She smiled at him. 'How are you enjoying your
visit?'

'Very much. I hope Mr Bellows is improving?'

'He seems much brighter today. Of course, Dorrie's
visit has done him good. I'm glad you're taking her out
tonight. She doesn't want to spend all her time in a sick
room.'

'We're off now, Mum.' Dorothea had shrugged into
a shawl-collared coat. Rob noticed she was wearing
high-heeled court shoes which made her taller than him.

'Well, have a good time.' Hazel nodded to Rob.
'Bring her back safe and sound.'

He avoided Dorothea's scowl of mock horror. 'Of
course I will.' He winced as she smiled sweetly at her
mother then dug her nails into his arm. 'Let's get out of
here,' she hissed.

They walked to the parked car.

'Mum persists in treating me as though I'm sixteen,'
she marvelled. 'In London she's fine, treats me like a
friend, but here at home . . .'

'She cares for you. I think it's nice,' replied Rob
quietly.

'In small doses, I suppose.' Dorothea, with a swift
change of mood, stepped back and put her head on one
side.

'What is it?' He felt uncomfortable.

'Just giving my new beau the once-over.' Dorothea
grinned as she opened the car door. 'You look
extremely smart, Mr Steyart, although I think the word
is "fab" now. Come on, let's go and knock 'em dead!'

As soon as they entered the dance hall, Dorothea collapsed into a fit of giggles. 'What is it now?'

She shook her head, then flapped her hands up and

down. Rob looked around the dance hall and then he was laughing too. Around them, couples, mainly teenagers, stared at them with puzzled expressions. Rob and Dorothea mopped their streaming eyes and staggered over to one of the few unoccupied tables.

'Oh, I'm sorry.' Dorothea groped in her evening bag for a handkerchief. 'I can't think what's got into me!'

'I can.' Rob pressed his lips together to suppress another wave of mirth. 'Control yourself, woman!'

'I can't. Did I say you were "fab"?' She choked. 'I thought Hull would be behind the times – King's Road has nothing on this!'

The band, four young men in purple suits and peculiar haircuts, struck up a Beatles' hit, 'A Hard Day's Night', and a crowd of youngsters surged on to the floor. Girls flashed long, long legs beneath incredibly short skirts. They tossed their wildly unkempt hair and peered at their partners through shaggy fringes. The clothes the young men wore put the girls into the shade. In blue Nehru-jackets, wearing psychedelic flared trousers and winkle-picker shoes, they eased their Indian scarves from around their throats and gazed impassively at the girls. The band changed tempo and the dancers, faces still expressionless, quickened their movements. They were dancing the Twist.

'I have never, *never*, felt so old in all my life!' Dorothea erupted into another spasm of giggles.

Rob manfully kept his face straight. 'I don't suppose . . .' He gestured towards the dancers.

'Oh, no. At least . . .' Dorothea tapped her feet to the music. 'Why not?' Eyes brimming with mischief, she looked at Rob. 'Are you brave enough?'

He grinned and held out his hand. 'Brave! You're talking to a man who eats snakes for breakfast!'

Ten minutes later the band brought the music to an abrupt halt and disappeared into the bar. Rob and Dorothea returned to their table, flushed and breathless.

'That was smashing, Rob. Thank you.'

'My pleasure.' He ran a finger around his collar. 'Would you mind if I took my tie off? I'm boiling.'

'Go ahead. Just don't go wearing strings of beads.'

They shared a broad smile which lasted perhaps a moment too long for both felt a tinge of embarrassment at the same time.

Rob stood up. 'I'll get some drinks. What would you like?'

'Martini, please, with just a splash of lemonade.'

When Rob returned from the bar a Cliff Richard record was spinning which made conversation easier. Dorothea was staring in fascination at the dancers.

'It was stupid to be surprised,' she murmured, accepting her drink with a nod of thanks. 'I should have remembered northern kids like to keep up with the times.' She smiled. 'I'm glad we came, it's fun.'

'So am I.' Rob sat down carefully. 'Don't know if I'll feel the same tomorrow, though. I think I'm tightening up already.'

Dorothea laughed. 'You're a good sport. Charles would never . . .' She stopped.

'He's a good friend of yours, isn't he? I've heard you mention him before.' He swirled the liquid round in his glass.

'Oh, yes.' Dorothea's voice was light. 'I've known Charles a long time.'

'I had the impression he was more than a "good friend".'

Dorothea's eyes narrowed, but she said mildly: 'We have a rather special relationship. It suits us.' She sipped from her glass. 'It doesn't really concern you, does it, Rob?'

He flushed. 'No, I suppose not.'

There was an awkward little silence, then Dorothea said, 'When do you go back to Australia?'

'In five weeks' time.'

'Will you be glad to get back?'

'Most of me will be.' Rob drained his glass.

'Because of Nicky, of course, but also . . .' He stopped speaking, looked over Dorothea's shoulder, moved the position of his chair slightly and continued, 'It doesn't suit me, not working. I want to discuss things with my partner and see if either of my two ideas make sense to him. If they do, then we're in business.'

'Going to tell me? Your ideas, I mean.'

Dorothea looked startled when Rob suddenly leant forward and hissed at her. 'There's a girl behind you, a very young kid with long hair and white lipstick.'

'So?'

'She keeps staring at me, Dorrie. I'm not being vain or anything, but I think she fancies me! She's certainly giving out some message. What on earth am I to do?'

His face reddened as he saw the merriment in her eyes. 'It's no joke. What if she asks me to dance?'

Dorothea deliberately pushed her bag so it dropped on the floor, then stooped to pick it up, darting a quick glance behind her as she did so. 'You're right,' she gurgled. 'She has a hungry look about her. Quick, I think she's coming over. You'd better dance with me!'

They hurried back on to the dance floor. This time, only Dorothea was laughing.

'We must be wrong, Dorrie. Look at her, she's only a kid!'

'Girls grow up quickly nowadays, Rob. And they often fancy older men.'

'That's ridiculous!' He sneaked another look at the girl. 'God, I hope she doesn't say anything to me. Look at her clothes – I can see her knickers!'

Dorothea snorted. 'You should be flattered. She's looking awfully disappointed. She's probably wondering why you're dancing with such an old woman.'

Rob pulled her closer to him. The records were still spinning and someone must have requested an 'oldie' for the strains of 'Smoke Gets in Your Eyes' drifted through the hall.

'I like this,' he announced. Then, in a lower voice, 'I like dancing with older women, too.'

Dorothea smiled. The nostalgic music and the whisky he had consumed were getting to him, she thought.

'Well, I like being older,' she confessed. 'When I was that girl's age I used to come dancing with Nancy. She was so pretty, so dainty . . . Do you know, I would never sit down because I loathed it when a little man would come up to me and ask me to dance. I was so self-conscious. Oh!' She pulled away from him, abashed.

Rob was puzzled until he realised, then he grinned. He drew her to him again. 'I'm not smaller than you,' he declared. 'It's those heels of yours. Anyway, I don't care if I am – I like older and *taller* women!'

They left the dance relaxed and happy but Rob had parked the car in the next street and when they reached it they were both shivering.

'Is it true that the sun *always* shines in Australia, Rob?' Dorothea watched as he unlocked the car door.

'Depends where you live. It's a big country, you know. England could fit into one corner of Australia.'

'Strange, isn't it?' Dorothea's voice was dreamy. 'We're all so involved in our own little lives, our own troubles, and yet, when you think about all the countries in the world, about wars being fought, famines, things like that, we should be ashamed of ourselves. Really, what importance have we?'

'A great deal.' Rob leaned against the car and looked at her. 'We can't solve world problems, Dorrie, but we can try and sort out our own lives and live them as decently and successfully as we can. After all, all our little lives make up the whole thing, don't they? So, in that respect, we are all important.'

'I suppose so.' Dorothea suddenly giggled. 'Listen to us, being all philosophical. I think perhaps we've drunk a little too much tonight, Rob Steyart.'

'You may be right.' He opened the car door for her. Instead of getting in, she came and stood in front of him.

'I still think I'm taller than you,' she declared.

'Don't think so.' He shook his head. 'I know, let's measure.'

Solemnly, they stood eyeball to eyeball.

'You still have your shoes on,' he objected.

'I'll take them off.'

Dorothea removed her shoes and giggled once more when the cold from the pavement chilled her stockinged feet. At the back of her mind she realised she was behaving uncharacteristically, more like a giddy twenty year old than a career women of over thirty. She decided she didn't care. She was enjoying herself.

'There you are. I *am* taller than you!'

'No,' Rob deliberated. 'We are exactly the same height.'

They stared into each other's eyes.

'Do you know,' he said softly, 'your eyes look positively green in the light from the street-lamp.' He paused then added, 'I never could resist green eyes.' And kissed her.

Dorothea stood stock-still. It's a friendly kiss, she told herself. Just a friendly kiss. And perhaps, at first it was. But then the pressure of Rob's lips on hers increased and he placed his arms about her and pulled her closer to him. Dorothea felt her body slacken. Her eyes, which she had closed, flew wide open. For God's sake, it was *Rob* who was kissing her! This was ridiculous. She struggled free of him.

'What's the matter, Dorrie?' His voice was light. 'Don't worry, I'm not ten years old any more. You enjoyed it, didn't you?'

The devil! He even knew what she was thinking. And it amused him. He was smiling at her.

'I think it's time we went home,' she said, and sat in the back seat of the car.

Rob drove home extremely carefully. He was sorry Dorothea wasn't in the seat beside him so that he could glance sideways and admire her long legs and smell her perfume. He really hadn't drunk that much whisky – was it Dorothea who made him feel dizzy?

But as he approached her home, he was suddenly sober. The door of the house was open, the lights were on. Neighbours were outside standing on the pavement and an ambulance was there. He slammed on the brakes of the car.

'Oh, God!' Dorothea was out of the car and running. 'It's Dad!'

Mr Bellows was already aboard the ambulance. As Rob reached the front door, Hazel appeared, a coat around her shoulders, her face pale.

'Mum.' Dorothea rushed up to her mother. 'What's happened?'

'He's in a coma. The doctor called the ambulance. You'd better come with us.'

Hazel's voice was steady. She grasped her daughter's arm and turned to Rob.

'It's all right, Mrs Bellows. I'll follow in the car.'

Dennis Bellows lingered on for three days. Dorothea and Hazel stayed by his bedside but he never regained consciousness. When his waxy face relaxed into death it was almost a relief. They returned home in a state of exhaustion but revived when they saw a good fire burning in the hearth, a meal in the oven and a pot of freshly made tea awaiting them.

'How can we thank you?' Hazel drained her second cup of tea. 'That was lovely. Tea in hospital always tastes funny, as though there's antiseptic in it.' Her voice wobbled a little but she smiled at Rob.

'I wasn't sure about the fire.' He gestured towards the hearth. 'It wasn't really cold enough to light it, but it makes the place more cheery, doesn't it? The food will be ready in about an hour, if that's OK?'

'Lovely.' Hazel stood and picked up her coat and scarf. 'I'll just put these away.'

'Have a rest, Mum.' Dorothea's voice was husky. Rob thought she looked more tired than Hazel.

'I think I will. Be sure to shout me when the meal's

ready. We mustn't waste Rob's cooking.' She left the room.

'It's only a casserole,' he said to Dorothea. 'I didn't know whether or not you would be hungry.'

'It will be fine.' She smiled at him. 'I can't say I'm hungry but after those hospital sandwiches . . . Where did you learn to cook?'

'You forget, I've been on my own with Nicky some time.'

'Ah, yes.' Dorothea walked restlessly towards the window. 'You've been a great help, Rob. We do appreciate it.'

'Nonsense. I've done little enough. I rang work, though, as you requested. I told them what had happened.'

'What did they say?'

'The usual things. Not to worry and don't rush back to work.'

She gave a short, painful laugh. 'That means they'll cope until after the funeral. Then there'll be daily phone calls imploring me to get back.'

'Life goes on, Dorrie.' Rob's voice was gentle.

'I know.' She ran her fingers through her hair. 'And I really wouldn't wish Dad back again. He hated being an invalid, but . . .' She shivered. 'Times like these, you realise just how *temporary* life is. Dad's always been there – now he isn't! Yet still, the birds sing, the sun comes up, you eat, sleep, go to work. What's it all for, Rob?'

'Hey!' He went and took hold of her elbows, gave them a little shake. 'Steady on, love. I can cook a casserole but I'm not clever enough to tell you the meaning of life!'

'Oh, you fool.' Dorothea's laugh broke on a sob and she turned and clung to him.

He put his arms about her. 'Go on,' he urged. 'Stop being brave, let it all out.'

Minutes later, she pushed him away, produced a handkerchief and mopped her face. 'I feel better now,' she said. 'Thanks.'

He brushed back her damp hair. 'Any time,' he said He found it difficult to look away from her and she must have noticed for she glanced downwards.

'I must look a terrible mess.'

'No,' he answered her honestly. 'Right now, you look just like the Dorrie I remember best.'

Without her usual clever, understated make-up he could see her face was rather too broad and her mouth over-large. Her eyes, usually so arresting, were dull and muddied by grief and fatigue. The skin beneath them was heavily shadowed. He looked, and at that moment knew without any doubt that he loved her.

Loving Dorrie was no new thing for Rob. As a boy he had loved her. Then it was because she was his friend and confidante, and because she alone cared what happened to him. In Australia he had loved her memory because she represented the happier times he had known in England. Then, as he had struggled through unfamiliar and hostile places and relationships, he had slowly forgotten the real Dorothea and had recreated her in his image of a perfect woman. When Irene's actions had disillusioned him, he had told himself that Dorothea would never have behaved so. Now he had found her again and realised that she was none of the things he had imagined her to be. Delving beneath the words of their carefully non-committal conversations, he had come to realise she had made almost as much of a mess of her personal life as he had done. And now this man Charles . . . Rob frowned. Where exactly did he fit into the scheme of things?

He kept his arms about her. He loved her! She had courage and guts. She had fought her way up to become a successful businesswoman, but she was no angel. She showed flashes of temper, she was impatient, she liked having her own way. Well, he suppressed a smile, she had always been bossy. But today, grieving her father, he had seen behind her cool exterior. He had seen her vulnerability and, seeing it, realised he loved her. She leaned against him, in a purely sisterly way, seeking comfort. In a brotherly way, he patted her shoulder and inwardly wondered what the hell he was going to do.

Chapter Forty-Two

The journey back to London passed without incident although both Dorothea and Rob were unusually quiet. Finally he broke the silence.

'I don't think you need worry too much about your mother, Dorrie. She's coped wonderfully well.'

'I know.'

Dorothea turned her sleek head towards him. Discreetly made-up, wearing an understated, dark blue outfit, Rob thought she became more desirable and more unobtainable each mile they drew nearer to the city.

'I asked her to come home with me, you know, just for a little while, but she refused.'

'Perhaps she's right. After all, she must have known . . .' Rob's voice died away as he negotiated a particularly tricky roundabout.

'I realise that. But it won't be easy for her, in the house on her own.' Dorothea's voice wobbled. She sniffed. 'Oh dear, what a crybaby I am.'

Rob laughed and gave her knee a friendly pat. 'Stop apologising.'

'But *I* should be the strong one, whereas Mum seems to be coping better than me.'

'Your mother can look back on a happy marriage.' Rob's mouth hardened. 'There's few enough of those, nowadays. And she knows your father wouldn't want her to make herself ill with grief. She's doing what he would want her to do. I gather she's already making plans. What's this about working in a dress shop?'

'Oh, that!' Dorothea's voice sharpened. 'It's a

ridiculous notion. What does Mum know about dress-making and serving in a shop? That, she tells me, is what she intends doing.'

'She used to make clothes for herself, I remember.' Rob waited for a reply but received none. 'She knows how to dress,' he continued. 'She always looks smart.'

'Oh, yes.' Dorothea turned her face away and looked out of the car window. 'She was always dressed up to the nines. I used to feel like a fat frump next to her.'

A frown creased Rob's brow. 'That was a long time ago, surely?'

Again she remained silent.

'Your mum's not old, love. She can't sit at home all day and grieve. She still has a lot of living to do.'

'But does she have to start doing it straight away? Anyone would think she's glad Dad's dead! Oh,' Dorothea gave a little gasp, 'don't listen to me. What a cow I am!'

'Don't worry about it.' Rob switched on the windscreen wipers as rain splattered against the front window of the car. 'Emotions get a bit churned up at times like these.'

They arrived at the flat. Rob took Dorothea's case from the boot of the car and carried it to the doorway of her flat, then he hesitated. 'Well, I suppose I'd better go. You'll have things to sort out. When will you start work?'

'Tomorrow, I suppose.' Dorothea's voice was listless. She looked at Rob, her face pale. 'Do you have to leave straight away?'

'Of course not. I just thought . . .'

She caught hold of his arm. 'Maybe I'm being horrible about Mum because she's coping so much better than I am. Please, Rob, come in for a little while. I don't want to go into an empty flat.'

Behind the door was a pile of envelopes. Rob picked them up. 'Popular person,' he commented, handing them to Dorothea.

'Not really.' Quickly she flicked through them. 'Nothing important, bills most of them. What's this?' She opened a long white envelope and took out the sheet of paper. 'Oh, it's a circular about Nuclear Disarmament.' Her tears began to flow again. Rob caught hold of her arm and led her weeping figure towards the sofa. He made her sit down.

'Look, Dorrie, I don't mind you crying but there's something more, isn't there? Are you going to tell me?'

'It's nothing.' She scrubbed at her eyes. 'Dad got on at me about attending Ban the Bomb Rallies. He was disappointed in me because I'd never been to one.'

'And . . . ?'

'Nothing.' She gave an impatient shrug. 'That's all.'

He stared at her. As quickly as she brushed one tear away another one appeared. She turned a bewildered face to him. 'Oh, Rob, I don't know what's the matter with me. I'm sad, naturally. And I can't help remembering how often Dad and me quarrelled, but why is it affecting me so much? I've coped with things worse than this. My baby – and Greg.' Her words were lost in another storm of weeping.

Rob's face was tender. 'Maybe that's the trouble, Dorrie. You've coped too well. I also get the feeling that you've worked yourself half to death over the last couple of years, never let up. You've kept things locked up inside yourself and now, with your father's death, everything has boiled over. You've got an almighty "blue". Sorry,' he grimaced when Dorothea raised her head and stared at him, 'I mean you're suffering from depression, you feel rotten,' he explained.

'Oh – you and your Aussie expressions.' She attempted a watery smile.

'That's better.' He hesitated. 'You must know by now how fond I am of you. Do you feel you can confide in me? I'm sure you'll feel better if you do.

449

And after all,' his smile held a hint of bitterness, 'I'll be leaving soon. You won't have to face me later and feel embarrassed.'

She shook her head. 'No, Rob, I can't.' She began to tremble.

He took hold of her hand. 'Are you sure? I'm Rob, remember? You can tell me anything.'

She bowed her head in a gesture of defeat. She sighed, then a moment later began to speak. Her voice was quiet.

'I was engaged to a young man called Arnold when I worked in York. Then I met an artist. He stayed at the hotel. His name was Gregory Paige.' She did not seem to feel Rob start. She went on: 'I broke the engagement and went off to London to live with Greg. I adored him, Rob, and I was positive he loved me. Anyway, we lived together for a long time. I had Jake then. Remember him?'

'I remember.' He kept his eyes fixed on Dorothea's face.

'Jake didn't like London and he hated Greg. It made life difficult at times because Greg wanted me to get rid of Jake, but of course I wouldn't. Actually, we rowed about all kinds of things but we were happy. We had a funny little flat covered with Greg's paintings. Life was exciting.' Dorothea swallowed. 'It was always absolutely great in bed, you know what I mean?' She kept her eyes resolutely turned away from Rob and colour rose in her cheeks. 'That's always been important to me. I know women aren't really supposed to . . .' Her voice trailed away.

Rob's eyes darkened. He almost said something, but checked himself. He squeezed her fingers.

'Eventually,' Dorothea continued, 'I got pregnant. Greg was furious. He couldn't help it. It was his work, you see.' Her eyes pleaded with Rob to understand.

'He needed space to work and he thought . . .' Her voice flattened. 'In the long run, it didn't matter. I became ill and the baby was born dead. When I was discharged from hospital, Greg was really sweet. He took me home. When I got back I found Jake had . . . died.'

Dorothea pulled her hand free and jumped to her feet. 'I don't want to think about it any more,' she whispered.

'Why not? There's more, isn't there? You can't stop now, Dorrie.'

She glared at him. 'Damn you – don't tell me what I can or cannot do! It's none of your business anyway.'

'But it is.' Rob went to stand before her. He put his hands lightly on her shoulders. 'In a funny way which you don't understand yet, it *is* my business. Please, tell me the rest.'

She shivered again. 'All right, if you must know.' Her voice was stronger now and hard. 'We had a friend – a lovely man, I thought. I used to tell him my worries. I trusted him.' Her smile was a travesty. 'I came home early one day. I remember I was happy because I thought things were improving between Greg and myself. It had been difficult. Somehow, ever since the baby died, nothing was right any more.'

She paused.

Rob gripped her shoulders. He could feel ripples of tension running through her body.

'Greg was in bed with this trusted friend. I couldn't believe it, you know. I just *couldn't* believe it! And the expression on their faces . . . Oh, not when they saw me. Then it was – horrible. But before then, when I first opened the door, they were gazing at each other with such *love*!' Her voice broke. 'God, I couldn't believe it! All those times Greg and I had made love, it had been wonderful. At least, *I* had thought so. Apparently he had found it disappointing.' Her voice was shaky. 'Do you know, Rob, on that awful day I felt as though I had failed as a woman.'

'Oh, Dorrie, you idiot! You bloody, stupid idiot!'

Rob's explosive outburst made Dorothea raise a startled face, and as she did so he brought his mouth down on hers in a long kiss.

She struggled free. 'No! Don't, Rob.'

He swore silently to himself. He had scared her. But still he held her close and spoke rapidly against her ear.

'Why do you always shoulder other people's guilt, Dorrie? Your father – you quarrelled with him so often because he was a cantankerous old devil. The chap you dumped for Greg – what else could you do? You didn't love him. You couldn't live a lie. As for Greg . . .' He gave her a gentle shake. 'How can you blame yourself for what happened?'

'But we loved each other, Rob. Greg truly loved me. How could he turn from me to a man?'

He groaned. 'I thought you had become a sophisticated woman, Dorrie? For Chrissakes let go of your hairshirt! I don't know Greg but I've met men like him. I guess he found it hard to face up to his true nature. In the end, he had to. Hell, I could almost feel sorry for him except for the grief he brought you! This talk of failing is crazy. Why, you must be one hell of a woman to turn someone with homosexual leanings into a good lover.'

She pulled back so she could stare into his face. 'But . . .'

'But nothing.' Rob wrapped his arms about her rigid body. 'Look at you – you're so brittle I could break you in two. Relax.'

He made her sit down again on the sofa and with his arm gently about her shoulders rocked her as one would soothe a child. 'You'll feel better in a moment, really you will.' She sighed and rested her head on his shoulder and he could feel her tension fading away like frost in the sun. Poor kid, he thought, and his desire for her was submerged by a rush of pure love.

'I've never been able to talk about it before.' She looked at him with a confused expression on her face. 'Why can I tell you, Rob?'

'Because we go back a long way.' Deliberately, he kept his voice light. He had almost spoilt things, kissing her like that.

'It's not just that.' Dorothea's voice was low. 'I feel

I can really trust you. And it's not because we both lived in Hull when we were young. Lord, that seems so long ago, it's like another life.'

Rob hesitated, aching to ask a question but afraid to break the closeness they were sharing. Finally, he said: 'What about Charles, Dorrie? You've known him a long time. Couldn't you tell him?'

'Oh, no. Charles is . . .' Her voice trailed away. She began again. 'I'm fond of him. He's funny and good company. We work for the same organisation so we know the problems we each have to cope with. We talk things over together. He cares about what happens to me and I care about him, but . . .' Again she hesitated. 'It's never really serious. It's as if we are playing a game; playing at being adults, but both really afraid of any serious commitment.' She sat up and pushed back her hair from her face. 'Maybe that's how we really are – I've only just realised it.' Her voice dropped and she looked downwards. 'We go to bed together sometimes.' She glanced at Rob as if daring him to reprimand her.

Rob's expression did not change but he felt shock at her words. He had expected as much; she was entitled to sexual gratification and the comfort and warmth of a relationship, but her description of her relationship with Charles and the bald way in which she stated the facts filled him with sadness.

'And that's what you want, Dorrie?' he asked. 'That's enough for you?'

She shrugged. 'It's enough. And it's better than being hurt again.'

He shifted, suddenly uncomfortable. Perhaps it was time for him to leave. Dorothea was regaining her composure. She'd be all right now. He stood up.

'Rob.' She clutched at his sleeve. 'You're not leaving?'

'Well . . .'

'Oh, God, I'm sorry.' She jumped to her feet. 'Of course you can go. You must be sick to death of listening to my hysterical outpourings. I can only apologise and thank you for listening to me. You've helped me, Rob. I appreciate that.' She moved towards the door. 'I'll see you out.'

He stared at her. Her face was drawn and completely devoid of colour. He hoped she had finally shed her burden of guilt but he could see she was now completely exhausted. And she had only just buried her father. He hesitated.

'What do *you* want, Dorrie? For me to go or stay?'

She did not reply immediately then she gave a strange little smile and wrinkled her nose, a gesture a small child might make.

'I'd like to go to sleep knowing you were right there, next to me. It's crazy, I know, but I'm so tired and yet I don't want to be alone.'

'Poor Dorrie.' He spoke to her as if she was that child. 'Come on then.'

He led her into the bedroom and helped her undress. He felt no flicker of desire as he drew back the bed covers and watched as she rested her head on the pillow with a tired sigh. He unlaced his shoes, removed his jacket and lay on top of the covers.

'Don't get cold. My dressing-gown's there.' Her voice was dreamy. She was half-asleep already. He pulled her dressing-gown across his body. He did not really need it. The weather was warm. But he could smell a faint perfume emitting from the folds of the material. Dorothea always wore the same perfume. He did not know the name but it was, for him, part of Dorrie and he liked the fragrance.

She was asleep immediately and Rob lay there in the soft twilight and listened to her gentle breathing. Dorothea's flat was in a quiet area and the only other sound came from the cooing of pigeons strutting in the small green park across the road.

It was early morning when she stirred. She yawned, stretched, then turned her face to him and smiled. 'That must be the best sleep I've had in years. But what about you?' She sat up, and as she did so, Rob caught his breath. Her sudden movement clearly revealed to him the swell of her beautiful breasts beneath the ivory-coloured silk slip she wore. This time, he felt a strong surge of desire.

'Have you had any sleep at all?'

'A little,' he lied.

'Poor Rob, what a trial I am to you. And yet,' she stared down at him with an intent expression, 'you never seem to mind.'

Rob returned her gaze without speaking. He struggled to control his feelings. He could hardly bear to look at her, and yet he couldn't look away. A frown appeared between Dorothea's eyebrows.

The small silence became charged with tension.

She shivered. 'I can't sort out how I feel about you,' she murmured. 'For years, you were just a kid I knew a long time ago. But now . . .' She placed her hand on his chest. 'Now you're back in my life and . . .'

'I'm not a kid any more.' Rob's voice was hoarse. Her touch burnt his skin like fire.

'No, you're not.' She smiled to herself. 'Sad, really. I was fond of that boy.'

'There's no need for sadness.' He stirred restlessly beneath her hand. He didn't want to talk. All he wanted to do was embrace her. 'The boy's still there, within the man. And we both care about you.'

Her hand moved in a caressing gesture. Part of Rob, the part trying desperately to keep control, noticed it had begun to rain. He could hear the large spots of water pattering against the window panes. The other part knew he couldn't take much more of this. He also noticed that Dorothea's breathing had quickened, keeping pace with his own.

'You unsettle me, Rob. I don't know . . .' Her voice trailed away.

He covered her hand with his own. 'You trust me, don't you, Dorrie?'

She nodded. Her eyes had widened. Those beautiful eyes he had remembered throughout all the lonely years.

'Then believe me when I tell you that I love you. God knows,' he tightened his grip on her hand, 'I can't make any promises. Neither of us knows what the future holds, but all I can think about now is that we are here together and – Christ!' His voice broke. 'I want you so much, Dorrie. Let me love you, please. I . . .' his voice faltered but she held his gaze and in her eyes he saw acquiescence.

He caught hold of her then and kissed her. He knew at once that she shared his desire by the way she responded to his lips and moaned in her throat when at last his hands explored the texture of her breasts. But, despite his exultation, he also sensed her fear. The fear she felt of being vulnerable again. So when he was naked and she was in his arms, he whispered words of love and reassurance. At first, their lovemaking was tender. They kissed and touched, then as their lips parted Rob could no longer contain his passion. With unchecked strength, he took her body and groaned aloud when he realised her passion matched his.

Then they slept and awoke in the full light of day once again to explore each other's body.

'I should be at work,' murmured Dorothea at last. And they both paused, shocked at the intrusion of reality. 'But I'll ring in,' she continued, winding her arms about Rob's neck and kissing his unshaven cheek. 'We'll have one more day.'

'We need it to sort things out.' His face was sombre as he returned her kiss.

'Yes,' she sighed. 'But let's not spoil things. I know,' she tried to recapture the wonderful feeling of intimacy they had enjoyed, 'we'll bath, then you make us an enormous breakfast. There's bacon and eggs in the fridge. And then I'll telephone work.'

Chapter Forty-Three

Adam Whitney frowned at the knock on his door, then smiled as Dorothea Bellows peeped in.

'Could you spare me five minutes?'

'Yes, of course. Come in.' He put down the accounts he had been studying. 'It's a pleasure to see you.'

It was true. He watched her as she walked towards his desk. How attractive she looked today. It was a pity, he mused, as he studied her wide-lipped generous mouth and beautiful eyes, that his nephew didn't appreciate her more. He knew Charles saw Dorothea from time to time. He also knew she was but one of his nephew's companions. Charles possessed too much charm. It was fatal to most females. The word 'fatal' reminded him he was one day away from his seventy-second birthday. Also, he started, hadn't Dorothea just buried her father? He looked at her again. She didn't appear to be grieving, he reflected. In fact, there was a positive glow about her . . . He coughed, realised he was staring.

'I was sorry to hear about your bereavement, Dorothea. How is your mother taking it?'

'She's coping extremely well.'

'And you? I hope you didn't find things too horrendous on your return?'

'No. That's one of the reasons I came to see you. This is the other.' Dorothea placed in front of him a small gift-wrapped parcel.

'What's this?' The old man's fingers fumbled as he untied the ribbon. 'Oh, my goodness.' He smiled broadly as the paper fell away to reveal a box of fudge. He picked up the birthday card accompanying his present and opened it. 'How did you know fudge was my secret weakness, and this very brand, too? And how did you know it was my birthday?'

'Jenny told me. Don't be cross with her. She told me last week, before she left on her holiday. As for the fudge, you mentioned it once, ages ago. I remembered, that's all.'

'It's kind of you, Dorothea. Thank you.'

Adam stood the card on his desk.

'I didn't know how many years,' she continued, 'so I played safe with the picture of a vintage car.'

'Most appropriate.' His eyes twinkled. No one had ever found out his real age and he knew his employees often speculated on it. Last year he had learned that the staff of one hotel had run a sweepstake on the subject but there had been no winner as his secretary had refused to divulge the necessary information. There were few people, he thought, apart from Jenny, Dorothea, Charles and a couple of old friends, who would dare to tease him about such things.

'Every year,' he said reflectively, 'I consider retirement, and every year the idea fills me with horror. I mean, what on earth would I do with myself?'

'I'm glad.' Dorothea gave him an affectionate look. 'It wouldn't be the same without you.'

'I don't know if the Board would agree with that statement, Dorothea. Or Charles!'

Seeing no change of expression on her face, Adam pressed on: 'Have you seen him since you returned to London?'

'No, I haven't. He did ring once but,' she shrugged, 'I've been so busy at work. He wants me to attend a party he's throwing next Sunday. I'll probably go. Actually, an old friend of mine is in London at the moment. He lives in Australia. He's the other reason I've come to see you.'

She paused, and although her attitude was relaxed Adam saw how eager were her eyes.

'I've completely caught up on my workload,

Adam. The only important event coming up is the Press Reception for the pop group The Crazy Crocs on Saturday. What I would really like is to take the rest of this week off. I want to show Rob around a little. Normally,' she smiled, 'I would have just taken the days off without consulting you but because I stayed over in Hull when Dad died, I thought I had better clear things with you first. It is all right, isn't it?'

'Certainly.' Adam leant forward and clasped his hands together on his desk. 'I don't know the exact number of days but I am aware there is a huge backlog of holiday time you have never taken.' He paused. 'Actually, Dorothea, this fits well into my plans. There's a new project I'm working on. We all know the enormous strides the tourism industry is making; well, I want to extend the scale of our operations. I've feelers out in several countries now with a view to acquiring certain hotel enterprises overseas. I intend chairing a series of meetings with departmental heads on the subject soon and I shall certainly want you to represent the press media section. So, by all means, ease off now and take a break.'

'Thanks.' She raised her eyebrows. 'From what you said, I'd better take a month! Well, I'd better go. Enjoy your birthday.'

When she reached the door, Adam called after her. 'What's the name of that group?'

'The Crazy Crocs.'

'Good God!' He shook his head gloomily. 'What is the world coming to? I remember arranging receptions for *real* stars, geniuses like Charles Chaplin and stunningly beautiful women like Greta Garbo. Ah, well, times change.'

Dorothea laughed, flipped her hand at him and left. Adam opened his box of fudge and popped a piece in his mouth. Rob . . . she hadn't mentioned that name before. He wondered if Charles knew of Rob's existence.

*　　*　　*

459

They spent five wonderful days and nights together, and during that time entered into an unspoken agreement to ban all thoughts of other people, work, and their impending separation. Like children, they took turns deciding what to do. The first day was Rob's choice. They went to a cricket match.

'This is the last thing I would have imagined you'd choose,' said Dorothea. She narrowed her eyes and lifted her hand to her forehead as she squinted at the score-board. 'Pigeon-racing was more the thing in Hessle Road, if I remember rightly, and I can't remember you ever being interested in cricket.'

'No, I wasn't when I was a kid.' Rob joined in a subdued round of applause as a dejected batsman plodded his way back from the wicket. 'But you must know Australians have a passion for the game. Also,' a trace of embarrassment crept into his voice, 'it was one of those funny images I kept in my mind when I was a kid. I mean, I had never been to a proper cricket match but it just seemed so *English*. I used to ride along some red, dusty road on my motor bike, miles away from anywhere, looking for work, and imagine I was at a cricket match, a cool drink in my hand, green turf, the smack of the ball on the bat. In some strange way, it helped keep me going.' He gave Dorothea a self-conscious, sidelong glance. 'I was only sixteen at the time.'

Dorothea was silent. She tried to imagine Rob at sixteen; alone and travelling to an uncertain future. He had been forced to grow up fast. No wonder he was now a calm and confident man.

As the distant white-clad figures moved about the green field and the sun played pattern games with the leafy trees, she studied his profile and watched the range of emotions which flickered over his face as he followed the game. In repose Rob's face was stern, almost grim. She felt a gust of sorrow blow through her like a wind for all that he had endured in his early life. And, as if he felt her thoughts, he turned to her and smiled. And he was young again. Young as a man in his twenties should be, with dancing eyes and no hidden shadows. She smiled back and took his hand.

The match ended when a beautiful stroke past cover point reached the boundary. Rob and Dorothea joined in the applause as the players returned to the pavilion then, hand in hand, they strolled away from the cricket ground.

'You weren't disappointed?' asked Dorothea. 'Sometimes, when you finally fulfil a long-held ambition, it's not what you hoped for.'

'It was exactly what I hoped it would be. Everything is.' They stopped walking and stared at each other. The sun was still high in the blue arch of the sky above them and Dorothea felt the heat from its rays on the skin of her bare arms. The intensity of emotion between them was so strong it was almost tangible. She drew a sharp breath, tried to defuse the tension.

'What now? It's still your day for choosing?'

'Let's go back to the flat.' He did not physically touch her but his gaze wrapped about her a mantle of love and desire.

The next day the good weather held and Dorothea plumped for a day at Richmond Park. They took a picnic and tramped miles to see the deer herd. They nodded to fellow walkers and smiled at young families also picnicking and enjoying the fine weather. They ate their picnic beneath an old oak tree. All was quiet. Nearby, a family of squirrels played chasing games. Rob and Dorothea did not talk much. They lay and watched the quivering leaves above them and listened to the chattering of the squirrels. It was enough to be together.

Then a family with four children arrived. The parents unpacked the food and the children, hot and excited, played games, rolled down a mossy slope and pushed grass down each other's backs. Finally, the two younger children burst into tears and their mother called them to her. Calmly and quietly she mopped faces, produced mugs of milk and fed them their food. When they had finished eating, they went to sleep, curled up together like two puppies. The two older boys went off for a walk with their father and the mother placidly took up her knitting.

Dorothea and Rob had watched the family with interest. She suddenly realised that at some stage of the procedure they had clasped hands, as if for mutual comfort.

'You'll see him soon,' she whispered.

'What?' The eyes he turned to her were blind. He was a long way away.

'Nicky, you'll see him soon.'

She opened her own eyes wide and removing her hand from his picked a daisy growing nearby, concentrating on studying its petals. It was difficult. They kept blurring.

'Yes.' He gave a hard, sharp sigh. 'It wasn't so much Nicky I was thinking about as his mother.'

Dorothea slowly shredded the daisy. 'Want to tell me? It might help.' She laid the denuded flower on the ground and buried it with a handful of soil. 'After all, I've shared my secrets with you.'

Haltingly, he told her. 'I guess we were both just too young,' he finished. 'But I'll never understand how she could walk away from her son.'

Dorothea couldn't understand either. She couldn't think of anything comforting to say and the sight of the tiny children so endearingly asleep close by, and her ritual burial of the daisy, brought an agonizing stab of pain as she remembered her own dead child. She jumped to her feet. 'Come on, let's walk back.'

The exercise raised her spirits and she was charmed at how often Rob and she found the same things amusing. They passed a curvaceous blonde struggling along the rough road on high heels, loudly berating her companion, a portly bald-headed man. 'I told you I'd rather have gone to Camden Market!' Dorothea looked at Rob and saw he was suppressing the same amusement she felt.

They entered the shopping area of Richmond and inspected the outside of a beauty salon, wallpaper shop and a wool shop, still sharing a delicious inner fount of laughter. Rob read the list displayed on the door of the beauty salon.

'Facial hair removed painlessly – hey, is that for men or women?' He rubbed his forehead. 'This place would make a bomb in certain towns in Australia I know!'

They pored over the wallpaper and picked out the kind they would like to buy.

'I've always fancied really crazy wallpaper in the loo,' said Dorothea. 'It's such a boring little room.' She gazed at a lurid roll of paper embellished with multi-coloured circles. 'What do you think, Rob? Could we manage to carry that home?'

'We could.' He looked solemn. 'But decisions of such importance need thinking about, Dorrie. Imagine facing that when you were suffering from a tummy bug or after a hangover.' He shuddered and gave a low whistle. 'Might lead to accidents.'

'Fool!'

At the wool shop they picked out various woollen garments for each other and Dorrie confided that she had never been able to knit. Then they linked arms and went to find a café.

That night they stayed in and Rob cooked a meal in Dorothea's kitchen.

'That was wonderful. Although,' she pushed her plate back with a sigh, 'you put loads of sugar in the pudding. I didn't know you had such a sweet tooth.'

'That's something else you've found out about me. I'll have no secrets left soon.' He grinned and started stacking the used plates.

But you will, thought Dorothea. You'll be gone soon and there's still so much I need to know about you. She had a sudden feeling of dislocation. What would she do when he had left?

'I'll wash up.' She jumped up, a sudden movement.

'No, you take it easy. I like washing up. Did I tell you how, when I first went to Coober Pedy, our water supplies were brought in by camel?' He carried the dishes into the kitchen. She could hear him whistling as he ran water into the sink. She pressed a button on the television and went to sit in an easy chair. She stared at the screen but saw nothing. She must be careful. She *had* to be careful. Being with Rob was changing her. In one way she knew it was for the better. She had kept her emotions on hold, but now she was opening up like a flower to all kinds of feelings. Mostly they were positive feelings, because Rob was with her, but what about afterwards? All she had really thought about for a long time was her work and yet now everything to do with it seemed unimportant. She bit her lip and stood up. She turned off the television set and as she did so Rob re-entered the room. 'Nothing worth watching?'

'No.' She stood without speaking and looked at him. We have three more days, she thought. Three more days completely on our own.

It was as if he read her thoughts. He crossed to where she stood and gently caressed her face. 'We might as well go to bed then.'

Each time they made love – it seemed impossible – but each time, it was better than before. Dorothea thought she had experienced every emotion possible with Greg but she was wrong. With Rob, she reached the same heights of passion but there was something more. A feeling of total trust, a feeling of mutual giving. It was if their bodies recognised each other. When Rob drew her to him and pressed his face between her breasts, she rejoiced in giving him her body as a gift for she knew he was also making himself a gift to her. Her dread of the future faded when she was in his arms. They were truly together, and at such times she felt nothing could part them.

The golden days slipped by. They explored each other's bodies and minds. They talked and walked. They wanted to know everything about each other. Their aura of happiness was so strong perfect strangers passing in the street stopped and smiled at them. Some lingered, tried to engage them in conversation, as if reluctant to leave them. Rob and Dorothea were polite to these people but they refused to engage in chat. They were within a charmed circle which no one else could enter.

On Friday, it was Dorothea's turn to choose what to do. She decided to take Rob to see Chelsea. Like the preceding days, the weather was kind. They strolled along the Embankment then sat down on an iron bench to eat ice-cream. The sun was hot on his face and Rob sighed happily. He looked about him.

There were tall plane trees to the right and left of him, and square white-fronted houses behind. The ice-cream was melting fast in the heat of the sun. He removed a trickle from his chin then grinned as, simultaneously, a red-coated Chelsea pensioner walked by, his boots squeaking, and a girl in a lime green trouser suit and a large, floppy hat rode by on a miniature motorbike. Dorothea had noticed his grin. She smiled back at him.

'The old and the new,' she commented.

He nodded. Once again, she had read his thoughts. He turned to drop his ice cream wrapper in the litter bin next to the bench. A sudden gust of wind teasingly fluttered several discarded sweet papers into the air and he thought how much they resembled a flight of bright butterflies. Poetry now, he thought wryly. See how love can change you! He turned to look at Dorothea. He could never get his fill of her. The beautiful weather, which had deepened the colour of his already tanned skin, had turned Dorothea's a light golden colour. Her freckles had increased.

'A tan suits you,' he commented. 'You could pass as an Australian girl now.'

She laughed. 'I don't believe it's always sunny over there.'

'It is most of the time, where I live.' He took hold of her hand. 'When you come over,' he said half-seriously, 'you must buy a big floppy hat like that girl was wearing.'

465

'Why?' Her lips smiled but he thought he detected a shadow in her eyes.

'Because if you don't, you'll end up looking like a boiled lobster. Even *this* sun has made your nose glow like a beacon!'

'Pig!'

He loved to hear her laugh. His teasing tap on her nose became a caress. Her laughter faded as his fingers followed the curve of her jawline and touched her lips. She pulled away.

'Please don't talk about Australia. It reminds me we haven't much time left. Oh, Rob – couldn't you stay longer?'

Like a candle caught in the wind his happiness spluttered out, leaving only the acrid taste of despair.

'I can't, Dorrie. I've been away too long as it is. I was selfish to come. Nicky's already lost his mother. I have to get back to him.'

'But you said he didn't mind. He told you to come.'

'*I* mind – and it's time I went back.'

Her voice sank to a whisper. 'And there's no chance of your coming to England to live?'

He shook his head. 'It wouldn't work.'

There was a short silence, then Dorothea sighed. 'Well, we still have two weeks left. Don't let's spoil them.' She forced a smile. 'By the way, have I told you? You're invited to a party on Sunday.'

'No, you never mentioned it. Whose party?'

'Charles, Charles Richardson.' She sneaked a look at him.

'So,' Rob's voice was enigmatic, 'I get to meet him at last, do I?'

'Why not?' She felt a sudden desire to wound him. 'You might even like him. He's a nice man. And, after all, I'll need someone when you're back in Australia.' She saw, with satisfaction, the skin about his mouth whiten.

'I thought we agreed to have this week, Dorrie. One perfect week before we . . .' His voice trailed away into silence.

'Before we what?' To her own astonishment, her voice came out loud and harsh. 'Before we talk reasonably, before we quarrel, before we both admit there *is* no solution? We have to face it. We have just two weeks before we part for ever!'

'*Don't!*' Rob clenched his fists and bent his head. 'We'll find a way, somehow. What about you, Dorrie? You've no family here except your mother, and she's a fairly independent lady. Would you consider coming to Australia? I know it's a lot to ask. You have your wonderful job here. But, with your talents, you'd soon be able to find something equally as good there.'

They stared at each other, conflicting emotions rippling across their faces, then Dorothea opened her mouth to speak. But Rob shook his head. 'Let's leave it, love. For today at least.' Their eyes met in wordless communication, then Dorothea nodded. He took her hand. 'See those birds?'

Above them, two birds with deeply forked tails circled languidly in the air. As Rob and Dorothea watched them, they swooped down and skimmed along the grass verge a few inches above the ground.

'Swallows, aren't they?' Dorothea watched their flight. 'Never seen them in Chelsea before.'

'They prefer farmland and meadows.'

'How do you know they like meadows?' Ashamed of her previous outburst, Dorothea leaned companionably against Rob's shoulder.

'I'm interested in them. Always have been. That old man I met on the mud flats, remember? He mentioned swallows. I told you about him.'

'Oh, yes. You tried to dazzle me with your knowledge.'

'It worked, didn't it?' He attempted a smile but she saw the strain behind it. 'He was interesting. He told me they go to South Africa for the winter. That's five thousand five hundred miles away. Yet see how small they are! He said they actually go back to find their old nest and original mate. Of course, the chances of two previously mating birds surviving a migration are extremely rare.'

'Oh.' Dorothea frowned. 'That's sad.'

'Yes. But there aren't too many happy endings in nature, are there? Still, I suppose a few lucky pairs make it.'

They watched the blue-black birds skim the grass. It had been freshly cut and there was a clean, fresh scent in the air. Then two small boys on tricycles raced by. Immediately, the swallows sped away, becoming black dots in the blue sky. Dorothea sighed then smiled brightly at Rob.

'What next, sir?'

'It's your choice today, Dorrie.'

She glanced down at their interlaced fingers. 'I'd rather it was *our* choice.'

'Well then . . .' He pulled her to her feet and they gazed into each other's eyes. 'We *are* the same height,' he murmured.

'If you say so.'

Their lips met in a friendly kiss which changed into something else. 'Let's go home,' she whispered.

The Press Reception for the newly famous pop group The Crazy Crocs had gone well. Better than she had anticipated, thought Dorothea. She had seen many overnight successes wilt and fade when faced with a battery of photographers and reporters with quick-fire lines in questioning. The Crocs had been articulate, well groomed and well prepared by their business manager for their ordeal. They were now in their suite of rooms, resting.

I wish I could, she thought. It was her first day back at work and she had been on her feet since seven a.m. She checked the appropriate handouts had been distributed to the media, ordered champagne to be sent up to the group and instructed Security to inspect the toilets and cupboards on the floor of the hotel on which The Crocs were situated. She knew how often stagestruck fans secreted themselves in such places.

468

Then she walked through the recently emptied reception hall. She was dogged by a feeling of unease. Had she forgotten something? She thought not. More likely her trepidation was generated by the fact that Charles and Rob would meet tomorrow.

The atmosphere in the hall was heavy with the odour of alcohol and cigarette smoke. Her nose wrinkled and she went to open a window, lovingly straightening the rose pink brocade curtains after she did so. Dorothea took great pleasure in the elegance of her surroundings. She never ceased to be thrilled by the sight of the huge, massed displays of flowers in the hotel and the beautiful rococo plasterwork of the high ceilings. She frowned when she saw some boor had ground out a cigarette on the newly laid wine-coloured carpet. What sort of person would do that?

She could see how impossible it was that Rob should like Charles but she hoped the meeting would not be too difficult. Charles would, she realised, be at his most suave which would make Rob glum and prickly. She sighed. Why worry about minor details? In ten days Rob would have left England. She felt a lurch in her stomach and tensed. She was hungry, that was all. She had left the flat without breakfast and at lunch-time had been too busy to eat. She and Rob planned to eat out tonight.

Involuntarily, her lips curved into a smile. He was a friend who had turned into a lover and she found the combination wonderful. They had healed each other, she truly believed that. But what to do next? Their week alone together had been almost *too* perfect. It had been like a honeymoon. They had simply pleased themselves, with no thought of the future. But now she was back at work and real life was different.

There was a broken wine glass pushed behind a fire screen and she spotted canapés trodden into another area of the new carpet. Again, she felt distaste. She felt it again in the ladies' powder room where the unmistakable smell of cannabis floated in the air. The cleaners would be moving in soon with their brooms and dusters. They would soon banish the seedier aftermath of the glossy luncheon party. If only life could be tidied up so easily.

This morning, she and Rob had disagreed about her work. It had started mildly enough. He had asked if she ever became tired of pandering to the whims of the idle rich. Didn't she, he had asked, ever fancy doing something productive? His remarks had stung. And what hurt most was she knew he had *meant* to hurt her. Even so, she knew and understood why. Their idyll was over. But she was miserable too and she had retaliated.

Wasn't he now behaving like one of those idle rich? she had asked. And what was so productive about digging up opals which would end up adorning the necks of the very people he despised so much? She had ticked off on her fingers all the difficult and worthwhile tasks she undertook each day, and then she had looked up and found him looking at her with such hunger they had ended up back in bed. That was one reason she had not eaten breakfast. The other was she had completely lost her appetite.

Their love-making had been so sweet. Despite everything, they had ended up laughing. How she loved to laugh with Rob. On the rare occasions, Dorothea suddenly remembered, that she had quarrelled with Charles, they had invariably made up but there had remained a residue of bitterness. Charles, she realised, had a faint streak of spitefulness in his nature. She shook her head. No, she was being unfair. Rob's personality had been tempered by his experiences. Charles had been indulged all his life. It was a wonder he had turned out to be as attractive as he was. She decided she was looking forward to his party after all. At least it would stop her thoughts buzzing about like a demented wasp.

'Miss Bellows.' A page boy hurried up to her. 'Your secretary asked me to find you. The Picture Editor of the *Daily News* is on the telephone asking for you.'

'Thanks.' Dorothea returned to her office. She forgot about Charles, Rob and the coming party and became the efficient Press Officer of the Coleridge.

She picked up the phone. 'Yes, how can I help you?' She listened. 'That's right, Marcus Beaumont, the MP *did* check in unexpectedly last week. Yes, it's true he was accompanied by a young lady.' Dorothea's voice remained cool but she began to smile. 'Yes, I think we can produce a photo for you to use. I'm sure your readers would be interested in a family picture of Mr Beaumont and his elder daughter.'

Chapter Forty-Four

Charles Richardson was even-featured, tall, slim, and splendidly nonchalant. Rob hated him. He glowered as Charles came over, took Dorothea's hand in his own and raised it to his lips.

'Thea darling, it seems so long since we met.' He smiled into her eyes then turned to Rob. 'And you must be her friend from Australia?'

Rob nodded. He noticed Charles had kept a firm grip on Dorothea's hand. What a jerk, he thought. But then Charles held out his free hand and Rob was surprised at the strength of his handshake. Looking upwards, another sore point, Rob thought he detected a hostile gleam in his host's eyes. He doesn't like me, he realised. Vastly encouraged, he beamed at Charles.

'Lovely place you have.'

Charles shrugged. 'It's OK.'

Rob looked round at the marble fireplace, the display of crystal and the luxurious furnishings. OK! He wondered how Charles would make out in Coober Pedy?

'Thea, I must talk to you.' Charles directed a tight smile at Rob. 'It's purely business, old man. Don't mind, do you?'

'Of course not.' Rob thought Dorothea looked tense. He smiled at her. 'You go ahead. I can amuse myself.'

Charles drew Dorothea into a quiet corner of the large room and began to talk. Rob wandered over to look at the collection of paintings which hung at the rear of the room.

'Cocktail, sir?'

The waitress wore a frilly apron and had a cap on her head. Rob had thought such dress could only be found in old thirties' movies. Not for the first time it struck him how far removed Dorothea's life was from his own. He gulped, reached for a glass, then hesitated.

'I'd rather have a beer. Is that possible?'

The waitress dimpled. 'I think so, sir. Just a minute.' She whisked away.

Rob glanced around the room. He was glad he had allowed Dorothea to help him choose a suit. He had bought new clothes in Sydney in preparation for his trip to England, but today, observing his fellow guests, he realised he had moved up into a different class. They were all impeccably dressed. The women looked grey-hound thin, their make-up was heavy and they sported long, red fingernails. Rob thought they looked unreal, more like dolls than women. All except Dorrie. When he looked at her, he felt his heart swell with pride.

She was the tallest woman in the room and she carried her height proudly. Her dark-green, severely cut cock-tail dress moulded her strong figure. Rob couldn't stop watching her for she created a disturbing, contra-dictory impression of authority, elegance and sen-suality. He felt a knot of anxiety gather in his stomach. He was seeing her in a new setting. She was surrounded by sophisticated, successful people and she was better than any of them. Rob clasped his hands behind him and shook his head slightly, a gesture of despair. Dorrie had achieved all her ambitions. She had competed with the best and won. And a few hours ago, he had asked her to consider throwing everything away and coming to Australia to be with him. How could he have done?

He glanced across at her again and she smiled her wide smile and wriggled her fingers at him in a sly greet-ing. He felt better. He might not fit in to the present company but, by God, he knew he had brought her happiness.

'Your drink, sir.'

He jumped. The waitress touched his arm and then offered him a glass. 'Thanks.'

'I am right – that *is* beer, isn't it? Fetch one for me, my dear.'

Rob looked round in the direction of the husky, amused-sounding voice. A small woman with a lively face and bushy, dark hair patted the cushion next to her. 'Do sit down.'

He took the vacant space on the sofa. 'Thanks.'

'I find most cocktails so disappointing. They come with exotic names, you await their arrival with anticipation, and they turn out to be dull, small and totally without interest.' The woman's large, brown eyes examined Rob's face. 'My name's Madge. I'm Senior Editor at Lawrence & Franklin. Now, let me guess who you are. You came in with Thea, didn't you? You must be her Australian buddy, am I right?'

'Thea?' Rob recollected Charles's greeting. 'Oh, Dorrie, you mean. Yes, I'm with her.'

'Dorrie?' Madge's eyebrows rose. 'My, you two must go back a long way!'

Rob gave his companion a sharp look but relaxed when he saw genuine interest mixed with the amusement on her face.

'We lived in the same town when we were kids,' he explained. 'But I went abroad when I was eleven and we lost touch for a long time.'

'Still, there must have been a close bond. I can't even remember *my* childhood friends.' Madge accepted the glass of beer brought to her by the waitress. 'Thanks.' She turned back to Rob. 'Cheers.' She raised her glass. 'And now you're back in England,' she continued, 'do you intend staying? I'm sorry.' She noticed his hesitation. 'I'm terribly nosey,' she confessed. 'And I'm fond of Thea. I've never seen her looking so good. I think, perhaps, you have something to do with that. Mind you, it's not often we see her at "dress-up" occasions. I keep telling her she's turning into a workaholic.'

Rob looked again at Dorothea. 'She looks wonderful, doesn't she?'

His companion nodded. 'I can see you're fond of her. It must have been strange meeting after so many years.'

Rob warmed to her. 'It was difficult at first, we've led such different lives, but after a little while none of that seemed to matter.'

'Will you stay in England, do you think?'

He shook his head and they sat in silence for a moment.

'Ah, well.' Madge took a bowl of nibbles from the low table in front of the sofa and offered it to Rob. 'You can still tell me a little about yourself. You may not believe this, but parties such as this one get incestuous. Everyone knows everyone else, you see. We're bored to death with each other. Now I know you're Australian and from Thea's past and there's a whisper going around that you've come into money. And that's all.' She grinned at him. 'You're an attractive stranger so be a darling and satisfy a little of my curiosity, and at the same time make the rest of the females here insanely jealous.'

Rob blushed, then laughed. He knew Madge was flirting with him and it amused him. She was fun, he thought, and extremely attractive. He glanced again at Dorothea but her whole attention was focused on their host so he nodded to the waitress to bring two more drinks and settled back in his seat.

Twenty minutes later, they were still deep in conversation.

'So you've definitely given up on your first idea?'

Rob was glad to hear the interest in Madge's voice. She had been such an appreciative listener he had wondered if he had run on too long about his ideas for the future.

'I think so. Oh,' he shrugged, 'financially my partner and myself did well from our opal finds, but we don't have the money to fund an operation on that scale. Also, there would be so much to learn. We just haven't the expertise to compete with the really big boys.'

'That's a pity.' Madge stared at Rob. 'From what you've told me, it would seem the ideal time to promote a string of hotels in your part of the country. You're right – people are becoming more adventurous. They do demand more from their holidays nowadays, and if accommodation is as rare as you say, you could make a fortune.'

'The hotels in the towns are OK, but in the Outback . . .' Rob drained his glass. 'Ah, well, it was just an idea.'

'You haven't talked to Thea about this, have you?' Madge put her head on one side and studied his face. 'Why not? She would be an ideal person to advise you.'

'No!' Rob's denial was so strong people close by looked round. 'I won't involve Dorrie in this,' he continued, his voice becoming quieter.

'But why not?'

He drained his glass. 'I can't explain. Lots of reasons. We have a really special relationship and it has nothing to do with business deals. Anyway,' he attempted a smile, 'I'll be damned if I'm going to sponge on her hard-earned knowledge and expertise to get me started. She made it on her own, and so shall I.'

'You're an interesting man, Rob Steyart.' Madge produced a cigarette case from her bag and offered it to him. When he shook his head, she took one for herself and fitted it into a cigarette holder. 'So tell me about your second idea.'

'This one could work, I know it could.' Rob could hear his own enthusiasm as he outlined to Madge his ideas. I really should stop talking so much, he thought. But his companion's face showed genuine interest and as he continued, his immediate surroundings faded for him and he was back in his beloved Bushland.

'City folk think the Outback is barren, harsh, but they're still fascinated by it. I want to set up a series of tours, show people what it's really like. There could be easy trips for "greenhorns" and tougher treks for the serious travellers.'

'It sounds a great idea, Rob.' Madge's eyes were intent. And neither of them noticed when Charles and Dorothea crossed the room and came to stand behind the sofa they occupied.

'I think so.' In his enthusiasm, Rob put his hand on her arm. 'You should see it, Madge. There's wild camels, there's dry areas where fish appear in lakes just one week after the first rainfall in years. There are parts of the desert awash with wild flowers after the winter rains. I'd like people to see all those things.'

'You sound quite poetic.'

Both Rob and Madge jumped at the sound of Charles's amused voice. They looked up.

'We came to suggest you both go through to the buffet in the dining room. Most of the other guests are already in there. I wouldn't like you to miss out on the food.'

Miserably conscious of Dorothea's stony silence, Rob mumbled something and stared down into his glass.

'We'll be through in a moment, Charles,' he heard Madge reply. 'We'll just finish our conversation first, and our drinks.'

'Of course.' Charles slipped his arm around Dorothea's waist. 'Take your time.' His gaze flickered over their glasses. 'I can quite see that food doesn't interest you. After all, beer and caviar don't really mix, do they?'

Snide bastard! Rob stood up and held out his hand to Madge. 'No, we'd better come now. After all, if you've underestimated the caviar, we might miss out on the Dom Pérignon too!'

'Did you have to be so bloody rude?'

Dorothea, having held her peace in the taxi home, flung down her jacket in a mood to quarrel.

Rob stood in the doorway. He was uncertain

whether he would be invited further in. 'I was rude because Charles was patronising.' He eyed Dorothea warily. 'You must have noticed.'

'I noticed how involved you were with Madge Lowell! You were so intent in telling her your plans to become a modern Robinson Crusoe out in the Bush, you never even noticed we had come to join you.'

Rob felt a thrill of satisfaction. She's jealous, he thought.

'I had to talk to someone. Charles completely monopolised you.'

'It was business talk. Charles had a problem with a decision he has to make.'

Rob looked down at the carpet. 'So have I,' he said quietly. 'And Madge was friendly. She was interested in what I had to say.'

'And I'm not?' The belligerent expression on Dorothea's face faded and left her looking tired. Rob stepped forward.

'Of course, you are. It's just . . .'

'Oh, stop hovering in the doorway. Come in and sit down.' Dorothea flung herself into a chair.

He went over to her and kissed her. 'It's hard for me to talk to you about my life in Australia, Dorrie. You know why.'

'Yes.' She sighed. 'It's all a mess, isn't it?'

He kissed her again. 'We'll work something out.'

'Will we, Rob?' She turned her face away. 'Do you really think so?'

'We have to, love. I can't lose you now. You're too important to me. There must be a way.'

'But you still won't consider living in England?'

He was silent.

'Oh, Rob.' She clung to him. 'Why do I always fall for men who bring me nothing but trouble?'

'I don't know. I guess you're just contrary!'

Her laugh broke on a sob. 'Let's go to bed. I'm really tired. All I want is a satisfying cuddle.' Her eyebrows quirked as she looked at him. 'All right with you?'

'Perfect.'

The dawn chorus woke Rob. He put his hands behind his head and stared up at the ceiling. The hours are ticking away, he thought, and we're getting more and more unhappy. Do I really have to go? But what happens if I stay? Even if I drag Nicky away from his safe little world and bring him over here, what then? What would I do? I can't fit into Dorothea's world, I'd hate it. I'm Australian now – all I love is over there. Except for Dorrie, of course. And, yet, how can I live without her? He rubbed his forehead with such a savage gesture of despair he disturbed Dorothea. She stirred and opened her eyes.

'Didn't you sleep?'

'Yes. The birds woke me.'

'Oh.' She plumped up her pillows and sat up. 'Noisy little devils, aren't they?'

'I like to hear them. You don't get much birdsong in my part of South Australia.'

'Why not?' She settled more comfortably. 'Tell me, Rob. You've never really told me about your life out there and I do want to know.'

He started to speak, slowly. 'I hated it at first. After England, everything there seemed over the top. The weather's extreme, the colours burn your eyes with their brightness. We were dumped in a God-awful place. Christ, you had to grow up fast.'

He was silent, lost in his thoughts.

'Go on,' she prompted him. 'Tell me about the good things.'

He smiled at her, and continued. 'I went Walk-about with an old Abo called Len. He was wonderful to me. Taught me how to survive.' He rubbed his nose, became embarrassed. 'He taught me about the land, about caring for the really important things. Money, success – Len didn't understand those words but he knew so much. I can't explain really. I began to see things differently. And I came to realise I could be happy there, happier than I had ever been in England.' He turned eagerly towards Dorothea.

480

'You *must* come over, Dorrie. I know you would change your mind about things if only you came to see for yourself. You'd . . .' His voice died away at the look on her face. 'What's the matter?'

'You're being unfair, Rob. I wanted to know about your life but you shouldn't turn it into a chance to make me feel guilty. My life's here. It's a good one and I've worked damn hard for it. Why should I even consider throwing everything away to go to Australia?'

'But if you only gave it a chance! Come for a holiday. It's not all desert, you know. We have some beautiful cities. You'd love Adelaide and Sydney. And there are countless opportunities for a woman with your talents. You could land a wonderful job.' His eyes gleamed. 'Hell, we could start up our own business. I've enough money. I . . .' He fell silent when he saw the expression on her face. 'What is it? What have I said that's wrong?'

'Everything!' She glared at him. 'That would be wonderful, wouldn't it, for *you*! I give up everything, you give up nothing. You would be in your precious Australia with your money, your son and your mistress. Because that's what I'd be, isn't it? You're not even divorced and yet you think I should give up everything for you. Perhaps you'd like me to live in a mud hut with you, out in the desert?'

Rob flinched. When he replied his own voice was cold. 'We lived in an underground cave, as a matter of fact. But it was comfortable, much better than a mud hut.'

Dorothea swore. She flung back the bedclothes and got out of bed. She pulled on her dressing gown and tied the belt with a savage yank.

Rob watched her. 'I'm sorry. I didn't mean to upset you. Perhaps I didn't realise just how much your career means to you. But, Dorrie, I still think you ought to consider what I said. Those people at the party last night – why are they so special? Maybe it's because I've been out of England so long, but I just can't understand the way they function. Why did Charles persuade you to change your name to Thea? Why should one name be better than another? Surely it's what you are, what you do, that counts? Back home—' He paused when he saw Dorothea's figure tense. 'I'm sorry, but that's how I see it. Back home, you're judged on your actions. I like that and I think you would too.'

'I don't want to hear any more, Rob.' Dorothea turned and faced him. 'I really thought you were different, you know. But you're not. You're just the same as the rest. And I've only just realised it.

'Oh, you say you love me. But it has to be on your terms, doesn't it? I give up everything, you give up nothing. Well, you can go to hell!' She put her hand up to her head. 'I want you to leave, now.'

'Dorrie.'

She swayed. 'Just get out.' She put out her hand as if seeking balance and Rob's eyes widened as her figure crumpled. She slumped to the carpet. The silk wrap settled like waves around her still body.

'Christ!' He leapt from the bed and ran to her. He checked her pulse and found it to be slow but steady. Her face was milk white, her lips ashen. 'Dorrie, can you hear me?'

He put a cushion beneath her head and fetched water from the bathroom. After a couple of minutes, when she had not regained consciousness, he started for the telephone, then checked. There was something at the back of his mind. Attacks – that's right, Dorrie used to have turns like this one years ago. He returned to her side and pressed her limp hand. He wiped her face with a damp cloth. 'Dorrie, please, please, come back.'

Her eyes flickered rapidly beneath her closed eyelids. Then her lips parted in a sigh.

Thank God! He gathered her in his arms.

Her voice was weak. 'Rob, what happened?'

'I'm not sure. You just keeled over. You'll be all right now.'

'Oh, Lord.' She rested against his arm. 'I thought I'd finished with all that.' A faint smile crept across her lips. 'See what you do to me,' she murmured. 'I haven't had an attack for years and years.'

'Oh, Dorrie.' He held her close and watched the colour steal back into her face.

Chapter Forty-Five

Rob's flight home was booked for Monday, the tenth of the month. He prepared for it by shopping for Nicky, and also bought presents for Kate, Peter and Boots. He made a final attempt to trace any records relating to his father's presumed death in the war, without success. He settled his accounts at the hotel and packed. Meanwhile, Dorothea worked long hours to ensure she would be free to spend the last week-end with him. They had both agreed to forget the hurtful quarrel and make the most of every minute remaining to them. Earlier, Rob had gone off in his hired car to find somewhere away from London for them to stay during that last week-end, and Dorothea had turned down two invitations to go out. One of them was from Charles Richardson.

'When's this friend of yours leaving? I never seem to see you now,' he complained.

'Monday.' Dorothea was at her desk. She drew a tiny aeroplane on her blotter as she listened to Charles. 'He goes Monday.'

'Let me take you out on Monday evening then?'

Her hand stilled. Then she drew fluffy, childish clouds above the plane. 'I don't think so, Charles.'

'Why not?' He waited, then receiving no reply went on: 'Tuesday then? Go on, Thea, say yes. You've been spending all your spare time with this chap. I've missed your company more than I ever thought I would. You'll probably miss him when he's gone, so come out with me.'

'Well . . .' Just below the clouds Dorothea drew a couple of thin vee signs, representing birds. They

485

reminded her of the swallows she and Rob had watched, so she took up her pen and scratched them through.

'All right,' she said.

'Great. I'll pick you up at your place, about eight?'

'Fine.'

Dorothea replaced the telephone and stared down at the little aeroplane.

On Friday morning, her plans looked like falling apart when Felicity Fowler, complete with entourage, booked unexpectedly into the Coleridge Hotel. A third-rate actress but enormously popular media star, Felicity always demanded maximum press coverage. When Dorothea went to her suite of rooms and announced that her assistant, Judith Roffe, would be handling publicity, Felicity was outraged.

'You *do* know why I'm in London?'

'Yes, I saw the item in a newspaper.' Dorothea's voice was cool. 'You've been cast to appear in a film version of a Restoration comedy.'

'Then you must know how important it is to have an experienced person co-ordinate my photo sessions, interviews, etcetera?'

'Judith is experienced, Miss Fowler. If you had let us know sooner that you intended coming here, I would have rearranged my schedule but I can't do that now.'

Felicity lit a cigarette, stared hard at Dorothea then launched into an attack. Dorothea watched her lips move and wondered if the director of the proposed film had ever heard her speak. When agitated, Felicity had a particularly unpleasant nasal whine in her voice which Dorothea thought boded ill for the complexities of Restoration Comedy. When the actress showed signs of running down, Dorothea prepared to leave. 'Well, I must get on. I'm sure you and Judith will deal famously together.'

She headed back to her office, longing for five o'clock to come and set her free.

486

Just before five, Dorothea's secretary buzzed her. 'When you were busy on the other line, I took a call from Madge Lowell at Lawrence & Franklin. Would you ring her, please?'

'Damn!' Dorothea hesitated. 'Did she say why?'

'No, but she seemed disappointed not to be able to talk to you.'

'OK, I'll see to it.' Dorothea dialled the number. Madge was a good friend and, remembering the party, Dorothea felt stirrings of guilt at the way she had behaved towards her.

'Madge? It's Thea.'

'Thea! Thanks for ringing back so promptly. Now, it's about that Australian buddy of yours.'

'What about him?' Goodness, her voice sounded sharp. Dorothea forced herself to relax.

'It's all right, darling.' Madge sounded amused. 'You needn't worry. This call is strictly business. Now, can you tell me where I could reach him?'

Dorothea hesitated. She glanced at the clock on the wall. What business could Madge have with Rob? Why, she had only met him once.

'Thea?'

'Sorry, I was thinking. It's difficult right now. Rob's out of London at the moment.'

'Oh, that's a pity.' Madge sounded disappointed.

'Can you tell me what it's about?' Dorothea was curious.

'I can't, love, sorry. I just have an idea in my mind and I want to see if anything could come of it. Do you think he could ring me when he gets back?'

'I couldn't promise. You see,' Dorothea took a deep breath, 'he's leaving England very soon.'

'Oh, Lord. I didn't realise he was going back to Australia *so* quickly.' Madge fell silent.

Dorothea waited a moment, then said: 'I'm sorry, Madge, but I have to go, I'm running late today.'

'I won't keep you then. Listen, if Rob *does* have a couple of hours to spare before he leaves, ask him to get in touch with me, will you?'

'Yes, I will. Bye.'

Dorothea put down the telephone receiver. She knew Rob would not have time to ring Madge. She avoided looking back at the clock. She was sure the hands on it were racing round at double speed. So little time!

Rob had found a place two hours' drive from London. The small hotel was surrounded by gently wooded hills and to the right of the building was a lake, complete with swans.

'Like it?'

She squeezed his arm. 'It's beautiful.'

They unpacked, made love, bathed and went down to dinner. The oak-beamed dining room was lamplit. There were candles on the tables, and the waitress served them freshly caught trout from the lake. They finished their meal and went into a tiny bar where they drank brandy.

'You couldn't have found anywhere better, Rob.'

He smiled. 'Pretty good, isn't it?'

They went back to their room.

'Even a four-poster bed.' Dorothea stretched out on it then laughed. 'It's not very long. If I lie on my back, I bang my toes on the end.'

'It's you, you're so tall.' Rob lay down next to her and kissed her. 'In olden days, women were smaller, compliant to their husbands. They did as they were told, not like you modern females.'

She tensed. 'Rob, I . . .'

'Hush.' He kissed her shoulder. 'I was joking,' he said. 'I wouldn't have you any other way, my love. And I told you, I like tall women.' He traced his lips down her body. 'There's more of you to love.'

Dorothea relaxed beneath his touch. 'You suit a four-poster,' she murmured. Amusement lit her eyes. 'You're the perfect counterpart of a mediaeval man: short, square and stocky.'

'Bitch!' He pinched her bare bottom and they laughed and clung together. Incredibly, their love-making was totally light-hearted. Somehow, with the shadow of separation looming large, they managed to create a perfect memory for the future.

Sunlight falling through the mullioned windows awoke them and they dressed, ate breakfast and went off to explore the surrounding countryside. They found an old gabled manor house which was open to the public and toured the place, exclaiming over the period furniture and the enormous cooking utensils in the kitchens.

'Your old-fashioned women can't have been that frail,' commented Dorothea to Rob. 'Otherwise they'd never have managed to lift those pans.'

'Ah, but there would have been short, stocky kitchen lads to do the heavy work,' he replied.

They discovered a gift shop in the grounds of the house and went in. Rob bought some lavender bags to take back with him. Kate, he told Dorothea, would love them. Then they went to the café and ordered two cream teas. They were served in the garden at the back, a peaceful place sheltered by tall hollyhocks and drowsy with the bumbling of bees.

'Surely you'll miss all this?' Dorothea turned her face up to the sun.

'Of course I will. This is heaven. When you're away, this is the kind of scene you always think of.' He gazed at Dorothea. 'Haven't you been abroad, Dorrie? I seem to remember that was one of your ambitions, to travel?'

She kept her eyes closed. 'It was, but somehow it just never happened. At first I couldn't afford to go, and these last years I've been so busy.'

'That's a pity.' He stirred sugar into his tea. 'I'd like to travel more. Maybe when Nicky's older.'

'Who knows?' Dorothea opened her eyes and held out her hand. Rob took it. 'Maybe one day we'll go together.'

'I'll hang on to that thought.' Rob cleared his throat. 'I know we said we wouldn't spend our last hours heart-searching, but I do want to apologise for my behaviour after the party.'

'It's all right. You were trying to find a way out for us.

Maybe I should apologise too. I reacted too violently.'

'No, you were right. I was being selfish. But somehow,' he shook his head, 'I have this gut feeling that it just wouldn't work if I came back to England to live. I know it sounds terrible. I say I love you, you *know* I love you, but . . . I still can't shake off that feeling. Maybe I'm just a pig-headed, stubborn male. I'm truly glad you've made a success of your life, Dorrie. I'm proud of you. But I can't imagine any way I could work over here and be successful, and I couldn't hang on to the fringes of your success. I couldn't live like that. The simple truth of the matter is that I'm an Australian now.'

He looked at her, willing her to meet his gaze, but she stared down at her hands, tightly folded in her lap. He sighed. 'We just can't get to sing the same song, can we?'

They sat in silence and listened to the droning of the bees, then Rob felt in his pocket and produced a small parcel. 'I want you to have this.' She took it from him, tore off the wrapping paper then removed the lid of the box and gazed down at the contents.

'Rob, it's beautiful!'

'It's the first bit of decent opal I found. I had it mounted on a pin. It's nothing as valuable as diamonds, of course, but it is unique. It's part of an opalised shell, you see. I thought you might like it.'

'I'll treasure it.' She fastened it to the collar of her dress.

'There, how does it look?'

'Beautiful. The perfect setting.'

His voice was low. 'Opals should be your birthstone, Dorrie. They always remind me of your eyes.'

'What, even the milky-coloured ones?' She tried a laugh which failed dismally for she began to cry.

'Oh, God – don't cry, Dorrie. Please don't cry. I can only be brave if you are.' He reached for her hand, and this time she gave it to him. 'I wish I'd never come,' he went on, his voice cracking with pain.

'What good have I done? You were fine until I showed up.'

'No.' She shook her head. 'No, I wasn't, Rob. I was empty inside. I feel terrible right now and I can't bear the thought of you leaving, but I shall never regret meeting you again.'

'You mean that, honestly?'

She nodded.

'Well then, I take back my words. Because it has been wonderful, Dorrie. I never thought . . .' He took a deep breath and began again. 'I want you to know, I'm not giving up. I'm going home and I'm going to sort something out. There must be a way forward for us. Maybe we're too close to everything right now. I'll give myself a chance to get my head clear. And I'm going to see about a divorce too. That should be simple enough. I haven't seen Irene in years. Hell, Dorrie, we've just got to sort things out. I don't know if you've realised it yet, but I want to marry you!'

Dorothea tried to remove her hand from his grasp but he refused to release her. 'Don't pull away. You must have thought about it.'

'Please, Rob,' she protested. 'You're hurting me.'

'Sorry.' He dropped her hand. 'I didn't mean to.'

'I know you didn't. And what you've just told me – I love you for that.' She fingered the gift he had given her. 'But you may see things differently when you get home.'

He frowned. 'Are you telling me I don't know my own mind? Or that you wouldn't marry me if you could?'

'No, no.' She shook her head. 'Of course not. But you're still a young man and you mustn't go making promises to me. These last weeks have been the happiest of my life but we can't live on dreams. I've got my work, and somehow,' she paused, 'I can't see myself falling in love again. But it's different for you. You're going back to your son and your friends and all the excitement of planning a new career. All I'm saying is

. . . don't look too far ahead. Take life as it comes.'

'I'll do that, Dorrie, but I'll be looking forward too. And like I say, I'm hoping we'll be sharing the future together.' Rob's mouth held a stubborn set. As if to close the conversation, he turned back to the table, seized the last piece of cream scone and thrust it into his mouth. Then he coughed, violently.

'Oh, for goodness' sake!' Torn between laughter and tears, Dorothea rose and thumped him on the back. 'Better drink some tea.' She handed him a cup. When the coughing bout was over she stayed beside him, her arm around his neck. She stooped and kissed the top of his head. 'I love my present,' she said. 'It reminds me of a little lad who, many years ago, bought some earrings for a girl he knew.'

He covered her hand with his own and they stayed there. The hollyhocks rustled in the breeze and the silence held a sweet poignancy.

Chapter Forty-Six

Dorothea slept late. Rob's flight time was five a.m. He had stayed with her until midnight on Sunday but had refused to let her accompany him to the airport. After his departure, she tossed and turned in her bed until four in the morning. Then, unable to bear the slow ticking away of the minutes, she succumbed to temptation and swallowed two sleeping pills.

It was eleven-thirty when she trailed into the foyer of the Coleridge Hotel feeling as dull and washed out as the weather. As she crossed to the lift that would take her to her office, she felt glad of the rain. She couldn't have borne sunshine this morning.

She heard the whine of the lift descending then cursed silently as the door opened and Felicity Fowler stepped out. Dorothea forced herself to smile.

'Good morning, Miss Fowler. I hope everything went well on Saturday?'

'Marvellously well. You were right about Miss Roffe. An extremely efficient young woman.' Felicity pulled the collar of her mink jacket close around her throat. 'Ugh, what a dreadful day! Peter—' She turned to her dark-suited, fresh-faced companion '—go and see if my car's outside. I have an appointment with Howard Dalton at the Savoy,' she told Dorothea.

'That should be interesting.' Dorothea had met Howard Dalton and knew him to be an intelligent though caustic theatre director.

'Yes, indeed.' Felicity patted her immaculate curls. 'He tells me he can't wait to meet me. I suppose it will be a nice change for him, working with me after all those terribly serious, dowdy character actresses. Worthy folk, I'm sure, but . . .'

She stopped talking and looked past Dorothea to where Peter was trying to catch her attention by the hotel entrance. 'I must go.' As she brushed past she added, her voice silkily feline, 'You should let Miss Roffe handle more of your work. You look positively exhausted, even after a weekend away.'

Dorothea stepped into the lift and pressed the button for the third floor. Felicity's remark did not upset her. Indeed, she felt a wry satisfaction when she realised that, despite her present negative feelings of loss and resignation, a thread of humour was struggling to surface at the star's bitchiness.

New displays of flowers had been placed along the corridors. Vibrant glowing colours, gold and dark red, shocked their way into Dorothea's self-absorption. She paused and breathed in the scented air. Did the same flowers bloom in Australia? she wondered. Rob . . . he would be well on his way home now. She remembered how he had commented on the displays of flowers the first day he had come to the hotel to find her.

She sighed. How long will I do this? she wondered. Pause in the middle of some job or other and remember a certain phrase, a joke, a tender moment spent with Rob.

When he had said he wanted to marry her, she had been almost shocked. That they had found love together was undeniable. The time they had spent together had been, for her, the most wonderful of her whole life and she hoped, knew, that Rob had felt the same. And yet . . . She sighed. Perhaps it was because she was older than him, perhaps because happiness had been snatched from her grasp before, she had never really believed it could last. Mentally, she realised, she had been preparing herself for this separation. But it was so hard to think she might never see him again. She closed her eyes as the pain crept up on her and pounced.

It was bad, worse than she had anticipated. Nevertheless, she determined it would not beat her.

The lift stopped and she straightened her shoulders and marched into her office. 'Good morning, Frances. Apologies for this late entry. Have I missed anything terribly important?'

Frances looked up from her typewriter. 'There's a couple of press releases on your desk for your attention, and a messenger brought a private memorandum from Mr Whitney. Oh, and Mr Charles Richardson telephoned. He left a message. Let me see,' she took a shorthand pad from a desk drawer. 'He says sorry, but he can't make tomorrow night after all. Something absolutely vital has come up that he has to attend to. He said he would ring again, about four-thirty, to explain.'

'Thank you, Frances.'

Dorothea went into her room and sat down behind her desk. And thank you, Charles! Absurdly, she felt like crying. She forced the tears back, angrily. If she would not cry for the loss of Rob, she'd damn well not cry for Charles's defection. But Charles was supposed to be her friend! Surely he must know that she could do with friendship at this moment?

She blew her nose then opened the sealed envelope which the messenger had brought. Adam's memorandum set forth details of a meeting to discuss and explore his proposed expansion into overseas markets, with particular reference to the hotel chain. Dorothea noted the date for the meeting in her diary. She supposed Charles would be there. She knew he was opposed to his uncle's ideas. He told Dorothea, in confidence, that he thought the old man was becoming senile. They were doing so well in the UK. Why risk a fortune overseas? Dorothea had argued with him.

She pointed out that Adam Whitney still held major control of the company and therefore the healthy balance sheets and increasing profits were all due to his leadership. 'Senile' was not a word one should use in connection with such a man. The forthcoming meeting promised to be lively.

She buzzed Frances and asked her to contact Judith Roffe. When, a few minutes later, the young woman entered her office, Dorothea congratulated her.

'If you can wring praise from Felicity Fowler,' she said, 'you've really made it! Well done. I can see I shall be handing on some important assignments to you in the future.'

Judith stammered her thanks. 'I won't let you down, Miss Bellows.'

'I know you won't.' Dorothea smiled at her. She liked Judith who reminded her of herself in her early twenties – ambitious, keen, and willing to work hard.

Her assistant left the room after reporting at length on the schedule for the continuing press coverage for Miss Fowler. Then Frances brought in a tray of coffee. 'It's a bit late for morning coffee,' she apologised, 'but I thought you could do with it. Oh, and Madge Lowell's rung twice.'

Dorothea groaned. She had been looking forward to having her coffee in peace. 'Did she say what about?'

'No, just asked you to ring her.'

'OK.' Dorothea consulted her watch. 'Give me five minutes then get in touch with her.'

Frances went out and Dorothea poured herself a cup of coffee. She sat back in her executive chair and kicked her shoes off. So far so good. She was picking up the threads of her work again and managing to keep thoughts of Rob at bay.

And immediately, as if to laugh at her presumption, the sense of loss came back. You can't work twenty-four hours a day, an inner voice whispered to her. And you know you can't rely on Charles. Dorothea slammed her coffee cup down on the saucer so hard the liquid slopped over on to the tray.

She felt affronted at her own thoughts. Affronted that she had even, for one moment, linked the two men in her mind. Charles had her affection; it was as she had explained to Rob. She and Charles were primarily friends, but it was a friendship spiked with sexual attraction – mutual gratification, if you like. But now she suddenly realised that their friendship must change. She wouldn't be able to go to bed with Charles any more. It would be a betrayal of what she and Rob had shared. Dorothea sighed. Charles would not understand. His affairs with other women had never touched him deeply. He would think she had gone crazy. Maybe she had. Being with Rob had changed her so much. And now, with him gone from her life, there really didn't seem much left.

She closed her eyes. She *must* be sensible. Of course she was feeling vulnerable, but it would pass. She must consider Rob himself. She didn't formulate the thought, but deep at the back of her mind lurked the difference in their ages. Rob was certainly mature for his years and when he had said he wanted to marry her, he had meant it. But he would go back home and pick up his life there. He was an attractive man. She suppressed the pang of desire she felt when she remembered just how attractive he was and how totally fulfilling had been their love-making. Life being what it was, he would gradually forget her and it was better so. He had endured one unhappy marriage. He had a small son. He should marry a girl in her twenties; a woman content to make a home for him and Nicky. He deserved that.

Dorothea knew she could never be that kind of woman. She had lived her life alone for too long. She had too much ambition, too much energy, to settle for being a housewife.

The burr of the telephone disturbed her thoughts and she raised the receiver gladly. It was Madge Lowell.

'Sorry to bother you again, Thea, but I really would like to talk to Rob. Last week I had just an idea to work on, but now I've got the go-ahead.'

Dorothea frowned, puzzled. 'What are you talking about, Madge?'

'Rob, of course, and his ideas. Listen, my

company's setting up a deal with a famous travel writer. He's been all round Australia describing the place "through his eyes".' Madge's voice held an amused note. 'His manuscript is OK in content but it's too short. We've talked it through with the author and suggested he interview a couple more Aussies at present in the UK. We've found one, a chap who lived out in the wild then found some sort of miraculous plant cure and is now in this country doing a deal with a firm of medical suppliers, but we need another. Then I remembered Rob.'

'But Rob's English, Madge. And, anyway, I know he's mined for opals but . . .'

'Oh, I know all that. But he'd be the perfect foil to the first man. *He's* about eighty years old. Rob's young and quite dishy. There would be photos, of course. He's lived in the Outback and has some good stories but his future's interesting too. He's got plans.'

'You mean his idea about taking city types out into the wilderness?' Dorothea paused. 'Yes, I can see it has possibilities . . .'

Madge interrupted her. 'It's his other idea, actually. This thing about opening hotels in out-of-the-way places. Places that are becoming accessible to tourists. I know he's ditched the idea for the moment – not enough money and lack of experience – but great scheme. Who knows?' She laughed. 'I might be doing him a favour. If the book's really successful – and, as I say, the author is a big name – Rob might attract backing. He might turn out to be the next Aussie millionaire! And that wouldn't do Lawrence & Franklin any harm. And if nothing happens, so what? At least the book would be the right length.'

Her quick-fire patter made Dorothea's head reel.

'Madge,' she interrupted her friend, 'I've only followed about half what you're telling me but I'm afraid it's out of the question. You see, Rob flew back to Australia this morning.'

498

There was a pause then Madge said feelingly, 'Shit!'

'I'm really sorry. I had no idea you were planning anything like this.'

'I wasn't last week.' Madge's voice had flattened. 'And when I thought up the idea, I couldn't tell you about it until I saw Harry Lawrence.'

'Will you be able to find someone else?'

'Have to.' Madge sighed, then laughed. 'Unless I can persuade the author to flannel away about mountain ranges and noble savages for another twenty-five thousand words. On reflection,' this time she laughed more naturally, 'knowing the guy, he'll probably jump at the chance. Don't worry, Thea. I'll come up with something.'

'I hope you do, Madge. Bye.'

Madge waited a moment before replying. Then she said, 'You OK, Thea?'

'Of course. Aren't I always?'

'Usually. But when I talked to your friend, I had the feeling there was something special . . .' Abruptly, she changed tack. 'Listen, give me a ring if you need company one night. We'll crack a bottle of wine together.'

'Thanks, Madge.' Dorothea smiled. 'I'll take you up on that.' She replaced her receiver and tried to sort out her thoughts.

Rob in a book? He must have made quite an impact on Madge for her to consider such a thing. And he must have really opened up to her about his ambitions. But then, Madge did that to people. That was one reason she was so good at her job. But plans for opening hotels? Why had he never even mentioned that idea to her? She stood up and paced about the room. Did he think she would laugh at him? Surely he knew better than that. She paused. She supposed it was quite a good idea. She remembered him telling her how difficult it was to get anywhere decent to stay, even when you were travelling on Highway One, the longest highway in the world! Of course, many areas of Australia were so sparsely populated, investment would be uneconomical but even so . . .

Dorothea opened her door and asked Frances to bring her more coffee. She also told her to block all incoming telephone calls. Then she paced up and down again. *Why* had Rob not told her about this? He must have thought about it and realised it was totally beyond his means even to consider the project. But on a small scale . . . He could have invested his money in a scaled-down version of the original scheme. She could have advised him.

She stopped walking and smiled to herself. Of course, he didn't want to be beholden to her. He knew she could find out things that might help him, things he couldn't find out for himself, and he wouldn't have that. He was stubborn. She admired him for that. It was a characteristic she recognised and approved of. But too much stubbornness could be bad.

'Thank you, Frances.' She nodded to her secretary but did not immediately cross to her desk. An idea was forming in her mind and she thought better on her feet.

She crossed to the window and stared out.

He had probably decided it would be too much hassle. His partner, she knew, was totally uninterested in increasing their modest fortune. He had enough to live on comfortably and that was all he wanted. Rob had told her all about it one night when they had been cuddled together after a wonderful session of love-making.

She had asked if Rob agreed with his friend's view of life.

'In some ways. I certainly don't think it's worth dying of a heart attack at fifty to prove you're a success. But,' he had grinned at her, 'I like a bit of a challenge in life. It would get very boring sitting on your backside fishing all day. That's what Boots wants to do.'

Oh, if only he were here and she could talk to him!

Dorothea went back to her desk and took up Adam Whitney's memorandum. She drank her fresh coffee and read with close detail the typed pages. The key points of the document were itemised:

Research into hitherto neglected possible tourist areas.
Development possibilities in such areas.
Full discussion regarding investigation and intensive forward planning with a view to implementing decisions reached.

Dorothea laid down the paper and smiled. Without asking Frances, she obtained an outside line and dialled Adam Whitney's secretary. She asked if he had any free time during the day. Jenny gave her an appointment.

After making notes, Dorothea laid down her pen and tried to contain her growing excitement. Her idea was fraught with problems and so many things could scupper it! She had to obtain Adam's agreement, the co-operation of several members of the Board, and there was her present position to consider. Dorothea remembered Judith Roffe and made another note on her pad. Primarily, of course, there was Rob. But it could work, it could!

Her old enthusiasm for a battle against all the odds surged through her. By God, she'd give it a go!

Frances gaped when her employer appeared in the doorway of her office. Dorothea had presented a wan and dismal face when she had arrived for work, but now she looked radiant. She smiled at Frances, her eyes sparkling.

'I'm going out. I have an important meeting with Mr Whitney at four-thirty.'

'Right, Miss Bellows.' Frances checked her notes. 'You've an appointment with the editor of the *Evening News* at 4.45.'

'Cancel it. Say—' Dorothea's smile widened '—something important, vitally important, has come up.'

'And Mr Richardson? He said he would ring back. Shall I tell him to try later in the day?'

'No, I don't think so.' Dorothea paused. 'When I leave Mr Whitney, I shall probably go shopping.'

'Oh?' Frances was puzzled. Miss Bellows was behaving in a most peculiar manner. 'What shall I say then?'

'Tell him . . .' Dorothea thought for a moment, and her smile turned into an irrepressible grin. 'Give him my apologies, but tell him it has become absolutely imperative that I rush out and buy a very large, very floppy hat!'